Gentlemen in Their Season

By the same author

THE BIRTHDAY KING
BROTHERLY LOVE
THROUGH STREETS BROAD AND NARROW
EIGHT DAYS
IN THE TIME OF GREENBLOOM

GABRIEL FIELDING

GENTLEMEN IN THEIR SEASON

William Morrow & Co. *New York,* 1966

The names and characters of the
people in this story were invented
by myself and are unrelated to
anyone whatsoever. The events are
all imaginary.

G.F.

 Printed in the United States of America. Library of Congress Catalog Card Number 66-17183

THIS STORY IS DEDICATED TO
THE HOUSE OF MORROW:
IN PARTICULAR TO SAM, JOHN,
LARRY, JIM, ADELE AND FRANCES,
FOR THEIR ENTHUSIASM, THEIR
SKILL, AND THEIR PATIENCE.

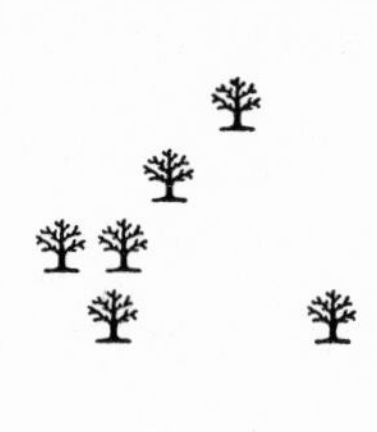

Gentlemen in Their Season

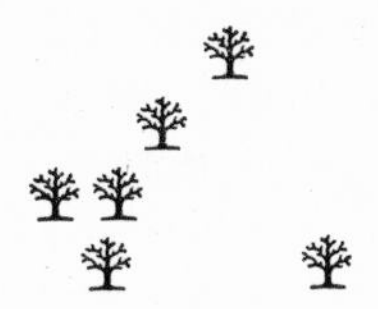

Coles was a watcher. His friend Bernard Presage was always telling him so, accusing him of joylessness, saying: "The good times come and they pass you by."

Presage was a Catholic who drank too much; he had a sadly happy wife, Helen, and two children, and Coles needed him. They met irregularly—hairy Presage and lined Coles—at Broadcasting House in London, where they worked, or at Shirreff's Wine Bar or the George or one of the clubs.

"Especially you watch me!" said Bernard, who had recently fractured an ankle. "Sometimes I think I get bashed about so that you can continue to live. But you do better than that, prison-snooping and not even feeling good about it or guilty. It's your tolerance I can't stand, Coles, your damned humanist tolerance."

"Your clock jammed after the Renaissance," Coles retorted. "Whether you like it or not, we're on our own now; we've got to be responsible."

But Presage quoted: " 'A time will come when men will be so weary of men that they'll weep at the name of God.' Two centuries of rationalism have made us long for the Bomb, Coles. Between you and me, don't you like to know it's there, too?"

They went on like this whenever they met until Presage moved off to go on drinking somewhere else or, more rarely, to return to his flat and continue his current monograph or talk to his young daughter, Cecily, or ring up Emily Minck, whom everyone thought was his mistress, not knowing that their real interests were gossip and theology.

Unless it was his prison-visiting night, Randall Coles went back to his home, to his home area and his wife, Lettice. He kept an eye on both. He was really lined with watching everything and often thought of himself as a juggler keeping half-a-dozen plates in the air at once, spinning on the ends of batons. There was his job at the B.B.C., which he had kept spinning off and on for nearly twenty years; his home life; his occasional painting; his prison visiting; and, in particular, his most recent prisoner, Christopher Hotchkis, who, since his transfer to the local prison, had become an obsession.

Coles did not include his wife Lettice in his spinning plates because he was never quite sure that he was spinning her. She was his partner, his colleague, and for twenty years they'd done most things together, including falling in love and getting married and rearing two children. They conferred about bills, jobs, schools, art, doctors, and income tax, about nearly everything except the things that were, as Coles expressed it, "separate, quite separate!" Though he did not certainly know what Lettice's obsessions might be, he suspected they were something to do with clothes and friends and possibly—thrown in—cultural ambitions and gardening.

But his own preoccupations, his secrets, hardly varied: they were sex, crime, and the idea-of-god, in that order, and had been so ever since he'd first discovered and resisted his temptations. And though he didn't know what he'd have done without them, with no sexual itch or urge to turn into pictures, no Famous Trials to mull over in wintertime, and a world in which the godhead had never been postulated, he did sometimes think that it was hard to find his obsessions growing rather than diminishing with age. For he toiled after Hotchkis and his murder-reduced-to-manslaughter as eagerly as at night, in his extreme youth, he'd studied the lives of the poisoners and Marshall-Hall's defense of Joseph Smith, the drowner of the Brides in the Bath. And now, at the age of forty-nine, he found himself ever more helplessly entangled, not with mere reportage, but with a living man who still held, somewhere inside himself, his violence and his moment: the actual instant in which the one had been given to the other.

Recurrently in Coles' day or night, quite independently of his moods, Hotchkis' face sprang up on the blank screen of his mind: the strong cheeks, the country eyes and the forehead over which the brown hair curled like a bull's, every detail as certain as a waxwork. At times, even on the six-fifteen from Charing Cross—crowded with commuters—he heard or almost heard the prisoner's voice and caught the scent of his body, that compound of the sea and washed armpits, of prison and shag, which he was getting to know so well.

So great was the fascination that in recent months he'd carried with him everywhere, amongst his scripts for the Department of Religious Broadcasting, a file in which he kept the cuttings relating to the murder and Hotchkis' first recorded remarks at the police station where he'd given himself up. He stored, too, the findings of the pre-trial psychiatrist together with his own most secret notes of his developing relationship with both Christopher and his wife, "Honeycomb" Hotchkis.

It was Christopher himself who had involved him with her. A day or two after Coles' last meeting with Presage, Hotchkis asked him if he would call in and see her sometime and Coles said: "Yes, I think that could be arranged, Hotchkis, with the Governor's consent. You live in Sumner, I believe?"

"Most of my life, Mr. Coles."

"It's not too far away. I might even make a detour on my way home from the prison one evening. I could tell your wife that I'd only just left you. It might knock down a few of the walls for you."

"Walls?" said Hotchkis. "There was only one and I knocked him down myself."

"A long time ago," Coles said, feeling the old excitement. "I was hoping you might not think of it so much nowadays—with your release coming up?"

Hotchkis smiled at him. "Paul Caine was my closest friend. You don't easily forget a thing like that."

"No, of course not. But it's essential to try."

"He left his cuff links in the bed. One, actually!"

"Yes, I remember, Hotchkis."

"Not gold—and in the center of the mattress, where the hollow is. The sort of thing that stays with you."

"Understandably."

"And against you too, Mr. Coles. That cuff link was dead against you. You couldn't even bring yourself to pick it up at first in case it was lying. Things can lie, you know, suggest something that didn't really happen."

"Indeed they can; I know exactly what you mean."

"I don't think you could—not until it's happened to you, Mr. Coles, not unless you've seen it."

"You mean that it's all in the thing itself, Hotchkis? In the experience?"

"Yes. Seeing the bedroom that day reminded me of the time when I was with the herring fleet off Yarmouth after the war. They hadn't cleared all the Jerry mines and the trawler next to us got done. After that everything looked different—not just the water with the bodies in it, but the wave crests and the birds . . ."

"The seagulls?"

"Them!" Hotchkis said. "Suddenly they looked as if they knew, as if they'd known all along what was going to happen, and you thought to yourself, 'By Christ! If I had a gun I'd knock all you bastards out of the sky.' "

Hotchkis was happy that night, very communicative. On his return to his wife, Lettice, Coles would tell her about it. He'd say, "Hotchkis was more than usually articulate tonight. That is why I stayed later than usual."

"If you do go and see Betty," Hotchkis said, "you'd better drop her a line first."

"Of course."

"Not a post card—she doesn't like post cards—but a proper letter so's she'll know you're coming, like."

"Certainly," Coles agreed, wondering how he would phrase such a letter.

He caught Hotchkis smiling to himself and took off his spectacles, coughed on them, and polished each lens with the little piece of chamois he kept in his left-hand breast pocket.

"I can just see her opening it," Hotchkis said. "She'll be sitting down on the couch under the clock with her knees apart, and when she's read it over a couple of times she'll knock on the wall to get Ireen over for a natter."

"A neighbour?"

"Yes. They've got no time for each other really, her and Betty. You see, Betty's dad gives Ireen all his money because he's been getting it from her for the past five or six years."

"He must be getting on, then, your wife's father?"

"He's knocking seventy. To see 'im tottering about there in his garden you wouldn't even think he could pull rhubarb let alone grow it."

"Extraordinary!"

"Cheers you up, though, Mr. Coles, don't it? I bet it cheers you up, sitting there hearing about it."

Behind his glasses Coles' eyes were sharp. "I must admit that it is rather amusing."

"I'll say! Especially when you're getting on a little, like you, or in prison, like me."

"And all this goes on in Sumner, in the village?"

"And more. You'd be surprised if you knew what people can cram into a village these days."

"Yet they're still on speaking terms, your wife and her neighbour?"

"Call them Betty and 'Reen, Mr. Coles. You might as well, since you've come in on it. You won't forget that letter, will you? It wouldn't do to catch her in her curlers, not Betty! And there's another reason—" Hotchkis was smiling with a slightly opened mouth. Coles could see many of his well-brushed teeth and his clean pink tongue.

"I'm sorry," he said, holding his breath a little. "You're thinking perhaps that your wife—"

"I don't know. Betty's a good girl, but she's only human, and I wouldn't want her to think she was being watched, that's all."

Coles picked up the notebook he had dropped and stowed it in his brief case with the rest of the Hotchkis file. He stretched his stooped shoulders and shook Hotchkis' hand before giving him the half ounce of tobacco and the quarter of bull's-eyes which he never forgot to bring. Hotchkis followed him out on to the landing and watched him descend the steel staircase.

It was Easter then and there were daffodils in the prison rockery surrounding the basketball pitch and over against the grey walls of the chapel, where the padre had fixed a large poster of the inside of the Holy Sepulcher. The prison lawn, which now covered the graveyard of the old hangings, had been freshly cut for the first time that year, and Coles, as he hurried past it, could smell the innocent mowings on the evening air.

The bell of the chapel's hideous clock tower chimed six as he paused to get his breath by the front gate. He noticed that his heart was thumping unusually fast, a little like a lover's, as if he were expecting a fulfillment of some kind. He held his brief case to his chest for a moment, considering all that it contained and the satisfaction it would give him later when, alone in his study, he expanded the evening's notes at his desk.

Waiting for the officer to unlock the inner gate, he studied the padre's poster. Inside the tomb a late-Victorian angel was pointing upwards and outwards towards its open entrance. Within the enclosing stone walls two apostles stood with their backs to the green world that lay behind them.

HE IS RISEN!

proclaimed the scarlet capitals beneath.

"Tactless! Very tactless!" Coles commented to himself as he walked out through the gates to his waiting Mini.

He drove away carefully, adjusting himself to the idea of his home and the reunion with Lettice.

They ate Boeuf Stroganov with rice and celery hearts. Lettice had been doing her welfare work at the old people's home, wheeling her trolley of books round the wards, talking to the patients, admiring their knitting and crochet. She had taken tea in the Sisters' room with one of her doctor friends, Geoffrey Cattermole, leaving in time to thicken the stew and write a letter to their son Malcolm, in his first year at Cambridge.

She talked eagerly throughout the meal and then together they washed up and sat before the French windows drinking china tea and listening to the Third Programme for half an hour. Then Lettice took her deerhound, Tyndal, for his evening walk down Coniston Road while Randall went upstairs to expand his evening's notes and draft the letter to Mrs. Hotchkis.

He took immense trouble with it, writing it out three times before he was sufficiently satisfied to lock it away in his bureau for further consideration at the weekend. At ten-thirty, when Lettice had taken her bath, he went into the bedroom to kiss her good night and then returned to his study to leaf once more through the papers in the Hotchkis file.

There were the press cuttings, with the first dated February 1957 and reading in part:

> Detective Chief Inspector Eric Browning said that when he spoke about the body at the house, Hotchkis asked, "Body, what do you mean, body? That's Paul Caine up there and he needs a priest."

There was the psychiatrist's report, also eight years old:

> He is a powerful healthy man with unexpectedly superior intelligence and surprisingly well-read. No mental abnormality was found though he has always been a somewhat inadequate man with a slightly inflated attitude to life as shown by the following brief biography I obtained from him. There is no history of mental illness or abnormality in the family.

Before he went to bed, Coles reread for the last time his letter to Mrs. Hotchkis, deciding that he would post it in the morning, that in view of her significance he could delay no longer. Awaiting sleep, he realized that he was desperate for a favourable reply. With his eyes open and his hands behind his head he lay there quite forgetful of his wife in her separate bed as he re-created the night of Hotchkis' crime.

He imagined his days on the sea, the ship lying out in the roads for the wind to drop, the berthing at dawn and the taxi out to the village of Sumner and Hotchkis opening the door of his cottage.

Often, in his determination to recall every detail, the old with the new, Coles had to start again at the beginning as a child does when it is remembering. But at last, with Lettice breathing gently in her matching bed, he was away, striding through the silent village to the cottage door, which opened only as he fell asleep.

Mrs. Hotchkis replied to his letter by return of post, writing with a ball-point pen on a pale-blue paper and envelope. Coles held it to his nose the moment he opened it, before tearing back the gummed flap, to sample the contained air of the Hotchkis cottage, to see if Mrs. Hotchkis used lipstick or smoked. A pink smudge and a shred of tobacco told him that she did both, and the letter, he found, smelled of her handbag, of face powder and aspirin tablets.

She wrote:

7 Albert Row
Sumner, Sussex

Dear Mr. Cole,

I am in receipt of yours of yesterday and you could come here on a Friday after seven when I have Marc and Debrah in bed. It is better then and we could talk. Well I don't think there is much anyone can do for me and Chris until he comes out but I am always willing to try. If you are coming by car leave it by the Assembly of God in Albert Row as the street is narrow and lorries can't get by.

Yours truly,
Betty Hotchkis (Mrs.)

Coles showed the letter to Hotchkis on the following Wednesday.

"Evidently your wife doesn't want me to come on one of my visiting nights here. She seems to prefer the weekend?"

But Hotchkis was not apparently listening to him. He was smiling to himself, holding the letter flat against the cell table under his hand, pinning it down.

"That's Betty," he said at last. "She was always willing to try." He looked up. "You'll be going all right, won't you, Mr. Coles?"

"It's all arranged." Although Coles was terribly tidy and found it difficult to change things when once he'd written them down, he added, "Unless you've changed your mind? I mean, you wouldn't rather I didn't?"

"I'd rather nothing. I was just wondering whether it'll do any good."

"I'm sure it will."

"If it's fair?"

"Fair to your wife, Hotchkis?"

"No, to you! That's what I was wondering."

Excitement began in Coles' fingers. They shook so much that he put the cap on his fountain pen and returned the pen to the clip in his right-hand breast pocket. Intuition always made his fingers tremble, and mentally he visualized the notes he would confide in his private diary, an addendum to the recent entries about Presage:

> Though they both know something about me, Hotchkis affects me differently from Presage. Whereas Presage despises my will to safety, Hotchkis has already got on to my weakness. After tonight there can no longer be any question that H. connives at events.

At the time he couldn't express it better and knew that he'd left out the real cause of his excitement, the certainty that he, Coles, was in some way "innocent." His intuitions always made him aware of eternity in himself, and when people discerned his deepest fears or desires they touched on it: they made him feel, for an undeniable instant, limitless and indestructible.

He played it down; he said, "I'm afraid Mrs. Hotchkis will only see my visit as an official one."

"You don't know Betty."

"No, of course not."

"She's very personal, is Betty; she doesn't get taken in."

"By people, you mean?"

"By men, Mr. Coles. She understands them."

"I'm sure—" Coles began, feeling his thighs tremble.

But Hotchkis interrupted him. "What I'm gettin' at," he said, "is that you've been my age but I haven't been yours. For all I know it might be worse . . ."

"What do you suppose he meant?" Coles asked Presage a day or two after his first interview with Mrs. Hotchkis. He and Bernard were drinking together outside the B.B.C. in the dingy club they frequented in the evenings.

"He's talking about his wife. He's not interested in you, Coles."

Presage was drinking whisky that night and looked depressed. He added, "This man killed for her. He killed her lover in order to—" He stared hard into the brown spaces of the club.

"I wish you'd finish your sentences, Bernard; he killed in order to what?"

"What's his religion?"

"I told you months ago."

Presage caught his smile. "Oh I see! He's one of us. He'll have killed in order to preserve the sanctity of his marriage; but by now he'll know that since you're indifferent to his beliefs, you're making a fool of him."

"In other words, he despises me."

"That's not what I said. He knows you're bound to be on his side and he doesn't really like it. Admit, Coles, that if we suddenly decided to execute him you'd have to start writing letters—agitating in a tasteful way."

"As a member of Amnesty, together with a number of Jesuits, I might remind you—"

"But don't write any of your damned little letters about me even when I'm alive to answer them. And don't come visiting me in my cell and reducing my immortal soul to the level of the *New Statesman.*" Presage almost shouted this last injunction, and one or two people who had been snapping at each other in earnest began to behave with calmness and sanity.

Coles sipped his bottled beer. "You're drinking far too much, Bernard. It's becoming impossible to have a conversation with you; you turn them all into diatribes."

"You're perfectly right; I'm depressed. Let us talk about Hotchkis' wife. Last time we met I could see that you were about to meet her."

"How do you mean?"

"You looked lustful. I told Helen that your marriage was in danger. 'He's involved,' I said, 'with a woman for whom murder was done.'"

Coles was delighted. "What on earth did Helen say?"

"She was incurious. But tell me about Mrs. Hotchkis. What was she wearing?"

"Scarlet," said Coles, simpering. "A jumper, I think, and a tweed skirt, quite well cut."

"Anything else?"

"Good stockings and earrings: white plastic chrysanthemums."

"What about her feet?"

"I didn't really notice."

"Feet are basic. Think, Coles. What was on them? Or did she perhaps discard her shoes?"

"I remember now. I didn't like them; they had straps."

"T-straps, or the kind favoured by the commoner members of the Royal Family?"

"Just straps; they embarrassed me."

"And rightly!" said Presage. "I'm doing a piece for *Vogue* on footwear and morals. Was Mrs. Hotchkis wearing costume jewelry for the occasion?"

"Yes, I think she was. One of those Harrods affairs of cut plastic and things that looked like raisins."

"An honest working-class woman." Presage got up. "You must tell me more next week. I have to meet Emily Minck. If I don't, I shall be in time for the meal Helen has cooked, and this might give her the impression that I have ceased to care." Abruptly, but with an affectionate smile, he thumped his way out of the club into the magical poisonous air of Regent Street.

Coles, feeling bereft, drained his glass and got out his journey-time whiff. Then, because he was feeling so deprived, he put it away again to smoke when he was actually in his train, speeding home to Lettice and supper. There would be honey on the table, he remembered, because Mrs. Hotchkis had given him a honey-comb when he was leaving.

"Go on," she'd said, not looking at him. "Take it, Mr. Coles! It's been ever so sweet of you to come and I'd like you to have it. . . ."

Sitting in the train, half an hour later, he remembered that first evening perfectly: the exact course of their conversation.

"Have you got children?" Mrs. Hotchkis had asked him shyly.

"Two. My son Malcolm's at Cambridge. He's rock-climbing in Cumberland this vacation; and my daughter Brett is in France, Bordeaux."

"They're that old, are they?"

"We've been married over twenty years."

"Heavens!" said Mrs. Hotchkis, only just catching the "H" and then remaining silent with her round chin in her hand.

"You sound very surprised," Coles said, surprised himself.

"More frightened really," she admitted, swaying her face on her palm. "It sounds so long. Don't you get lonely with your children away; doesn't Mrs. Coles?"

"Oh no, I don't think so. My wife's always so busy."

"Wish I was. I never learned how to be busy. My neighbour now . . . Ireen's always polishing and cleaning. You could see your face in her floor if you wanted to, but I don't see any point in it, never have."

Coles found that he was looking at her legs. They looked idle, smooth and lazy. There wasn't even the smallest of ladders in her fine stockings.

"Bored too," she had; "that's my trouble—I start dreaming."

"Dreaming," Coles had said without meaning to.

"Do you like music?" she'd asked, turning up the volume of her transistor set. "I couldn't live without music."

Coles recognized an aria from *Madame Butterfly*.

"I leave it on even when I go out," she said, "so that when I come in again it's there, as if there was people."

"You're bound to be lonely until Christopher returns."

"Don't," she said; "I'm sick of it—after nearly eight years. It's all I ever hear, and how does anyone know that I'll want him back again when I don't even know myself?"

"They don't, of course, but—"

"I'm not Madame Butterfly, not likely. Stupid bit, going and killing herself like that. She should have started over."

Coles smiled. He was feeling a little mesmerized, as if not too late in life he'd let himself go at a fun-fair. He grappled with the long view, seeking to span a gap.

"You forget that she had to withstand the weight of religious tradition," he said. "Poor Butterfly felt herself dishonoured, Mrs. Hotchkis."

She raised her sulky brown eyes. "Religion's all men. They invent it to suit theirselves. That's why I wouldn't let them start on the children. I told Christopher and that priest, 'The day you start indoctrinating the kids, I leave.' "

"Christopher didn't insist, did he?"

"We're still arguing about it, or we were until I stopped visiting him. I said to him the last time I went, 'Now look where your religion's landed you! You're worse off than if you'd never believed in anything. You've got to confess to the priest as well as the police.' "

"And what did he say?"

"He said, 'Not yet I don't, not until I'm sorry.'

" 'That's good,' I said; 'you kill your best friend and you're not even sorry.' And he said, 'No, not for him and not for myself.' And then he looked at me, Mr. Coles, and he said, 'Are *you* sorry, Betty?' "

Coles had been longing to get out his notebook, but instead he'd crossed one leg over the other and sat back in the red wing chair trying to look so relaxed that it would never occur to her to stop remembering. It was some moments before he noticed that her gaze was fixed on his face. She had forced her left foot half out of its shoe and was slapping it rhythmically against her shining heel. She'd been smiling into his eyes, and for the first time he'd noticed that she had a very slight squint. He found himself smiling back at her.

"Do you have to wear specs?" she asked. "All the time, I mean?"

"I'm afraid so."

"You might look a lot younger if you was to give them up. You've got young eyes, haven't you?"

"I'm a worrier, I'm afraid."

"You don't want to be too serious, do you? Not really?"

"Not if you can avoid it."

"I expect you think I'm never serious. When you get home you'll tell your wife, 'She hasn't got a thought in her head.' " She paused. "But then perhaps you don't tell your wife everything?"

"I don't, as a matter of fact."

She smiled again. She slid on her left shoe and got up indolently. "I've got some coffee in the kitchen; would you like a cup?"

He hesitated. From the doorway, leaning against it, she said,

"You want me to talk about Paul Caine. That's what you're waiting for, isn't it?"

"I did hope you might answer Christopher's question."

"About being sorry for him? Of course I'm not. What's the good of being sorry for anybody that's dead? You might say they was missing all the fun, but they don't know they're missing it, so what's the use?"

"You're sorry for yourself, perhaps, Mrs. Hotchkis?"

"Betty!"

"Betty," Coles said.

Her voice came through from the kitchen now: "I don't think about it much. Paul was all right, but he got careless. I said to him, 'Now don't you start getting serious about me, Paul. I'm not that sort. If you get serious you'll get careless and you won't care where you land yourself. . . .' "

The train drew in at Coles' local station, where the Mini was parked in the yard.

He drove to his home, Half Yoke House, in Coniston Road and went upstairs to wash before greeting Lettice. It was an understood thing between them that such greetings should not be too informal.

When he came down again, his sand-grey hair neatly parted, his face and hands fresh with soap, he found Lettice at her bureau preparing the guest list for the first summer party in June.

She said, "I was wondering whether you would want to invite Bernard Presage this year?"

"I'm not sure."

"Well, please don't leave it to the last minute. I'm allowing for six of *your* friends, but I shall want at least ten days' notice for the catering."

Coles kissed her stiff little neck just above the pale-blue collar of her blouse. Her stiffness must be her response, he decided, as her fingers tightened on her fountain pen and she sat up straighter.

By the time he had put her glass of sherry beside her she was at work again listing new names.

"This year I thought we might have readings from *The Threepenny Opera,*" she said. "You might borrow recordings of the music from the corporation library."

"I'll make a note of it."

"I was playing with the idea of calling it 'Words and Music.' Putting it on the invitations, I mean."

Yes, he thought, it might help to fulfill the longings of your doctors and schoolmasters.

"Supper in twenty minutes," she said.

He left her there in her room, contained and efficient, the spring sunlight silvering her hair, making grey her lavender-coloured eyes. He was grateful to her for sitting there, for such certainty, the opportunity it all gave him to rebel a little.

Already the French windows were open, and he strolled out through them to look at her border, at the green shoots tender against the soil, the weedlessness, the trug basket on the terrace. In three or four weeks their guests would be strolling the length of it with glasses of wine in hand and Lettice would be here and there among them like summer lightning, so English and so temperate. Then there would be the long lull until the first of the winter parties in November, the month of the dead.

Now the horse chestnuts at the end of the garden were studded with unopened candles, but by then they would be nearly bare, and before the last leaf fell he would be free to get on with his life, to do some more reading and have another try at Fabers with his poems. And in November too, he remembered, Hotchkis would be released; his obsession with the man would have been either unwound or deepened, the conversations with Presage would have taken a new direction. Perhaps this year he would risk another rude refusal and invite Bernard to the June party.

Let me see, he thought. *By now he will be with Emily Minck in her flat.* He wondered what was the precise nature of their relationship and what, on that particular evening, they might be saying to one another.

As it happened Bernard at that moment was telling Emily Minck about Coles' meeting with Mrs. Hotchkis. Emily, nearly forty, a most accomplished lutenist and composer, was just back from an American tour which had been a great success. They were sitting in her flat in an unfashionable area of North London.

Bernard said, "I warned him to be careful and told him, above all, to avoid comparisons with Lettice. I told him that if he must take such risks he would be advised to get mixed up with a typist rather than some welfare-state Emma Bovary."

"Well," Emily said, "it's a change from everybody going to bed with their best friends' husbands and wives. With the increased facilities for travel I can't understand how incest should have caught on so."

"All the same, Coles worries me," Bernard insisted. "He might imagine he was moving into reality."

"I, since my latest success," said Emily, who always followed her own lines of thought to their inspired conclusions, "I, as you know, fly everywhere."

Bernard looked at her neat little body, appreciating her enormous eyes and the ashen fluff of hair above her pale forehead.

"And he is past ripeness," he went on; "there can be little hope of a conversion when one considers Lettice."

Emily was wondering if the New York line suited her legs.

"And I never insure myself," she said. "I insure my diamonds because they are objects and it would be improvident not to do so; but myself I leave to the Holy Spirit."

"It might occur to him that he has despaired. Lettice, who has known it for years, ought to be warned. I'm not sure I shan't accept her next invitation to one of those horrible parties."

Emily concentrated on Coles. Her thoughts ran down the shining web of her mind like a spider to a long-enmeshed fly.

"Randall Coles has been behind bars for years, Bernard. I really can't think he should be helped now."

"He has pathos. He calls forth my attenuated charities."

"You waste them," Emily said, "on worthless people. Never forget that God loves his little humanists and that you, Bernard, should keep half a step behind the Holy Spirit."

"In my own case He's always been so slow."

"That's because you don't pray."

"Helen does."

"As you know," said Emily, who had enjoyed his wife Helen's friendship for ten years, "I've never had much time for Helen; in my opinion she's gone under and I'd sooner not talk about her. In fact, Bernard, I've decided that it's time you and I regularized our own relationship—for the sake of my position in the Church if for nothing else."

He leaned back further into Emily's blue Maples armchair and looked at one of her more bewildering abstracts—a present she had been given by a German physicist in Oak Ridge.

"You're right," he said. "We should start an affair this evening."

Emily looked pleased. So recently back from the States, where they had made her feel "very famous and nice," she told people that her new riches had made her even lonelier than her talent. And now she looked affectionately upon Bernard and, in her most clear-cut voice and with her most blurred smile, said: "An affair? What a nasty bugger you still are, Bernard. It's too late. I'm too well known now, and besides, quite apart from my convictions, you were never on my list."

Bernard looked hurt. "I didn't know you had one. Who's on it?"

"Bertrand Russell," she said. "He's got a mind. Influencing him would liberate me from carnal desires and dirty thoughts."

"Ah, repressions!"

"Suppressions," she corrected him. "As a Catholic one must be accurate, Bernard. One cannot knowingly repress; suppression is the conscious act. Repression is a function of the—"

"Oh all right!" Bernard looked at her more appreciatively than ever. "You know, lately you're looking even prettier than usual. Other things being equal, I wouldn't mind marrying you tonight."

Emily examined him. She thought that he looked untidy in her armchair, altogether too masculine. Suddenly he offended her chastity. As a little girl she had been precocious, but having always found men so much less intelligent than women she'd never been able to decide whether or not they were worth the necessary sacrifices. But her loneliness still occasioned her pain and she still dreamed of finding a distinguished husband who would resolve her dilemma.

She got up. "You are offending my chastity, Bernard. You must make up your mind either to be my *cavaliere servente* and look after me affectionately or you must take your place among my friends."

"But you don't like your friends; they only irritate you."

"They are my friends nevertheless. Now I will make you a cup of tea and you then must go home. It is nearly eleven o'clock and I still have a little work to do."

"Just a little gin, please," Bernard pleaded.

"No. At this time of night it is pointless. And, besides, it affects my fingers the next day. I cannot play."

He closed his eyes and sank back into the enormous cushions, making them look small. Emily glanced at him secretly, wishing she'd never met him. Had she been more emotional she might well have sobbed a little; but as it was she did not even sigh. She only hoped that he would not leave too soon.

"Play to me now," he begged. "Play as only you can, while I brood about Coles and my darling Helen."

"And if I do, will you consent to my terms?"

"Anything. I need you in my life. We need one another."

"That is true."

She went into her music room and came back with her lute and the little stool on which she rested her foot when she played. She also visited the lavatory and resmudged the mascara round her wise, tearful eyes in case Bernard should wake up and regard her.

"I will play for you on my lute. I will even sing for you Yeats' 'Golden Apples of the Sun' in a new setting by my friend Desmond Dupré. You shall be the first person to hear it on this side of the Atlantic."

"I'd rather have 'The Owl and the Pussycat.' "

"No, Bernard. Tonight I'm feeling serious. We both are, and for that reason you must promise me that afterwards you'll go."

Bernard opened his eyes. The last drops of the day's alcohol were being filtered through his kidneys and there was no prospect of any more until he got home. Helen would be in bed. Emily's pupils were feline, very slightly spear-shaped, he noticed; her ashen hair was as fluffy as candy floss.

"But I would much rather have 'The Owl and the Pussycat.' "

Emily only smiled to herself before removing the rings from her tiny hands and touching the lute strings. Then, as he dozed in the chair, she sang to him in a voice that was as clear as the wavering light from the sky full of the London stars.

II

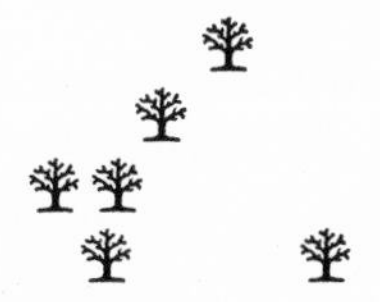

It was August and Coles was being foolish. He had started smuggling comforts into the prison for Hotchkis: razor blades; powder for his plate, on which there was but a single tooth to replace that knocked out in Liverpool Docks; shampoos for his dandruff; white balm for a leg muscle he claimed to have pulled in the weight-lifting class; some pile ointment and liquid paraffin; corn plasters; a pair of eyebrow tweezers; and an extra toothbrush.

"We get through a lot of toothbrushes for our tinder boxes," Hotchkis explained. "The handles are inflammable, see? When we're banged up with a flint and a razor blade we can always get a light."

With one of Coles' cigarettes he showed him how it was done.

"Pencils come in handy too," he said. "We plug a pile of graphite powder into the cell bulb and get a light that way. Ask Betty to send me a couple of 2-Bs next time. Oh, and some penicillin ointment for me back."

"What's the matter with your back?"

"Acne. It's playing me up since the warm weather started."

"Have you been to the doctor?"

"It's not worth it."

"I think you should, Hotchkis. In three months you've had dandruff, acne, athlete's foot, constipation, gum rot, pulled muscle, backache, and now acne again."

"Rheumatism too," said Hotchkis. "It's gate-fever probably. What's the matter? Betty cribbing or something?"

"No, no. I make most of these small purchases myself, but it's getting a little embarrassing. Last week the chemist told my wife—Lettice, you know—that he was worried about my health."

"I'll tell you the truth, Mr. Coles—"

"No need for the 'Mister,' please! We're not on those terms now."

"Since you started seeing Betty?"

Coles did not reply.

"Well, I'll admit that most of these things are for my friends," Hotchkis went on. "I don't ask any questions, but that liquid paraffin—"

"It's quite all right. Please don't explain."

"A coloured boy wanted it. They get through bottles of it, and who are we to judge? After all, in a prison things get concentrated, don't they?"

"Of course. One should always remember that society gets the kind of prisons it deserves."

"It's not that I'm excusing myself, Mr. Coles."

"I think you'd better call me Randall. After all, your wife does."

But Hotchkis, sitting back on his bed with a crucifix above his head, appeared not to have heard him: "I know I'm still in sin, of course. I took Paul's life and I can't give it back and I'm still so mean that I wouldn't even if I could—not yet."

Cole stretched out his legs and considered his well-polished shoes. He said: "I think it's a great mistake to think of your action as a sin. It would be much healthier to look upon your crime as a momentary lapse in your humanity—your manhood, if you like. It happens to all of us. We live in the process of readjustment, or civilizing ourselves and accepting those elements in us which—"

Hotchkis flushed suddenly. He took his back off the cell wall and looked at Coles hungrily.

"I felt sinful all right," he said. "And I liked it. It was great. It was as though I was kicking down a cathedral when I slammed him. I thought—no, I didn't think; I was just doing my thoughts, if you get me? As if they were me. And although I was mad, I was *clear* mad. I went through my conscience purposely. I didn't have it any more."

Coles felt remarkably calm. "Appreciation is the better word," he suggested. "Nearly all crime is a failure to appreciate a particular situation, whether great or small. I, for example, by bringing these things in for you without the Governor's consent—"

"I've been wondering about that. Why do you do it?"

"I'm not sure. I've been trying to work it out. I think that perhaps with your release getting nearer—"

"No, it's not that, Randall."

Coles kept stiller than ever, trying not to look at the photograph of Betty Hotchkis on the locker. She had said, "You're doing it for me as much as for him, Randall. You needn't think I don't know it, and I'm ever so grateful; I am, really."

"It's Betty's got round you," Hotchkis said. "I've seen it happen before, remember? It was the same with Paul; he stopped taking my duty-free fags off me and started giving me things."

"Really? I—"

But Hotchkis reached out his hand and gripped Coles' forearm. "Don't worry about it! Take it easy. I'm not blaming you, am I? And, look, if it's making you sweat, give it a miss. Tell Betty there's to be no more of it, just so long as you don't stop seeing her —not at this stage."

"I've been thinking it might be better if I did."

"It wouldn't. I wouldn't want it, see? And not just for my sake, but for yours too. You've been good to me, Randall, and I know there's no harm in you."

Coles was so embarrassed that he dropped his chamois polisher on the floor, and Hotchkis jumped over to pick it up for him. Coles polished his spectacles in his lap and then put them on again. He felt that he was very near an overconfidence of some sort, a total understanding that might destroy temptation. He only just managed to resist the impulse to confession. He said, "Please don't underrate me, Hotchkis. We're all in the dark. I mean, I have my problems, too, or, rather, my—"

"Difficulties?"

"Yes, difficulties."

"You wouldn't be a man without them, would you? You wouldn't be able to do yourself no good, let alone me, if you weren't full of things. Just don't let them build up, that's all, and when you go over there next time give Betty a kiss from me. Tell her—" On the landing beyond the half-open door of the cell a bell shrilled. "Ah, there goes the ruddy bell for the bang-up. What was I saying? Just tell her to wait for it, Randall. It's only fourteen weeks before I'll be eating her up myself."

Leaving the prison, Coles drove home a little faster than usual. He felt as self-assured as if he had passed some not specific preliminary interview, quite ready to meet Bernard and all Lettice's guests at Half Yoke House, quite satisfied with the immediate past and the things he had kept to himself.

It was the night of the second summer party, August the thirteenth, when in view of family holidays the guest list was inclined to be more eclectic than usual.

"I like to choose a thirteenth if it falls on a weekend," Lettice had said. "It could be inverted superstition, I suppose; but then one can suppose practically anything, but at least the children have grown up with none."

A little later in the conversation, they'd had a disagreement about inviting Bernard a second time in the same year. Though he'd failed to turn up in June, he'd told Coles that he would very much like an invitation in August.

"Well," Lettice had said, "he's your friend, so there's really no point in arguing."

Coles had said nothing. In previous weeks he had confided constantly in Bernard, hinting at his increasingly narrow escapes from Betty Hotchkis and asking him if he believed in the male climacteric.

"What?"

"The male climacteric," Coles had repeated. "Do you suppose I could be going through it?"

"No. You are merely restless and randy, as are most of us."

Coles had been as exasperated then as he was now in his red

Mini, floating through the green lanes at thirty-five to the gallon of the cheap and one pint of the best oil per every twelve hundred miles. Queen Anne's lace was out in the hedgerows and meadowsweet and burdock and the tall, tall emerald hemlock. The countryside was quiet, the shadows deep across the roads, and he dreamed now of Betty Hotchkis as he had seen her only three nights previously. On an evening just like this, with blackbirds singing in small trees and the smoke from the village ascending undisturbed, she had taken him over the road to get another honeycomb from her father's shed.

"Over the road?" Coles had asked.

"You needn't if you don't want to; suit yourself."

"But I'd like to."

She had tweaked his trousers as she opened the door.

"It's nice over the road. Different somehow."

The narrow street was empty, but Debrah, Hotchkis' ten-year-old daughter, was looking out of an upstairs window, watching them blankly.

"You always wear red," Coles said, "don't you?"

"It depends."

"On what?"

"Who's coming."

"It suits you."

She opened the little green gate. "Of course it does."

"Why?"

"I'm dark. Hadn't you noticed? Close the gate, please. He's funny about the gate, is Dad."

Coles stood under the crab-apple tree in front of the cottage. He felt a little short of breath, inclined to look back over his shoulder.

"What's the matter? What are you looking for?" she asked.

"I was admiring the cottage."

"Where I grew up," she said. "I was here twenty years until I met Chris twelve years ago and I'm still here. What a life!"

"But it's beautiful. People in London would give their ears to spend their lives here."

"Not me! I hate every stick and stone of the place." She opened the door. "There's not much to see; but you can look round it if you like."

Coles stepped in on to the red brick floor. He saw the sink and the copper, the latched doors, the half-timbered screen between the scullery and the living room-kitchen.

"We have a downstairs bedroom too," she had said, leading him over to the fireplace. "But nobody sleeps there, not now."

Coles was smelling the cottage. He rarely smoked and his nose was acute. He could smell old wood, old fires, brickwork, just-damp from the August rain, and tobacco.

"Your father smokes a pipe," he said. "When does he get in?"

"He's at the pub. The Cross Keys. He goes there Tuesday nights for the cribbage. Won't be back for hours."

"He's lucky to have you so near."

"You try and tell 'im," she said. "I expect you think it's funny to have a bedroom on the ground floor. He won't use it, but I do when the children are at school. I've done a lot to it really and I always keep the bed made up."

"Do you?"

Smiling to herself, she moved to a low door and opened it.

"Seeing's believing," she said as they stood there together, looking through across the fitted carpet to the new divan bed with its deep white candlewick bedspread.

"Lady of leisure," she said. "It's nice, isn't it?"

Coles was silent, taking in the tableau wallpaper, the flounced dressing table, and the white plastic camellias edging the rimless circular mirror. On a bedside table there was a second transistor set. She switched it on and closed an open window.

"It's where I dream, somewhere where I can think about things. Do you think I'm nutty?"

"Certainly not. Does Christopher know about it?"

"What do *you* think? He'd want to know where I'd got the money."

"Where did you?"

"Not what you think, not altogether." She sat down on the edge of the bed. "Not often, that is. Why don't you come in and shut the door behind you?"

Coles was thinking of Lettice, her austerity. She wore face cream at night and, several times a month, an ivory silk scarf to keep her hair in place when she'd washed it. Although she was only thirty miles away, he found it difficult to believe that she would really be going to bed in his presence that night, her cheeks moist with cream, her hair curling over the edges of the silk.

"And if you're thinking about Paul, you're wrong again," Betty said. "We didn't never come over here, only over at my place or out in his car."

"I wasn't thinking about him."

"You were thinking about something."

"My wife."

"If that's the way it makes you look, you shouldn't!"

He smiled at her impudence. He said, "It's over now."

"Well, come and sit down then." She was on the bed, leaning back against the swell of the pillows beneath the counterpane, her feet, with the shoes half off still on the fitted carpet.

"Not now," he said.

"Come on; I won't bite you."

"I know you won't."

She turned off the wireless, suddenly earnest, strangely apathetic. "Well, come and get it over then. Give us a treat, something to remember."

"Not tonight. I couldn't."

"It's Christopher, isn't it? You're thinking of Chris, and if he ever knew he wouldn't care."

"How can you be sure?"

"He wouldn't—that's all."

"But I can't possibly. Not this evening. I really can't."

"Think I'm bluffing then?" She rolled slowly over onto her left hip, drawing up her knees over the mattress. "I've got fond of you, that's what. I know what you're feeling and I'd like to help. Chris wouldn't mind that."

Coles sat down beside her and she drew his head down to her face, her palms closing over his ears.

"I can't hear you like that," he said.

She uncovered his ears and he looked into her deep-brown eyes, in which the cast shone like a child's.

"I was telling you not to worry, not to take yourself so serious," she said. "There's plenty of time. Just try me and see."

He gasped in her arms. He wasn't sure that he mightn't sob in her scented breath, in the scent of cosmetics and Virginia tobacco.

"You're lonely," she whispered, "like me. You don't need to tell me."

He lay on her red-swathed breast, his lips just touching hers. "My God! You're so right. When it comes down to it, there's so very little."

"There's nothing," she said. "You don't need to tell *me*."

"Nothing," he repeated, not hearing anything—not the sounds from beyond the windows or the tick of her bedside clock, but only the thrust of the blood inside the bones of his temples.

For five or ten minutes, silent and without making love, they lay there together and then, as suddenly, got up again, dragging themselves back into the room. They went back across the road with the honeycomb from the shed. In her own cottage she made him a cup of tea, which he only half drank, and kissed him good-by. Before he stepped out into the road again she brushed her lipstick from his lips with his handkerchief and said she'd wash it for him.

"You'll have to come again now," she said. "If you want to pick up your laundry . . ."

Remembering it all now, Coles looked at his watch. He was going to be late for the party if he wasn't careful. He drove faster but found himself looking restlessly at each of the pubs which divided him from Lettice and home. After passing the station entrance he did a thing he hadn't done for years: he stopped at the Railway Inn, only five minutes from Coniston Road. He guessed that Bernard might be in there, topping up after his journey from Charing Cross. As he'd said himself, he preferred to meet people "in a haze of self-satisfaction, because then they appear to be as charming and significant as they really are. What is more, I do too."

Coles parked his Mini beside the village taxi and went into the Saloon Bar. Presage was in there all right, talking to the Foleys, who had themselves been on the same train and who, though new to the village, had been on Lettice's guest list for several weeks. Coles had only heard her speak of them as "worth while; the new Cambridge, you know: young but not 'beat.' Though they're rather spoiled, they're quite interesting. He's in advertising and she's *enceinte* for the first time—rather striking-looking, but neurotic."

Presage was wearing a light flannel suit. His thick hair was parted steeply, and Coles noticed that he'd had his ears plucked and his eyebrows trimmed. The vertical furrow between his eyebrows looked as if it had been only recently sustained, young and clean.

"Magnificent timing, Coles!" he said as if their meeting had been arranged. "If you've got the car with you, we've time for a final round. Mrs. Foley, what will you drink?"

"Whisky, please."

"Another!" her husband said. "Darling, don't you think it would be wiser to have something else?"

"Oh, Charles!" she sighed.

Coles thought she looked ill, as ill as some of the early Picassos and as beautiful.

"If whisky agrees with me," she said stubbornly, "it probably agrees with the baby too."

"But you know how dreadful you felt last night."

"Except when I've had whisky I always feel dreadful. Thanks to you, I've felt like death for three solid months."

"And as lovely!" said Bernard sententiously.

Her husband, in Coles' view, absurdly dressed, good-looking, young and inadequate, seemed to be used to these interventions. Coles was certain somehow that he'd have felt at a loss without them.

Mrs. Foley left a pale lenten stain on the rim of her glass and looked down her long italianate face. They all three studied her hungrily. The two older men noted the frayed black back-swept hair, the childish neck, the violet eyelashes, and the dead-white cheeks.

"The lady is not Indian; she's ill," Bernard quoted.

Coles said, "By the way, I'm Randall Coles, your host actually." He would have gone on to talk about Lettice, her pregnancies, his comfortable memories of morning sickness in the evening; but Presage, obviously in his best form, steam-rollered him.

"In all great portraiture, Mrs. Foley, there's an element of malaise, a suspicion of mortality."

She looked at him with interest; but her husband, who was a little stupid, wasn't sure if this was culture or rudeness.

"Do tell me the rest of the quotation," she asked Bernard.

"Strictly, it's

> "*She* is not Indian, she's ill.
> Tis death has darkened that pale cheek of hers.
> No sun of Indian Summer in a trench of climate tropical
> Has made her brown, that was so pale and fair
> A Northern girl."

"Lovely," she said; "it gives you that little shiver."

"The *frisson,*" said her husband.

"I said 'shiver,' " she reminded him contemptuously.

Coles tried to fill in the gap. "I think it's rather morbid. I never did care for Stevie Smith and her Anglican mythos."

But the girl was apparently only interested in Bernard. "I really do like it," she insisted. "It's so lovely to be neither Indian nor ill. As a matter of fact, I *am* a northerner myself; I was born in the North Riding."

Presage bought her a bag of crisps: "Eat the lot before Coles drives us back to his Lettice." He opened the packet for her. "With Helen I always found that a little something in the stomach—also, you must sit down."

"I'm always telling her not to smoke so much," her husband said, "but she does exactly as she likes."

"I don't exactly like having babies," she reminded him.

"Now how could you possibly know that until the process is complete?" Bernard asked. "Until you've had it?"

"I don't. But I'm quite convinced that even at the end of it I shall only produce something as meaningless as a rabbit."

Coles was a little shocked, but Bernard was only more sympathetic.

"You must be feeling so frightful that I can think of no way of effectively comforting you."

"I am!" She glanced at her husband. "I feel as if I'd been poisoned months ago and it was still going on. I can't even enjoy my moods any longer."

"And you've been to a doctor?"

"Oh God, yes. They ring the changes on all kinds of pills and capsules."

"Which you don't take," put in her husband.

"Only because I find whisky so much better. Without it I'd sooner be dead."

"Then certainly you're not dying yet," Bernard told her. "If you were, you wouldn't be sooner dead, and what's more this party's going to be a success."

"It won't be if we stay here much longer," Coles said. "I promised Lettice I'd be home half an hour ago."

But Presage was only interested in Mrs. Foley.

"If at any time during the evening," he was telling her, "you should feel in the least faint, nauseated, bored or vertiginous, then seek me out in preference to your husband, who, quite understandably, irritates you at this time."

She smiled up at him. "I will."

She did. In the middle of Brecht's "Mack the Knife," when Lettice was passing round the raspberry shortcake she'd rolled that afternoon while reading *Le Milieu Divin,* Hera got up dreamily and privately and walked along the terrace to be sick into the roots of the anchusa.

Presage, keeping his promise, followed her, while everyone else, including her husband, who was dealt with by Lettice—"No, not you; she'd hate it"—sat on inside, talking of the noösphere and pregnancy. Two of Lettice's doctors, Geoffrey Cattermole and Norton Baird, held their seats, while Bernard, wiping Hera's ashen lips, was falling in love with her heavily and not without hope.

As he put it to Emily a day or two later, Emily looking interested and sour: "It was her timing as much as her weakness. I've often suspected that women unconsciously choose their moments for these displays. Lettice was being nauseating about 'complexification' when it happened."

"And she fainted too, of course!" Emily said.

"She was completely sick," said Bernard with satisfaction. "The prawn *risotto,* the black-currant syllabub, the retsina—everything."

"What else did you have?" asked Emily, kindled.

But Bernard hummed "Mack the Knife" and remembered Mrs. Foley in her cottage, once he'd got her free of the pack, leaving her husband behind at the party, at her insistence.

"Charles, her husband, bores her," he said, "after only two years."

"I thought you said they'd been married only six months."

"They lived together for over a year when they came down from Cambridge. They're rather an old-fashioned couple really: it's the sort of thing people did in the Twenties."

"Do they quarrel?"

"I think she dislikes him. There was the usual abortion."

"Was it his?"

"That I did not ask her. It's just possible she might have been offended."

"It will all end up with the smell of old goat," Emily said. "Bernard, you are boring me."

"But I'm not boring myself. Sad as I am, I enjoy their pain. It seems only right and proper somehow. You must admit that if it worked it would be one in the eye for us."

"You are being narrow and uncharitable."

"That's because I'm in love with her!" And he sang:

> I am crooked, I'm fifty, a funk,
> But I'm in Being, even when drunk.

"Only just," said Emily. "Lately you have ceased to develop. I can see that our friendship is coming to an end."

"Then you must pray for me."

"I do. You come in with Himmler and Dame Edith, whereas once you were with Bertrand Russell and Calvin."

"Pray," said Bernard, "that in her dreams Hera Foley may accept me, unshorn of all my accidents, the bruising disparity of the years. Pray that one night when her husband is possessing her she may cry out hungrily, "Bernard! Oh, Bernard!"

"I thought," said Emily coldly, "that your object in going to the party was to advise Lettice about Randall."

"Ah, Lettice and Randall," said Bernard sadly, "forever on the parquet, forever contemporary. When the doctors and the dentists and the lady magistrates had departed, when Tyndal had had his run, when Lettice had brewed the china tea bought by Randall in Old Compton Street, they counselled me. It was a long headachy night."

"Then you must have behaved very indiscreetly."

"I put her to bed and drank Scotch with her. We listened to Radio Luxembourg and talked about marriage."

"When *I* reach the change—" began Emily.

"Not with Lettice, with Hera Foley, that sweet spirit, that tarnished bride."

"Bernard, you are at your worst when you attempt the baroque. I don't think I want to see you for a week or two. Do not be surprised if my morning secretary makes excuses when you telephone me."

But Bernard was quite carried away. Merrily he left Emily's flat to catch a train to the West End and a late drink in Rules: to dream of his moments with Mrs. Foley . . .

"You see," she had told him, as in her dressing gown she had prepared not for bed but for a row with her husband on his return, "Charles is a good lover, otherwise I'd never have married him."

Beneath the thatch of the pretty, conceited cottage Bernard sat on the foamy counterpane of the low double bed, fascinated by his reflection in the various looking glasses, which were full of flowery wallpapers, hand-blocked by her husband, of windows, of twilight and trees. He'd thought for a moment that he might be having a kind of affair with himself to which she was incidental. In this light he looked about thirty-eight, he believed, or forty-five, or possibly sixty; and he decided that it depends who you believe is looking at you.

Before her dressing table, sick and graceful, Hera was doing something to her hair, which had gone lank with pregnancy.

"At Girton," she resumed, "we classified lovers according to voices."

"And your husband was a baritone?"

"No, a tenor."

Bernard glanced at his flannel-clad body in the double mirror. "I would be a bass, I suppose?"

She looked at him. "A double bass. I'm not being horrid. We all agreed the heavies would be worth a trial."

"What about altos?"

"Oh, they were mostly dud poets. I tried two and they bored me terribly."

"And so you married Charles?"

"He gave me such an attractive prospectus. No steady job, no dreary fidelity, and nothing about babies."

"How were you going to live?"

"We weren't, not in that sense. We were going to write, act, paint, drink, and fall in love with people."

"What went wrong?"

"Nothing *went* wrong. It's only that Charles *was* and I didn't realize it because he was so good in bed."

"But you're so intelligent."

"I may be, but I'm not intellectual. Charles ought to have been an art master at Eton. Even that couldn't have been worse than this cottage and the garden studio."

"I'm not with you, I'm afraid."

"Oh, for God's sake, can't you see that I hate compromise, that I'd rather he humiliated me properly, painted all the time, and took mistresses and drugs?"

"Why?"

"It would give me an excuse to decide about my life. He might do something so convincing that it would be worth staying with him. He might make me feel I couldn't manage him."

She ground her cigarette into the carpet. "That's my bitchiness, I suppose. There's a part of me that enjoys his weakness, the feeling that I can destroy him any time I want to; but the rest of me resents it because I know I'm guilty."

"And what do you do about that?"

"Go on going to bed with him, looking after him, cooking his meals and having this bloody baby."

Bernard was silent, and she looked at him curiously.

"Have I shocked you?"

"You've made me wonder about my own wife."

"Did you say 'wife' or 'life'?"

"I said 'wife'—though they're the same thing really."

"They oughtn't to be," she had said. "The strong go under for the weak. I don't want Charles' life to be under anyone's control, least of all mine. I want a prince; all women do!"

"How do you know he wouldn't be a prince if you gave him the chance?"

"Princes don't need chances; they take them."

Bernard asked for a drink. He got up and, standing in front of the mirror, straightened his hair with a little comb of which he was ashamed. She took him downstairs and, because she was now feeling a bit shivery, they drank by a small electric stove.

"I was furious at being sick in the middle of 'Mack the Knife,'" she said. "Do you mind if I put it on the gramophone?"

They sat on, waiting for Charles to return, until between them they'd finished the whisky. When Bernard got up to go she said she wished he would come again. He sketched in his week for her and told her about Emily.

"Oh, I love her music," she said; "she's so clever. Why don't you stay a little longer and let me play you some of her records?"

"I know them all. They're Emily's public self."

"How I'd love to meet her."

"We'll have to arrange it. How often are you in London?"

"As often as you like. My mother's got a house in Lowndes Square. I go there whenever I find Charles too boring."

He kissed her and trundled off into the luminous summer's dark beneath the warm stars. Moths flew and he heard the whistling of owls. Along Coniston Road lights were on in the bedrooms, and Bernard, singing "Mack the Knife," planned his next meeting with her as, exultantly, he returned to Half Yoke House. He was glad that Coles would not be able to confide in him until they were alone in the morning train; he did not want to discuss Mrs. Hotchkis.

III

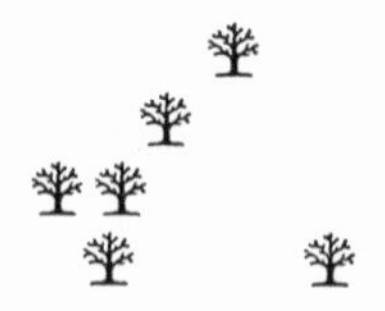

Thirty miles away, late as it was, Betty Hotchkis was entertaining Mr. William Smeed of Westminster Rugs and Pavlova Detergents Ltd., whose product was "gentler than feathers." He was forty-five but looked older because he dyed his hair—a man of many parts. In pubs he boasted of this: he'd say, "When you've had as many agencies as I have, you're more than a good mixer; you've got no class at all. You're accepted everywhere."

Betty had met him about four months earlier. It had started then and had been going on ever since he'd sold her a giant bottle of carpet shampoo a fortnight before Randall Coles' first visit. She liked Bill Smeed's voice, his commercial sympathy, his gentle, businesslike love-making.

"It's like his shampoo," she'd told her neighbour, 'Reen, as they were hanging out their washing. "It gets down to the dirt without ruffling."

She and 'Reen had been "speaking" at that time, and though there'd been a quarrel since then they knew it wouldn't last forever, that, other things aside, they needed one another.

"You wouldn't believe the things I've bought off him," Betty had said. "A foam-latex shampooer with a yellow handle, a plastic bucket with a free duster, an instant spot-remover—and now he's trying to sell me an electric wringer."

"Paying for him, aren't you?"

"Only on the H.P."

"But you give him his installments, I'll bet."

"Not unless I'm in the mood, and I don't half play him up when I'm not."

"They expect to have it all ways," 'Reen said. "Send him over to me and I'll give him electric wringers."

"Not before Christmas. It's my bad time, is Christmas, and I never feel like it then."

"You make up for it in between, though, don't you? Who's that other fellow you've got on the hop—the one that comes in the Mini?"

"Randall Coles. He thinks he's going to bring Chris and me together—a prison visitor or something. You can't see his face for lines, but he's not so bad."

'Reen pegged up a pajama jacket. "They think love is blind," she said. "Get anything out of him?"

"I don't want to somehow, not that way. He keeps offering me presents, but I tell him, 'Give them to old Chris.' "

"What's he like then, this Randall? He looks real lemony to me when he passes the window."

"There's plenty of pips in a lemon," Betty said, waiting for her to laugh, trying to keep faith with the particular vocabulary they employed. "I suppose you'd say he was educated, really. I know he works me to death trying to keep up with him."

"You've gone cultured, have you?"

"A bit maybe. It cheers him up, though, poor little fellow. From what he says about her, he's got a wife like a clotheshorse. At least it's not what he says so much as what he doesn't. He's after a fling really before his kids make him a grandfather."

"Will you give it him?"

"Well, he's done a bit for Chris."

"Chris indeed! You want your head testing, Betty. He's got what it takes, has Chris. If he was mine I'd give him the top brick."

"For a year or two, maybe—but not after. You'd find he expected too much of you."

"They all do, once they've got you."

"Not the way Chris does. He expects you to submerge yourself like a ruddy submarine."

'Reen had laughed under her deep fat. "In the oceans of his love!"

"In the sink," said Betty.

"You're right there," 'Reen said. "Just look at this wash, and I haven't put the dinner on yet."

"Nor me, and I've got the backache, and not with what you think."

"Well, so long now, and give my love to Mr. Gentle as Feathers . . ."

But that had been several weeks ago, and now in the half-dark, in the cottage living room illuminated only by the hundred-guinea radio-cum-television-cum-record-player bought by Hotchkis ten years earlier and already long out of date, Betty sat with Mr. Smeed on the sofa, discussing Randall Coles.

"He's nice," she was saying. "He rather intrigues me."

"Intrigues you; come off it, Betty."

"Interests me, then. But that's what he does; he makes you think of new words, working on the B.B.C."

"What's his other name?"

"Coles. He lives near Etchingham—Coniston Road."

"I'm doing that area next month; I'll call. But what's he got that I haven't got?"

"It's not like that with him. He seems to understand me. He says I've never really caught up with myself—words to that effect."

"I know, Betty."

He did know. Often enough he'd said that sort of thing himself and it had paid off.

He drew her closer, his fingers, with their home-manicured nails, insisted on by the firm, tightened in her armpit. He could feel its classless warmth and dampness as he swallowed dryly. He had an idea that she was going to be difficult tonight, and in order to distract himself a little he looked at his brief case, just visible on the dusky window sill opposite. It contained his order books and the Novice's Handbook of the Westminster Rug Company, which he was supposed to have off by heart before the next sales conference at H.Q. in Holborn.

He recited to himself:

> The successful representative never mixes business with pleasure. Unprofessional intimacy, irrespective of the party concerned, brings short returns on long odds. Offer your prospects a cigarette, but be careful to retain the packet. Remember christian names but do not use them.

"Betty," he said, "sweetheart!"

"He's got a smashing voice," she said. "When Randall's talking, he makes everything sound different."

"Yes, darling."

He pulled her a little closer, his gaze fixed on her round chin, her barely moving lips, dark as a wound in the chamois-grey of her face. Her left shoulder rode on his right chest as softly as a ripe melon; her cheek against his own was as smooth as his daughter's. Nuzzling it, he was glad he'd shaved again before dropping in. Betty didn't like bristles, and he'd shaved in a lane with his razor plugged into the dashboard socket of the firm's car.

> The accessory provided for all our representatives to emphasize the sales value of a neat turnout.

Let her talk, he thought. *For God's sake, let her go on talking. Let her talk her silly head off about this square from the B.B.C.*

He kissed her cheek and the side of her nose, smelling her clean breath. In minutes or moments, depending, he'd work round to her mouth, and that, unless she'd got a mood on, would be it. Betty was dodgy: he knew it instinctively; the best ones always were. You must never let them think you were taking them for granted.

He looked at the clock made by Christopher Hotchkis in the prison Hobbies Class a Christmas or two ago. He couldn't see the face, but he knew it must be close on eleven by now, as it was a long time since it had struck. He hadn't got too much time, but he couldn't risk withdrawing his right hand from her armpit to look at his wrist watch. It would mean starting all over again.

She was talking all right, on and on about Randall and Ireen; and he was as attentive as the firm could have wished.

Always be ready to listen. A minute's listening can be worth five minutes' sales talk. Never forget that many potential customers are lonely. Westminster reps are good listeners.

Ten minutes, he thought. *Multiply by five and you get fifty. Just about the time I've been here, and yet I'm nowhere. Last month I made it in twelve minutes flat and nobody talked.* He decided he'd go into action the next time the clock struck.

Interruptions can clinch a sale. Do not let them distract your approach. A burned or scalded child sympathetically and promptly treated may result in regular orders. Always carry the vest-pocket tin of dressings supplied, replacing them as necessary at the firm's expense.

The clock struck eleven, and in the silence ticked out by the brass pendulum he said: "Come on, darling! Give! It's getting late."

He slid his face round to her dark mouth and got his arms to work on her shoulders.

"Don't," she said indistinctly; "I don't want messing."

She pushed him, shaking her head, collecting herself on the small sofa. There was just enough light for him to see that she was smiling, and he went on hoping. But she said: "I'm a woman dreaming and I don't want messing."

A woman dreaming! he thought. *So that's what Mr. Coles is telling you.* He got out his king-size cigarettes and lighted one for her in his own mouth, sliding it glowing between her lips.

"Dreaming? What about?"

"Christmas, if you want to know."

"You're always dreaming, and it's not healthy. You want to give it up, Betty."

"Can't."

"What's up then? What's up with Christmas? It's four months off."

"It's coming, though." She bit a knuckle. "Everything always happens to me near Christmas."

"You want to forget it."

"I've told you. I can't. You don't understand, but *he* would. Old Coles is sensitive; you can talk to him."

"You haven't tried me yet. Get it off your chest now. Is it your husband; is it Chris?"

"No." She was scornful. "He always used to tell me I was dippy."

"He's one to talk. A Catholic nut-case. Now come on. Pretend I'm the doctor or something. Tell me everything."

"I've told you before. As much as there is to tell."

Wait for it, he thought.

> Though the good representative is always in a hurry, he never appears to be. He knows that although time is money there's plenty of it.

He looked at the toys bundled in the corner, just visible in the dial lights of the radio relaying dance music from Hamburg. There was a Raggedy Ann doll, a plastic space gun, the remains of a telephone set, and an intercontinental ballistic missile with broken fins. There was also a gentleman doll with a bowler hat and a brief case.

Toys have changed, he thought. *Myself, I had Meccano and bricks.* Charlie, when he was young, had an electric train set that cost a fortnight's commission. Charlie was his son.

"There was Mother," said Betty. "Two years ago this Christmas."

His son, Charles Pollard Smeed, he remembered from his last letter, had just got a good job with a tire firm. He'd be up for the management of the Exeter Branch in a few years. He was earning very good money.

"You mustn't live in the past," he told Betty.

"I don't," she said, "except this time of the year."

The firm had nearly turned Charlie Pollard Smeed down on account of his flat feet, but he'd stuck to his remedial exercises and improved sufficiently to pass the medical. His mother, Norma Smeed, had wanted him to be a male nurse.

"Betty! Sweetheart, you loved your mother," he told her. "You must have done."

"I didn't love her enough. I know I didn't. She went the twenty-seventh of November two years ago and I never cried."

Charlie would have made a good male nurse, but he'd had a business head even at sixteen. ("There isn't the money in it, Dad. There's security, but the money's rotten.")

"You were numb," he told Betty; "that's all. People are—it's natural."

"Death!" she said. "It's horrible. You can't believe they've gone. You keep expecting to hear from them, and they don't never give you a sign."

How the hell could they? he thought.

> Bereavement need not necessarily spell No Sale. Give what comfort you can and remember that gratitude, though not immediate, is often inevitable.

He understood what "often inevitable" meant: it meant "more than sometimes." He would stick it out.

He wondered, in passing, whether Betty's mother had been cremated or buried and, for some reason, hoped that she had been buried whole. It was the kind of thought that came to him when he'd done too much; it was a sign that he ought to slack off a bit.

He said: "You don't want to worry, darling. Whatever it was, she'll be at peace now. Your mother's at peace, sweetheart."

But she was miles away. He doubted if he'd get anywhere even if he spent the night there, which would be taking a risk with the village.

"She looked so little," Betty was saying. "When Ma Baily laid her out, there was nothing of 'er. That's what I can't get over. She was over the road on the sheet in her own bedroom and she looked as though she'd never done anything. You couldn't believe she'd ever *been,* really."

"You don't want to worry, darling. Your mother'd had a full life, must have done. She'd had work and a husband and children and you. She'd had *you,* Betty! And you loved her. You love 'er still, sweetheart."

She was sobbing into her handkerchief. "It was her feet," she wailed. "Her feet and her face, as if they'd never been used. And when I went up there to say good-by she looked as if she was telling me something I couldn't hear. I kept saying, 'Oh, Mother; oh, Mother!' "

She sobbed on and Smeed allowed it, waiting moments before he whispered, "You don't want to *dwell* on it, darling."

He put his hand back into her right armpit and she came over against him, her whole body sagging with warmth and grief against his exultant breast. His heart flushed and saliva gushed into his tobacco-flavoured mouth.

"I couldn't believe she'd given me myself," Betty whispered. "She didn't look big enough, and I thought of the years she'd given us: all that cooking and Dad getting drunk and the rows. I said to 'er: 'How did you ever stand it, Mother? You've got to tell us before they take you away.' But she lay there as if I was finished too, as if she thought she'd given me nothing."

He gave her his handkerchief when he felt her tears trickling down his shaven cheek into the right-hand side of his mouth. "There, there," he said. "Have a good cry, sweetheart. Use this. It's clean on today."

He mopped her drenched eyes, lashes, her dark red lips, and then held the wet handkerchief for her to blow into like a baby before he planted his mouth into her silent one, holding it there and getting no response, no resistance, only the enormity of her grief and wonder. She pulled away from him. "Don't. It's not decent. It isn't right."

"It can't harm 'er now. You know it can't. You know she wouldn't like it. You know she wouldn't want to see her little girl crying her eyes out after nearly two years."

She got up. "Oh Gawd! I look a sight, I know. Lend me that hanky again."

He sighed, stretching out his not-long legs in their hopsack trousering, looking at his wrinkle-free stockings and new shoes shining in the radio light. In front of the dark mirror she was combing her hair, drying her thick eyelashes. He watched her blow her nose as unashamedly as a man or a long-married woman while he wondered whether she'd sit down again beside him or go through into the kitchen to make the tea. He looked at his watch as the clock struck the half-hour, and anger stole up in him, making him feel ready for anything, for the toughest assignment.

Never acknowledge defeat. There is always another time. There is this time.

She sat down opposite him, too collected by half, too tidy and with too much attention to the lipstick she was applying now that she'd switched on the light.

"Besides!" she said.

He waited, watching the pendulum of the clock, feeling as flat as if he'd just made it. *Half an hour to midnight and then another day,* he thought. *It hits you.* He had a lot of country to cover if he was to make up the week. It was the w/e again already and he was down on his orders. Weekends always stirred his conscience: he'd never liked Sat/Sun; only Fri was tolerable.

"Besides what?" he asked.

"You've got a wife—that's what."

"So?"

"So Paul hadn't," she said.

"And now he's dead. So what?"

She laughed at him, reminding him of the playground at school years ago, one of the girls scoring off him.

"And you're not dead and your wife isn't neither," she said. "Norma, or whatever you call her."

He concealed a belch. It was hours since he'd eaten.

"Norma—that's her *name!*" he said. "There's no whatever-you-call-her stuff about it."

"*You* ought to know after nineteen years."

"I do know."

She giggled. "Maybe. But I only know what you've told me, don't I? That's all."

"Listen," he said. "There's no call to get insulting just because you're not in the mood and nobody's given you a drink yet."

But she was obstinate: "Norma! Mrs. Norma Smeed of Five High Street, Belling near Horsham, age forty-two. Now what else has he told me about her on his visits to my place?"

"Give over; I don't know what's got into you."

"She's got blood pressure and she's in the change," Betty went on, beginning to sway her round chin in her hand, "and the pills the doctor's giving her have made her frigid and she's got no use for you—at least that's your story."

"Well, it's true, isn't it? What of it? What's the matter with you, Betty?"

"Nothing. I'm just remembering, that's all. I'm remembering the things you told me, and there's no harm in them or why'd you have told me?"

> Never lose your temper no matter what the circumstances and/or provocation. A lost order can be made up at the next door call. A lost temper poisons an area.

"If you hadn't of wanted me to know, you wouldn't have told me," she said, wagging her crossed leg in its unladdered nylon stocking. "You've got a son too. Charlie, isn't it? And he's got flat feet."

His face was flushing and he rather liked it.

"That's a lie for a start. He's got over them."

"And when he was born his ears stuck out. He had to wear a helmet affair."

Smeed got out his car keys and picked up his brief case.

"Shut up, Betty; for God's sake, shut up. I've had a tiring day."

"You're not the only one. You off, then?"

"What does it look like?"

"Drive carefully," she said, "or you won't be here next week. . . ."

As soon as he'd gone she went across the road to her father's cottage, where she had a room on the ground floor. She took her cigarettes and transistor with her and a post card that had arrived that morning from her elder sister, Pery, who worked in a Hampstead club.

The post card was a photographic enlargement and had been posted in Ostia. It showed Pery with two thickset men beside a private swimming pool. The men wore shorts and sandals, the hair on their chests was touched with grey, and one of them was smoking a cigar. Pery lay full-length in a canvas hammock with a striped canopy; there was wine in an ice bucket on the table beside her. One of her long legs was drawn up, and she was wearing sunglasses.

On her divan bed, in the room across the road, Betty got out her album and pasted the card onto a blank page. Then, with the wireless playing softly, she started again at the beginning of Pery's life: the first weekend in Brighton, 1952.

She was glad she'd riled Bill Smeed.

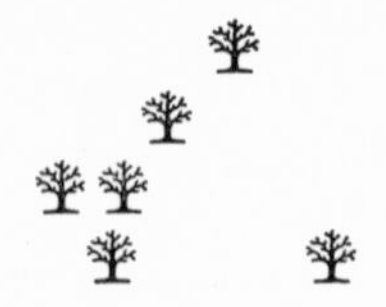

On that same morning at six o'clock, Helen Presage, Bernard's wife, was returning from her daughter Cecily's convent school, after the all-night vigil which had prevented her attending the Coles' party. A beautiful woman whose maternal grandmother had been Polish, she was seven years younger than Bernard, green-eyed and fair-skinned. Though she was seldom happy and could not see that she ought to be, she had always enjoyed the present more than the past. The future did not interest her very much. She did her best to put it all into her prayers.

Now, on the London bus, she yawned on the five-thirty communion, long dissolved completely in her stomach's fasting juices, and thought of Cecily's lovely little face, seeing in it the hope of some visible justification of her life.

Cecily herself looked at the younger workmen on the top of the bus, wishing they would sometimes look at her instead of at the racing fixtures in the morning papers. Wearing her mother's black lace mantilla, she could see her reflection in the window whenever the bus passed a building in shadow; she thought she looked rather lovely.

Her face looked spiritual and luscious at the same time, she believed. Her eyes were enormous and her lips, even when not stuck out, desirable. Framed in the irregular edges of the mantilla, trembling over her forehead, she must surely look very exotic. For all the workmen knew, she might just have returned from abroad—Rome probably—and her mother, pale and self-contained, could be her chaperone: a duenna who had accompanied her on the instructions of her "real" mother, "the Principessa." They were only on the bus because they were economizing. They both spoke several languages.

The workmen swayed and smoked, they greeted one another as they got on, and they said, "Mind how you go," as they got off; but in between they said little. Only one of them so much as glanced at her and, seeing her response, a deep look followed by hauteur, began to take an interest in her. She kept an eye on him for the rest of the time, saw him drawing on his cigarette with his pleasant mouth, and became ever more conscious of his glances, equally divided between herself and his newspaper.

He said to his friend, "No, I'm not doing him, not this season. He pulled a muscle at the Oaks." Then he went on staring at her questioningly, as if he were asking, "What are *you* doing up so early, anyway?"

Unlike her father at this hour, he'd already shaved. His hair curled round the back of his neck, and his left hand, holding a cigarette, had TRUE tattooed across the backs of the fingers, one letter to each finger.

She tried to read the right hand, but it was at the wrong angle, so she made it up; obviously it would be FALSE. What a clever idea! Though it would have been best the other way round: "false" on the left, "true" on the right.

He moved his right hand at this moment and she saw that the word was LOVE and that he was smiling. With the same hand he began to beat out a meter on the seat in front of him, his fingers flickering and the thick gold ring on the little one gleaming in the interrupted sunlight.

Cecily studied her reflection again and tweaked at her mantilla to hide her face from him. She was very grateful for his interest. He was open and mysterious, she thought, as mysterious and nice as all men doing manly things. He reminded her of all the soldiers she'd ever seen on television documentaries, clutching the sides of lorries or landing craft with ringed hands and cheerful frightened faces, about to invade something.

"Oh, I do feel exhausted," she told her mother so that he should hear her voice.

Helen squeezed her hand; she was not going to compete, even though she was half asleep herself. She was thinking about the angels in the reredos of the convent chapel. Cecily's school fees, she supposed, had helped to pay for them, and they had been very expensive, the work of Adam Kossowski, the Polish artist. Perhaps because of her own Polish blood these particular angels had excited her more than any in her collection. They had been severe, with dark eyes and sheathed swords. They'd stood fifteen feet high at least, seeming to fill, like those described by Claudel, "the space between the sea and the sky."

"Angels exhaust," Father Detriman had suggested some time after midnight, "because if they exist they must be a purely spiritual creation. It is hard to be interested in them with so much else going on in heaven; but personally I think I might find them restful after God and saints." Then he had corrected himself: "I would be wrong! For all the evidence suggests that to be exposed to angels is an even more exhausting experience. They might make one want to sit down."

"Quite exhausted," Cecily repeated, and went on to herself, as if she were speaking to the workman, whom she had promoted to the rank of Warrant Officer First Class, "by my long flight, you see. I left the airport at Rome only three hours ago, at three-thirty this morning, because my mother, the Principessa, asked us to economize on this brief visit to England."

But the workman was only wishing she were older and said to his friend, "With this mist you can bet it's going to be stewing-hot later."

"Why worry? They'll put us in the shade, oh yes!"

"In the boiler room, under old Beefy."

"And won't he be sweet, losing that packet at Catford on Golden Rain?"

"That dog dried up halfway round. She dropped dead on him and he done her heavy. When his old woman finds out!"

"Gawd, Beefy's old woman! Here! Did you know he calls her 'is pullet? He used to, anyway."

"Some pullet!"

At Hyde Park Corner they both got off to go over the river to Battersea Power Station, where, from the four fluted chimneys, the smoke rose peacefully as a sacrifice.

Cecily and Helen rode on past St. George's Hospital and into the park, where a troop of the Household Cavalry was returning from morning exercise. Cecily watched the silent men in their uniforms, each man moving asynchronously to the soundless trot of his horse. She lowered the window in time to catch the jingle of their spurs and harness, to hear the horses' steel-shod hooves knocking on the tarmac.

Thirty men on horses looking neither to the right nor to the left, their heads as stiff as statues on their shoulders. They would smell of horses and tobacco and beer perhaps: nearly all men did; or they might smell of whisky, like her father when the B.B.C. cheque came, or of after-shave lotion, like some of his friends. She would marry a horseman, a horseman or a nice workman like Beefy, who'd call her his "pullet."

As in a Victorian print, she saw the horsemen back in the Palace stables with the stone urns on the high containing walls. She saw each man in shirt sleeves and breeches tending his particular horse. Rows of stalls and bales of straw, water in country buckets, mangers full of crushed oats; beneath a high-beamed roof chaff and dust floating through shafts of sunlight.

Over towards the Serpentine the sun lighted up the tree-high mist—pale as milky water—and touched the crowns of the trees. Beyond, the distances lay hidden in distance and whiter mist, the dew refracting the light on the roofs of Park Lane.

In the Bayswater Road they got off the bus and walked along the silent street to the top-floor flat in one of the houses. Helen cooked them a big breakfast and Cecily begged a post-vigil cigarette from Bernard's box. In front of the kitchen mirror she brushed her hair straight and then went into her bedroom to play with her make-up, wondering what was the secret of looking older.

Helen sat on over the breakfast table drinking coffee and smoking. The cat sat on the sill of the dormer window squinting out into the risen sun. On Cecily's plate baked beans and bacon rind were a golden mess, and over the sink was a good picture of some Byzantine angels. In the sitting room through the open door she could see those she'd bought at the convent sale of work: their close-curled heads against blue silk, their hands long and thin, disembodied in blessing or praise against that blueness. Lazy and irritable as she was, the nuns' blue caught her mind. It could be the colour of what "is," she thought, the secret that's in distance, what the Italians saw when they looked at the medieval sky. And, although they were not there in that particular needlework, she saw golden fourteenth-century birds with trailing tails and enamelled breasts flying against pale Lombardy poplars and dusky mountains, the hinterlands of christian vision, studded with olive groves and eremitic chapels.

She had one more angel given her long ago by her uncle, a great traveller. He had brought it back from Mexico and it was made of silver. The head and shoulders were feathered; the fine feathers of his hair curled up a little from his forehead and ran down like a peruke to the roots of his wings. His arms were cleanly muscled with a skin that suggested it would grow plumage rather than hair. In the folded forearms there were the sinews of a man who waits with confidence, as if he waited out of the Mexican past, Indian and adamant, the keeper of himself.

She wondered when Bernard would get back and how she would behave when she saw him. She always had to be careful when she'd been to a vigil, because it made him suspect blackmail or witchcraft, some sly advantage.

But Emily had once told Bernard, who had told Helen, "Helen goes to vigils in order to excite you. It doesn't do for married women to lark about in convents. It only makes them sensual."

She remembered this as she went into her bedroom, to make up for the night she had lost. It was not altogether true . . .

Bernard came in as she was undressing. She heard the flat door open in the hall, his pause in the sitting room, his "where are you?" from the kitchen.

"Here," she said, lying down on the bed so that she could sit up as he entered.

"I just sat down, darling; I'm so sleepy. I hope you've had breakfast?"

"Toast and coffee with Lettice and Randall." He kissed her on the neck pleasantly. "Where's Cecily?"

"She's playing about with her make-up. I think she's at work on her Great Love Stories again. I wish you'd tell her to get to bed."

"She went to the vigil with you?"

"Yes, poor little thing. I suppose it's self-indulgence really. I love looking at her."

"It'll do her no harm," he said. "Did you miss me?"

She yawned. "I'm so terribly sleepy."

He kissed her and quoted:

> "I feel a mortal isolation
> Wrap each limb in desolation,
> Sight, hearing, all, suffer a fall."

They lay back crosswise on the wide bed. Helen followed in her mind the rest of the verse:

> I see the pretty fields and streams,
> I hear beasts calling and birds singing,
> Oh not clear but as a prisoner who in a train does pass
> And through the glass peer.
> Ah me, so far away is joy, so near.

Bernard was seeing Hera Foley's ashen cheek with its violet eyelashes, her lips. Kicking off her sandals on to the floor, Helen opened her eyes as he kissed her and looked up at the bedroom ceiling.

"Do shut the door," she said.

As the ceiling receded a little further she thought, *I'll get up and shut it myself,* and then noticed that Bernard was looking distracted. Perhaps it wasn't going to be necessary to close it after all.

"What are you smiling at?" he asked.

"I was thinking you looked tired."

"I am, but not as much as all that."

With an effort as definite as someone rubbing a statement off a blackboard he eliminated the mental image of Mrs. Foley.

"I've just realized that I haven't done the shopping," she said. "There's nothing for lunch. Also it's the middle of the month."

She got up and went over to the dressing table, smoothing her hair and watching herself in the mirror.

"You knew that when I came in," he said.

"It's just that I don't want the whole day to be disorganized, darling. There's always tonight."

He dragged himself upright and followed her to the dressing table, where the dormer window was reflected with its long view of chimneys and clouds.

He remembered the flowers and trees round Hera Foley's cottage. "And besides," Helen was saying, "we haven't the stamina of men."

He wondered if something in his manner had given her a clue; his uncertainty reinforced his determination to make love to her.

"We're not doing anything this evening, are we?" he asked. "Nobody coming? You're not going out?"

He wasn't going out himself that night. Not yet. There had been no definite date.

"I'm going nowhere," she said. "But I'm frightfully tired and it only makes me irritable. Why don't we wait till we're both fresher? Tell me about last night."

"It was just the usual thing," he lied. "Worse than a vigil really."

"Whom did you meet besides the Coles?"

"No one of interest." He put both hands on her hips. "I'll tell you all about the party on one condition."

Without a word she went over to the bed and lay down. "The door," she said. "The telephone, and perhaps the curtains . . ."

Through the wall in her own bedroom, sitting at her grandmother's desk, Cecily turned over the title page of her book:

GREAT LOVE STORIES OF THE O.T.
A transalation from the English—
With notes and comments by
CECILY PRESAGE

She flicked over the pages to reread her last entry:

JUDITH (CONTINUED)

The best part of Judith's prayer begins:

> "The sword of Holofernes. Lord, if it might be his own pride's undoing! Be the eye he casts on me a lure to catch himself, the professions of love I make, his death."

That opening phrase is a battle cry in itself. The sword of Holofernes! It conjures up a tall warrior with a fine ignoble face in which the devil shines like an angel. And Judith, who knows all about marriage herself because she's a widow, is not intimerdated; but "in her place of prayer" begs the Lord her God that *"his eye"* should be a lure to catch himself. "The professions of love I make, his death."

Oh dear, how difficult this is to pin down and understand. It is not Judith's eyes that are to be Holofernes' undoing—though she's obviously made them up with orrisroot and olive oil—but his own eye, and, I suppose, beauty would be no good if we were blind, though I've always hoped that it would be my own eyes that would make a man choose me.

And next Judith goes on to pray that all the sweet words she makes up for Holofernes shall be his death! She prays to tell lies about love and asks the Lord her God to let love bring death in its train. We can only suppose that Judith is contrasting the kind of love she feels for Holofernes with the other sort she has for her own people. It is exciting that God allows her to use it too.

It will be noted in Chap 10, before Judith puts on her make-up, that she calls her maidservant to her and goes downstairs. Perhaps she was on the flat roof praying prostrate in the moonlight. The editor does not feel it was likely she was in a temple—probably on a hillside with little steps cut into it and many scented plants growing across them. At any rate, Judith does go down from her place of prayer like after a vigil, which can be extremely boring.

Next Judith throws aside the sackcloth and flings away her widow's weeds, which tells us that she must have been a tidy wife and wasn't hoping for another husband or she'd have no use for such clothes. Still, we can't help envying her that trip to Holofernes' banquetting hall, which, since he was a general with his armies, was probably a *tent!*

I've always loved tents, even ordinary ones on the Isle of Wight. But Holofernes' tent would have been vast, with Persian carpets spread on the grass floor and tapestries and cloth of gold lining the walls, a fit place for what Judith had to do, and here I must admire her foresight in taking her own food with her and not drinking any of his wine, because when people drink even cider they never get on with things, even when it's not murder. Also she was careful to take her maidservant with her.

Coming back to her getting ready (see Chapter 10):

> "She bathed herself, anointed herself with the finest myrrh, parted and tied her hair. The garments of happier days she donned anew, put on her sandals, took bracelet and anklet, earring and finger ring, decked herself with every ornament she had."

We sympathize with that "garments of happier days," and anklet and bracelet and the single earring, but we feel that she perhaps overdoes it when she goes on to wear all her accesories: unless it was the fashion. We can't help feeling, however, that she must have wanted to look like a harlot, so that if she did fall for Holofernes and go too far she could tell God later that it was not her real self she gave him but only tartery.

And God cannot have disapproved because it goes on to say: "The Lord Himself lent grace to her mien. . . ."

And at this point, feeling sleepy, Cecily stowed her journal and the Knox Bible away in the lower left-hand drawer of the desk. She went through into the sitting room, paused outside her parents' door, and heard them talking away in there as usual. She decided to have a snack from the refrigerator before going to bed. In the evening she would go to the swimming pool and practice her diving.

V

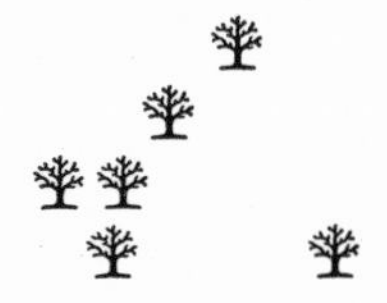

For October a friend had lent Betty Hotchkis' elder sister, Pery, his rather small villa at Praia da Rocha on the south coast of Portugal. Miss Bowles-Johnson had tacked on the "Bowles" for business reasons soon after her entry into London's clubland thirteen years earlier.

"It's not exactly class," she'd told Betty at the time; "that's out of date. It just sounds better."

"Go on; what's wrong with 'Pery Johnson' anyway?"

"You ought to know. You never liked 'Johnson' yourself. Remember how, when you were engaged to Christopher, you were always practicing your signature? 'Betty Johnson,' 'Betty Hotchkis,' 'Betty Johnson'!"

"That's different."

"Oh no, it's not," Pery had said. "There's plenty of better reasons for improving your name than becoming some fellow's sink-slug. I'm intending going places."

And she had: a steady progress from agency modelling via film commercials to West End Clubs. For holidays, Brighton had been succeeded by Jersey, and Jersey by Ostend, Deauville and Menton.

This summer she had the Portuguese villa offered her a year earlier by her ex-friend Colin Phipps-Cable when their friendship had been at its height. Though slightly tarnished by the repercussions of a recent political scandal, he had remained faithful to his undertaking—faithful but absent.

"He's still close to the Shadow Cabinet," Pery had told Betty on one of her flying visits to the cottage in Sumner; "but he has to watch his step, poor old boy. When I ring him up these days, he's always 'in conference'; but even when his secretary puts her hand over the receiver you can hear his pulse in the background." She laughed a little sourly. "Funny when you think of it. That place in Portugal must have cost him a fortune and he never did get me to it."

"They can't stick the pace, if you ask me."

"Don't you believe it! Colin was a demon while it lasted. I don't know whether it's pills, but they seem to get worse as they get older."

"It's a pity you didn't pick someone in the Home Office," Betty said. "He could have done something for Chris then, while it still counted."

"You have to take it in cash and presents, dear. Favours don't pay. I must say, though, he was as nice as nice when I wrote to ask him if the villa was still on this year." She had thought back: "What d'you mean, 'while it still counted'?"

"Christopher's release. It's going to be my lot, that is."

"Well, I told you that at the time. Look at the money I sent home, and the fun I've had with it."

"I've had some myself these last few months. But when Chris gets out—"

Pery lighted a black cigarette. "Cheer up; I'll send you a p.c. from Praia."

"Who you taking?"

"No one. They take us, dear. Max."

"Who's he?"

"He's in fashion photography. He gets two hundred a week, and he's still only twenty-eight."

"D'you like them that young?"

"It makes a change. And it gives you confidence too if you can get them."

"Confidence! I haven't got any. I went to the doctor about it last month," Betty said. "And he sent me up to hospital to the psychiatrist. *He* said I was suffering from 'loss of reality.' "

"What you want is a bit of life, darling. If it wasn't for Debrah and Marc, I'd take you with me next week. Fix you up with a nice executive to pay your expenses and leave the rest to nature."

"It wouldn't do no good."

"You've still got your figure. You only want to see the fellow who does my bras. Properly made-up and with your hair done up-to-date you could still pay your way."

Betty helped herself to a black cigarette.

"I wish I could. I think that's half my trouble—the life you lead! I can't get it out of my head. Don't send me any more post cards, Pery. Please don't."

"Whatever you say."

"You could bring the kids something, though, poor little devils."

"I was going to—some dolls from Lisbon airport. They say they make them lovely in the convents there. Well, darling, take care of yourself. Not to worry. Things'll be better when Chris gets back."

Pery was sleeking on her make-up for the drive back to London, standing there in front of the mantelpiece mirror in her blue cut-away blazer and narrow mattress-ticking trousers.

"You look marvellous, you do really!" Betty admitted, despite herself. "Sometimes when you've gone I feel like a bloomin' ghost thinking of you."

Betty looked beyond her, out through the window and along the street, to the chapel of the Assembly of God, where Pery's MG, with the hood down, stood waiting in the long shadows.

"Don't go yet. You don't know what it's like when you've gone, Pery. I get to thinking about Mum and when we was kids and knew nothing."

In a fit of memory she saw Pery in her home-knit yellow bikini on one of those wartime August evenings over by the water. "Remember those summers when they used to call you the 'Goddess of the Gravel Pits'? Remember that song you used to sing?"

Pery smoothed down her tinted hair so that it clung round her face as if she'd just got out of the water. She pretended to shiver and allowed her teeth to chatter. She pulled in her stomach and stuck out her breasts, singing:

> "What's mine's my own!
> When you get home in summertime
> Be sure you phone or leave a note in school.
> Remember I'm no fool! What's mine's my own for
> keeps;
> Unless you buy the bloomin' best I'll moan,
> I'll make you blue. You'll know when I am
> through,
> What's mine's my own."

"I can still do it," Pery said, "and it's as true now as it was then."

"It took me right back. I don't half wish things was different. Sometimes I think you're living my life for me. Whenever I read something about the club in the papers or you send me a bunch of snaps from Rome or somewhere—"

"I'd have thought you'd have had enough of the papers after the plastering they gave you over Paul Caine."

"I don't know. I've often wondered. I felt alive then. I felt real."

Pery kissed her. "It's not all roses. A lot of the time it's fantastically boring. You have to listen by the hour and you always know how it's going to end up—in bed with a headache and some fellow sleeping his head off with his false teeth shining."

"At least you don't have to get up and get the bloomin' breakfast."

"It's hoping keeps you going," Pery said, "and I'm just hoping right at this minute that Max and Portugal's going to be different."

"All the same you're lucky. If Chris ever gets himself done again I'm going to put the children in care and come up to London. I'm going to start all over."

"You'd never stick it now, Betty. You cling on to what you've got for the sake of the kids." She opened the door into the street. "I must push off now or I'll be late. I don't want Max in one of his moods. He can get really mean when he's cross."

A fresh cigarette between her fingers, her grey lizard-skin handbag swinging beside her trouser-clad legs, she walked gracefully with Betty up the street to the MG.

"Be good!" she said. "And wish me luck with Max."

Betty leaned against the windscreen. "You wouldn't want to marry him?"

"Why not? It's about time; but really I just want it to be different, I'm tired of the same old thing."

With a final wave, with the sound of the engine dying away and the silvery dust hanging in the air, she was gone.

Three days later she sat having photographs taken by Max on the parapet of the fort at Praia da Rocha. She was brown, wearing a straw hat she'd bought in Lisbon and a sunset-pink Italian bathing suit paid for by David Heim, the owner of the club.

Max was very brown too; his teeth and his eyes gleamed above the hooded lens of his camera.

"Roll your left shoulder. Roll it, for Chrissake! And can't you pull up your left bra? You're 'anging out of line. There's too much contour on that left nipple."

"That better?" She yawned.

But he didn't answer; his brown forehead was sweating, and there was a trickle or two running down through the black shield of hair on his chest.

"Your suit's riding over your left buttock, you've got that leg too high, and you should've shaved again."

"Oh God!"

"Well, I have to do it, don't I?" Max always emphasized his Cockney when he was irritable. "Listen, I 'aven't got staff with me, see—no one to put pins in the bloody dresses and tighten up the sags. Your figure's going; that's the trouble."

"It isn't."

"It bloody is. Anyone'd think you'd 'ad a family the way you're looking this evening."

"Do you mind!"

She watched the sardine boats going out, far below, the men aboard swaying with the hulls, tossing as they rounded the promontory. She could see their pink tartan shirts and naked feet. Octopuses hung drying in the rigging with bunches of fish baskets, like huge brown grapes. The men looked up at the fort, casual unsmiling stares, as if they were riding lorries to work.

The sun descended like a moonstone into the pale-green horizon over the sea and she thought, *A night on the water.* She adopted a new pose, pointing her toes downwards, sliding a heel into the instep of the other foot, glancing downwards at her stomach to look demure and sad, as if she were posing long ago by the gravel pits, as if she were waiting to rebuff some boy she had taken in by her demureness and sadness.

You don't change, she thought. *You haven't changed at all, really.*

"If you weren't out of frame now you'd be better," Max said.

She was conscious of his movement round her. She heard a table grate on the concrete. She was aware of him as though he'd been a shadow himself. He might have been that boy over the gravel pits coming up on her so solidly that his advancing shadow seemed to disturb the grass.

"Now keep it like that, kid. Keep on thinking whatever you was thinking. Keep your little thoughts in your head and before long we'll 'ave a picture. I've only done three spools so far. No! Don't tighten your lips; leave them the way they was and you'll make the cover."

I'm losing it, she thought. *Why can't they stop talking? God, the hours I've spent listening to the devils.* Remembering the faces of the men in the boats, she chased her thoughts as if they'd been a tune or a poem.

"Cor strike it! Just when I get the setting you go and move your head. 'Ow many more times do I have to tell you? Keep your eyes in the shadow of your 'at. I want mystery, pathos; I want poignancy, the end of summer. Just keep looking at your fortune the way you was. Think of your lost opportunities."

The sardine boats had strung out like a flight of birds, like the curlew that used to come in off the marshes at sunset in those wartime summers. She couldn't see the men now, only their boats riding out into the dark part of the sea, where the sardine shoals flickered to the surface at the approach of night.

"I'm cold, Max. If you're much longer I'll get goose flesh."

"Think deep, darling. Concentrate! Just now you was thinking somethin' and it came out in your face. Well, for Chrissake, think it again. The light's just right for the filter. We've got five minutes before the sun goes down. Come on, kid, for my sake."

He wheedled her. They always did at dusk. All men changed their voices at nightfall. They got round you, they made promises, they became friends.

She heard the clicking of the shutter, and in the breeze she could smell his body, young, sweet still.

"You can put on your dress then and go for drinks. If you're getting the 'ab-dabs' here, we'll move on to Seville Saturday, so long as you'll just get back to where you was when you moved yer head."

"I can't, Max. I'm trying but I can't. It won't come."

"Of course it will. What were you thinking? You 'ad beauty from it, and I didn't mean that about your figure. A woman like you can never lose her rating."

"It's no good! It was the men in the boats; I was thinking of a night on the water."

"A night on the water? Go on, then."

"I was thinking it must be nice to be out there all night doing something real. They say they sing when they're pulling the nets back in."

"What else was you thinking?"

"When I was young."

He had been on his haunches for a low shot, but he jumped up. "Young! Pery, that's it. It came out in your face; you looked young. Now get your head down and get back there." She felt his gaze upon her, his gravity. She heard his breathing as he waited with the camera poised between his hands.

The past moved jerkily through her mind: the shadows of the boys over the gravel pit, Betty being noisy because they were standing her up in favour of Pery, the cries of the homing curlew, the black surface of the water in the pit reflecting the bodies of the lounging couples.

She tried to hold the memory, but through it all came the shadows and shaded lights of clubs, the taxis and the long convertibles, the figures of men beside her whispering or noisy or quite silent on the drives back to the different flats.

She could smell the sea, hear it. There was that hush again as the lowest edge of the sun touched the soft line of the water far out; and she saw that the ocean was not still, that it writhed, turning over upon itself in slowed motion as if something were about to come out of it.

Max saw her through the reflex of the camera; she was perfect. There were green tones on her shoulders and on the round of her drawn-up knee. Against the pink of the suit she was taking the light lime of the unclouded sky. She was all washed pinks, greys and greens; the laxity of the pose was just right, her expression—what could be seen of it in the mouth and the crescents of the shadowed eyes—dead clever for the commission. Her age did her a favour, leaning into it as she was, blurring just enough at the edges for *The Queen* autumn cover. If the picture came off the way he imagined it, she'd make the younger women envious and the older confident.

"You've done it!" he told her as he packed up. "Darling, you was perfect. One of that last spool's a genuine Max Stamford. Come on! Get yourself decent before we eat." His hand stroked her hair. "I like to have something to work on."

They danced to the jukebox in The Fort. The place was practically empty; the barman and the waiters leaned against the walls watching them. The records were three years out of date, tunes they had moved to in 1962. But the floor was as smooth as ice and the lights were low. They ate seafood and drank carafes of lobida.

"I'm feeling better now," she said. "Just for a minute it got me down—out there on the terrace."

"That's what I wanted. It's the secret; you don't get a picture before the subject's broken down. Know what I say?" He held her closer, waiting. He was sorry for her not being younger, for being near the first edge of it, for coming up on "thirty-two"—"add five." "I say to them all when I'm jumping round them, pushing that bloody shutter, I say, 'You got to remember, that's what! Once you start remembering, *I'll* start taking.' They don't realize that for the first half hour I've got a stopper on the film. It's 'ow I made my name, kid. That and something else."

"What else?"

"Visu'lization. Bein' able to see how it's going to look in chemicals."

He let his lips brush her bare neck, where as yet there were only the earliest lines. A shiver came through to her, and she knew it was going to be all right after all. By the third day you could always tell, and this time it would come off because of the work, being partners. There would be no need for Seville.

She let herself ripple against him, her hips and her stomach.

"It was those men," she said, "out in the boats. They looked I don't know what like, as if they really didn't care. You know what, Max?"

But he was at her neck again; she could feel his teeth and his tongue. She'd have to slow up his drinks if she wanted to prolong the dancing. She wanted to talk before they went back to the villa; she needed to.

"I'm listening," he said.

"Well, for a good five minutes I felt like they were worth having. I was telling them: 'All right, boys, you win.' "

"Poor sods."

"And I thought I'd write Betty in the morning, send her a letter instead of the usual p.c., and tell 'er to go with it with Christopher and the kids."

He straightened up as the record changed. "I was asking this morning down at the quays. Do you know what they get for six nights' fishing a week? About a thousand escudos a month, about three ten a week. Work that one out with a wife and four or five kids. It's no wonder they have a dictator here."

"Don't spoil it, Max."

"Don't worry; I won't. I'm a Tory myself really, some kind of a one. Know why?"

"I don't know and I don't care."

"Because, kid, they don't believe in politics—not Tories . . ."

They were high when they left. Full of the light-red lobida, they walked back along the front in the moonlight with the moon laddering the sea. The air was scentless and the water flat-calm in the dropped wind. Max wore his calf-high leather boots, making a padding sound as soft as an animal's. Pery's straw zapotas clapped on the concrete.

The night was beautiful as a tropical film and the moon clear as a high note. On the edge of the cliff there was a never-completed hotel with unglazed windows and enormous empty rooms. Over the years fig trees had grown up from the cellars as far as the first floor, their leaves black against the dark sea, the moon silhouetting their branches.

"It's eerie; isn't it eerie?" she said.

"It's good, but it's 'ackneyed. I thought about it yesterday."

"I meant the people that never came, the couples on honeymoon."

"And good-timers like us." He kissed her in good time and heard her catch her breath quickly.

"I was only thinking," she said flatly, "that it seemed such a waste. There should be cars and waiters and music in there. Think of the view from those bedroom windows."

"Trimmings!" he said.

They went on past the bare places of the cliff, where the leaden sea with its single ladder of moon stretched to a just-lighted horizon. The sardine fleet had anchored for the night and rode motionless, each boat with a lamp at the masthead. They stood off from the eroded cliffs in a serpentine skein, as still as floating sea birds.

Pery dragged. "I don't want to get there really; it's so beautiful it makes me feel I want to bring it all down some way. Does it get you like that?"

"It used to, but I stopped it with the pictures."

"I feel heavy and I feel light. I want to get there and I don't."

"I turned it into lolly and why not?"

She held his arm, dragging at him again as if they'd been back at the gravel pits. "We've got to make it last, Max."

"We're going to."

"Not just that, but this, just walking like this. There ought to be some way."

"I could eat you."

They stood there joined above someone's back yard, a long kiss above a lonely house on the forefront of the cliffs, where there were four white turkeys sitting out on poles between rows of globe artichokes. There wasn't a light in the windows of the house. With its white walls it stood there, crouched in the moonlight on the very edge of the land with the black sea behind it, private and, in some way, suggestive.

Lust dizzied them like alcohol. Max wanted to kick the pavement with spiked shoes as if he were an athlete starting a short race. Pery wanted certainty; it had to be perfect, more than itself, so that she would know.

They swayed, stuck there in the moonlight. He saw the bed in the villa, five minutes away; he saw the loose ropes of the sheets, the whole area of the mattress, the mirror on the wall twisting and trembling as if something had just fallen into it.

"Come on, kid; don't let's muck about. We're not teen-age."

"I was thinking we'd have a cup of coffee first; I'll make it the minute we get in. And I want a bath too."

"You try it!"

"I won't be more than five minutes, Max."

"As long as it takes me to use a fag, and that's your lot."

He'd sit in a deck chair and watch her get the coffee. With another ten days to go there was no hurry really.

They walked on again, more slowly, holding hands, convinced.

In the morning Max went into Portimao to buy a film. Pery remained at the villa, sitting beneath the sun blind over the porch, writing letters. She sent a long one to Betty back in Sumner and then, remembering that it would soon be his birthday, she wrote a post card to Christopher. It was in rhyming couplets and a little flirtatious; it suggested good times.

VI

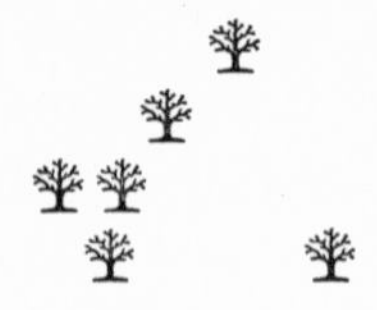

Hotchkis was getting restless and Pery's post card was one of the last straws. "Not the last straw," he admitted. "Who worries about the last straw when you're carrying the stack? Last straws are what God sends when your back's already busted."

So he went to see 405 Bushnell on "A" Landing. He cut the Art for Leisure Class arranged by Miss Coakley and he cut the ping-pong tournament and the "spider" or safe-busting conference in the Quiet Room. Purely out of politeness he knocked on the unlocked door of 405 Bushnell's cell: purely out of politeness because Bushy couldn't lock it anyway; it was on the "double" with the big steel tongue sticking out two inches. The light was on and Bushnell was sitting on his bed, thinking.

Bushnell, with his beard, was sitting on his bed brooding beneath the coloured photographs of the royal family. That Christmas there was much patriotism in the prison, a consequence of the loss of the Empire; except in the petty larceny cells, Sport had gone down: there wasn't a boxer, a wrestler, or a footballer up in "G" Hall that November—just royalty. Prince Philip, Annigonni's Queen in the robes of the Garter, and the "Pudding," or heir apparent, with smashing little Princess Anne and the good old corgis.

Everybody was feeling loyal, and some of the younger officers had memorized the royal genealogy, and some of the spider boys had copied them and could rattle off the German connections as fast as the bloodstock tables.

Many of the older officers disapproved of this flush of patriotism: they said it spelled trouble and was more dangerous than religion. There'd be a riot, they said, or a lockup strike with everyone refusing to associate or even slop out—except the fairies, who couldn't abide their own excreta.

But, despite his photographs, 405 Bushnell was not a real enthusiast. Although, with the exception of the latest prince, he'd got all the royal family—including the Queen Mother outside a Scottish castle which looked just like Pentonville—he admitted when questioned that it was only because his bird was dragging and that he believed the pictures might help.

"That's right," Hotchkis had told him. "It shows you're committed, boy. Go on plastering your peter with them like a Catholic with medals. It's one way of retaining sanity."

"Sanity, Hotchkis?"

" 'anging on to your head by means of contemplation. There's the actives and the passives: passives, various saints; actives, the Count of Monte Cristo and Legless Bader, D.F.C., D.S.O., R.A.F. and bar."

But Bushnell had mixed up the royalty with his own wife, Stella. Stella was in a number of positions in a bikini and without it. In the ones without it, owing to prison regulations, the prints had been touched up: the areolae of her breasts had been blurred out and between her legs there were shadows like ectoplasm. "Much more suggestive," Hotchkis had pointed out to one of the officers, "than the real thing, Officer Dalrymple."

"I know, Hotchkis, I know."

"Much more likely, sir, to inflame the inmates than a straightforward life study."

"They ought to come down, Hotchkis," Officer Dalrymple had said. "And when this governor gets his transfer and we get the admiral in his place, they will."

But Bushnell was very proud of Stella. Often the boys dropped in to have a look at her, admiring her as if she was a work of art: her three measurements, her painful Camberwell smile. They would look at her with awe and at Bushnell with a fearsome respect. They would look; but, until later, they would say little, as if a visit to Bushnell and Stella were a kind of sharp constitutional after the dinner break. Bushnell, sensing their disquiet, sometimes challenged it a little blindly, like a ringed bull: "Stella's all right," he would say. "There's nothing wrong wiv Stella!"

And the men would whistle outside the door before coming in. They would whistle to each other, sibilants of surprise, holding up their hands as if measuring the girl on the wall.

"He's morbid," they would say as they clattered off along the "A" Landing slates. "Bushnell's morbid."

But Hotchkis would tell them, "He's not morbid; he's an artist. Bushnell's an artist."

"He's not. He's morbid. Hanging her up like that in there!"

Hotchkis would move along with them, retaining the argument and not allowing his feet to clatter with theirs. "Each man kills the thing he loves," he'd say with a stagey sneer. "That's what comes of putting a ponce like Oscar Wilde in prison. Did I kill my Betty? Not likely. I killed that bastard, Paul Caine. And that was more or less an accident—like a lot of things a man does on purpose."

Having set them off along the pale-mauve slates beside the green suicide railings, he would leave them and return to Bushnell and charge him with this last thought. "When you strangled Stella," he'd say, "you did it entirely accidentally. Anyway, that's your story, you big lug. Why don't you admit, at least to yourself, that like everything else it was a half-purpose? Then they might of believed you."

But Bushnell, in his cockeyed way, stuck to his story, and grew his beard ever bigger and bushier, saying that Stella's death was a hundred-per-cent accident, that if it hadn't been for some neighbour's knocking at the door of the flat and asking after Stella, he'd have taken his thumbs off her windpipe thirty seconds earlier.

"Yes," Hotchkis would agree, "but, look, why did you put 'em there in the first place?"

"To teach 'er."

"Some class, some blackboard." Hotchkis would turn his grey jacket collar up and then down. "But perhaps it's better that way! To leave you in ignorance of yourself with your monument on your chin."

"Monument?"

"*Her* monument. The hair that murderers grow: Stalin, Lenin, Trotsky and Hitler—a tombstone to your ignorance, you bum."

"Oh, get out, 'Otchkis; you make me tired."

But this evening, Hotchkis, full of his own problems, was intent on being polite to Bushnell. He knocked on the cell door at a good moment: ping-pong going full swing on the ground floor, and the Art for Leisure Class in the Tower House, and the spider conference in the Quiet Room. On the governor's orders no officers were allowed in the Quiet Room; decorated in postwar Cunard, it was one of his many conceits—simultaneously snobbish and vaguely religious: a good place for planning big jobs.

Hotchkis was feeling physically comfortable; there had been a thick welsh rarebit for supper with tomatoes and cocoa. The new central heating, installed by the Home Office at a cost of thirty thousand pounds, was going full blast, and the prison had really settled in for the winter like a refitted steamer on a long voyage.

So Hotchkis, with the post card and a book of Villon's poems in one hand and his snout tin in the other, knocked in perfect good faith, and Bushnell, underneath dead Stella in her polka-dot Bikini, called out: "Who is it?"

"Ah, Bushnell!" said Hotchkis in his padre voice.

"Drop it!" Bushnell growled. "I'm feeling tired."

"Tired! Me, I'm worried, old son."

"Look, 'Otchkis! If you can't be normal, bugger off!"

Hotchkis held up his tobacco tin as if it were a microphone and spoke into it: "Testing, testing, testing! This is Marconi speaking; can you hear me, Dimbleby?"

"What you want? Busting in again."

"I told you: I'm worried. Even without a day's lost remission I'm powerless to sort things out."

"Well, give us a fag, then."

Hotchkis rolled him a generous one, about the thickness of a knitting needle. He stuck it through the beard into his mouth and lighted it for him. Bushnell closed his eyes and bit on it, drawing in a quarter of an inch of it without a rag of smoke's appearing.

"I'm getting nowhere," went on Hotchkis. "They gave me just a bit too long, and things are building up outside."

"With Betty?"

"With her and her sister, Pery. She's a bad influence. I got this card from her this morning."

"What's it say?"

"Read it! Oh, I forgot; you can't." Hotchkis addressed a royal photograph: "You see, your Majesty, without me the poor slob can't even read. It says, Bushy:

> " 'Well, another year has gone; it's one you must forget. I feel the year that's coming will be your best year yet. I know it won't be easy to do the things you planned—but, Christopher, I'm sure you know I'll help you all I can. Today I will be with you—although we're miles apart. The distance has no meaning, for you are in my heart. So, "Happy Birthday Darling." I'm sending love so true. I know you'll find fulfillment in everything you do.' "

"I'd forgotten it was your birthday," Bushnell said.

"It was last week. Pery's gone to Portugal with some ponce with a camera and a long prong and she's stirring it with Betty again. Coles told me."

"What can you do?"

"Plenty. I'm going over the wall."

"With six weeks to go? You're nutty."

"Not nutty. I'm converted, that's all. I've rotted long enough. All you've got to do is to get me a boiler suit out of Stores."

"It's not on."

Hotchkis sat down beside him on the bed. "Come on, Bushy! I've listened to you long enough and done my best to help you sort things out."

"You keep Stella out of this. And take your 'ead off her legs! You're putting grease on them."

Hotchkis got out his blue prison handkerchief and rubbed at the photograph gently. "I'm sorry. Now, where were we?"

"We was nowhere; it's just not on—not Stella, and not your break. It's barmy."

"It's my birthday, Bushy. You got any of our brew stowed away? Any of the old apple juice?"

"It's in the ventilator, but it's not ready yet. The apples wasn't ripe."

Hotchkis clambered on to the bed, but Bushnell, who was younger, beat him to it and pulled a quart bottle out from the shaft beneath the window.

Hotchkis sloped over to the door and took a look both ways along the landing and over the rail. He saw the ping-pong balls bouncing on the table and the blue hats of the officers walking about down below. Returning, he took the tooth mug from the table and slumped down again on the bed, fumbling in one of his pockets for a bottle of surgical spirits.

"Coles brought it in for the slipped disk I got weight-training."

"That stuff? We'll be as drunk as a fiddler's bitch."

But Hotchkis emptied the little bottle into the cider and stirred the mug with a toothbrush.

He drank and passed it over to Bushnell.

They lay there slumped on the truckle bed, hearing the sounds of the other men echoing up from the basement. They sagged, swinging the mug from hand to hand, mouth to mouth.

Bushnell felt himself relaxing. Hotchkis had always affected him like this, stirring him up and then settling him expertly, making him talk, making him remember.

His influence had grown ever since their first meeting in Wandsworth, where, in for similar crimes, they had become mates, full of quarrels and sympathy, more than friends.

Between them they'd shared fourteen birthdays in different prisons, always with a drink of some sort and an extra tobacco ration, taking it turn and turn about to provide the stuff. Their crimes had been sudden, irremediable and had made them think. Hotchkis was already a Catholic, but Bushnell, up to the killing, had been nothing until Hotchkis had explained to him that murder, like martyrdom, might be a kind of "baptism."

Bushnell's grandfather had been a Baptist, and the word had run down to him through his family like water. Hotchkis' use of it had touched off a sensibility inside him, making him thirsty for something he felt he deserved for his murder. Until that moment, back in Wandsworth, he'd never believed he might get anything out of it. He'd come to believe that he was more dead than Stella.

Now Hotchkis opened his book and Bushnell settled back with his head between his pictures.

"I'm going to read to you, Bushy, so pin your ears back."

Bushnell rolled himself another cigarette. "I've been thinking about Stella again. What you said about getting forgiveness."

"Never mind that; listen to this: it was written by a French grafter more than five hundred years ago when he was in prison himself:

> " 'Love now and wenches I forswear:
> War to the knife to them I meet;
> For death (and not a rap they care)
> Through them treads hard upon my feet.
> I put my lute beneath the seat;
> Lovers no longer I'll ensue;
> If ever I with them did treat,
> I'm none henceforward of their crew.' "

"He was bitter!" Bushnell said. "Same as us. There's nothing to it."

But Hotchkis read on:

> " 'I feel the droughts of death draw nigh;
> Gobbets of phlegm, as white as snow
> And big as tennis balls, spit I—' "

Bushnell sat up. "It's disgusting! If you're going to read stuff like that, you can get out. I thought you'd come in here for a jaw about me and Stella."

"What about her? We've been over all that before and I've told you where you stand, Bushy." Hotchkis topped up the mug with cider and passed it over.

Bushnell drank it all, as of right.

"This about forgiveness," he said. "Eight years you've been telling me things would be all right if I could see what I'd done. You said that in the end I'd get my forgiveness."

"Absolution!"

Bushnell belched. "Absolution, then. With you gone, where do I get it?"

"You don't. Until you realize what you've done you can't start."

Bushnell stared out through the half-open cell door.

"And if I did realize it?"

"You won't, not on your own, not just thinking about Stella. To get absolution, you have to be bigger than what you did. The way you are, you can no more forgive yourself than I can. We're both stuck with corpses, with people; and forgiveness doesn't come from people. It's something they use. It's God's."

"Well then?"

"We're back where we started, with the actual killing. Was you right to rape and strangle Stella?"

"I told you, I was keeping 'er from screaming."

"You're burning your fingers, Bushy; drop yer stub."

The cigarette had reddened two small semicircles of the skin on the squat fingers.

"I was only keeping her quiet. That's all. She was used to it and she liked it that way sometimes. Stella liked it roughish."

"But was you right?"

"She was finished. She was no good."

"Well, that's it, then. You're still stuck with 'er, playing God. You don't get your absolution."

The tapping of the ping-pong ball ascended; all the sounds of the activity in the block.

Bushnell was looking alarmed, sitting bolt upright. Hotchkis, lying back, could only see his grey serge shoulders, his white neck and the brown bush of beard in front of his ears.

"I'd have give her another chance," Bushnell said. "But for Enid hearing her screaming and keeping knocking at the door, I'd have let up on her. I was actually saying at the time, I was asking her, 'Had enough, Stella? Are you sorry for what you done?' "

"Screaming! Bushy. Stella screaming. What with, when she couldn't breathe? Or weren't you blocking her that hard?"

Looking for the cigarette tin, one of Bushnell's hands crabbed over the bed sideways and found it. He rolled himself one and accepted Hotchkis' light in silence, lolling back like a wounded man. After a few moments he got up again and walked round the cell a couple of times. He stopped in front of a small photograph on his bedside locker: Stella in a white blouse in the woods, coy behind bracken, holding up in her ringed hand some kind of toadstool. He said: "What were we talking about then?"

"You know!"

"It was a lot of bloody insults the way Stella lived. She'd had 'alf a dozen before me and more after we got married."

Hotchkis took another drink and rolled it round his mouth before swallowing it. "Did you know that when people are doing it they nearly always whisper?"

"What's that got to do with it?"

"A lot. When people whisper it's either because they're lovers or because they're frightened or praying."

"Well, Stella didn't whisper. That night she'd been screaming at me, telling me I wasn't a man, that she'd only taken the job with that bastard in the shop because he was better than me."

"She was frightened, Bushy. And the other one was frightened, the one that interrupted you, knocking on the door."

"Enid," Bushnell said. "But for her . . ."

"A woman with a mouse can be frightened, let alone being strangled. If you think back, Bushy, you'll see it was all in the scream. It went out through the flat the way it went out through Stella, frightening everybody in the evening the way she was frightened."

"I tell you she'd been insulting me and throwing stuff and I took it all until I saw 'er face change. I saw her look over me as if she'd really made up 'er mind, as if she'd decided I was more than just *her* mistake."

"And that was when you started, wasn't it? That was when you put your hands on 'er neck."

" 'Course it was. I 'ad to do something to stop 'er, to make her see me."

"And when she went silent, you was waiting to give her another chance?"

"You know I was. I've said it all along—I've always said ever since Wandsworth—that if it hadn't been for Enid I'd have let up."

"And then what?"

"Nothing! For God's sake, 'Otchkis, it was too late."

"That's right. But if it hadn't been, you'd have been quiet even if she was dying. Nobody says nothing when they're dying except forgive you. People can't ever believe it. They can't believe they nearly went out. They just lie there. It would have been like the two of you looking down a well and seeing your faces at the bottom, and you'd have thought, you'd both have thought, 'We nearly —Christ! We nearly finished it.' "

Bushnell sat down on the chair, watching him, his hands on his knees. Hotchkis lolled across the bed with his head back on Stella's thighs. "Maybe," Bushnell said. "But she'd have made up for it later. I'd have had a lot of her mouth later."

"You don't know, though, do you? Because you didn't happen to hear it and neither did no one else. Whatever she'd have said when you were lying there on the floor whilst she was still alive, nobody ever heard and nobody never will."

"Nobody."

"It was the same with Paul Caine. I stopped his words before he was finished, and because I still can't see him but as a bastard I don't get my absolution either."

"Nor you, neither."

"And yet," Hotchkis went on, "I can think about Stella better than about him. I can feel sorry for her. I can think, 'God have mercy on us; we're full of the devil!' I tell you, Bushy, I keep seeing her still getting stuff in the shops, keeping up with everything—"

He rolled over on the bed and upended the cider bottle, wiped its mouth clean on the blanket and passed it over. "We ended the story and we've both got to regret the way I do with Stella—"

There was silence. The cell was full of cigarette smoke, and from below they could hear the night staff coming on duty; the shouting, the rattle of key chains.

"And that's why I'm going over the wall," Hotchkis concluded.

"You'll be lucky!"

"Maybe!"

"Where will you go?"

"Anywhere. Just around and about, sooner than expected, in charge of myself. They'll get me, of course; but when they put me back in again for an extra month or two I'll know I've stopped rotting. I'll know I could be alive enough to believe it, to get the forgiveness to forgive Paul."

Bushnell yawned. "It's five minutes to bang-up. You'd better get into your peter."

"Is it a deal? The boiler suit?"

"It's a deal. But you better make up your mind where you're making for."

"I've got it all worked out. It's no good breaking without somewhere to kip."

"Well, where, then?"

"I'm going to Coles' place. I think he'll wear it."

"He may, but what about his missus?"

"I don't know. She's called Lettice. From what he's said, she sounds all right, full of good works, a sport."

VII

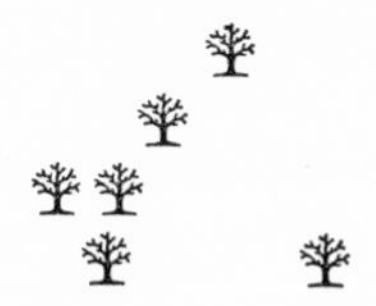

Lettice Coles, as it happened, was finding her life getting neater and neater. Sometimes she had a vision of herself living at last with Randall in a small private bungalow on a private estate. Though she found it increasingly hard to keep her plans up to date, the bungalow would have mostly glass walls, she had decided; but it wouldn't be open-plan, since open-plan had gone out some years earlier, just when Lettice had been thinking of going in for it. She had been put off by an *Observer* article on the problems of lavatory noise.

But the house would have oil-fired central heating or possibly, unless it was superseded by then, the new electric storage-heating. Certainly there would be lots of laminated wood and plastic resin which she saw herself pointing out in the roof frame at the winter and summer parties. "Laminated wood," she would say. "No, not Frank Lloyd Wright; later, more Pacific Coast, and absolutely coleopter-proof: beetles, even the deathwatch, simply give up."

The bungalow would sit in the middle of a largely "stone-finished" concrete garden. There would be a stone trough or two collected by Randall from local farms—or from Wiltshire if necessary—filled with moss and hardy succulents in the winter; while in the summer they would brim with "Botticelli" flowers—annuals like petunias, anything reminiscent of Primavera. There would, too, be a few shrubs planted in lacunae in the concrete and a bay tree for ornament and cooking. There might even be a herb garden and a small lawn for Randall to shave with an electric mower. But it would have to be very small because "we both realize that as one grows older, energy is limited, one has to live more and more in the mind."

There would be a guest room for the children and a toy cupboard for the grandchildren. Occasionally, no doubt, when the children were going away somewhere, the grandchildren would come on their own and stay for the weekend—or all the "brood" together for Christmas. Such times would be occasions of quiet influence; all the—by then—old-fashioned principles—vitamins, prophylactic injections, mild sedatives for overexcitement—would be tactfully instituted.

On Christmas day the traditional picnic would be held for the new generation and there would be the walk in the woods. Probably the children and their spouses would have to alternate, Christmas by Christmas—Brett and her husband one year, Malcolm and his wife the next. Randall would drive—or Lettice—and the children would sit in the back with the grandchildren—or the latter might sit in little seats fastened to the backs of the big seats. In the woods, by the brown bracken and the bare trees and the green, green moss which never withered, they would all get out of the car and start walking—as they always had done in healthy protest against the Christian festivities.

Brett and her husband would take a hand each of the toddler—or Malcolm and his wife of their toddler—swinging him over icy puddles and noting the winter bird song. She could see it all: Randall, always in front, striding bent and keen, would pick a leaf or two of pennyroyal and Lettice would tell the small ones about "the Ruins." How bright the young cheeks would be, pinker and pinker as the short walk progressed; and surely Malcolm or Brett's husband, if it was his turn that Christmas, would pickaback a baby as the little line of them strung out down the path by the black wood to the abbey in the hollow.

That November, when it was still five or perhaps more years away, Lettice saw all this bleakly and beautifully. Brett was not even engaged yet and Malcolm, who was still at Cambridge, was still quite unable to make up his mind whom to marry.

It was a Wednesday morning and Lettice was preparing Marmite and whole-meal-bread sandwiches and a blue-and-white bowlful of celery-and-apple salad for her lunch. In the electric oven there was a quite large caramel cream which would do for supper as well.

But she was lost in her "remembrance." She had told Randall once, "When I think of the future it's always a kind of remembrance, because, fundamentally, things always go on the same—fundamentally, I mean."

"But surely—?"

"Oh no, Randall. We don't change; we only become more ourselves. Mankind progresses to himself. We've always believed that, haven't we?"

"I suppose so, in a way."

"But it's not 'in a way.' It's simply that history is slowly permitting us to become ourselves by a kind of process of discard; the more we discard, the more real we become."

Randall had agreed as much as he ever agreed, as much as it was in him ever to agree with any of Lettice's thoughts. That is to say that he had slid his index finger up along his cheek to a point just above his right eyebrow where a long forehead furrow ended. Through his spectacles she had seen his evasive smile and welcomed it as a sign of his humility.

But she had returned now to the contemplation of the bungalow. *And too,* she was thinking as her wooden-handled knife sliced through the crisp celery, *and too there will have to be a "religious room." The poor darling won't be able to forgo that after all these years—untidy though it will be.* And she determined that in the bungalow they would really make a feature of it. Randall's Ethiopian goatskin—relic of an African commission—with the painted "Song of Solomon" etched out in the saddle pattern between the hairs, would hang on the wall above the bentwood desk. The Ten Commandments in bronze, a circle of sculptured figures brought from Israel by a rabbi who had spoken on the Third Programme, would be suspended around the ceiling light. Pointing it out, Lettice would be able to continue very quickly to quote her old observation: "One of them, of course, is broken! But not by Randall."

Because everyone knew that she and Randall were humanists, this little joke was always a success and was often followed by Lettice telling her guests that they were both "well aware" of the Ten Commandments. "They were brought by the Israelis from Egypt," she would explain. "In the Middle Kingdom there were no less than forty-two purely negative commandments. Hence the emphasis on the 'not' in the Jewish ones. Specifically, 'Honour thy father and thy mother' is a matter of eugenics; there's no need whatsoever for the homily that follows: longevity has nothing to do with filial devotion and 'the land that the Lord thy God giveth thee' is begging the question. After all, man was in the world before God—I mean, demonstrably."

Yet, despite these reservations, she was perfectly sure that Randall had in fact never broken any of the Ten—even in his youth; he was too "decent." "Randall is decent, you know," she would tell her closest friends. "Given half a chance, men *are*." And it was not that she had never "interfered" with him. She supposed in a way that merely by marrying him she had. But she'd tried not to let it go beyond that: to take only what Randall had been willing to give her—his passion, his poetry and his income—and not to demand his mind as well. "People have a right to their minds," she always said. "And that right is not surrendered by marriage."

Lettice thought a lot about her mind, and lately, when she couldn't remember a quotation exactly, she was in the habit of saying, "How I miss my mind." But when Brett, at seven, had asked her, "Mummy, what happens to my thoughts when I'm dead," Lettice, instead of answering, had taught the little girl how to make *choux* pastry. "Distraction is better than frustration," she had said.

She liked to be busy herself; she believed in it. She attempted definition and crispness in every action. Snap-snap her joints went, as her arms, hips, wrists and hands performed their tasks, her vertebrae swaying on her pelvis as she swept a floor or rolled out ready-mix pastry. "If one keeps busy, one is not disturbed," she said. "The only times I've ever doubted myself have been when I was forced into inaction by the terminal stages of pregnancy."

She was tidy too, more orderly really than Randall, whose office in the Religious Department of the B.B.C. was a studied chaos, designed to reassure visiting clerics. In Lettice's kitchen even the cracked Bognor mug had a hook on which it always hung. In the cupboard under the stairs, the jumble-sale box—filled every spring with castoffs—had been in position since before the children. It dated back to her mother's marriage and bore a late-Victorian label: "Edwards' Desiccated Soup." In her bedroom in a cupboard above her sewing machine there was the button jar, a prewar Kilner, which never held anything but buttons. There was a sweet jar too, which had also belonged to her mother; and the sewing bag, patched and repatched; and an old cake tin used for boiling down soap pieces at the end of every quarter.

Her thrift and business she supposed to be an Edwardian legacy. The Edwardians, she knew, had had no respect for neurosis—only a variety of happy names for it, like "highly-strung" and "acidosis." She boasted, in fact, that she'd never taken a tranquillizer in her life, only a little benzedrine in her final year at Girton. It was not that she'd never been tempted; of course she had, during periods of stress or, as she preferred it, "strain." She had been strained by Randall's pneumonia, during Brett's mastoid, and throughout her mother's exhausting death. She had been strained, too, throughout the unnumbered phases of her infants' infancy, as who wouldn't have been in the new middle class, constrained, as her mother had pointed out, to "hand-rear its offspring"?

In the past Lettice had thought a great deal about this particular development, and in her thirties she had even gone so far as to found a woman's luncheon club on the notion. For seven or eight postwar years the ladies who "managed" on their own—the wives of local doctors, schoolmasters and "executives," with babes, infants or toddlers—had met monthly to eat, smoke and talk. It had been the era of Dr. Spock, of morning helps and "coping." There had not been a member who couldn't recall the nurseries, nannies and maids of her own childhood, who had not a mother of her own "stunned" by her daughter's lot. Or, if there had been, the daughters had either kept quiet about it or invented an appropriate background.

But now that was all over. As would be Lettice within a few

years, the senior members of the luncheon club were now themselves preparing either for grandchildren or for hysterectomy: the nappies, teething rings and strings of grey "educated" washing had vanished; even the guitars of the fledged teen-agers were in the attic with the typescripts of luncheon talks on early Christopher Fry or latter-day Cocteau. The members had more time to dress, to be publicly charitable and sometimes privately aghast at what Lettice termed their nearness to the "head of the battle."

This phrase had been one of her mother's, to whom, on this particular Wednesday morning, she found her thoughts so often returning. Abruptly as a door slamming somewhere in her head, a voice now pronounced the words, "But mother is dead."

Her hands closed on the untidy green celery leaves and dropped them into the waste bin beneath the sink. Suddenly she had no clear idea as to when exactly that death had taken place. It seemed simultaneously to her that her mother had been dead for as long as she could remember and also that she had never died at all, that she was still at The Poplars Nursing Home expecting to be visited on the Wednesday.

There would be the bottle of "good" vermouth to carry along the corridor that was so like the aisle of a church with its gratings for the central heating; there would be the winter jasmine or perhaps some florist's flowers wrapped in tissue paper—two parcels to bring to the room where the smell of the unknown aged suddenly ended and Mother's own presence, going back three-quarters of a century, began.

And in all those visits, she now suspected, nothing had been accomplished at all. She even whispered the words aloud as she whipped over the top of the stainless-steel draining board with an impregnated dishcloth: "Absolutely nothing! Nothing at all." For she could scarcely remember a thing they'd ever said in the whole of that last eighteen months at The Poplars. She could not recall a smile, a greeting or a disappointment. Their one real point of contact had been, she supposed, the B.B.C.—and not because it was Randall's job, but because they'd been able to discuss together programmes which they had heard separately, as if the transmitter had been a common origin, an ancestor.

"The Spanish on the Third on Monday evening was worthwhile,

I thought," Lettice might well have said. Her mother, she believed, had taken a detached interest in Randall's series, "About Religion." But for the rest, all the other points of contact which there must surely have been, it seemed now that her mother's had been a death by drowning—the aftermath of shipwreck which had left both of them floating quite peacefully in a common ocean, within sight but too far apart for conversation.

"She insisted on being admitted," Lettice had told the luncheon club at the time, "when the bedsores developed. They were down to the bone and she thought it would be too much for me. I'd have kept her, of course, upstairs with her own things; she still has those at The Poplars, but it's not quite the same perhaps. It was nothing to do with Randall; he was quite equable. It was her pride. One forgets that the Edwardians were really Victorians. One forgets that we ourselves are really Edwardians—because of the time lag, I mean."

In the nursing home her mother had shed her ghosts: the ghosts of her husband and children, Lettice's brother and her elder sister, Eleanor. In some way all these personages had become detached from her, as if The Poplars were too hot and hygienic for them. Yet, during her weeks in Coniston Road, before her buttocks had broken down, the whole family had somehow existed in the spare bedroom.

"Quite honestly," Lettice had told Randall, "when I was strained I used to feel that we were all up there, that in a way, through Mother, you were sharing my childhood with me. But now she's down at The Poplars there's been a kind of clearance. It was the continuity, I suppose, or sentimentality or, more probably, association of ideas."

"Though it was a strain," she had told the luncheon club, "it was not that it was too much for me; it was too much for Mother. But I'm sure it was right—in principle."

What exactly had happened to Mother's things? she wondered now. Eleanor had taken the silver, Henry had gone off with the Birkett Fosters, and, officially, Lettice had been left with the Coalport and the two pieces of chipped Rockingham. But there had been more, much more, a whole houseful, which over the subsequent years must have got scattered—her mother's ship sinking so slowly that some of the cargo had drifted over the horizon before the passengers themselves had taken to the water.

It's sad, really, Lettice thought now as she looked at things, as her gaze, lavender-coloured, shifted round the drawing-room walls past the curtains, the water colours, the mirror, the console, the bookcases and chairs. *So sad!* Because in so many of these very objects her mother's taste persisted. They had not exactly chosen the curtains together; but at Liberty's, years ago, she had felt her mother approving of that particular damask with the pale urns and cherubs and had chosen it almost with her father in mind—as if, with her mother, she had been furnishing not for Randall but for "Daddy."

The room itself, long before her mother's death, had been a reminder of her, a re-creation of Lettice's own childhood. For here, apart from the bookcases, Randall had not been allowed to obtrude. It had been an unspoken agreement between them that the drawing room was to be Lettice's testimonial to her own upbringing. In the old days, before her mother's illness, she had liked to imagine her there, as if, absurdly, she the daughter had made an exquisite nursery for the parent in which, in a world so woefully changed, she might by Lettice's grace still be at home.

Now, in this recollection and sadness, she went unhurriedly through the hall to the front door to open it and take what she knew would be a registered parcel from the postman. It happened so regularly: people would send their manuscripts to Randall's private address instead of to Portland Place. But it was not the postman; it was, initially, just the figure of a man standing out there in the open. He narrowed into focus quite slowly: a brown Harris tweed overcoat, a leather brief case and a nasty little green cap.

"Mrs. Coles?"

"Yes."

"Good morning."

"Good morning."

Against the enormous greyness behind him, the man smiled. "I've already called twice before, but I must have been unlucky."

"Yes?"

"But I know how it is! You ladies are kept so much on the go in the mornings. My name is Smeed, by the way—William Smeed. Do you mind if I step in for a moment?"

"What exactly—?"

But he had already stepped past her into the hall, still smiling and morning-fresh. She could smell after-shave lotion and noticed that the Harris tweed was not Harris and the brief case not leather. She was feeling a little strained, unable to cope. Men had always affected her like this; that was why she had married Randall: there had been nothing "sudden" about him. He had entered her Cambridge life almost unnoticeably. Mr. Smeed was taking off his hat—or, rather, cap—the green one with the top stitched, not buttoned, to the peak, the kind her friend Harriet Harvey referred to as "Inland Revenue"—the kind she herself had forbidden Randall to buy two years earlier. Mr. Smeed took it off hesitantly, with tact, as if he were awaiting the permission he knew she could not refuse. Lettice wondered what he would do with it. Would he put it down on the oak chest or hold it in his hand?

"I'm sorry," she began, "but I really haven't—do you perhaps wish to see my husband?"

As if he were a conjuror, a card appeared between his fingers. She took it from him and read something about Pavlova carpets and shampoos; but she was really watching him. Continuously throwing out little easy remarks, he was making formal practiced movements in the hall. Over the edge of the pasteboard she saw him stooping to look at the hall runner.

"Very nice little rug," he was saying. "But those vacuum cleaners! See the fringe? They nibble them, suck them in and comb them. It's the domestic problem. Pieces like this were meant to be brushed, cared for, Mrs. Coles. Am I right when I say it came from a good home?"

"My mother's." She said it quite involuntarily. "My father bought it in Ispahan just after the Great War. He—" She pulled herself together, remembering as she did so that this too had been a phrase of her father's when they were young: "Pull yourself together, Milly! Eleanor! Lettice!"

She proffered Mr. Smeed his card, but he did not take it; his eyes were everywhere but there, taking in everything in the hall, flashing through the open doorway at the far end into the drawing room and returning back to Lettice again, not starting at the top or bottom and working down or up but watching her face intimately.

"We really don't need anything—any carpets," she said. "Very soon I have to go out; I have an appointment."

He was opening his brief case with a practiced hand and she realized suddenly that to him she was not a person but a "prospect." Anything that did not fit in with this idea of her he simply didn't notice.

"Now these will interest you," he was saying, "and they'll save us time. The firm I represent are carpet specialists and our business is with anyone who owns or has a carpet—whether it's a piece like this one, an heirloom, or just something you put on the floor, something for people to walk on and keep the draughts out."

She now had a handful of brochures and was reading them in the automatic way she read cereal packets at breakfast or the print which always found its way into the lavatory:

Pavlova: Pavlova Service:

You trouble.
WE SAVE
Your carpets/Cash.

"I shouldn't keep you now and I won't. Just a jiffy, though—"

Even as he was speaking his gaze had wandered yet again along the hallway through the open door to the floor of the drawing room. An expert, he walked in there and stooped down, his not-Harris tweed overlaying the carpet as he did so. He fingered the selvage. "Axminster, but still quite bright, and two nice little rugs—not antique, furnishing quality, but still worth preserving. No cottons, I'm glad to see. Now with cottons even *we* don't mind stilleto heels."

She had followed him and was standing there behind him, quite undecided.

"No tapestries"—he sighed—"but I see a nice little sampler in the corner. Now what else have we got? I never trespass upstairs in the absence of the man of the house."

Through the open drawing-room door Lettice could see the open front door, which purposely she had not shut, and beyond it the stillness of the outside morning, grey as an ocean and as reassuring.

In the opposite direction she could see the end of the kitchen table, the white formica set with a single place for her lunch. Mr. Smeed had noticed this too.

"Like everybody else," he said. "I see you've gone over to tiles in the kitchen. Better than the old-fashioned lino—keep their colour. Are you going to turn off the kettle?"

"A jelly," Lettice lied, "for tonight."

"And your husband, Mrs. Coles? If you don't get the time, he might care to look through our literature?"

"My husband?"

"Mr. Coles, Mr. Randall Coles."

"You know my husband?"

"I know *of* him."

"Oh, I see. You've heard his programmes on the wireless?"

"The steam? We don't have it any more. We went over to telly twelve years ago. On Sunday mornings perhaps, while we're dressing, we might turn on the transistor, but that's all. No, Mr. Coles and I have never actually met; I haven't had that pleasure."

"Then?"

"Our paths have crossed, that's all; but not through the radio, though Norma, the wife, remembers his name. She listened a lot when she was in hospital; he was a favourite in the gynae ward—amongst the women, you know."

"Naturally!"

"I'm sorry?"

"I only meant that it could scarcely be amongst the men in that part of the hospital."

"According to Norma, they lapped him up in the mornings. They went over to telly in the evenings. They had a viewing room for the ambulants."

As if he himself were taking part in a television play, Mr. Smeed sat down in Randall's armchair. Lettice felt bound to go to the kitchen and turn off the gas. She walked in there as crisply as a nurse, flicked off the tap and returned.

"My husband rarely participates in his own programmes. He's a producer."

"I know, Mrs. Coles."

She waited, bound now to watch him. He began to explore the

leather band on the inside of the cap, holding it upside down in his lap, revolving it slowly round his exploring fingers. "We have a mutual connection," he said, "part business, part pleasure."

She said nothing.

"As you'll know," he added.

In a moment I shall get rid of him, she promised herself; quite suddenly, even without anybody's doing anything, he'll go. She caught the very faintest smell of celery from the kitchen and, in her hunger, became resolute. "If you'll forgive me, I really must get on, Mr.—"

"Smeed."

She'd already memorized his name. It was quite fixed in her head as a necessary key to the conversation she was going to have with Randall. She was walking purposefully towards the drawing-room door and the hall, listening as she did so to hear him getting up, following. "And I shall tell my husband when he gets in that you called about the carpets, though I'm afraid he may not be terribly interested."

Clip-clip went her heels over the wooden gaps between carpets and rugs. Clip-clip. Then she heard him get up and knew that he was following her. As if she too were in a television play, she knew that the moment she had closed the front door on him she would lean against its inner surface for a moment, her lips tightly closed, a hand briefly on her breast.

"He'll be late," said Mr. Smeed behind her. "This being a Wednesday, Mr. Coles will be late home tonight, won't he?"

"I beg your pardon?"

"The prison. It's your husband's night for the prison, isn't it?"

"I still don't understand."

"I meant Betty, Mrs. 'Otchkis—Hotchkis, our mutual friend."

"I see." She was feeling very strained, quite faint. She needed very much her Marmite, brown bread and celery and a telephone. The feeling in her knees reminded her of her days as a W.A.A.F. during the air raids, when she had had to hold the muscles in tension to stop them from wobbling. She thought of her father again, his attitude to everything: "Grit!" This was no worse than an air raid and she was not a child. She would see it through, not even hurry Mr. Smeed out through the door.

"And Betty needs it, believe me," he was saying, "appreciates it, Mrs. Coles. I don't think your husband can have any real idea of what his visits have meant to her. I was there this morning—no, yesterday morning—and she was telling me how much trouble he'd taken on Kit's behalf."

"Kit?"

"Her husband, Kit or Christopher—Kit for short."

She smiled out into the late winter's morning. For ten minutes or more, for perhaps half an hour, the coldness from out there had been stealing in through the open front door; the whole house was icy with it.

"Peculiar girl, woman—Betty, Mrs. Hotchkis," he went on. "To look at her, you'd think—"

"I have never met Mrs. Hotchkis."

"To look at her, you'd think she hadn't anything in her head! It could be that she's not a talker, definitely. Myself I'd say she was a reader, library books. Some people are, secretly. Betty's like that, Mrs. Coles, a secret reader who appreciates conversation." He paused, preparing himself for departure and reminiscence: fastening his brief case, pulling out the flaps of his overcoat pockets, and screwing his cap back onto his brilliantined head.

"You'd be surprised the people I meet in the course of my work: old ladies with animals and secrets—very nervous; young women living with older men—lonely. But Mrs. Hotchkis, I'd say, owing to her circumstances, is in a class by herself."

"No doubt."

In no hurry, he smiled. "She goes for educated talk. She was telling me only yesterday that without your husband's visits she could never have managed."

"How fortunate." She opened the door a little wider for him, a polite, nearly imperceptible gesture which he noticed at once. Moving towards it, he began to talk very much faster.

" 'Randall—Mr. Coles—explains things so beautifully,' Betty told me, and I said, 'Well then, I'll have to take lessons from him, won't I?' 'I don't know what you mean,' Betty said. 'He only comes for Christopher's sake. He's old enough to be my father.' 'And so am I,' I said."

Still talking, still facing her, still as if he were acting in some new television play, he stepped out backwards on to Lettice's terrace. "So tell Mr. Coles that I'm sorry I missed him today but that as soon as I hear from him we'll rendezvous to suit his convenience." His smile was expectant, reddish, in the frosty air.

At the last minute, just as she was going to close the door on him and lean against it with her mouth tight shut and her hand on her breast, Mr. Smeed suddenly extended his right hand and took Lettice's left hand, on which were her wedding and engagement rings. His hand was warm and urgent, quite different from Randall's; his grip held her motionless in the doorway.

"And of course," he said, "you won't forget to let him know how much his kindness is appreciated? Tell him from me that without his help Betty's morbid streak could have triumphed. Tell him she could have gone the same way as Pery."

She did not try to extricate her hand. It felt like a trapped bird. "I'm afraid I haven't the least idea—"

"You don't know Pery, Mrs. Coles?"

"My husband has never mentioned him to me."

"Well, you'll have to ask him about her."

"Of course." She smiled.

"Mind you, in all fairness, he may not have met her yet himself. But with all the publicity she gets"—he raised his cap and jingled the keys of his car—"sooner or later he will."

She watched his brightly polished golf-club shoes cross the terrace and descend the steps to the gravel and did not wait for his last gesture, whatever it might have been. She closed the front door gently and went back into the kitchen busily. She started clopping things on to the formica top, fitted ten years earlier by Randall: pepper, celeriac salt, a packet of french butter, oatmeal biscuits, gruyère, honey, and her vitamin capsules—food for every eventuality. She still saw herself spread-eagled against the inside of the front door, suffering recognizably.

She found that she was eating standing up, chewing ravenously a stick of celery as if she were in a station buffet—Victoria Station with a train for home already by the platform. She forced herself to sit down at the place she had laid, to analyze her emotions. The ingredients of her meal were on the table; she must be masculine and label her feelings too. There was anger, of course; fear, as well; and something else that she could not at first identify. She was aware that her heart was very small, quite tiny and working very hard, as hard as it had done in her childhood. Though she had no specific memories, she had apprehensions of hiding and excitement. Whenever she had been excited, her heart had worked like this at the expectation of discovering or being discovered: parties, hunt-the-slipper, hide-and-seek, sardines—her wedding.

She had been married in white for the sake of Randall's parents, who had been conventional Christians. Under the white bodice, full of anticipation and curiosity, her heart had worked like this. Curiosity—that was what, until now, she had missed in herself: quite definitely an excitement. Seated there alone, munching things in no particular order, she stared back into her marriage as if it had been the morning itself, seen through the open front door, the persistent mist veiling its familiarities.

She had spread an oatmeal biscuit with butter and honey and was eating it together with gruyère cheese. Honey reminded her of Randall again; she remembered the honeycomb he had been given in the summer and sat there for a moment motionlessly, like a television heroine. She had to do something original; she simply must break the continuity. She rushed into the drawing room to the white telephone and was put through to Randall's secretary. Mr. Coles, she was told, had cleared his desk in the morning and would not be returning that afternoon. He had no programme going out until Sunday, but he had got a number of outside appointments.

Lettice drank a small glass of unsweetened gin and then rang up Harriet Harvey, her closest friend, a founder member of the defunct luncheon club.

Lettice had never confessed to needing anyone before; though she would never, even in a private diary, have written, "I pride myself on my self-sufficiency," she did in fact believe that she was self-sufficient. Despite the sudden strain of Mr. Smeed, she had spoken gaily to Harriet Harvey, caressing Tyndal's head ungently as she talked into the telephone's white mouth. Tyndal had suffered it and Harriet had understood, interpreting Lettice's laughter and talkativeness correctly and promising to come over the moment the jobbing gardener arrived. "He's so deaf," she had said.

"I shall just have to *show* him the dahlias if it's not too late already. I've asked him a dozen times."

Lettice had talked about dahlias too: "Randall's so good like that. There's an excellent gardener's diary I get him every Christmas. It's simply a question of reminding him to look at it at the weekends." She had wanted to mention Jorrocks too, with his "Blister my kidneys, the dahlias is dead," at the start of the hunting season. But this was not for Harriet, who was neither literary nor county. She wouldn't have understood the nostalgia for something which Lettice's antecedents had never, in any case, enjoyed, but which they had sufficiently approached in Edwardian times to entitle the whole family to a kind of seasonal mournfulness in October/November. But, then, Lettice had chosen Harriet as her closest friend because of Harriet's problem with Edward, who was unfaithful about once a year and drank in between. Their friendship was based principally upon unspiteful disagreement about nearly everything. Harriet did not even like her own children, and when Lettice had said that they "made" a marriage she had replied, "How do we know? We've both had them. We might easily have been far happier without."

"I'm sure Edward wouldn't agree with you."

"Edward behaves as though they were an excuse for everything except sex."

"What do you mean?"

"With me," Harriet had replied obscurely.

Lettice had wanted to say something beginning with "Randall" but had managed to stop herself in time.

She had always been quite sure that every member of the luncheon club envied her Randall, his tired youthfulness, his reticence and fidelity. She didn't realize that her own complacency did not apply to her friends, that consequently she was outside the general run of lightness and amusement that women felt for their friends' husbands. Lettice approved of Randall in the way she liked the Coniston Road house: as far as it was possible she had decorated him to suit herself. She had no idea that her friends all imagined that they would have done him up very differently had he been theirs, or that the reason she was "popular" was because their husbands looked upon her only as a warning and thereby felt a little easier in their own marriages.

Harriet Harvey, big, intelligent and catty, was in fact the only woman amongst them who was in any real sense fond of Lettice for her own sake. She put it about that Lettice was the only one who really "got away with it," meaning that triumphant feminism lay not in rebellion and career insistence, a room of one's own, but in the absorbed narcissism of her kind of life. "The skill!" she said. "The conviction! It's the successful English alternative to the American system. Randall's as happy as a fly in amber and it's everyone's duty to see that he never wakes up, however tempting it might be to disturb things."

She really was really fond of poor Lettice, loving her not only for her certitude but for lesser reasons too: her asceticism, defenselessness and innocent ruthlessness—in a word, her "antithesis." She was Harriet's exact opposite, the counterpart of that side of herself and "of them all" with which they struggled as middle-aged, middle-class English wives. "Sex, greed and resentment are no problem to her," she said. "Lettice remains as we all intended to remain when we started: slender, chaste and dutiful. We shouldn't merely not hear a word against her; we shouldn't *think* it!"

So, in response to Lettice's telephone call, Harriet came, "almost immediately," about two hours later. She saw the gardener, picked up her two youngest from the day school and whisked them home to an austere, starchy meal presided over by her "sewing lady," and then rushed into the shops again to buy some crumpets to furbish up Lettice's china tea. After tramping into the house, she threw her big black coat with the astrakhan collar over one of Lettice's ladder-back chairs and fairly plunged herself into the kitchen to make the tea.

"Your call was a *cri de coeur,*" she said; "I recognized it at once. But you're not to do a thing or say a word until we're all cozy and safe. Just toast the crumpets while I make the tea."

Yet she threw out questions just the same. Was it the guest list for the winter party on Saturday next? Or Brett or Malcolm? A failed examination, an illness or a pregnancy? She placed these last three questions in what she knew would be Lettice's order of tribulation, the nastiest first. But Lettice, who had had time to recover herself while waiting, was quite snappy. With an indoor plastic watering can she watered the azalea, brought in from Randall's little glasshouse for Christmas, and turned the potpourri in the chinese hawthorn bowl and said, "Certainly not! As for the winter party, I don't think we'll have it this year."

"Well, well! How are the crumpets doing?"

"They're not."

Waiting too, before the fire, knees far apart in the largest armchair, Harriet toasted the crumpets herself. She paid great attention to the buttering of the first one, sprinkled it with salt and ate it daintily, as she always did. "It's one thing to like food," she believed, "and another to show it." This was a defensive attitude because she suspected that Lettice watched her with disapproval. But this evening Lettice was totally concerned with herself; she was trying to avoid having to say, "It's Randall." This would be altogether too like the television, and Harriet's presence, so warm and substantial, made her determined not to feel "wronged," or at least not to appear to feel so.

"It's Randall, then?" Harriet asked in between mouthfuls.

"Yes."

Harriet said nothing, knowing that this best suited Lettice's tempo. Hot with curiosity, licking her finger tips like a greedy little girl, she sat there lazily toasting a second crumpet—for Lettice.

"I don't want it," Lettice said. "I don't feel like them. It's one of his prisoner's wives. As far as I can gather, he seems to have got himself involved with her. A man, rather dreadful, called about some carpets this morning, just before I phoned you. *He* told me about it."

"You make it all sound so impossible."

"It *is* impossible; that's just what worries me. I simply cannot understand it. Since I rang you, I've tried three times to get through to Portland Place; but he's still not back. His secretary was most vague and evasive."

"Begin at the beginning, please," Harriet begged. "With the arrival of the carpet man."

Lettice did and Harriet said, "You'll have to handle him very carefully. When Edward started—"

"There's no comparison." Lettice flushed. "Randall's not like that; I mean he's not that kind of a man."

"They all are. It's just a question of opportunity."

"Randall's had heaps of opportunities. He simply doesn't see them, that's all."

"Doesn't or daren't?"

"Randall's always been perfectly free. He's always known that I've never intended to interfere with any of his weaknesses. We've shared them just as we've shared our enthusiasms—as far as it's possible, I mean."

From a crumpled paper packet in her handbag, Harriet took a saccharine tablet and dropped it in her tea. Idly she buttered herself a third crumpet. "When you say 'involved,' how much do you mean?"

"I don't know. I can't imagine that he's been to bed with her. It would be too disgusting, and he wouldn't in any case."

"But you feel he's headed that way? After the usual time lag, Edward's always admitted that—"

"Randall's an idealist. If he's got himself involved with anyone, then it must have been because she appealed to him through his work."

"Or his hobby?" Harriet suggested.

"I don't know what you mean."

"Well, Randall does have a hobby. This prison-visiting thing of his isn't exactly the same as his real job in life, is it? I mean he does devote a good deal of time to it out of hours?"

"Not at all. In a way, they're exactly the same thing. Randall does his religious programmes as an academic exercise. It's precisely what the corporation pays him for. With any denominational belief there would be bound to be prejudice. So as a humanist and a non-Christian he has to apply his own private principles to his prison-visiting."

Harriet was silent. While she knew that it was because she was so forthright, so broadly Church of England, that Lettice valued her opinions, she was very sensible of the point of no return. When she spoke she used her most disarming tone of voice.

"I should have thought that might be rather dangerous?"

"No, only consistent. Randall and I are very keen on being consistent. We don't like muddled thinking."

"Well, I still think it's dangerous, I'm afraid. Edward always says division has been his undoing, that half his trouble is having to split himself up between London and home—that and the dreary drinking executives seem to have to go in for. But if Randall divides himself up between your beliefs and his work, then surely—"

"*Our* beliefs," Lettice said.

"I meant yours, shared. But never mind! The point is really whether or not he's been unfaithful or is only thinking of it."

"I can't make these distinctions," Lettice said. "All I'm concerned about is his getting himself involved with someone else; it's so untidy and horrible."

"It makes a big difference, you know."

"Not to us."

"But it does, my dear. When it's only the preliminaries, you can afford to hold your hand, to be cautious and fairly gentle. When they start real adultery, you have to be quite adamant: separate bedrooms and sustained ill temper for weeks on end."

"That wouldn't be my method."

"What would, then?"

"I don't know; I haven't decided."

"Well, take my tip," Harriet said. "Before you say or do anything at all, find out if the beast has been unfaithful."

"I must have a cigarette," Lettice said. "Randall forgot to bring any home last night."

Harriet handed over a squashed packet from her handbag and Lettice lighted a cigarette with the table lighter.

"I can't imagine how one would know—about actual sex—even if it were relevant."

"It's perfectly simple. The further he's gone, the more attentive and understanding he will be with you. At least that's the first stage."

"The first stage?"

"Until they become hardened. After that they're beastly to everyone except the children."

"How disgusting."

"And then there are the timetables," Harried went on. "Quite casually, as soon as they come in, they fill in every minute of their day for you—or night, if necessary."

"Randall is never away at night."

"Not ever? Not just very occasionally, after the Sunday Quiet Spot?"

"Only very very occasionally."

"One must never underestimate the mornings," Harriet said; "even for middle-class women they can be deathtraps: one's so rested."

"Randall—" Lettice began, and stopped herself just in time. It was a principle never to discuss her sex life with anyone except Randall. She got up and switched on the lights as a signal that the consultation was over.

Fifteen minutes later they parted fairly affectionately.

VIII

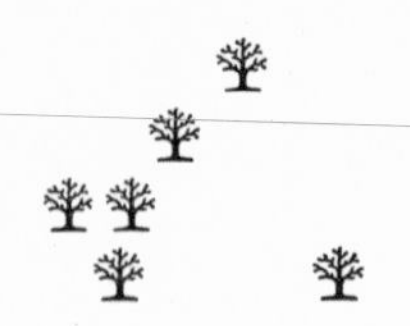

That evening, Coles was still with Bernard Presage in the B.B.C. club. They had eaten tongue sandwiches, drunk coffee and were now drinking beer. The room was empty; soon the steel grille would be lowered and clamped to the top of the bar. They would have to move on to the M and L Club.

Presage said: "Go on, Coles; please keep on talking."

"There's no more to be said: Hotchkis has absolutely no idea of her true feelings, her boredom. *She* hasn't a notion of his complexity; as far as one can tell, she sees him only as a bully."

"And that is what *you* have decided?"

"An opinion only," Coles protested, silent, drinking his beer quite fast.

"Well, go on."

"With what?"

"My dear Coles, I want to know what *you* are feeling about the Hotchkises. After all, you are the only person who is regularly seeing them both; their only living means of communication."

"True." Coles suppressed a wriggle of discomfort.

"An enviable position," Presage affirmed. "Unique."

"Quite."

"You must tell me, sometime, about their letters, give me an account of the kind of things they write."

"They don't very much. But I rather suspect that when they did they wrote in verse, simple rhyming couplets. It's a working-class thing."

"Interesting. Later on, when you have time, you might try and collect me a few examples. But tell me now what conclusion you've reached."

"None. So far none at all."

"But you have a preference?"

"For what?"

"For one or the other. For Hotchkis or for his wife. You are more deeply involved with one than with the other?"

"Oh really!" Coles began. He looked over his tankard to see Presage's right index finger pointing at him like an elder brother's.

Bernard lowered it. "Or perhaps she has ceased to attract you?"

But already Coles was mentally across the road in Betty Hotchkis' dream bedroom. He felt like saying, "Bernard, you won't tell anyone, but . . . ," or, "Look here! As a matter of fact, Betty and I . . ."

The novels he had read at school, the fictional language of the early Thirties nearly overcame him. He wondered why it was. Lettice had admitted to him that lately she was constantly seeing herself in television situations and had wondered if over the years they might not have "conditioned" the children too. He perhaps ought to expose himself a little more. It might change his visual vocabulary.

Presage's question came to him like a pistol shot: "Then you have not committed adultery yet?"

"Good God, no!"

"Only heavy petting?"

"What?"

Coles completely forgot his beer. He forgot everything; he was again lying scrupulously with her in her scarlet on the white-and-coffee folk-weave coverlet of the divan bed "across the road." He began an urgent, confidential speech.

"As a matter of fact, it's been rather a near thing, Bernard. You see, I've got so frightfully deeply involved, and there's no one, absolutely no one, I can discuss it with. And yet, at the moment, I can't discontinue the relationship and I don't want to."

"I know how you feel. I'm in a somewhat similar position and it's difficult to know to whom I should go."

"Really?"

"I could discuss it with a number of priests, with Helen, or of course with you."

"Confession?" suggested Coles.

Presage flushed. "No. Not confession."

"I only meant can you confess, discuss, a thing before you've done it? That was all."

"What?"

"I was suggesting–"

"I heard you, Coles. I was being evasive. The answer is that under certain circumstances you should–or, rather, *I* should."

"You, but not me? I don't count?"

"No."

"You mean I'm a pagan."

"A pagan? No, no. You're something new in the world, my dear Randall. You have no gods, no distraught choruses; you'd find it hard to disturb even your psychiatrist."

Coles refused to be sidetracked; he stabbed his finger into Bernard's upper arm. "Surely you don't confess an inclination?"

"A disposition, Coles: an intention. Already, during her first pregnancy, I've mentally seduced Mrs. Foley three times over smoked-salmon sandwiches."

"Bernard, I was hoping you'd be serious this afternoon. I really do need your advice."

"It began in an empty bar on the Great North Road," went on Presage. "The landlord thought she was my daughter."

"Lately I've been sleeping badly, too," Coles insisted. "I simply can't get Mrs. H. out of my head. And, apart from that, it would be such a frightful breach of confidence."

"But I was not humiliated," went on Presage. "Mrs. Foley does not think of me as a father. On the last occasion she was perfectly willing to sacrifice herself in the car park. She undressed swiftly and gracefully. Had the landlord been an abolitionist and read of it in the Sunday newspapers—"

"Frankly," Coles said, "if it wasn't for the fact that Christopher Hotchkis will be out for Christmas, I think I'd have to drop my prison-visiting altogether. And, quite apart from that, there's my marriage."

"Her husband, little oaf, suspects nothing," said Presage, "and Helen, of course, would forgive me and fly to Loch Derg to do penance during Lent."

"Lettice will know," Coles said. "Sooner or later she's going to sense a change in me."

"But if I persist, Coles, then sooner or later I shall have to face the priests."

"And of course there's Hotchkis himself. He trusts me implicitly."

"And, quite apart from the priests, there's Emily. Somehow I shall have to convince her."

"Oh, Emily; oh yes." Coles was feeling a little dizzy. "Well, what do you advise me?"

"Another drink—somewhere else." Bernard glowered round the room at their contemporaries in their dusty suits and thinning hair. The whole club looked grubby: too many ash trays, too much winter sunlight. "The M and L, where it's dark," he finished.

"I hate the place," Coles said, rising obediently.

Hands in pockets, books or brief cases under their arms, slouching like sixth-formers changing classes, they walked out into Portland Place.

"Why don't we go back to my office?" Coles suggested.

"No."

"I have a conference with the head of religious broadcasting at three-thirty. We could have coffee somewhere."

"No."

"I don't want to get drunk this afternoon, Bernard. It's my prison night, and I have to go on to see you-know-who afterwards."

Presage stopped as suddenly as if he had been hit by a falling brick.

"Betty—Mrs. Hotchkis," Coles corrected himself.

They were outside the Kardomah Cafe. Roasting machines were

turning in the window; there was a background frieze of women in hats. Presage looked gloomily at the thousands of frosty imprints on the winter pavement. "You'll undo us both," he said as they increased their pace, turned the corner and hurried, out of breath, into the uncomfortable darkness of the M and L.

Coles risked a Pernod. It had been an extraordinary slip, reducing the whole thing to the level of one's school days: "You-know-who!" But then, after all, conspiracy was inevitable in these matters and conspiracy was always juvenile.

"Conspiracy," he said to Presage, "is inevitable in these matters. One slips back into the language of one's childhood."

"*You* slip. *Your* childhood."

"It's the social guilt," Coles insisted. "You know what I mean?"

"Why 'social'?"

"Why not?"

"It is awe," said Bernard.

"Fear, perhaps."

"Awe, Coles. Without it we are as the beasts. The human act is not to be confused with the traffic of the mating cage. Think of your honeymoon."

With the aid of the Pernod, Coles searched his mind. It was a good point: the honeymoon with Lettice twenty years ago. At first he could only remember that she had made conditions, one of them that she should be allowed time to put in eighty pin-curlers every night. To this, supposing that his sacrifice might be his contribution to her femininity, he had agreed. It was a pity, though, that now, twenty years later, he should remember only the curlers. Yet there had been other images, he supposed, or there would not have been the three poems the following winter. And the black poodle—she had insisted on taking that along too: not a miniature but a "standard" one; miniatures had not then been in the fashion.

But mainly, he remembered, he had been worried about his "performance." Quite distinctly he had equated Lettice's satisfaction, approval, with that of his mother. But undoubtedly they had been very much in love too; for months, despite the poodle and the curlers, he had connected Lettice with white jasmine. "Her body, innocent as ivory," as he had written in one of the three poems, had alarmed him as much as some separate "condition"—as if she had said, "And as well as Stalky and my curlers, I must be allowed to bring my body too."

"Predominantly," Coles said, "with Lettice I felt only guilt, not awe."

"You had a Freudian honeymoon, Coles, because you had been reading Freud. Had you been reading Adler, you'd have had a power honeymoon—a battle for dominance."

"And I'd have lost it." Coles snickered. "Perhaps that's the explanation." He ordered himself another Pernod and drank it exceedingly fast. "Bernard! Do you suppose I could be trying to overcompensate with Mrs. H.? I mean, having lost the battle with Lettice?"

"How should I know? Examine your conscience as I examine mine."

Coles did. Mrs. Hotchkis had said, "Give us a treat." Into the prospect of that treat, like lilies sliding towards a weir, the whole cottage, the village, the lost nonchalance of Coles' entire life, seemed to have drifted. He could see it clearly on the stretched, mote-filled silver surface. But at her invitation he had shrunk back, and now he could not discover why.

"There is always Jung," said Presage, "whom, in company with Graham Greene, I bypass as respectfully as he himself bypassed Rome."

"A great humanist," Coles said cattily.

"And for me there is Emily," continued Bernard, "at whose feet I shall lay my own burdens this evening."

"Hitherto," Coles said, "I have always shrunk back from final committal with Mrs. H."

"Repeat that!" whispered Presage, shaking. "Repeat that sentence!"

"It's no more sententious than 'laying one's burdens at somebody's feet,' " Coles said, feeling really nasty.

And a little later they separated.

IX

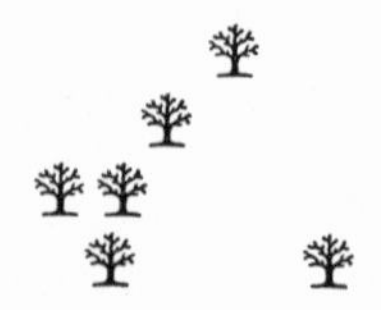

Bernard had observed that when Emily Minck was especially angry she made many small jerky movements: fussing with the cigarettes she burned rather than smoked; pushing at her forehead hair as if it had been some vexing victorian thing she found a handicap; or popping her chin on and off her musical little left hand, on which was a childish ring. Emily herself had observed all these things too; but, as she said, "I do them nevertheless, and even when I am not angered." And when Bernard had protested that to be "angered" was not the same thing as being angry, Emily had said: "I knew you were going to say that. I do not lack insight; but I am entitled to my conveniences."

Bernard, half believing her, had continued to love her for the almost permanent anger her insight gave her. He had told Helen, "Her insight is like a new razor blade. Once, when she was being particularly silly, I was imitating her to myself. And although I hadn't moved my lips at all and was looking at her affectionately, she suddenly drew me up short by saying, 'Bernard, you are imitating me to yourself. I know exactly what you are thinking. You are inventing my absurdity with me as we go along, and I don't like it.' "

"Do you think of Emily as a child?" Helen had asked.

"Certainly. That is her secret." He had added to himself, "And mine too."

This was not entirely accurate, for although he often saw Emily as a little girl he sometimes imagined her as an old lady, by no means harmless: the kind with opinions, with anger and little sorrow. Really, he supposed, she was neither a little girl nor an old lady—more a figurine whom he was bound to propitiate.

When her concerts took her to Munich, New York or Stuttgart, he was always as uneasy as if she had been purloined or stolen. He had even told her this, and she had said, "You mean kidnapped," and Bernard had said, "No, stolen." They had laughed together until mascara-dyed tears had coursed down Emily's cheeks into her glass of gin and fizzyade.

But later, when she had followed his implication to its conclusion, she had been angry, had disappeared for three weeks and instructed her morning secretary, a coloured girl named Patrice, to say in answer to all his inquiries, "Miss Minck has gone to stay with old friends in the country. She apprised no one of the date of her return."

"Dearest Emily, why didn't you tell me at the time?" Bernard had asked her as soon as she had relented. "You joined in with me, you appeared to have caught the exact flavour of the verb 'stolen.' "

"Upon reflection, I had. And I warn you, Bernard, that I am not to be trifled with."

"But, dearest, it's because I take you so seriously that I can afford to—"

"As a woman, Bernard."

He had been about to say that he did not like her to leave even her flat, that it was necessary for him to know she was there in all seasons. But he'd thought better of it. Eventually she had forgiven him, warning him, however, that he was not to imagine that their quarrel would not recur and that when it did it would not be "fatal" to their relationship.

"She means," Bernard had thought at the time, "that she's unable to forgive me for having accepted her stylization of herself.

Night after night, she likes to imagine she's giving herself to her art while I remain like a ponce in the cupboard."

And now, after his afternoon with Randall Coles, he hummed a broken tune as he stood remembering all this outside Emily's front door in North London.

Emily always kept people waiting a long time on her doorstep. It was a principle with her, one of the few actions in which she was not "immediate." She replied to letters and answered telephones without hesitation and never put off consulting doctors or dentists; but when people called she kept them waiting while she decided not about them but about herself. For she usually knew exactly who her visitor would be and needed time only in order to renew her make-up and determine her attitude.

Bernard hung about patiently in his old tweed overcoat, glancing up at the stuffy lace curtains and watching the plumes of his frosty breath in the dim fanlight. *She'll be angry,* he thought. *As usual I shall have interrupted her in something vital and beautiful. When she realizes that I've come to confide in her about Mrs. Foley her fury will be dangerous. Yet eventually, as a direct consequence of my confusion and weakness, she'll love me more than ever. I shall be a step nearer carrying my little nun over our sinless threshold.*

For Emily, being so very musical, mystical and bitchy, always occasioned such surprising thoughts in him. It was as if, in her, his male battle between truth and the flesh were being carried out femininely. And sometimes he reminded Helen that they were both very fortunate to have Emily in their lives. "With her help and a few drinks," he had been able to say, "we shall be spared my making a fool of myself in my fifties."

"One of those intellectual communions, you mean?"

"Exactly! And within the Church."

"I told you, Bernard," Emily said now in her open doorway, "that when I am working, my friends, if they wish to see me, must make appointments with Patrice. Because you have made no such appointment I am afraid I shall have to send you away. You will have to go."

But he saw that she had shampooed her hair and done up her

eyes, that she was framed beneath the light as becomingly as a television lady.

He took one of her hands in both of his and kissed it respectfully. "I had hoped you'd allow me to confide in you. It is pressing."

She looked at him brightly. "You can stay half an hour," she said as they went hand in hand up the staircase. "You have interrupted me."

In her sitting room, beneath an ornately plastered ceiling, she dropped his hand and stood eagerly in front of the midnight-blue alcove which framed her collection of Chelsea heads, all little girls with hair as thick as fleece. Though she looked distraught as well as eager, she talked as precisely as if she were explaining something to herself: a set speech she was rehearsing for some imagined platform.

"I was rearranging for my cittarone, a madrigal of Peter Warlock's composed at the beginning of the century, just before his suicide. My ideas for the notation of the bass in E-Flat were taking shape—a dying fall."

"I'm so sorry, Emily."

"So you see, don't you, that you are a nasty inconsiderate bugger to have interrupted me."

"I do indeed."

"And that the conception may well have been lost."

"Your hungry sheep—" Bernard began for her.

"Look up and are not fed," she chanted. "My idiot public in New York, the same."

Now that the ritual was half done they dropped their affectation and she greeted him properly, kissing his cheek, settling him in one of her vulgar armchairs and fetching him, as conveniently as a mistress, a drink that tinkled with ice. He thought he had got off lightly as she settled opposite him, taking an american cigarette from a golden case as thin as a biscuit. But she had no matches and he patted each of his doggy pockets in turn before heaving himself up again and padding obediently round the room.

"The music room," she instructed, "or the kitchen, and I want you to put the kettle on. You know I have to be propitiated."

He filled and plugged in the electric kettle and prepared two cups of coffee with tinned milk and american coffee essence.

"Black!" she called out.

He rinsed one of the cups under the tap and put another teaspoonful of coffee in the bottom. Then he lighted a taper from the gas stove and took it through to her and lighted her cigarette. She drew on it and handed it to him. He took another from her case and placed it between her lips.

"How is Helen?" she asked.

"Helen–" He hesitated.

"I hope you've done nothing silly."

He lighted the second cigarette and blew out the taper.

"I have."

"With the girl who was sick?"

"I am in love with her."

"With Hera Foley?"

"Yes."

"How nice." She pushed up at her hair. "Tell me everything."

"I have," Bernard lied.

"I must know first of all if she was actually sick upon you, Bernard. Your shoes, for instance?"

As usual she was right; he saw again his rubbed suede shoes by the roots of the anchusa. He remembered that he had wiped them clean on Lettice's grass verge.

"It was quite unintentional," he said, remembering exactly Mrs. Foley's ashen face, her shy, sly smile as she saw what she had done.

"And that was when it happened?" Emily asked. "You fell in love at the moment she was sick on your trousers and shoes?"

"I said nothing about my trousers."

"I know you didn't, Bernard; but I am right?"

"The left turn-up."

"Go on."

"Her fingers," he said. "Apart from her fingers, she is flawless."

"Tell me all about them."

"She bites the skin at the base of the nails–must have done it for years, ever since she was a child. They are–"

"Ugly?"

"Astonishingly so."

"And you have kissed them?"

"Bitten them gently," Bernard admitted, "on several occasions."

Emily stabbed out her cigarette in a Melanesian mission ash tray. "I hear the kettle."

Bernard took his drink through into the kitchenette and poured hot water into Emily's coffee cup. It was going to be a rough night and he was getting too old for it. It was time he retired properly into middle age and undeviating faith. It was altogether too much to have to endure Emily in addition to Helen in addition to Mrs. Foley. Why couldn't God make things easier?

Hera Foley had sighed up at the night sky as, gently, he had bitten her permanently inflamed finger tips. He had bitten them like this because they were the mark of her mortality and so constituted the junction between their generations; they had been more touching even than her consent as she had lain upon his breast like a drift of snow, of blossom, of newly flayed furs. She had whispered not a word, but deliberately had sought his lips, smiling at him without hope in the half-light.

"Bernard!" It was Emily's voice, not Hera's. "I am waiting—and not for coffee."

"There's so little to tell. You know that as well as I do. One is either in love or one is not. I mean *I* am either in love or I am not; I've contracted that damned pronoun from Randall Coles."

"It should be Randall who is contracting things from you. But never mind; I want more details."

"Very well, then. She's very secretive, full of despair."

"But she has confided in you?"

"A little, yes."

"About what?"

"Oh, her marriage, her husband." Bernard emerged into the sitting room and handed Emily her coffee. She took the cup and saucer without looking at it.

"And about her menstrual cycle?"

"No. *Not* about her menstrual cycle. She happens to be pregnant."

"Had she not been, she would have done," said Emily, who had not flinched at his shout. "I know the type."

"What are you suggesting? A spell?"

"Of course." She flashed him a cruel smile. "Pour a little whisky into the coffee. You'll find it in my bedroom—I don't know that I should allow you in there—next to Saint Charles Borromeo."

Large and dusty, he padded through on the just-wrong purple of the fitted carpets. Emily's taste was confined to the immaterial; it was this in her which he would have bitten gently, had it been possible. He looked at the bed with the flounced silk pajama case propped on the big homely pillows. He noted the large rosary hanging from the converted candleholder, an altarpiece with a bison-skin shade. Saint Charles Borromeo, in Italian aluminum alloy, stood on the mantelpiece, just taking off on one of his shorter flights. Beside him stood the bottle of Long John, labelled "Export Only: Bottled and Distributed by Whitney Balliatt Limited, New York City."

He took the bottle back to Emily and poured a little into her coffee, then recharged his own glass.

"I dismissed the idea of a spell because she is a romantic," he said.

"Novice though she is, you were unwise."

"I am in love."

"At fifty."

"At forty-eight and three-quarters," Bernard corrected her.

She flicked open her golden case and took another cigarette. Her hand darted to her hair again, pushing at it irritably as she gazed into her past.

"I too," she said precisely, "when I was younger, was immoral. You should have known me, Bernard, before my conversion."

"Agreed."

"Though I never really enjoyed it, even when I had learned not to respond."

"Quite."

"And that took me ten years. How old is this tart?"

"Twenty-three."

"Quite old enough, then, to realize that you are a failure?"

"I persuade myself that, in essence, she doesn't see me like that. That is why—"

"Lust and magic, Bernard, you must counter with the sacraments. Your place at this moment is not here in my flat but in the confessional."

"I need to discuss it a little first. I have reached the age where the prospects are diminishing, where so little happens to one."

"Discussion in such a case is connivance. I will have no part in it."

"I need an intermediary, Emily darling. You make the world so bare."

"And Helen?"

"Emily, you must not be unintelligent and unfair."

She got up. "Before you come to see me again you must be shriven. I cannot afford to consort with the confused."

"For God's sake, sit down. Let me try and explain."

"You have no need to. You are in search of a compromise which you know is not permitted."

"In France," Bernard began, for he had always relied on the French, "the Eldest Daughter of the Church—"

"I must remind you that you were born in Pinner," said Emily. "God did not make you a Frenchman. Quite evidently your sexual needs were to be catered for by Greater London."

"Greater London," said Bernard sadly.

"And Helen," concluded Emily.

She took his whisky glass from his hand and sipped at it, smiling at him as a good teacher smiles at a pupil, with as much angelic intuition. "And now you may, if you wish, take me out to dinner, provided that it is somewhere nice."

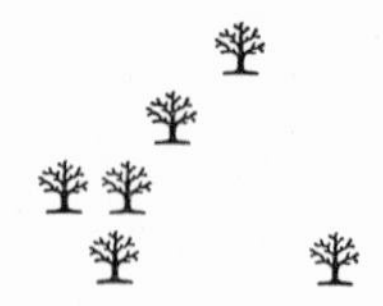

Some weeks earlier, in September, Hera Foley had lost her baby in the fourth month. She had been admitted to a private room in a London hospital, and on the day following she had asked to see the foetus. At first the staff had demurred; but eventually, when she had smiled coldly at the obstetrician and insisted that the baby was, after all, her own property, a staff nurse had brought it in to her in a bottle, suspended from a piece of grey wax by the umbilical cord, floating in methyl alcohol.

"Put it by my bed," Hera had commanded. "I'll look at it later, when I've finished my letters."

"It's not usual, Mrs. Foley."

"Neither are miscarriages, frightfully. At least, it's only *my* second."

"But–"

"Why? What are *you* going to do with it?" Hera was wearing a translucent black chiffon nightdress with a pitch-black narrow lace collar; above it her skin looked yellow, through it, sooty like a sweep's. Like an arrow, her black and gold fountain pen was poised between her nibbled fingers as she waited for the staff nurse to reply.

"Well, they usually go out with the other specimens—unless one of the medical-school museums—"

"Where to?"

"I'm not really sure."

"Exactly! Some incinerator or a council dump."

The staff nurse held her ground. "Of course, after the fourth month, Mrs. Foley, it's a legal question."

"This was not after the fourth month."

"And religious. Roman Catholics like to have them baptized."

"How ludicrous!" Hera stored the fact away for future use with Bernard Presage. "Well, it's not going to happen to *him*. And he's not going to end up in the boilers, either. I told Mr. Saddler-Halfpenny on his morning round that I'm taking him home with me . . ."

Alone, she had stared into the bottle not quite as into an aquarium: without a tear, with a curiosity as chill as vengeance. The tissue, boy-shaped, seemed to her to be the final evidence of her reproach.

"Of course I lost it," she had told her husband, Charles, on his first visit a day or two later. "What the hell did you expect?"

"But darling, after the first time I was rather hoping—" His words slid into silence as he caught sight of the specimen on the locker. Then, because he had learned in her presence never to rise to the outrageous, his eyes slid away from that too.

"This time," she said, "unless it was a consequence of that, was an accident. At least I suppose it was, unless my thoughts could have had anything to do with it, or that other beastly abortion."

"You were sick, darling."

"Yes, sick of everything, especially the baby."

He stood, as she had supposed he would, helplessly at the foot of the bed, looking elegant and awful. She found that she hated his clothes: his short overcoat, laceless shoes and tiny hat. For a time she had quite approved his earlier, Regency phase: hair brushed forward on the temples, straight waistcoats and absurd stick with a silver knob. She had even encouraged it for a few months, as though casting him in some private play of hers. But whatever she had done with him he had remained so young and pale and dull, his acquiescence itself a bore. She would not have minded him if he had not been her husband; as a visitor, he might have been as amusing as he had seemed to be at first, when they were only living together. How on earth was she to have known that he would turn out to be like this? So stupid that he couldn't even appreciate the depth of her dissatisfaction.

"As soon as possible we'll get away somewhere," he said then. "France, Switzerland, the Tyrol. I've told Phillips at the office, and he's been wonderfully understanding."

"France? With you?"

"Well, I–"

"No, thanks. London, yes–permanently; but no holidays together. Ever."

Seeing it all, the country of their experience, as flat as a map, she wept angrily. Where was the adventure with that voice at her ear? There was only the repetitive, transiently thrilling, ultimately boring love-making and the possibility of fresh pregnancies. She tasted her furious tears and, as she might have guessed, as she had in fact suspected he would, he took them as a cue for tenderness. She bit his encircling arm, closed her sharp teeth briefly on his wrist and sat up higher in the bed.

"That cottage!" she said. "The whole poisonous country after the promises you'd made."

"Darling, I'll take you anywhere. We'll move wherever you say."

"Yes, wherever I say. It will have to be *me,* won't it? Originally I thought our life would have come out of both of us; but now there's only me, and wherever we went I should loathe it."

"I'll change," he said. "I could if you'd let me."

"That's the point. You would; but it would only be *you* changing."

"Or you."

"I lack a dimension," she said with awful truth, "and you failed to supply it."

"And that's my fault, I suppose?"

"Yours or God's, if there is such a thing. No, you'll have to find us somewhere in London: Hampstead or Chelsea, where we can spread ourselves out a bit. Until you do I'm going back to Lowndes Square."

"You can't possibly."

"I arranged it with Mummy on the telephone this morning."

Still flushed with anger, he was holding his bitten wrist. It amused her, as tangible an evidence of his hurt as was the baby for herself. He even moved over away from the foot of the bed to examine the bite mark in the light of the big window. In the silence they could both hear the traffic passing up to Piccadilly, as active as her thoughts, in which she could imagine his.

Already he would be telling himself that the bite was a good sign, showing real disturbance on her part. In a moment he would be believing that she was having one of those postpregnancy upsets, would see her as the outraged mother in the nest with a dead fledgling beside her. The bite was a love bite; it was an advertising situation, something that Charles could turn into an uncomfortable but basic slogan for Phillips, the head copywriter. God! Why in those earlier months had she ever done more than get into bed with Charles?

"My God!" he said.

"Your God, what?"

"I don't know. There was no need to bite me."

"Why not? It was at least truthful; putting your arm round me, as far as I'm concerned, was a lie—probably as far as we're both concerned."

He was still struggling with himself, hopefully waiting to humour her in the light of his continuing thoughts. With as much familiarity as if they had been middle-aged, she awaited his apology.

"I'm sorry, darling; perhaps it was the wrong moment. I know how you must be feeling."

She laughed high. "If only you could." She meant: "If only you could hate me; if there were only something in you I might find worth persuading." But she said, as so often before, "Did you bring anything to drink with you?"

He produced a half-bottle of whisky from his overcoat pocket and poured a stiff one into the glass on the top of the locker. He said: "I won't, if you don't mind. Not before lunch."

"I don't mind in the least. Put the rest in the locker, please."

She drank half the glass and lighted a Gauloise cigarette. She was seeing herself as a Colette heroine: yellowed, not so much a man-hater as someone quite beyond sexuality—a witch perhaps, a French witch. She was getting bored and saw clearly that the brief charity of the whisky might allow her to get rid of him sympathetically. Certainly, the French witch now knew he wouldn't leave until her hostility ceased.

"I'm feeling tired, Charles."

"Of course, darling."

Why couldn't he even see that he too was just very slightly relieved? She gave him her "rueful" smile. "Thanks awfully for bringing the whisky."

"That's all right. By the way, do you want me at Lowndes Square, too? While we're waiting—for the sale and so on?"

"It's up to you. I suppose it might be easier. My mother would have no objection. She might find it reassuring—if she's there at all."

"Well, tomorrow then, at the same time?"

She had put up her unpleasant face to be kissed, really hating herself for a moment. She even steeled herself to listen to his whispering, longing for him to finish it and go.

When he had done so she threw her pen and writing paper to the end of her bed and drank the remainder of the whisky, staring meanwhile at the baby within the glass. . . .

But on Bernard Presage's arrival the following day she had behaved very differently, not, she told herself, because she was insincere, but because she wanted to please him. He had brought her not flowers or fruit but a little piece of Staffordshire ware, a holy-water stoup flanked by male and female saints, very ingenuous—the price, he explained, of a bottle of whisky and so much more permanent. She exclaimed over its pinks and indigos. "How sweet of you to make such a complete sacrifice."

"Do you mind its being religious?"

"I don't think so—not at this stage. What exactly is it? A font?"

"No, a piscina for holy water. They kept them in their houses to bless themselves with."

"Oh."

They caught one another's eyes and she was suddenly aware that she was looking very beautiful and, to him, sad. She supposed that before her anger and behind it she had every reason to be so in his thinking. She had an idea that women were only "feminine" when they were with men and that one day she might find the necessity tiring.

"Holy water?" she said. "I think I prefer whisky. Do you want some?"

"I'm always game."

"It's in the locker. Charles brought it yesterday, if you don't mind sharing the glass? I don't get on too well with the nurses."

It was only when he was pouring it out on the top of the locker that he noticed the foetus.

"What's that? It's not the—?"

"Yes," she said, taking the glass slyly and drinking from it, "a boy."

She handed him the glass as he sat down a little heavily beside her on the bed, his attention rivetted by the other bottle on the locker. Absently, he drank from the glass she had passed on to him as she tried unsuccessfully to read his thoughts. He leaned forward to see more clearly. "Good God!"

She smiled to herself out of excitement and slipped the glass again from his fingers without his being aware of it. She held it in both her hands like a brandy glass, leaning her lips down to it with her eyes on his face.

"You shouldn't do things like that," he said, catching the gaze she had prepared for him. "You really shouldn't."

"No?"

"What made you?"

"Curiosity."

"What else?"

"Nothing else."

"Has it satisfied it?"

"It's made it worse—or better. It's such a starting point, isn't it?"

He looked round for the whisky and saw her sipping at it again. She passed it back to him unmistakably, lying back against the hospital pillows, her blue-lashed lids momentarily closed above her sallow cheeks, then half-raised again. The glass and the whisky spilled unnoticed over the white counterpane as he kissed her cold, opened lips. She lay half beneath him passively, one hand hardly resting on the hairy nape of his neck: her eyes closed, her breath against his cheek.

"Oh," she whispered, "that was right."

He closed her lips again, kissed the hollows at the base of her neck, her eyelids and her ears. They rescued the glass from the thick folds of the counterpane and refilled it.

"We could still drink to something," she said, lolling back and nuzzling his cheek.

"To what?"

"Just to something. A baby, for instance. Yours."

"Impossible."

"Of course not. If it had been yours, I couldn't have borne it. I mean, to lose it like this. I'd have been desperate."

He kissed her again. "Are you sure you're not?"

"Not in that way. It doesn't mean anything to me, except as a kind of focus for disappointment with everything. I'm in love with you, I suppose. Ever since we met I've felt breathless, breathless and hot, as if I were physically ill. Not immediately, but gradually. It was the way I'd always imagined I'd feel with someone; but it hasn't happened before." She paused. "Charles said—"

"What?"

"He suggested taking me away somewhere, to recuperate."

"What did you say?"

"Not with him, that's all."

In terms of resolution not sin, Bernard compared himself with Coles and saw, even as he did so, that it was not the comparison that decided him, but desire.

"I'll take you. To France."

She slid halfway out of the sheets and lay on him. "Are you reliable?"

"Not as a rule."

"This time?"

"Yes."

"When will you take me?"

"As soon as I can arrange it, as soon as you're well enough."

"I'm well enough now, in some respects." Her dark hair dimmed the daylight as she kissed him. "Give me a fortnight," she whispered, "for complete recovery and the necessary lies."

"Oh Lord."

"But, darling, one can't avoid them."

"Not 'one'; *you* can't, *we* can't," he corrected her.

"No one can avoid lies. They're as necessary as money."

"I suppose so." He got up and looked down at her. "What are you most frightened of, do you think?"

"Growing old. No, not growing old, but being alive for too long; I'm so horrible, so vicious, even though I'm still young."

"Doesn't the fact that I'm nearly fifty matter to you?"

"It's not like that; you couldn't understand, I wouldn't expect you to, but we don't remember it when we see someone, loving them. It's only when I think of living on and on with Charles that I find marriage and being alive intolerable. With someone else I might never have thought of it. But with him—oh, let's have another drink!"

"Discussion's usually a bad idea," he suggested.

"Very. Let's agree not to, at least not about the other part of our lives."

"Only one thing," he said. "D'you think it's possible that it's nothing to do with me, nothing to do with you? That in the other part of our lives there might be something waiting to be born? My God! I know really that this kind of thing isn't an excuse or even an irrelevance, but a substitute for what we've already got."

"I don't know; I've often been tempted to think like that, but it's too painful, too much of an effort. What I want is to go away with you. That'll be heaven."

"Heaven," he agreed uneasily.

"Don't *worry!* Just look forward to it, enjoy it and then, if necessary, forget it. That's what I do."

"Forget it and forget you?"

"Why not? Nothing's lost. Anything I've ever found lovely has remained lovely—more so, when I think of it afterwards." She kissed his hand. "D'you want to know why I really kept the baby?"

"Very much."

"It's simple; I kept it because I didn't believe in it. How could you when you hadn't even seen it?"

"And now that you have?"

"Oh, everything. It really is extraordinary; I could think about it for hours, off and on for the rest of my life if I were an invalid or a prisoner. The baby's a prisoner; it's done absolutely nothing so far—no story at all. Probably, quite without meaning to, I'm responsible; I stopped it just as I stopped the first one, by not accepting it, by hating my life. But I shan't think about it much after this."

"Quite right. You'd either go mad or you'd get very bored or religious."

"Not as bored as I would thinking about God, if that's what you mean; but that's where we differ, isn't it?"

"Yes."

"If I ever do think about him, it's only to hate him. When I look at the baby, I feel it's blasphemous to bring God into it. As far as I'm concerned, God would be more comfortable if I never spared him a thought. He gets nothing that anyone would want from me." She smiled, with pleasure, to herself. "Take yesterday—"

"When you were with Charles?"

"I was foul to him. Just as I was really hating everything, he walked in. I felt sorry for him in a way, and I used my sorrow to humiliate him quite deliberately; and that was wicked, wasn't it? I mean to experience sorrow and intentionally turn it into hatred? But when he'd gone I felt much better, and now you've come I feel marvelous."

"Feel?" he asked. "No point of rest."

"None, except for the baby. But who wants a point of rest? It's not the idea of life—or if it is, God's mad or devilish or both." She looked up at him. "You think I'm frightful, don't you?"

"Only as frightful as we all are and so much more truthful than most. I love you, I adore you."

They held one another for minutes on end, silently: the traffic passing unendingly below the window, the sounds of the hospital heard faintly along the passage beyond the white door.

The telephone was ringing beside the bed: her mother, Claire, concerned and tired—the tired elegant voice in the earpiece. Hera kissed him and spoke back into it collectedly, her voice small and cool. In her free ear he whispered that he would see her during the weekend, and then he left, guilty and exultant.

XI

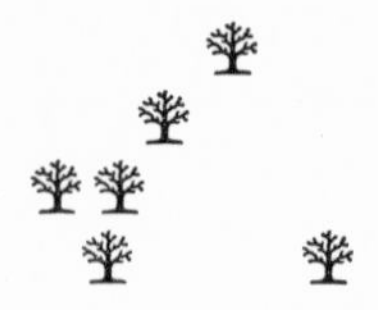

Bernard's exultation was not short-lived; like his guilt, it was recurrent, the two emotions alternating sickeningly, plunging him back into the kind of late adolescence he had found so tiresome in Randall Coles. As Emily had often observed, Bernard was not "far advanced in spirituality." The days in which he had seen his shortcomings as causing God pain were as distant as his last conversion ten years earlier—he experienced conversions within his faith—and at present there was not another in sight. Nowadays the motions of human suffering were his only means of guessing at divine.

He watched Helen suffer after he had confessed his love for Hera Foley. She received the news in silence and slept from that night onwards in the spare bedroom, gradually removing herself from him in every way possible. They had conversations verging on intimacy, but as often withdrawing again, trickling off into an habitual silence. Sometimes the warmth of these conversations surprised him; they would be on the verge of talking as if there were nothing amiss, sharing the perpetual secret, when suddenly he would see that his wife's face was especially bright and remote, as if a stranger had entered the room, someone she was watching a little warily.

When, at nighttime, he heard her moving about in the other bedroom he would try to guess exactly what she was doing and what thinking as she did it. She had a way of getting into a nightdress impatiently, throwing her arms up and letting the thin fabric slide over her body swiftly, like the foam of a breaking wave. She often left her shoes and stockings in the bathroom, and he would find them there with his damp toothbrush, if, as was usual, she had been unable to find her own. Most nights she brushed her long hair briskly, not in front of the mirror on the wardrobe, nor looking at him, but doing it as she had been taught by her mother and grandmother—a nightly chore.

But now he scarcely heard any sounds from the adjoining bedroom: her shoes and stockings were no longer left in the bathroom; she bought a new toothbrush, pink-handled and with soft bristles. Even her underwear disappeared from the airing cupboard, and after a time he had a fantasy in which he played with the idea that he had been widowed and was living with his daughter and an attractive but circumspect housekeeper. His guilt flowered; he became more considerate, drank less, and returned home earlier on the evenings on which, for one reason or another, it was impossible to see Hera. Then, after a few weeks and the conversation with Emily in which he had carefully suppressed reference to Mrs. Foley's earlier miscarriage, he became angry with Helen.

"I can understand you refusing to sleep with me," he said. "But I think it's damned unfair to deprive me of small change."

"What small change?"

"The day-to-day currency of our life together."

"For example?"

"To refuse literally to sleep with me."

"You said 'day-to-day.' Sleeping with you would be night-to-night, wouldn't it?"

"I said *sleep!* I wouldn't expect more at the moment."

"You can't have it both ways," she said.

"I'm not trying to."

"Really?"

"No. And why be so damned neat and tidy after twenty years of leaving your things about?"

"Just an instinct. As you say, I don't awfully like the thought of you at the moment."

"As *I* say? I didn't say anything about it."

"At the moment," she said.

He was eating the fricassee of chicken she'd prepared for him, all the more delicious for his diminished drinking. He couldn't help enjoying it, despite the circumstances: the brisk look of his wife waiting to clear the table, a suggestion of outgoing make-up on her face. She and Cecily had already finished supper before he came in, and he now realized that recently, even when he was only ten or fifteen minutes late, this had nearly always been the case. Although it was a simple move on Helen's part, quite unworthy of their mutual subtlety, he didn't like it.

"Would you mind getting your own coffee?" she asked. "I'm late already, and Cecily's doing her homework."

"Where are you going?"

"Out. Some friends."

"When will you be back?"

"Does it matter?"

"Of course it does."

"Why?"

"It's so damned unoriginal, so suburban." He was imagining some violent scene with Hera Foley, a prolonged and satisfying dialogue.

"Marriage is," Helen said.

"Suburban?"

"No, boring. As boring as adultery."

"Which friends are you going to?"

"Ones you don't like."

"I wouldn't like any of your friends at the moment."

"It would probably be mutual." She was whisking things off the table and putting them on a tray. "You realize that that is boring, too? Friends take sides whether one lives in the suburbs or not." Her sharp-heeled shoes pattered backwards and forwards across the wooden floor, reminding him maddeningly of Lettice Coles.

"Well," he said, "so long as you're not priest-hopping."

"Does that include Benediction?"

"No. Not unless you go and make an unnecessarily frank confession at the same time."

"By 'unnecessarily frank' you mean at your expense, I suppose?"

"Sort of."

"Yes or no?"

"Yes."

She flushed. "These days I never need to bring you into my confessions, even indirectly."

"These days?"

"You're in charge of yourself. You had twenty-five years without me when I didn't even know the colour of your hair or how you made love."

"They can read between the lines, you know. At Westminster they're particularly good at it—so many of the faithful 'shopping' away from home."

"Shopping? Are priests any worse than whores?"

"No, of course not. She's married and she's not honest enough. They're hard workers."

He moved his chair back from the table. "Darling, from the inside, it's not like that. I'm in love with her."

She looked at him, a steady glance that reminded him of their first passport photograph, in which the same innocent gaze had somehow penetrated the camera.

"We both know how little that counts."

"So much in love with her," he continued, "that so far I haven't, that neither of us—"

"It's nothing to do with me; it's to do with you. We're both of us on our own, as we were before we met, as one of us will be again."

"Please, you've got to understand that I'm powerless. It's not as simple as lust or a straightforward love affair."

"It never is."

"It's her despair, darling; I'm snarled up in it in some way."

"Try mine! Have you had enough supper?"

She left him sitting before the cleared table, listening for the whir of the ascending lift. . . .

He finished his cigarette and went into Cecily's room. She was sitting at the little bureau she had inherited from her grandmother.

The room smelled exotic and young: a mixture of eastern tobacco and scent.

"What's the scent?" he asked.

"Gloire de Dijon. I saved up for it. Do you like it?"

"Not bad."

There were squads of young men over the bed: signed photographs of horse guards, grenadiers and Coldstreamers. He congratulated her silently on the absence of guitars.

"Do you want a cigarette?" she asked.

"Where's Mummy gone—d'you know? You shouldn't be smoking."

"I'm not really; it's only an experiment. I like Egyptian best, but they're so terribly expensive. You can have one if you like."

"Where's Mummy gone?"

"I'm not sure. I think she may have gone to meet Emily. She rang up earlier to ask her to have drinks with her in the West End."

"When?"

"Sometime this afternoon."

"Are you sure?"

"Yes, I think so."

"Was that what she asked you to tell me?"

"Yes."

"Is it true?"

"I don't know. But it easily could be; the telephone did ring and I did hear her talking to someone."

"But was it Emily?"

"I don't know."

His daughter was yawning and restless. He had the sense that he was scarcely there for her, an interruption in her evening of work and imagining. He began to look at her more closely. She was wearing a pale lipstick and had drawn Egyptian lines out from the corners of her eyes in dark-blue mascara. Her dark hair was glossy and immaculate, drawn forward below each cheek into points sharp as the folded flight feathers of a bird. Her eyes questioned him idly.

"Daddy, what's it like to be in love?"

"In love?"

"Yes. What happens to a person?"

"It's unavoidable, really."

"How?"

"I'm not sure. Once it's happened, it's there inside you like a mood you can't get out of."

She was drawing a girl's head on an open exercise book. "Even if you stop seeing the person?"

"You don't want to."

"Well, what happens then?"

"I'm not sure. Cecily, have you been listening?"

"Not specially. You both talk awfully loudly sometimes. I kept hearing words through the door." She gave the girl long eyelashes and a small hat. "Will it end up in divorce or something? If you can't get over it, I mean?"

Her pen hesitated over the drawing and then sketched in a hand holding a cigarette, a table with a glass of wine on it.

"You know perfectly well that Mummy and I would never think of getting divorced."

"Well, separation." It was scarcely a question. She was fiddling with things on the bureau, had opened a drawer and taken out a blue scarab brooch given her by Randall Coles for Christmas a year or two earlier. Bernard was quite astonished by her boredom and preoccupation.

"Have you really considered that?" he asked.

"Of course." She clipped the brooch on to the bodice of her dress and squinted down at it. "Naturally. I was thinking of writing to Giles about it."

"For God's sake, don't."

"No, I wasn't going to in the end. It might stop him working for his exam; and, besides, you can't make it sound right in a letter. I only got halfway."

"Let's see."

"It's in the wastepaper basket. I crumpled it up."

She sat very still as he fumbled for it beside her feet.

"Is this it?"

"Yes."

"Dear Giles," he read . . .

I hope you are well and happy. I'm working very hard and nothing much seems to happen to me. Life goes on and on with exams and things as if it would never start. The old folk are just the same apart from Daddy, who is not drinking half so much. Apparently he's fallen in love with someone else who is married too, much younger than he is, in fact not much older than you are. If it wasn't for Mummy I could sympathize with him in a way, but it's all rather like one of those bad films where you find yourself crying and worrying despite your better judgment. They are both behaving automaticly as if they couldn't get out of it either. I haven't worked out the end yet, but I've put a male saint in charge: not s. Joseph because how could he understand but s. Augustine for obvious reasons. Daddy is taking more trouble with his appearance, but he is not slimming, I'm glad to say. He came home the other night with a society journalist, a real self-regarder who wanted to know how many calories there were in everything. Don't worry too much about M and D. Just pray for good things for this girl; then God might give her a disaster.

I haven't met anyone exciting yet this term, but . . .

"Do you mind if I keep this?" Bernard asked.

"You won't show it to Mummy? At least, not until afterwards?"

"No."

"Do you really like it?"

"Yes. Cecily, do you and Giles always think of us as 'the old folk'?"

"We call you that, but we don't think it all the time. In the letter I was only trying to be laconic, but it came out too flat. I just wanted to give Giles the facts so's he could pray for you both."

"Me and Mummy?"

"No—it's in the letter—you and this girl you're after."

"I'm not after any girl."

"The one you're in love with, I meant."

"You don't believe that I am?"

"Oh, I suppose you could be. I know it does happen; there are heaps of examples in the O.T. David, I mean, and Uriah's wife. After they'd committed adultery he got the husband killed."

Bernard sat down on her bed. "I'll have a cigarette."

"Oh good! Let me light it for you. I love lighting them. It's the best part—so far the main reason I smoke, really."

He watched her do it as he worked out a line of attack.

"Cecily, if you really want to understand what's going on, I'll have to try and explain."

With some reluctance she passed him over the cigarette, allowing the smoke she had retained to drift out slowly between her open lips. It occurred to him that she was wondering how she might get rid of him without hurting his feelings.

"I do understand, Daddy. Honestly, there's no need for a session."

"I've no intention of indulging in a 'session'; but I think I ought to give you a clearer idea of my difficulties."

She concealed a sigh and settled back patiently in her chair. She picked up her pen, preparing to doodle again, and suddenly Bernard gave up. She saw his preparations for departure and became instantly apologetic, for the first time a little nervous.

"Please, Daddy, don't be hurt. We know all about it at school. Nowadays we simply have to because of television and the Eng. Lit. course. It's this middle-aged thing, isn't it?"

"In this case, it's a little more complex than that."

"But that's what everybody thinks. I mean, *I* don't really believe I'm adolescent: things like this brooch and my cigarettes. But when I look at them by themselves and say, 'This is me doing it,' I have to realize that I *am* 'teen-age' and everything else. So although I don't believe in it inside, I take it on trust. Although it doesn't help, it cheers me up to think it must be only a phase in my life and that one day it'll be over."

"You're right," he said. "I'm sorry, Cecily."

"It's nothing; I'm just a bit tired tonight. I got carried away by my journal and couldn't really concentrate on what you and Mummy were saying, so if I've been stupid, making you feel a fool, it's not what I really believe. However it feels, however horrible it is for you, I just want you to get over it." She paused. "I'm going to have a bath now and watch the television in my dressing gown. Are you going out?"

He kissed her on the forehead and walked across to the door.

"Will you be all right if I go over to the pub for an hour or so?"

She looked at him with polite surprise. He saw her eyes flicker round the confines of her room: guardsmen, china favours and a holy picture.

"Of course," she said. "I'll tell Mummy if she comes in before you."

She smiled at him compassionately, with the kind of flair a sister reserves for an elder brother. He closed the door and went out to the lift. But he did not wait for it to return from the ground floor; instead, he walked slowly down the stairs, smoking her Egyptian cigarette, stepping out into the night-lit street thoughtfully.

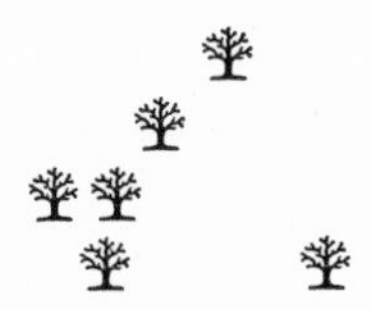

Coles would have thought it impossible for Lettice to become any more efficient; but of late, undeniably, she had—both brisker and busier and, in a sense, wilder. Though he believed he'd noticed it almost immediately, he found it difficult to date the change precisely.

In the midst of his own preoccupation with Hotchkis and Betty Hotchkis, both of whom were alarming him at the time, he had a memory of returning home late one evening and finding Lettice sitting beside the fire in the big room, smoking a cigarette. As a matter of fact, he'd been so "exercised" that it was only when he had taken off his grey overcoat and grey woollen scarf and hung them in the boot room that he'd remembered the cigarette. He had gone upstairs to the lavatory to freshen himself up before coming down again to have the glass of dry sherry before supper when it had suddenly struck him that his wife had held a just-lighted cigarette between the fingers of her left hand. He thought about it as he washed: Lettice hadn't smoked since their engagement days in Cambridge twenty years ago and had dropped the habit voluntarily on their honeymoon in St. Helier. "Only virgins should smoke," she had said; "in a matron it looks loose."

Before the mirror, Coles brushed his greying hair with a tortoise-shell-backed wedding-present brush; he straightened his tie and regarded himself for a moment. Betty Hotchkis had told him that his hair was nice, "crinkly," and had got into the delightful habit of stroking it. He looked a little tired, he supposed, but otherwise there was no outward sign of the stresses within. Confidently, he descended the stairs and went back into the drawing room. He kissed Lettice and went over to the drink table to help himself to the decanter.

"Sherry, darling?"

"No, gin, please."

"Gin?"

"Yes, the unsweetened. It's in the cupboard."

He poured it out obediently and returned to her, walking delicately as had Agag in the cave.

"Enough?"

"Quite, thanks."

"What sort of a day have you had?"

"The usual. Rather busier, if anything."

Coles took off his glasses, polished them and put them on again. It seemed to him just possible that Lettice had on a little make-up. He made an excuse to get nearer to her by warming his dry hands at the fire. Distinctly, there was a pale ring of lipstick on the filter tip of her cigarette.

"You're smoking," he said, sniffing the air.

"Yes."

"It's not herbal, is it?"

"No, virginian. Geoffrey gave me them."

"Geoffrey?"

"At the hospital last week."

"Oh yes, of course."

Coles had forgotten about her hospital days; she hadn't mentioned them for weeks. It occurred to him that they lived an enormous part of their lives separately. For a moment he couldn't even remember which of her doctors "Geoffrey" was; then he placed him as a guest at the last summer party, the one at which Bernard

Presage had become involved with Hera Foley. He couldn't remember his surname but believed that he had been an E.N.T. specialist, a large man with bristling eyebrows who had talked about golf and dogs. Lettice preferred consultants; much as active work in a parish provided some women with ecclesiastical friends, so Lettice's medical chore had opened the clinical horizons.

"I've decided to cancel the winter party," she said then. "I've managed to ring most people up, but there are still one or two London guests outstanding: Bernard Presage and the Foleys, for example. Perhaps you could let them know tomorrow? It saves on the telephone bill."

"Cancelled it?"

"Deferred, really, for a fortnight. Instead of Saturday the thirty-first, Friday the thirteenth."

"But why, darling? What decided you? You didn't mention it this morning."

"I hadn't decided this morning."

She drew clumsily on her cigarette, coughed briefly and wiped her eyes with one of the irish linen handkerchiefs their daughter Brett had given her for Christmas. Coles patted her thin back, noting that it was very much bonier than Mrs. Hotchkis'. He was immediately and disproportionately worried by her cigarette. "Why don't you put it out? You're not really enjoying it, are you?"

"Don't be silly; of course I am." She drew on it again. "I cancelled or, rather, deferred the party for a number of reasons. For one thing, I'm feeling strained; for another, Malcolm's written to say he's coming down that weekend, the thirteenth one; and, also, Geoffrey can't manage the original one."

"Geoffrey?"

Lettice turned and snapped at him: "For heaven's sake, don't keep on saying 'Geoffrey' like that every time I mention him."

"I'm sorry, darling."

"Also, I want to organize it better this time. I'm tired of people just coming here and eating and drinking everything in sight, then talking and going away again. I want you and Malcolm to arrange a game of some sort, something intelligent and original."

"I see." Coles emptied his glass and refilled it. "Darling, there's nothing wrong, is there? You haven't got any big worries?"

"No, it's simply the party."

"But they've always been such a success. I don't really see any necessity for a change. Admittedly the play readings weren't very rewarding, but I'm not sure that at our age, games—"

"That's exactly what I mean. We've got to do something to brighten them up. Something constructive that will give people a chance to use their minds. I've noticed lately that with the exception of the younger doctors all our guests are getting older and older each year."

"But so are we, darling."

"Are we?" She spoke ironically, but he decided to ignore it.

"It's inevitable. One can't possibly put back the clock."

"I don't want to discuss it, Randall. I just want you and Malcolm to arrange it. If you haven't got any ideas yourself, then he'll think of something. I have an instinct about it, that's all. . . ."

Since then there had been a number of additional clues which Randall, had he been less *affairé* with the Hotchkises, would have followed up more immediately. As it was, he temporized and confined himself to trying to sleep with Lettice at the weekend—and was refused. In the cold darkness he made the journey across to her narrow bed but didn't get very much further. She would scarcely move over for him.

"I'm tired," she said. "Quite frankly, I don't feel amorous tonight."

"It's not necessarily that, darling. I mean, apart from anything else, I'm cold—the bedroom's cold."

"No colder than it's been for the last ten days."

"It feels colder."

"That's your fault. You will keep the windows open."

'But you like them open. We've always had them open, ever since St. Helier."

"I can't help it."

"Just to get warm!" he pleaded, kissing her in the usual way.

She suffered it for a moment and then he felt her teeth close: a hard plastic barrier, made by Mr. Blue, their local man, whom Lettice did not consent to know other than professionally. "One knows one's doctor, possibly," her mother had always said, "but rarely one's dentist." Betty Hotchkis had her own teeth, filled, he remembered; it was one of the things she cared about. "Lose your teeth," she'd told him, "and you lose your charm. You might as well give up."

"Please, darling," he said to Lettice.

"No, I can't. I'm not going to."

She had wanted to say, "Certainly not, you deceitful pig!"—all the quite brutal words Harriet Harvey evidently employed during Edward's infidelities. But she managed to hold herself inflexibly, to yawn and sigh with a normal kind of exhaustion. Although she was feeling so bitter, she could not help remembering her mother's warning the night before her wedding: "Never refuse in the bedroom, dear, or they will look elsewhere." Randall had looked or was looking elsewhere already. Twice that week he had been even later than usual and given her nauseatingly exact timetables of his supposed movements. For all she knew, he was hot from the chase, about to employ the familiar techniques with someone else. How absolutely disgusting it was! Quite involuntarily she brought one of her thin knees up sharply and felt it collide with his warm groin.

Randall gasped.

"Oh, I'm sorry," she said. "I was only trying to get comfortable. I didn't mean to hurt you. I simply want to get to sleep if I can." She would have liked to try again, more accurately next time; she was quite astonished by the violence of her feelings as he fumbled for and switched on the light between the beds. With extreme pleasure she watched him as, with one hand holding up his pajama trousers, he stumbled out of bed and limped into the bathroom.

"Why are you so tired?" he asked her on his return. "What on earth have you been doing to get so tired?"

"I went for a long walk with Tyndal on the golf links this afternoon. Geoffrey very kindly gave us a lift in his car."

"Geoffrey?" Randall asked before he could stop himself.

"Yes, Geoffrey. It was his afternoon off, so after I'd finished the morning library in the surgical wards and lunched with the staff, we went out to get some exercise together."

"A walk on the golf links?"

"Yes, I've told you. We weren't playing today. Geoffrey brought

Wolf too. And please don't parrot me and say 'Wolf.' Wolf is the Cattermole bull terrier."

"Oh, I see. Geoffrey Cattermole. I'd forgotten his surname."

She yawned again, audibly. "Good night. Is your leg all right?"

"It wasn't my leg."

"I'm so sorry. Are you sure it's all right? It's stopped hurting?"

"They haven't." Randall was feeling inexplicably angry. It had obviously been accidental—everything was—but Lettice didn't sound really concerned. He remembered his undergraduate days at Caius, rugger and the running for which he had got a half-blue just before he had met Lettice.

"You hit me straight in my balls," he said.

"Please don't be coarse with me; it doesn't suit you."

"I can't help it; they're extremely painful and I could only find cold cream in the bathroom cupboard."

"There are some aspirins if it's as bad as all that."

"It's not."

"Well, good night, then."

"Good night. You seem to be seeing a good deal of Cattermole lately."

"Yes, I am. He has difficulties at the moment. Outside his work he's rather lonely. You don't mind, do you?"

"Not in the least." It was what he deserved at present, he supposed; though in other respects it was a little disturbing, morally it made him feel just very slightly easier. "He seemed to be quite a decent man," he added.

"Of course he is. If he was in the least bit suspect, one of those unpleasant, hinting, womanizing men, I wouldn't have anything to do with him."

"No, of course not. All the same, one has to be careful."

"Only if one is loose oneself, lacking in principle, I mean."

"Exactly."

"What do you mean 'exactly'? Are you suggesting that either of us *is* lacking in principle?"

"Of course not. But it's possible to be bored, to get bored."

In the darkness, Lettice sat up. "With what?"

"With life," Randall said.

She forced herself to lie down again. This was her testing moment, the one in which Harriet Harvey would have indulged herself as unedifyingly as in crumpets. Lettice changed the subject.

"By the way, did you manage to contact Bernard Presage and the Foleys about the party?"

"Yes; they're both coming on the thirteenth."

"Both?"

"Both or all three—I don't know which. I rather think they're having an affair."

"Who? Bernard and that girl?"

"It looks rather like it."

"How disgusting."

Coles said nothing. It was a crucial moment; a less contained man might have been tempted to make his own comment, a general plea of some sort.

"Does Helen know?" Lettice asked.

"Probably. Bernard's pretty honest with her."

"Or a coward," Lettice said. "If a man's going to behave like a pig, he might at least manage it with dignity, like the Victorians. Dirty as it is, the one really unforgivable thing is to let it come out."

Randall half sat up and lay down again. He spoke as casually as he could: "Do you really think so?"

"Yes. I can't bear clumsiness and cowardice in a man. But then of course Bernard's a Roman Catholic; their habit of confessing everything makes them careless and soft."

"Yes."

"Don't you agree, in principle?"

"Bernard's never struck me particularly as being either weak or soft, but—"

"He drinks. What's that but weakness? There are times when I feel very sorry for Helen."

"Darling, I'm tired and still in some pain."

"Well, I'm sorry. Good night."

"Good night, darling."

But Lettice did not return the endearment. He knew that she was thinking as furiously as he was himself; yet he had no inkling of the cause of her anxiety. She lay there a few feet away from him, playing out her secret grievance in the darkness. It occurred to him that in the old days there would have been the making of a poem in the event. They lay there in their separate beds as if in separate hives, their heads surrounded by gently moving bees. All was dark; the wind whispered round the eaves and a thin gust of it touched their faces, the external casements of the thoughts which circled and moved continually, turning over and in upon themselves as on an underlying comb of sweetness.

XIII

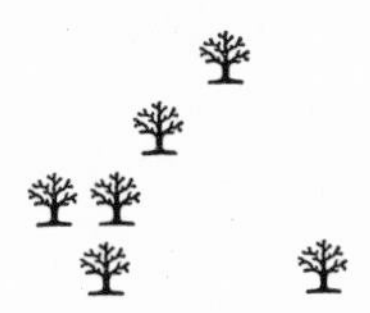

A few days later, in his office in Langham Place, Coles confided some of his uneasiness to Bernard. "What do you suppose it means?" he asked.

"The make-up, the cigarettes, the friendship with the consultant and the marital refusal all add up to a change in the pattern which can mean only one thing: Lettice is on to you."

"Ah, a change in the behaviour pattern," Coles said with relief. "But how on earth could she have found out?"

"Take Helen—" Bernard began.

"But you told Helen yourself. Lettice, by the way, considers that a sign of weakness."

"She may be right. I preferred it to the necessary lies and, anyway, I have the instinct to confession. You're lucky, Coles; you don't have to consider anything but the finite. All you've got to do is to muddle through to the final coronary. You don't even have to consider the possibility of a pathology of the soul."

"No, thank God."

"It would never have occurred to you that even now, as we're talking, we might both of us be very slightly out of true, the information we're acting on falsified not so much by our sins as by our excuses for them."

"I don't see it," Coles said, twisting his foot.

"The new word for it is 'insight,' whether in the confessional or on the psychiatric couch. With it there's hope, without it, none."

"Scarcely relevant, I should have thought."

"Then remember the fools you meet on the train. Speak to them and they won't hear you. It will be only a gabble, a quacking; they will see geese everywhere, large white geese in a green field."

"Oh well, of course—"

"Stop twisting your foot under the table. It's time you made your confession, Coles, to someone other than yourself. The fountain cannot cleanse itself."

"Need we bring religion into this?"

"With me, yes. You must allow me to talk in my own terms, as you do in yours."

"What about Hotchkis?" Coles asked.

"I don't know him. Is there any comparison?"

"You mean in his attitude?"

"Yes."

"On occasions he's talked in the same way," Coles said. "As a matter of fact, I'm worried about him at the moment. He's been behaving extremely oddly. He talks continually of what he calls his 'night.' "

"In a metaphysical sense? The dark night of the soul?"

"I hardly think there's anything mystical about it. He's still quite impenitent."

"A strange choice of word? For you?"

"Unregenerate, then. But Hotchkis Night seems to him to be a prelude to some kind of action, even the action itself. Also, he's influencing a fellow prisoner, another murderer, a man called Bushnell. I suspect he's disturbing him quite dangerously; he catches me on my way in and out of the prison and gives me messages."

"Such as?"

"Oh, things about not dropping Christopher on his release, hints of various kinds. Last week he even referred to Lettice by her

Christian name. He asked me if I'd taken her into my confidence yet."

"Delightful!" Presage said. "Let's go and have a drink somewhere."

"Not this afternoon; I've got too much on. I never think drink's a good idea when one's worried. You see, I can't help sensing a kind of threat behind it all, and I'm not sure what steps I ought to take to protect myself."

"Yourself!"

Coles flushed; his foot twisted like a cat's tail. "There's no need to be offensive, Bernard. It's simply that I'm not sure of my position, I don't know what to do under the circumstances."

"Of course not. Now, as I've suggested, I do and I won't and you don't and you can't."

"I've told you," Coles said, suddenly furious, "that at the moment I'm under considerable stress, both personally and publicly."

"Confused," Bernard said, "and godless."

Coles started sorting out his "In" tray. "Let me make it quite clear that I don't believe in your 'other level,' your religion, your soul, or your bloody confession. All I want is some sane and rational advice. And, incidentally, I've got the hell of a lot of letters to write about the damned sacraments!"

"Good," Bernard said. "There's hope for us yet. I'll see you tomorrow."

Most irritatingly he patted Coles on the back of the shoulders and sidled off along the corridor.

His anger cooling slowly, Coles sat on over his cooling cup of tea. Bernard's continual references to confession had touched him on a particularly sore spot. As he well knew, only in September, at the Senior Producer's Conference, the head of R.B. had suggested that the Sunday Quiet Spot should prepare a new series for the Christmas season. Someone had thrown out the idea of the seven sacraments, to run throughout December/January. The transmissions would "go out" on the Home Service at the peak hour of ten forty-five, just before the public switched on its electric blankets and boiled up its malted milk. The eighth in the series could be a "filler," very matey, with even the nonconformists giving their views. Coles himself, it had been suggested, should preside and hold the clerics together.

Under considerable pressure, he had been forced to agree even to such short notice. He had started soliciting scripts by letter and telephone the next day, and now the first four sacraments were piling up in his "In" tray: Baptism, Confirmation, Confession, and Holy Matrimony. He had had to reread the Book of Common Prayer, the Penny Catechism and the Roman Missal before seeking more personal contact with the contributors.

There had been "jolly" lunches with the Anglicans in Knightsbridge and what he had described to Lettice as rather "quelling" tea parties with the Jesuits in Mount Street: invariably, muffins and rhubarb jam. In addition, there had been a particularly trying coffee morning with the Anglican Bishop of Holborn, who had wanted to slide Father Willie Morgan into the "filler" programme. Father Willie had recently been taken for a ride by a group of Americans who specialized in fund-raising. They had left the church commissioners about ten thousand pounds light on the deal and so incensed the parish that the church was now completely empty. Father Willie had lost the deanery he was in line for and reverted to the violent Welsh nationalist politics of his youth. Dr. Standish, a left-winger himself, had heard of it and arranged for his transfer to a particularly horrible new town in his own diocese. The Reverend Morgan was about the last person the B.B.C. wanted on any kind of programme.

The whole project was stretching Coles' humanist tolerance to its limits. He had told Lettice, "It's this wretched ecumenism. They're all so horribly polite to one another nowadays. When they were all at each other's throats, one knew where one was. But ever since that peasant pope started the ball rolling, the department's been thrown into complete disorder."

"You must look upon it as a development, disillusion, a desperate closing of the ranks in the face of reason. Logical, really."

"Quite apart from that," Coles had said, "there's the vocabulary: grace, contrition, penance—all the meaningless jargon of doctrinal theology. It's like living in a Roman seminary."

"Treat it simply as an assignment. Don't get involved."

Coles had thought for a moment. "I've been wondering lately if I'm not seeing too much of Presage."

"Wondering!" Lettice had said. "I should have thought it was obvious."

But now, sorting out the dictation for the next day, Coles congratulated himself that even in his anger he'd had the good sense to withhold some things from Bernard. In the confidences about Hotchkis he had managed to suppress any reference to the Pery Bowles-Johnson business, his undertaking to give her Christopher's message that evening at the Dolphin Club in Swann Street. He was looking forward to it really; it distilled some of the excitement of the earliest meetings with Hotchkis. Thinking of it, he was aware again of the lump in the center of his chest, the dry granular sensation in the back of his throat, the sense that out of the vital indiscretion there might come rest, peace, reconciliation to what Presage had termed "the private pathology."

Coles often thought that he would have liked to have been a spy rather than an observer, a Graham Greene character with a mixed conscience, hounded across Europe to a secret death. His life, then, his work—a reserved occupation which had spared him military service even in the war—the domestic pattern with Lettice would all have made sense. As a minor communications official in the diplomatic service, an agent, the very normality of his social existence would have been as deceptive as the lugsail of a Q-ship with guns beneath the rigging. But as it was he had been forced to do his best, to unite his hunger for significance with his principles as a humanist, to do good stealthily with his heart in his mouth.

Before setting out that evening he changed his clothes in the overnight bedroom provided by the corporation for those on late duty. He put on his best suit, the navy worsted he had worn for the coffee party with the Bishop, a pair of dark suede shoes, a dull-pink silk Cardin tie with deep-red silk socks to tone, a touch of Monsieur after-shave lotion under his armpits, and, over all, his american mackintosh and an english trilby. The hat and the mackintosh were important: they conveyed cosmopolitanism, they suggested yawning jet flights and overnight stops in foreign capitals. When they were removed, there was the transformation: the flawless midnight-blue suit, the softly glowing tie, the hint of Paris in the lotion.

Leaving that morning, he had lied to Lettice. "Another Jesuit evening," he had told her, "together with the ex-editor of the *Catholic Herald,* Michael Compostella, to discuss the Matrimony script." Compostella, he said, had rung him up in the morning, wanting to discuss the question of the "pill." "It's the sort of thing one can only discuss over dinner."

"Expenses?" Lettice had asked.

"Yes. But of course the Jesuits are always a little fly and Compostella's horribly close."

"Then you'd better take three pounds with you, hadn't you? If you cut out taxis and short drinks, it should be ample."

He wondered now how far three pounds would go with Pery Bowles-Johnson and decided to eat first in the Garden buffet in Victoria Station. It would fill in time; he didn't want to reach his destination much before ten and, besides, the contrast of the "safe" meal and its possible sequel afforded him pleasure. He and Lettice usually ate at the Garden on their joint trips to London for Christmas shopping or Poetry Society evenings. It was, as Lettice explained, "sensible: after all, we've never been competitive."

Tonight, just as if she'd been there with him, he ate baked beans with two slices of toast and H.P. sauce, a compote of tinned fruit salad and custard followed by a cup of black coffee. Then he took a District Line train to Swann Square and went into an expensive pub, where he spent five more shillings on a slow double Martini. He managed to waste an hour and a half watching people and "tuning in" on their conversations. At half-past nine he walked up Swann Street and descended the red-carpeted stairway of the Dolphin Club.

The owner, David Heim, welcomed him rudely. Although Coles knew him slightly, he had asked his secretary to ring him a week earlier and ask if it would be all right for him, as a nonmember, to drop in and see the floor show. Heim, an inveterate self-publicist and the author of two or three dirty plays, scenting the possibility of a broadcast, had said that although there was no floor show Coles could drop in on any evening he liked.

This evening he was sitting beside the bar, waiting for the club to warm up. He said, "I was wondering when you'd show up. Your secretary said you wanted to contact some girl or other."

"Miss Bowles-Johnson."

"The Bowles girl? She doesn't usually come on until eleven. She's slowing up; they do in the middle thirties. What's the matter with your secretary?"

"She's strictly a secretary."

"Ugly or old?"

"Neither. Is Miss Bowles-Johnson in the cabaret?"

"We don't *have* a cabaret," Heim drawled, "and if we did that whore wouldn't be in it. We're strictly a rendezvous here. What are you drinking?"

"A Martini, thanks."

"D'you want a table booking?"

"Well, not really."

"I should." Heim signalled his headwaiter. "It will cramp her style if you don't. MacKendrick! You might reserve a table for Mr. Coles."

"By the wall, sir?"

"Oh, anywhere."

Heim winked. "MacKendrick's not what he seems; he's a very discerning man. A failed novelist, as a matter of fact; I picked him up in Soho."

"What exactly does she do, the Bowles girl?"

"Neurotics mostly. The lonely men from Ruislip and places north. She's rather good at picking them off without letting them know."

"Know what?"

"That it's going to cost them. Finesse: no hurry about it. A relationship before the sex, sex well before the presents." Heim turned his blank gaze on to Coles' face. "What's your interest? One of those vicar-meets-whore programmes or purely personal?"

"Purely personal."

"Well, you could do a lot better with one of our amateurs. They roll in about one A.M.: young marrieds from Chelsea or advertising girls with a mummy and daddy in the country."

"Frankly," Coles lied, "I had nothing particular in mind, just a scout round for a possible series we may be putting on. Certainly I'm not looking for a woman in the accepted sense."

"Your mother might believe you, but your father wouldn't," Heim said. "But it's all of my business. If you want a documentary, though, you'll have to be careful, because you've come to the right place."

Coles snickered. Heim's clever compromises were beginning to amuse him. He was like a conjuror who apparently was compelled, every now and again, to throw away the act. Coles' obvious pleasure now drove him on to further self-revelation.

"My middle-class stuff's largely a cover-up. You realize that, don't you, boy? Don't tell me; I know I'm right. The hard core of my trade stretches from Shadow Cabinet level down to the mobs."

Coles drank his Martini airily. "Cutting it a little fine, surely?"

"Why should I care? I'm a good boy, aren't I? Lost the pack at Auschwitz. What's Society to me? I'll tell you, Coles: all we need here is a good scandal and we'd have it made."

"Risky, I should have thought."

"I was never taught to be cautious. I'm not a Mason. We watch our journalists and our cops; only the top-flight are accepted for membership. By the time they've swapped their women for a month or two they're in our pockets. But for the Corporation you'd never have got in here in the first place. Which reminds me, now that we're really talking, what's the business with the Bowles girl tonight?"

Coles was flustered but firm. "I'd rather not say, if you don't mind, Heim. I can only assure you that it won't in any way prejudice your interests."

"If it does I'll get you the sack overnight. Your programme boys like their ferrets to keep their tails clean."

He moved away to welcome his incoming patrons. But in a few moments he returned with his *mot* for the evening.

"As a humanist," he asked, "have you ever thought how clever it was of God to make the holes in a cat's fur fit exactly over its eyes?"

Coles' own eyes crinkled with pleasure. "You're not orthodox, are you, David?"

"Now I ask you," said Heim, discarding his drawl, "can I afford to be, boy, with my living to earn in a Christian democracy?" He paused. "Mac's given you a table by the wall—number twelve. Don't lay the Bowles woman before midnight; she'll cost you double. . . ."

Half behind a pillar, Coles sat at his table eating pearl onions and sipping white Bordeaux, watching the businessmen, executives and Chelsea dudes beneath the discreet lighting. Here and there were solitary men like himself, the "Ruislip fringe," he supposed, waiting hopefully for one of Heim's unattached girls to take them on. Heim, he knew, did not employ "hostesses." Apart from two or three seasoned professionals like Miss Bowles-Johnson, he relied solely on the amateurs, young women of good or not-so-good family, married or unmarried, who came in parties, a man or two short, as soon as the pubs closed.

As the evening wore on, the lights dimmed even lower, the music became more suggestive and the dancing more static. Couples with only their hair or scalps shining stood glued paunch to pelvis, undulating hardly perceptibly: hands crept up backs, mouths drooped open and eyes closed flaccidly.

Coles dreamed of Betty Hotchkis—her boredom, naïveté, directness: "Give us a treat," she had said, "something to remember." Presumably she had said the same thing to Paul, the friend Hotchkis had killed eight years ago; yet when she referred to him now it was with a smile of condescension—condescension and distaste. "He got silly," she said, "careless. I've forgotten what he looked like, Paul."

"You'd forget me too, wouldn't you," Coles had said, "as soon as we'd—"

"Now don't say it! Ooh, you haven't half got a dirty mind."

"But you would, wouldn't you? Forget me completely?"

She had yawned. "I might. Who's to say? The same as Pery, I do get tired of men; and I haven't had half so many."

Recently she had talked a lot about her sister. Now that the date of his release was so near, both she and Hotchkis seemed to have become suddenly mindful of Pery.

"Pery fancies Chris," Betty had said. "Always has done. Provided I get my housekeeping again, she's welcome. She'd be clever enough too—able to keep up with him and his weird ideas. I'm simple. I know what I want and that's it."

"What do you want?"

"You!" she had said. "And it's her fault—Pery and the television. They get in here and leave their ideas behind them, right in the bloomin' kitchen. You can't escape. I often wish—"

"What?"

"Nothing."

"Tell me, please."

"Just mother in the cemetery. She was satisfied. She had a rotten life, but she knew where she lived. . . ."

Coles was so lost in his recollections, the anguish of his longings, that he didn't see Miss Bowles-Johnson approach. He jumped when he heard the well-modulated, classless voice and rose hurriedly to face the slender woman standing by his table.

"Miss Bowles-Johnson?"

"Pery," she said. "You must be Randy—Randall, I should say."

Coles pulled out the chair for her. "Would you like white wine or something stronger?"

"It's early yet." She glanced at a tiny golden wristwatch encrusted with rather small diamonds. "I never touch shorts before midnight."

"A meal, then?" he asked as he poured her a glass of Bordeaux.

"Just egg mayonnaise and an omelette. I have to watch my figure." She looked at him: her tired little face, her light-brown eyes, cooler than her sister's. "You don't have to worry; you're slim."

"I wouldn't have thought you had to either."

She was wearing pale green, low cut in the front. Lettice made her party dresses out of yard goods, usually a length of sale velvet blown together with a few stitches and tucks on the sewing machine left her by her mother. She was inclined to disapprove of what Harriet Harvey called "clo'es." As a university woman she felt obliged to dress as a "graduate"; she was not "competitive."

"I look all right only if I cut down on undies," Miss Bowles-Johnson said. "I'm a night bird really; so it's that and goose flesh." She gave a picturesque little shiver, as if to say, "there's not much of me, is there?"

Coles fussed.

"It's not too warm for me, even here in the Dolphin," she went on, "maybe because I haven't got warmed up yet."

"Would you like to dance? I mean, you haven't a wrap or anything?"

"I'll be all right. I'd love to dance." She rose gracefully, sipped at her wine, and put her long cigarette in an ash tray. She fell to him easily, professionally, moulding her body to his as they clung somewhere in the center of the crowded floor space.

"You're tall, aren't you? You can't guess what a relief it is to have someone lean and quiet at the start of an evening."

"The start?" Coles asked quietly.

He was breathing in her scent—rather subtle: it might suit Lettice if it wasn't too expensive. He was feeling the ripple of her stomach against his midnight-blue waist and comparing her neck with Betty Hotchkis'. Her fingers tightened on his own, as soft as his daughter Brett's. For a moment, filling him with memories of Lettice in May Week twenty years earlier—the dances, the mooning walks along the Backs—Pery Bowles-Johnson drew him closer, then relaxed again.

She gave him a pretty, sideways smile. "I'm going to like you. Perhaps it runs in the family."

"It's mutual."

"We'll have to watch out then, won't we? I mustn't fish in Betty's preserves or she'll do her nut. How is she, lately?"

"She's getting a lot of headaches and sleeping badly."

"Poor Betty. It'll be gate-fever. You wouldn't think of the wives' getting it too, would you? Yet it's obvious, really."

"Yes, of course."

"Definitely. Underneath, Betty's very nervy. A lot of people don't realize it, but she's always been the same. I feel guilty, really, that I haven't dropped down to see her again, but I don't like to go too often; she gets jealous."

"Does she?"

"Didn't you know? I thought, knowing her so well, you'd have been bound to notice."

"It hadn't really occurred to me."

"She's never grown up, hasn't Betty. She thinks London and the clubs are all roses. Some people do; they think someone else is having a better time. They don't ever think of the snags." She drew away from him a little. "Randy, does she ever talk to you about me?"

"Oh yes, quite often. She told me about your Portuguese holiday with someone or other."

"Max, that would be Max." He felt her quiver and saw her teeth for a moment.

"Max?"

"Definitely. He was the fellow who took me to Lisbon and Praia da Rocha in the summer. Dirty little beast!"

"I'm sorry," Coles said. "Did he—"

"You don't need to be; I was the fool. I fell for it all. *Me!* Wedding bells, a home, a family."

"You were very attracted by him, I expect?"

"It wasn't just him; it was his professionalism. There's something about a man with a real job to do. And Max was good; he makes his models feel good, all of them. Then there was the place too. We used to go to the fort together in the evening and watch the sardine boats going out at sunset. It did something to me, seeing all those men going out there to work on the water. I can't describe it really; it was like something coming true before you'd even thought of it. Can you understand?"

"Of course I can. It's in us all. Poetry. I'm so sorry he let you down."

She nuzzled his cheek, her own warm and soft, lightly scented, as smooth as he remembered Lettice's.

"That's why Betty's so silly," she went on. "She's got a family and a future; she could do something with Chris if she tried. I know I could; I just know it. But, instead of trying, she spends her time dreaming and envying me, *me,* Randall!"

"You must try not to resent it. It's what's known as a transference. People identify themselves with someone else they're fond of. There's always resentment."

"You're clever, aren't you? Betty always said you were clever; but all the same I don't think you'll be able to straighten her out where Christopher's concerned."

"Where do you think she's gone wrong with him? Apart from the obvious mistake, the business with Paul."

"Ooh, that was bad, wasn't it?"

"Unfortunate, very unfortunate."

"Not just getting caught, Randy; but doing it in the first place when she had a man of her own—even if he was away a lot."

"Of course," he said.

"What she did," she went on, "was immoral, definitely immoral for a working-class woman; but her big mistake was not understanding Chris."

Coles was really on the trail again and caught himself wishing that Presage had been with him or that at least he had brought his notebook. Exact conversations were increasingly difficult to remember as one grew older; perhaps he would borrow a sheet of paper from Heim and jot down Pery's remarks later.

"Christopher's always said it was her innocence that caught her," she went on. "When he was first after her he used to tell me he knew there'd been others. You couldn't expect anything else, he said, in England now. But Paul was different. He was a Catholic. Some other fellow, Chris said, he'd have let go, but not Paul, because Paul knew what he was doing."

"In that case it's probably just as well that Betty didn't know."

"I'm not sure," Pery said. "Maybe if she'd accepted Christopher in the first place, the way I'd have done, she wouldn't have wanted to have known anything outside of him. She'd have been different; the whole story would never have happened."

"I can't accept that, I'm afraid. It's not logical."

"You're not a woman," she said. "I sometimes wonder if I am myself, the way I live."

"You mean the impermanence?"

She looked at him angrily. "No, I don't! I mean the monotony with nothing to show for it—no kids. You're married, aren't you?"

"Yes."

"And children?"

"Yes, two."

"Well, ask your wife."

"Marriage doesn't prevent boredom," Coles said; "you're making it all too simple. I mean, I myself—"

"I know, Randy; somehow I know all about it from the outside, from watching, perhaps, and listening to so many men. That's why in Betty's place I'd have given in to Chris from the first."

Coles prodded the conversation. "Perhaps you should have married him yourself?"

"Give me the chance," she said. "I'd never have looked back. He's a man, is Christopher. What's this message he gave you for me?"

"It's rather vague, I'm afraid. As far as I can gather, he's thinking of coming to you first. I think he's hoping you might be able to put him up in your flat for a time. Originally, he was going to have gone straight home; but now, in view of Betty's attitude—"

"She's playing him up, that's all. If he wants to shack up with me in Earl's Court for a week or two, tell him it's on, and tell him to write to me too; he never even answered my birthday post card."

"He'll be very grateful."

"And Betty won't mind. She knows about me and Christopher. I'm no temptation to him."

The dance was over. She gave him a smile he couldn't quite define—of commiseration perhaps, of conspiracy too, touching and well-mannered.

"Let's forget it all," she said. "You didn't come here just to talk about Betty and Chris all the time, did you?"

"Not entirely, I suppose."

"Of course not. Like the rest of them, you came to have a night out, away from your wife and children. Let's have a drink together, something that'll take your mind off Betty."

Her generosity disarmed him. "Betty!" he admitted. "That would be difficult."

"You want to watch your step there, Randy. Innocence doesn't go on forever, and you don't know my little sister the way I do."

They drank whisky at seven and six a glass, Coles' money thinning in his pocket. They danced for an hour or two and agreed to meet again on another evening. Pery said that she had to earn her keep and left him brightly.

XIV

A week before his escape, Hotchkis changed his mind about climbing the prison wall. Instead, he was driven out through the front gate by the part-time medical officer, Dr. Lait, at ten o'clock at night. As a long-sentence man, nearing his release, he had been entrusted with the supervision of the Thursday-evening intake from Wormwood Scrubbs. In parties of ten, the prisoners had to be taken from Reception over to the hospital block for medical inspection and documentation. Hotchkis, after handing over the last group to Officer Dalrymple, simply climbed into the boot of the doctor's waiting car and closed the lid, preventing it from fastening by wedging one of the tire levers into the lock.

The doctor, an elderly practitioner who was himself nearing retirement, drove straight home and ran the car into the garage, which was separated from the back premises of his house by a passageway leading to the surgery. Hotchkis, cramped as he was, allowed him half an hour to eat his supper and settle down in front of the television set with his wife. Then he let himself into the adjoining waiting room and surgery.

Doctor Lait, a thrifty man of the old school, had not moved with the times; his premises were neo-georgian in their simplicity: two or three wooden wall benches and a small gas stove in the waiting room, a weighing scales and a desk and chair in the surgery. On the shelves there were half-a-dozen bottles of stock mixtures for coughs and constipation and hundreds of old samples of more up-to-date medication supplied free by the manufacturers. There was also a drawerful of old corks and another of used envelopes which the doctor reused for his own correspondence.

Hotchkis changed in the patient's dressing room, a small cubicle divided from the surgery by a faded green curtain. He put on the navy-blue boiler suit snatched by Bushnell from the clothing store and packed his own prison clothes into an empty crocodile-skin bag labelled "Obstetrics: K. Lait, M.B." From behind the surgery door he took an old porkpie hat and a long tweed overcoat, relics of the doctor's more active days in a largely rural practice. Then he returned to the car with the gladstone bag and spent half an hour rewiring the ignition so that he would be able to start the engine without a key. At a quarter to eleven by the dashboard clock he scouted the front of the house, peering through the bay windows of the sitting room between the gaps in the curtains.

It was known in the prison that Dr. and Mrs. Lait distrusted one another so profoundly that they rarely spoke at all. Their marriage was a kind of box of silence, like a submarine, so complex and dangerous that as they navigated it beneath the surface they concentrated only on the controls. Silence and caution had become so much a part of the doctor's habit that in the prison or out of it he rarely addressed his patients, saying only such things as "take this" or "do that." This evening he sat opposite to Mrs. Lait in one of a pair of rexine-covered armchairs, drinking a mug of meat extract and eating unbuttered water biscuits. His wife was stitching up a black coal glove, cut from an old pair of the doctor's trousers, while he was counting his certificate money, stacking little piles of sixpences from his surgery cashbox on the top of a table and entering the totals in an old ledger. On the mantelshelf, over the dull red mouth of the fireplace, was a large cardboard clockface with adjustable hands. It was inscribed: AS OUR GUESTS YOU HAVE BEEN WELCOME, BUT WE RETIRE AT: The hands were set at eleven o'clock.

In a few moments Mrs. Lait looked into her husband's mug to see that it was quite empty and put it back on the tray with her own and the biscuit plate. She swept up such table crumbs as she could find and ate them, then went through to the kitchen in the back of the house. The doctor dropped his sixpences into a small canvas bag and tucked it out of sight beneath the cushion of his chair. With a pair of tongs he removed two pieces of half-burned coal from the fire and stowed them neatly on the hearth. At once, as though they were performing a well-rehearsed *pas de deux,* his wife returned with a colander of wet tea leaves, damped the coals down, and fetched the fireguard. In silence, one behind the other, they went upstairs to bed.

Hotchkis waited until twelve-thirty and then rolled the car down the sloping drive to the main road. He started the engine quietly and drove south towards Brighton until he came to an all-night transport cafe, where he spent some of his hoarded pay on a long-drawn-out meal. Afterwards he drove along a series of side roads into a heavily wooded countryside, where he parked the car in a forestry track and made himself comfortable in the back seat, listening to Radio Luxembourg until he fell asleep.

A little before ten A.M. he awakened and switched on the news: there were no police messages. He smoked three thin cigarettes and went to sleep again, not reawakening until four o'clock, when it was already growing dark. He polished his shoes with car wax, shaved dry with the razor he had brought from the prison, and washed his face and hands in a forestry commission fire butt. He even damped his hair and combed it neatly before resuming the doctor's porkpie hat and overcoat; then he hid the gladstone bag in a haystack and, after regaining the main road, thumbed a lift in a lorry travelling north back towards London.

With the last of his money he bought an evening paper and a single ticket to Etchingham, reaching Coles' house on the Friday evening, just before the last of his guests arrived for the winter party.

There were about a dozen cars parked along Coniston Road and three or four more at the head of the short drive. A white five-barred gate lettered in black, HALF YOKE HOUSE, stood beneath a georgian lamp fixed high to one of the supporting posts. The near end of the house was screened from the drive by an unclipped yew tree, silhouetted sharply against the picture window Randall Coles had given his wife on her fortieth birthday. Just to the left of it, standing pale in the moonlight, was the greenhouse Lettice had given her husband in commemoration of her mother's death.

"It wasn't," as Coles had once told Hotchkis, "that we thought she would have liked it. We *knew* she would. My mother-in-law was in the nursing home at the time, and my wife suggested it to her. She was extremely pleased." Lettice had in fact said, "We can do the whole thing out of the estate for fifty pounds—unheated. When the time comes it will be in use for hardy alpines, the sort of thing Mother would most have liked—a kind of renewal." "My mother-in-law," Coles had explained to Hotchkis, "refused to have even a rose tree planted after her cremation. With my wife and myself she believed that death was a purely private matter."

Hotchkis walked fast up the drive and went into the greenhouse. A fine rain was falling, drops as thin as dew, a distillation of the November mist hanging in the tops of the larches and making hazy the lights from the windows. The greenhouse held pots of white chrysanthemums and smelled of winter. On a tray at the near end of one of the shelves there was a mound of loam and a paper bag, stencilled, JOHN INNES POTTING-ON COMPOST; on top of it there was a trowel and a pair of elbow-length black rubber gloves.

In the moonlight Hotchkis looked through his evening paper once again and smoked his last shred of tobacco, rolled up in a matchstick-thin cigarette. His nose close to the print, he rechecked the STOP-PRESS COLUMN: there wasn't a line about any prison escape. By this time the police would almost certainly be combing Brighton; they might, though it was unlikely, have set up roadblocks south of London, and, intermittently, they would be watching Betty's cottage. He didn't think that at this stage they would have thought of contacting either Coles or Pery.

He crumpled up the newspaper and stuffed it into the potting-on compost, closed the greenhouse door and crept up the flagstone terrace which surrounded the house. He was worried about the dog,

Tyndal. Coles had told him that the deerhound was a house pet, never missed a party and was only put out last thing at night.

He turned as a Mini car came up the drive. It was driven by a large woman with a plump man beside her on the front seat. Hotchkis doubled back behind the greenhouse. If when they went in the dog came out, he'd have to give up the idea of catching Randall on his own, he'd have to join the couple who had just arrived. It might break Randall's nerve, it might throw everything; but he'd have to risk it.

The big woman slammed the door of the car shut, and her husband got out stumbling on the other side. They stood for a moment collecting themselves by the front door.

"It may be a bore for you, darling," the woman said, "but for me it's bliss. Promise me you'll talk to Randall if you can get him away from Lettice. Find out all you can about this woman he's seeing, Mrs. Someone-or-other."

"Hotchkis," said the man, sliding his hands deep into his overcoat pockets, standing still and slack in the damp air.

Hotchkis smiled over towards him, his smile secret as the moonlight. He tilted the doctor's porkpie hat a fraction and listened intently. *Old Randall,* he thought. *I hope to God he's the one answering the door tonight.*

The husband stood there dumpily beyond the yew tree, a long-sentence man. He said something like, "I really fail to see, Harriet—" Then his voice dropped into a well-modulated mutter, the end of his sentence so much breath, a plume in the grey light.

"Gossip," his wife said, her voice dropping too. "No, not gossip, just interest." They laughed together as if this were an old joke.

"Do you think we ought to ring?" he asked her.

"I never ring. Good heavens! Lettice and I are practically sisters."

"I insist," he said suddenly. "I get a bit sick of you and Lettice together. I'm not going to be—Harriet, you won't let me down tonight, will you?"

"I promise I'll be good, darling. Lettice is very strained at the moment."

"Strained!" he said. "My God!"

"Strained," his wife repeated, tittering again. "Poor Lettice."

They rang the bell. Hotchkis flattened himself against the back of the greenhouse, ready if necessary to stride out into the drive, a late and unexpected guest.

Coles came to the door. An inner door opened with dresses behind it, bare arms and necks, an egress of chatter and additional light. Coles closed the hall door behind him. He stood there, dogless and lined, hanging a little as if suspended by a thin rope under his armpits. Very dapper in a dark-blue suit, he smiled out into the night, his greying, crinkled hair shining over his gold-rimmed spectacles. The fat woman swept up to him and hugged him briefly, her husband shook his hand, and they went in.

Hotchkis cased the house from the terrace, peering into every window. The closure of the front door implied that the party was now complete, there would be no more guests arriving. He must allow things to settle down and run through the arguments most likely to convince Coles. "I'm grateful for all you've done, Randall," he'd tell him. "And this'll be the last. I won't get on to you again after this lot. We'll have *done* something then—together."

Looking through the windows, he saw that the guests were drinking glasses of something, sherry or wine. There was a big man, square, with a seamed face and clear eyes beneath heavy eyebrows; a pale black-haired girl was with him, carelessly intent on him, watching him all the time he wasn't looking at her. "Deathly she looked, deathly!" Hotchkis would have told them back in "A" Block. "One of those dying bints from Hampstead or Chelsea."

The man would probably be Randall's friend, Bernard, the B.B.C. fellow. Possibly there might be other radio men at this party; but he betted there wouldn't be clergy, police or prison staff. Over the last year he'd studied Coles, and there were a lot of things Randall didn't want to know.

The dog was spread out in front of the fire, enormous, getting in everyone's way. People had to step over it, talking and holding glasses, playing a kind of hopscotch when they came to its long grey legs. The dog cocked an ear every now and again—the ear would flick suddenly, stand up, collapse and prick up again—and its nostrils were working too.

A woman in grey silk, some kind of a two-piece Betty wouldn't have been seen dead in, leaned down and stroked its head, talking all the time, her lips moving, opening and shutting without pause. Lettice Coles for a certainty: Randall's wife.

Hotchkis watched her. Well, she was thin, a thin one and tired, a fast mover. She had a tortoise-shell comb in her bun, stuck into the loose knot high, pretty. "Pretty," Hotchkis would have told them back in "A" Block. "Here! They give these parties all the year round, you know, not just Christmas and Easter and not relatives and no real reason."

Mrs. Coles had a thin neck, half concealed by the little flappy collar of the grey dress, and earrings of tortoise shell to match—a set to go with the comb. She was smoking clumsily, waving the cigarette about between her fingers. She put it between her lips to stroke the dog's head and her face flushed, thin in the firelight. A red-faced man standing over said something and she laughed up at him. In a few moments they went into the kitchen together.

Outside on the terrace Hotchkis followed them. The tall man could just be a policeman, but he didn't think so: a doctor more likely, surgeon type, big and breezy. They chatted in there over a table with dozens of little casseroles on it. A cardboard box on the floor was full of straw and more little casseroles: it was labelled "Mason's Hire Service." The man started getting more out and Mrs. Coles stopped him. Using a large silver ladle, she was filling the pots on the table from a stockpot, pouring white stew into them, a chicken mixture it looked like. She talked all the time and caught her companion's eye over the tray of casseroles, very excited, her tortoise-shell earrings trembling with every movement.

After a minute or two Coles came in from the big room and was given something to do. His wife looked across at him and there was a little pause, a stiffening. They all three looked at one another, their eyes joining up in glances and then giving way again quickly. The dog, Tyndal, had followed Coles in there and was sent out again. Mrs. Coles looked angry; she put down her ladle and clapped her hands together smartly at the dog.

It stood there, questioning her, its ears cocked; then it went back into the sitting room, moving carefully between the guests. Just to make sure, Hotchkis followed it back along the terrace and saw it collapse again in front of the fireplace: just fold up and sprawl out as if it had given up.

Coles had left the kitchen too. Perhaps he'd been asked to fetch something, a corkscrew or an apron. He threaded his way out between his guests and went alone into the hall, shutting the door behind him. Hotchkis' moment had come. He doubled round to the front door and knocked on it softly.

Through the hall window he saw Coles hesitate on the staircase; then the door opened and Coles stood there looking at him. He was so flustered that at first he didn't recognize him.

"Yes, who is it?"

"It's me, Christopher!"

"I'm sorry; what do you want?"

"It's Hotchkis, Randall. I've come, that's all—the way I said I would—before time." He took off the porkpie hat and Coles stepped back, crumpled a little at the knees, as if the rope holding him up had suddenly slackened.

"My God! What's happened?"

"Plenty. I've bust out. I took a lift in the boot of the doctor's car. My night, remember?"

"But your release—you're not due out until—"

"Twenty-eighth, a fortnight." Hotchkis paused, suddenly uneasy. "Where d'you want me? We can't start gaffing here."

Coles looked round the hall: at the three doors, the staircase. "You'd better come upstairs. Quickly."

He took him up to his son Malcolm's room: a truckle prison-type bed, climbing equipment on the walls—ropes, *pitons,* an ice axe. The room reassured him a little. He was about to say, "Look here, Hotchkis; what is it?" But he stopped himself in time—because it wasn't relevant, because they were too intimate. Hotchkis might want anything, everything; he looked fit, as confident as if he had a commission of some sort, a right to be standing there in Half Yoke House. He stepped over to Malcolm's bed and fingered the climbing rope.

"You've got a good pad here all right. Everything."

Coles was sharp. "This is my son's room. Good God! Hotchkis, what on earth made you do it?"

"Easy, really. I was getting too comfortable. I couldn't tell you direct, naturally; but I thought Bushy would have done." He was still looking at things appreciatively. "There was Betty, too."

"Betty?"

Coles saw her suddenly. The threat of Hotchkis' arrival had changed his idea of her. For the first time in his life he was aware of class warfare, of betraying himself. He imagined her awaiting him just inside the door of her cottage, neatly dressed, her hair shampooed. She seemed free of all but the crudest sexuality: a wife, not a woman.

"When it gets too tight," Hotchkis said, "you've got to do something. You've got to change the pattern." He was still fiddling with Malcolm's climbing rope. "It's like this rope, in a way. It can mean anything to a prisoner, from an escape to a topping—some kind of a change, anyway!"

Hotchkis was fumbling inside his mind. He was thinking of death, of absolution, of a break-through back to something he could only just remember, not innocence exactly, but optimism—a kind of certainty.

"All this gear," he said. "It puts you in mind of mountains."

Coles saw the mountains: he saw them as judicious risks, things that were quite external, and tried to avoid the implications, to stick to immediate facts.

"You should have taken your home leave as I told you at the time," he said. "You'll get nothing out of this but a fresh sentence."

"What's two or three months?"

Coles shifted his weight. "Apart from that, there's my own position to consider."

"That's no 'eadache. If they ever catch up with you, you can tell 'em I told you it was the Governor, that he made me change my mind about taking home leave. If necessary I'd back it up; but it won't be, because by the morning I'll be gone, I'll have shoved off to Pery's place."

"Tomorrow morning, you mean?"

"Tonight, if you like." Hotchkis replaced the rope on its nails, festooning it carefully from one to another. "You might have done the same thing too, Randall, if you'd ever gone as far as I did."

Coles was only half hearing him. He was thinking about the party downstairs. He dared not think of the possibilities, of Lettice's reaction, of the police. He must get hold of Presage at once; he must get down there, take Bernard on one side and say to him:

"Bernard, I need your help. There's been an unexpected development; things have got rather out of hand."

"It's doing it makes the difference," Hotchkis was saying. "You do the job without thinking; you do it for yourself, really. While you're on it you only see yourself, as big as a giant, and then afterwards you get tired. Everything makes you tired—people, for instance: they seem like photographs, dead ones in a wallet." He broke off, suddenly animated. "Here, while I was in the garden I was watching them all through your windows and I got interested again. It could be because I didn't know them or it could be because I was right to break!"

"You were in the garden?"

"There and in the greenhouse. I was thinking about the dog, see? And checking the stop-press in the evening papers. They were dead clear, not a line so far."

Coles flushed. "Hotchkis, if you don't mind, I'm going to consult someone, a friend. I've just realized that there might have been a police message on the B.B.C. If anyone heard it . . ."

"Oh, I've covered that. You could tell people that I'm one of the fellows you helped in the past, and that I came over to look you up —gratitude and all that."

"That won't be necessary with Presage. He knows about you."

"Oh, Presage. Would that be the thickset fellow I saw, with that Chelsea girl on his arm?"

"Yes, he's always wanted to meet you. It's just possible he might give you a lift back to London tonight, to Pery's flat."

"I'm willing."

Coles collected himself; it was a vital moment. He wanted the introduction to be a success.

"It's important that you should go on just where you left off," he said. "Bernard's trustworthy; but he can't stand lies."

Hotchkis smiled. "I can see."

"What d'you mean?"

"Don't worry; you're a good sport, Randall. I was only thinking about your job. It must come hard when you can't have a rehearsal."

Anger stirred in Coles. As he ran down the staircase he saw himself as a misfit, a slum missionary, a man whose inadequacies drive him into mixing with his inferiors, a victim of absurd adventures. Now he had to face his guests again and he realized that, apart from Bernard, they didn't interest him, that he didn't much like them. They represented the concessions he had to make to his marriage; but for them and all they represented, he might never have reached the present impasse. There would have been no hunger, no guilt, no inconsistency. From the first he had been victimized by something of which Lettice herself was only one manifestation.

For no reason he thought of Hotchkis waiting outside in the garden, peering through the windows into his house, above him the night sky, the cold stars, the emptiness. It made him pause on the staircase, halfway down; it made him straighten his tie and polish his spectacles. He must pursue the thought no further. All his friends must continue to be deceived, to see him as they expected to see him, as Randall Coles, Lettice's husband, thinker of no mad thoughts, a minor poet only.

He opened the dining-room door and went straight across the room to Bernard, smiling placidly, every line in his face benevolent and normal. From her buffet, where she and Cattermole were handing out her damned casseroles, Lettice saw him and called out: "Did you get it, darling?"

He had forgotten what "it" was. "No, I didn't; I couldn't find it. I need Bernard for a moment."

"Well, do hurry up. We want to organize the game. Won't Malcolm do?"

"No, he won't. I want Bernard."

Everyone laughed—at something in his tone, he supposed—but he had Bernard's attention and he thought, *I'll make you see me yet—you, Presage!* The Harvey woman giggled—he felt her small brown eyes on his face, hot with curiosity—and he knew beyond any doubt that it was she who had been responsible for the change in Lettice. Fat and knowing, she was exactly like a woman he had once included in a programme on spiritualism.

He took Bernard into the boot room. It was an instinct to delay with him on some neutral ground, somewhere between Hotchkis upstairs and the other, "sane" part of his life downstairs in Lettice's drawing room. Lettice was to be pitied really. He saw her as a pretty calcium shell on the tide line of a deserted beach: elegant, white, empty.

It was extremely fortunate that Bernard had decided to come. He thanked God for his presence as he got him into the boot room amongst the gum boots, galoshes and raincoats, the vase of bull-rushes picked years ago by the children. He explained things to him rapidly.

"It's a little more than I can handle," he said. "I had to talk to you."

Bernard studied himself in the mirror above the washbasin.

"How do you think I'm looking tonight? Personally I think I'm carrying my years rather well. There's a clean-lived look about me: the whites of my eyes, the texture of the skin. Give me your honest opinion, Coles."

"Bernard, Hotchkis is upstairs waiting. What the hell am I going to do?"

"That's the question!" Bernard had taken out his little comb and was straightening the steep iron-grey sides of his parting. As Coles had done, he twitched his tie into the dead center of his waistcoat. "We're in deep. Both of us. But when the trap's closing the great thing is the outward appearance. Villainy these days is smooth."

"All right," Coles said childishly. "You're not going to help me, then?"

Bernard smiled at him. For the first time in their friendship he struck Coles as being handsome. He found himself admiring the clearness of his eyes, his thick cheeks, whiskered over the broad facial bones, the affection of his smile. He saw that, more than his help, he wanted his approval; he even wondered if from the first Presage had not been the necessary audience. One did not perform in a vacuum: beyond the silent studio there were the listeners, the composite intelligence.

"The trap," Bernard said. "Yours this time, constructed with an exact knowledge of your difficulties—a kind of poetry. But unless you nip out in time, a killer just the same."

"For God's sake, Bernard, there's no time for rhetoric."

"I was thinking about myself, about Hera, my Persephone. For some reason she makes me think of gentians—the violet-dark tunnel to the underworld, the annual visit, the risk. You know what I mean?"

Coles ignored it. "The point is that Christopher's escape is much more than a gesture. He's only got a fortnight to go. *I* can't understand it."

They went up the stairs together and Coles introduced him to Hotchkis, standing well back in the familiar bedroom. They got on well from the beginning. Bernard asked, "Just tell me why you broke out at the end of an eight-year sentence."

"It was the children and Betty, Mr. Presage. I wanted to go back into my own life in my own time, not on the day. There was Paul, too. After nearly eight years he's still a knot in my life, the sort you can't undo even with your teeth."

"You mean you were in a state of despair, depression?" Bernard asked him. "You saw the doctor?"

"Despair nothing! I could eat all right, sleep, smoke and want a woman—laugh too. I had some good laughs in there with old Bushy and the others. It's hard to explain to anyone, but I believe in God and I was used to more than that."

"But how is it now?" Bernard asked. "Since you broke out?"

"It was the answer. Even if you've done nothing, you get times when you want to bust out and change everything."

"And you want to get up to London tonight?"

"Yes, but I wanted to see Randall first, because he can get out to Betty's without any trouble. He could let me know how much they're watching her place."

"Right; I'll give you a lift as soon as the party's over." Bernard turned to Coles. "He'd better come down with us? You could lend him a suit."

Someone came up the stairs fast. Coles moved over to the door, but it was too late. It was his son, Malcolm, pink-faced and officious. He stopped in the doorway, looking at Hotchkis, at Bernard sprawled on his bed.

"Daddy, Mummy says you simply must come down now. They want to start the game in five minutes."

Coles looked at him irritably.

"Tell her we're just coming—a friend of mine, Mr.—"

"My name's Bicknor," said Hotchkis, just in time. "Your father's been a good friend to me ever since I was in Wandsworth, and as I was in the area I dropped in to look him up."

Malcolm hesitated—he seemed to be about to argue—and Coles noticed that his ears were red. "Well go on," he ordered him. "Don't hang about up here."

Reasonable, mastering himself, Malcolm did what he was told. It wasn't until he had gone that Coles realized he would almost certainly send Lettice upstairs.

"Bernard, could you go down and make sure Lettice doesn't come up? I don't want to have to—"

"You mean she's easier to handle in public?"

"Yes. You could start distributing the clues too, with Malcolm. My God! I'd forgotten about the game. It's going to be rather embarrassing."

"Change it, then."

"I can't; it's impossible."

"In that case, why don't you go down yourself? Just give Hotchkis a suit of clothes."

"Call me Bicknor," said Hotchkis. "Old Bicknor was harmless; I knew him when we were in the 'Ville. No one's liable to have heard of him."

"You don't understand," Coles said, going through to his own bedroom and returning with a dark suit on a clothes hanger. "Lettice insisted on this damned game, and it's going to upset people."

"What is it?" Bernard asked.

"It was a way of getting people to circulate, really. Murder."

There was silence. Coles looked at Malcolm's climbing rope. Bernard looked at Hotchkis.

"Does it embarrass you?" he asked him.

"Not me. I was wondering if there was a prize?"

"What?" Coles asked.

"He wants to know if there's a prize for the winner," Bernard repeated.

Coles took off his glasses and rubbed the lenses furiously. "As a matter of fact there is; but I can't see that it's frightfully funny. Our guests, the whole evening—" He was interrupted by Lettice's voice from the hall.

"Randall, you've simply got to come down. Bring Bernard and whoever it is with you."

"Two minutes," Coles called.

"Playing Murder!" Hotchkis began.

Coles turned on him. "By now they'll know you've done time. Malcolm will have told them, or my wife."

Hotchkis was contrite. "I was only joking, Randall. With me leaving tonight, you've nothing to worry about."

"He's right," Bernard said. "As things are they'll only be impressed. Play it as it comes, Coles. Don't advance and don't retreat. Just ride it and we'll back you up. But get down there."

"Very amusing," Lettice was saying as Coles re-entered the drawing room. "Darling, it's most piquant."

"What is?"

"One of your prisoners arriving like this. There was really no need for all the secrecy."

He didn't even trouble to answer her. As they clustered round him he felt like a dog that has escaped from the kennels and then been locked back in again: an object of envy and inquiry to the others. Even Tyndal got up and sniffed his shoes and trouser legs as he lost himself among their guests. But Harriet Harvey, eating Lettice's zabaglione greedily, would not be shaken off. She pursued and almost physically compressed him, pushing him into a corner, so bulky and inquisitive that she protected him from the others as he caught up on the cooling chicken casserole.

He was still shaking with fury and anxiety. His glasses had misted over, but this time he didn't trouble to wipe them: the haze was appropriate. Mentally he was still up in Malcolm's bedroom with Presage and Hotchkis, wondering what they would be saying. He saw them now as a composite, two men, a twin conspiracy.

"Thrilling," Harriet was saying. "What had he done when you knew him?"

"Who? Bicknor?"

"Your prisoner."

"I don't know. One forgets these things. One isn't interested in the actual crime. I daresay it was larceny, some petty theft or other."

"Oh, is that all?"

"He could have been queer," Coles said nastily. "If that's an improvement?"

"It's not." She glanced at him as though she had scored. "I never imagined things of that sort would interest you. I always thought you were after bigger game. After all, it's been quite an obsession with you over the years, hasn't it?"

My God! Coles thought. *Why do people always attack me?* He said: "What would you have liked yourself, Harriet? Murder or rape?"

"You're cross, aren't you?" She ate the zabaglione as fast as a cat, her teaspoon flashing in and out of it like a little silver tongue.

"I'm tired, that's all."

"Poor Randall!"

"Men do work, you know. The fact that we can't bully our wives about it—"

She changed her attack. "But when are we going to see your prisoner? And how old is he?"

"He's in his thirties."

"And good-looking? Attractive? Or one of these little sneaky men?" She was watching him with amusement. He had a feeling that he could not escape from her, that she knew everything. Looking at her enormous breasts, he found a biblical phrase in his mind: "Blessed are the paps that never gave suck."

"I know I'm being horrid to you," she said.

"I don't know what you mean."

"If you'd tell me about him, I'd stop. I'd leave you in peace."

"There's nothing to tell. He's been in prison, that's all—as anyone else might have been."

"All the same it must have been rather gratifying to have one of them come back like this. The ten lepers, or was it nine?"

Lettice's voice interrupted them, as intimately as if she had been at his elbow.

"Quite a number of Randall's ex-prisoners are grateful, even if it's only by post."

Coles hadn't noticed her. She was quite some distance away, but he was reminded now that over the years she had developed this facility of overhearing his conversations, the more especially when he was harassed or, as she put it, "on the defensive." As with Malcolm's intrusion he found that her intervention filled him with coarse emotion, an inner bad language. *Damn it!* he thought. *Leave me alone! Get out of my hair. I've had enough. I need no help. I'm guiltless.* But really he was wondering how much longer they would be, Presage and Hotchkis.

They came in a moment later and the guests took it well. The Cattermoles, the Harveys, the Scott-Roberts, the local headmaster, all the guests, with their aging bodies and marriages, behaved impeccably. Conversations ran on without a pause, exploratory glances were not more than normally curious, and Lettice, as though Coles himself had "started" her, was magnificent. As a producer he couldn't fault her. She and Cattermole provided the two men with food and forks; Malcolm gave them pencils and notebooks as Lettice made the introductions.

"Now everyone ought to have their clues ready," she announced. "We're a man short, so I'll pair with Mr. Bicknor. Malcolm, give him the spare clues."

The guests circulated in pairs, reading and copying Malcolm's typed notes into their booklets. It was, admittedly, a little uncomfortable: there were not only the slips of paper, the pencils, and the threepenny stationer's notebooks; there were also the cups of coffee and the glasses of calvados. Some "detectives" propped their books on their partners' backs to write the entries, the partner holding both cups of coffee and both liqueur glasses whilst this was done; others temporarily abandoned the drinks on the sideboard, revisiting them at intervals for a sip or a hurried gulp. But gradually they all completed their stories and paired off to work out their solutions to the crime. It was involved and very boring, but loyalty to Lettice kept everyone working hard for the best part of an hour.

Lettice herself took Hotchkis to the love seat left her by her mother. It was a pretty little piece with dark rosewood rests and stretchers, the seats and cushioned arms upholstered in mauve velvet. Lettice sat there beside him, rather upright, facing in the opposite direction, confident but alert.

"Unfortunately," she told him, "although I didn't help them with the clues, I do remember the solution, so you'll have to do nearly all the work yourself."

"I'll have a go."

"We mustn't cheat, I mean."

"I wouldn't know how to, not with this," he said.

"You did copy them all out, didn't you? You haven't missed anyone?"

"Well, if I have, there's still plenty to be going on with. And some of them—well, they're a bit dodgy."

"They should all be perfectly clear."

"They're clear all right, but it's hard to know where to start."

She became helpful, leaning over him like a schoolteacher. "Take the medical evidence first, I suggest. There may be one or two technical words. I know Malcolm took a lot of trouble with them. There we are, on page three. I can't read your writing, I'm afraid, so you'll have to."

Hotchkis took the book from her.

"It says, 'Dr. Horder stated the wound penetrated the left ventricle of the heart one inch inside the left nipple line.' " He paused.

"Well, go on," Lettice insisted.

"I was thinking it doesn't say whether it's a man or a woman."

"That will be in the constable's evidence, I expect. I think Mrs. Harvey had it. She's the one on the sofa with Mr. Cattermole, the large woman."

Hotchkis looked across at Harriet. "That's what I meant. With all this about anatomy it could make a lot of difference, Mrs. Coles."

"Of course," Lettice said placidly. "My son's very conscientious. At Cambridge he has a number of friends reading medicine."

"I meant if it was a woman, Mrs. Coles. With women . . ."

"It was a male," said Lettice sharply, "a murdered *man*. I thought you knew that."

"Oh, I see. I'm afraid I'm a bit slow." He paused. "If you don't mind me asking, who did the clues? Were they all done by your son? By Malcolm?"

"My husband helped him a little, I think; but Malcolm's really responsible."

Harriet Harvey signalled them. She was eating a chocolate; her face was flushed, her eyes were moist as she leaned forward to attract Lettice's attention.

"There seems to be some trouble above motive," she called across the room. "Unless you rely on the doctor's evidence, Geoffrey and I can't find anything definite about it. And the doctor's evidence seems to suggest something rather horrible."

Her husband, Edward, was smoking his pipe by the mantelpiece. In the silence he took it out of his mouth and said, "Mutilation," and then replaced it.

Mrs. Scott-Roberts, the lady magistrate, took off her spectacles and said precisely: "We think that chronology seems to be the vital factor."

"Chronology." Lettice sighed. "You mean the time factor?"

"Yes. The victim's wrist watch had apparently stopped at eight forty-five; but Inspector Marples mentions that the clocks had been put back the night before. Now I wonder if there's any means of knowing whether or not the bedroom clock—"

"We spotted that," Bernard Presage said; "it's in the vicar's evidence. He noticed that the alarm clock in the bedroom was ten minutes slow by the church tower."

"Oh, we're allowing for that," Mrs. Scott-Roberts said. "What I meant was—"

But Bernard interrupted her sonorously: "Our difficulty is with the position of the body: one statement says it was in a sitting position on the pillows, the other that, before the doctor moved it, it was prone on the bolster with the left leg hanging over the edge of the bed."

Lettice sat up higher in the love seat and lighted a cigarette. "Randall, can you elucidate?"

"I can," he said irritably. "People aren't meant to discuss the solution aloud. The game's meant to be played privately until the end. After that Malcolm no doubt can clear up any difficulties."

"Yes, of course," Malcolm said. "I can assure everyone it's absolutely accurate; we did it together."

"We did *not* do the medical evidence together," Coles contradicted him. "That was your field."

"Yes. Grey's *Anatomy* and Harvey-Pratt's *Jurisprudence.* I can't see why anyone should be having difficulties."

The young man's eyes were flashing behind his glasses, and Lettice sprang to his defense. "Darling, we know it's accurate, and we know it doesn't do to be squeamish; but there does seem to be rather a lot of medical detail."

From her place on the window seat beside Bernard, Hera Foley spoke coolly.

"I don't think there's too much, Lettice; but did the murderer rape her first? A sex motive, after all, would account for a lot; but the bloodstains on his"—there was a pause while she referred to her notes—"clothing weren't the same group as the ones on the bed."

In the renewed silence Lettice got up. "Would anyone like tea? After working so hard, I mean."

"Tea would be lovely," Harriet Harvey said.

"Malcolm's been a little too thorough perhaps," Lettice went on. "The game was intended to be more like an Agatha Christie."

"Or Dorothy L. Sayers," Bernard suggested.

"I'll help you get it," Harriet said.

"No, Malcolm will."

"I can't, Mummy; the game isn't finished."

"No, darling, I know. But—"

"I've spent a week on it; it's all based on facts; there's absolutely nothing in those clues you wouldn't find in the Sunday papers."

"It depends which newspapers," Lettice said shortly. "I don't think it would quite make the *Sunday Times* or the *Observer.*"

"But we wanted to get the thing accurate. After all, dammit, murder is murder. Daddy knows that. There's no point in—"

"Come and help me with the tea," Lettice said. "Nobody's criticizing you, Malcolm; it's only that you've been a little too thorough."

But he stood still in the center of the drawing room, pink-faced and furious.

"Dear Cambridge," said Mrs. Scott-Roberts. "How wonderful it is that it should never change."

Before he followed his mother into the kitchen, Malcolm suddenly turned on her.

"It wasn't Cambridge; you can't blame it on Cambridge, Mrs. Roberts. We did it together, my father and I."

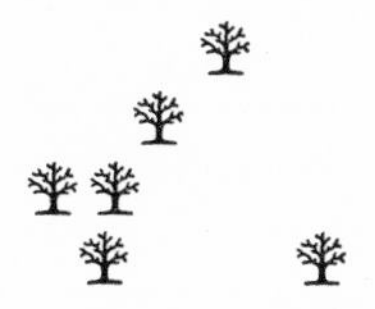

"Let Christopher sit in front," said Hera Foley after the party.

She and Bernard were using her new Mercedes, a recent present from her mother, Mrs. Philip Boarzell, a compensation for the crisis in her daughter's "marriage to Charles." Ever since Hera's wedding her mother had always referred to it like this—perhaps because of her own divorces. There had been her "marriage to Humphrey," her "marriage to James," and her present one to Philip, already showing signs not of breaking up but of "loosening" a little.

"As you like," Bernard said, hurt. "I'll sleep better in the back."

He had no intention of sleeping; there hadn't been enough to drink, since, as Lettice often said, "by 'enough,' men mean too much." Obeying Hera, he deliberately chose the near-side corner, the better to see her profile, dramatically shadowed by the lights of oncoming cars. He'd noticed that she'd seemed unaccountably excited ever since he'd confided in her Hotchkis' true identity, and he was afraid of the consequences. She would either show off or sulk.

They had been amongst the earliest guests to leave, preceded only by the Scott-Roberts, who had pleaded Court in the morning—Mrs. Scott-Roberts' magistracy. For Hera, Bernard and "Mr. Bicknor" there had been a waving party in the Half Yoke drive: the youth Malcolm, Randall, looking nervous, and Lettice, hollow. Unable to miss a moment, Harriet Harvey had come out, too.

"I hope we didn't break things up," Bernard said from the back seat.

"They were broken up anyway," Hera said. "A fairly quick getaway was the only answer. And it was entirely his fault."

"Whose? Malcolm's?"

"No, not Malcolm's; with those parents, he's the only one I felt any sympathy for. It was *his* fault—Christopher's!"

"What did I do?" Hotchkis asked.

She put her foot down a little further on the accelerator; the pale-black road, the broken white lines slid faster under the car as she turned to him, dark-lashed, barely smiling.

"You killed someone, didn't you? A man."

That settles it, Bernard thought. She's going to show off.

"Paul Caine was a man all right," Hotchkis agreed.

"Marvellous! Anyone got a cigarette?"

Bernard passed his packet over and Hotchkis saw to it for her.

"Light it for me, please," she said to him. "I never take my hands off the wheel."

She didn't know why she'd said "marvellous!" like that. It was dated. Perhaps it was the word "man." She had such mixed feelings about them; they'd all been so sweet to her, so tiresomely indulgent. Her "fathers"—her mother Claire's successive husbands—had been so overwhelmingly nice, each of them in turn; and with each marriage Claire had been ever more adorable too.

"Not so marvellous," Hotchkis said. "Aside from what I did to Caine, something's been done to me, and *I'm* still alive."

She spoke coldly: "Something's been done to everybody—particularly to Randall Coles. You've got right in amongst him. He identifies himself with you so strongly that he affects even his own son. They must have hatched up that game together without any idea of their motives. They'll be analyzing themselves for weeks to come."

She was analyzing herself, too. Really she'd objected most, she supposed, to the use they'd made of the men—Claire and herself. Her "fathers" had come into their lives overladen with generosity and affection and then, almost as suddenly, but with thrift and bitterness, left again. With each new father there'd been a change of house, the necessity for new interests and friends. With each she and her mother had changed, too, an utter transformation after each wedding which had left both of them exactly the same, only more horrible.

Yet Claire continued to hope that she, Hera, valued men, liked them. She was nearly sure that she didn't, that, inside herself, she nursed a profound distaste for them, like a baby. She was afraid that one day she might bear it and that, having done so, from then onwards she might be honest enough to become a man-hater or some kind of lesbian.

She drove a little slower now; she would step up the pace again when they reached London, frighten them both. Sometimes she drove Charles like this when they went out together in the evening. It amused her to ferry him dangerously to some restaurant or party—helpless, too immature to protest.

The divorce was rather hanging fire in her mind, not because she was undecided about it, simply because she hadn't quite finished with him yet. Besides, before she told him, she wanted to go to France with Bernard, free from the detectives Charles would inevitably hire. At Claire's suggestion she had herself already briefed an agency to watch Charles, and, even if that evidence wasn't used, Claire would settle the bill: so that was all right.

Hotchkis was watching her in a working-class sort of way. She could sense it and enjoyed it mildly.

He was thinking that in seven years he hadn't had the chance of a good look at a woman and was comparing her with dim memories of Betty. They were both dark-haired, white-faced, but this one was a lot thinner, smaller-boned and worse-tempered too, he bet. When Betty was "down" she just sulked, but Mrs. Foley's moods came up to the top like ice in a pool, colder and colder.

The way she was driving; the way she'd got into the car, slamming the door; her certainty that she was in charge of them, of himself and old Presage lumbered in the back; and the speed they were moving—you'd think that for a brass one she'd whisk them both to hell if she felt like it . . . the first lorry, the first tree.

Back in the prison they'd talked about women a lot: wives and girls at that distance had merged into a composite, the wives—or most of them—as desirable as the girls, taking on, in anything from six months upwards, the original dimension. Many of the married men brooded over their photographs as fondly as the bachelors and, no matter how old the marriages, found themselves writing love letters again.

"Things look good," Hotchkis had told the men once, "when you've stopped being in them. Here, I'll tell you, when you're in prison Eden was yesterday. And why not? If it wasn't, you wouldn't want to go back home."

Mrs. Foley herself put him in mind of Eve. What had Eve said when the first murder was committed? He'd noticed that it hadn't seemed to worry Betty a lot either.

"They say women are stronger," he said suddenly to Mrs. Foley. "I thought a lot about it when I was inside. Eve and all that."

"Eve?" Hera asked. "What on earth d'you mean?"

"Eve. You know, Adam and Eve."

"Oh, I see. You're wondering why I said 'marvellous' like that?"

"You meant it, didn't you?"

"Yes, in a way I did—because of the circumstances. But I can't honestly see what Eve's got to do with it, although she started everything off. I mean, I don't see where she could have got her resentment from. She was a daughter without a mother."

"You're dead on. She had no parents to get in the light, no trouble to begin with. Just her own self to decide out of."

He was struggling with words, things he knew but couldn't express, and gathered himself together as if he'd been back on one of those long gaffs with Bushy in "A" Block.

"Here," he said. "We all come into the world direct and with a dream like Eden, chasing it. Take weddings and 'oneymoons. It's not so silly. People still believe in the Bahamas, don't they?"

She looked at him suspiciously. "For ten days perhaps."

But he was convinced. "And getting married in the first place. It's what people want. Nobody forces them; they invented it theirselves so they could promise 'forever' when there was no real need."

She put out her cigarette and gripped the wheel harder. She smiled at him with hostility.

"I always find talking about love rather boring. Tell me about hatred instead."

She put her foot down again: houses, pubs and black elms whispered past the windows of the car. The dark horizon was astonishingly clear, cold with starlight.

Ahead lay London, the house in Lowndes Square, with Charles rattling about somewhere in there in the top flat—or more probably out. She hoped he'd be out with someone; for weeks she'd avoided sex with him in order to break up his stubborn attention. Tonight she wanted to change the pace with Bernard. She needed to convince herself of his limitations. He must be made to commit himself.

"Hatred's easy," Hotchkis said. "You can bet on that. And anything easy's wrong, a sin. That's why people only play with it."

"I don't," she said.

"Then you'd better watch out, then. Even when you're only playing it can get hold of you, and when it does you don't only lose the game, you're different yourself."

"How disappointing you are. I'm not being rude, but I really am disappointed in you. You're the first man I ever met, apart from soldiers, who's killed another one. You committed what the French call the 'crime of passion'—perfectly clean and sudden. The sort of murder that gives everyone a lift when they read about it."

"Maybe it does, but if it gives *you* a lift afterwards you can bet you're nutty—bent even before you did it."

Bernard listened to them, fascinated, watching her face. She had, he thought, five or six expressions only, and their range was further restricted by the half-darkness and the contemporary make-up. Yet her sentiment was continually astonishing and made him long for her more than ever.

"You were talking about mothers," Hotchkis said. "Don't you like yours, then?"

"We don't see much of each other. My husband and I are living in her house at the moment, but she's nearly always away."

In recent years, she thought, Claire had been mainly a voice on the telephone, a tired sound coming through the European static.

"Not that I mind," she added. "It's because she was always so nice to *me* when I was growing up that I now find her such a bitch."

"What she done then? To *you?*"

"Nothing. She was never there, really. She was so guilty about her divorces that she could never afford to neglect me."

"But there must be something else. You can't think of your mother like that over nothing; it's not natural."

"Well, perhaps it was when I was eight or nine—I don't know; but I began to notice that we were both using the same methods with her husbands. But whereas I liked them, she didn't. I really loved my father even when they were having rows and he took it out on me; but she never forgave him anything, and in the end he left, he married an American."

"Did your mother give him his freedom?"

"Yes. But she never gave me mine."

She was thinking of the Lowndes Square house again. She always thought of it as of an hotel, not her home. The house of her childhood had been in steep country; the gardens, the grass, rocks and trees had been as familiar as the furniture. And the whole lot had been sold after the first divorce, when the pampering began.

Her present stepfather, Philip, who was rather a dear, had provided Lowndes Square for her to grow up in during the school holidays.

"I'm a textbook case, I suppose," she said now.

In the back of the car Bernard sat up. "Of what?"

"Mother-rejection. Do you know about it? It's quite simple, really. We take revenge on men for having given in to our mothers. All men are our fathers."

She was animated, gay in the darkness, thinking of those vanished gardens and rooms of her home before the first, the only real change. She needed a moment of frankness to tell them both what was true.

She said, "Don't imagine that because I can see things like this it makes any difference. The more clearly I see my mother, the more like her I become, and even though I can see it happening it never stops me—not even my divorce."

They were silent and she thought of Eden. It came into her mind quite without warning as things did at night after sex or too many drinks. She saw Hotchkis in hanging gardens—a kind of Alabama landscape with the trees festooned with Spanish moss . . . but with many rivers, the colours principally blue and green.

After "finishing" in Chillon she'd painted at Heatherly's for a time herself, hoping for a break-through. But she'd soon got bored with it, frustrated, particularly after being taken in by Charles and discovering how hopeless his work really was.

Hotchkis had thought over her remarks. He said: "I don't get it. We talk like this in the prison—especially the library boys and the university types. We're always on about rejection and not being adjusted and I used to get fed up with it because I'd know that you can't explain evil. It's there inside you from the start. The way we jawed you'd get to thinking it was a subject like geometry or something."

She hardly heard him because she was still thinking about Eden, imagining Bernard now as Adam. He'd be a little plump perhaps, but he had the right legs, long and sturdy with curly hair on the thighs. Adam as Pan—but without whimsy. Bernard was what she and her friends would have called "a hell of a man." He was not merely sexy and sensitive; just possibly he might be noble too.

The blues and greens dripped in her mind, flowing exquisitely down the canvas. All the wash of christian myth, so primitive and so spoiled. She accelerated again, her lower lip nipped between her teeth.

"I know exactly what you've been trying to do," she said. "You've been trying to drive me into a corner about christian marriage."

"Driving!" Hotchkis said. "My God, you're doing that. I've wanted to get out half-a-dozen times."

"It's been discredited for you too, then. You know that it's no longer relevant even to a fast car."

They said nothing.

It was possible she'd silenced them but more probable that they were only as bored as she would have been herself. Rome was as boring as most fashionable things; but she must be careful not to betray naïveté. Her anger amused Bernard, but her ignorance always gave him an advantage.

They were whipping up Knightsbridge now towards Earl's Court. There was warm light everywhere, the glow from shop-windows, the intimacy of cars and taxis slipping between the high buildings on either side. On the pavements there were people, well-dressed, assured. . . .

A few minutes later she asked Hotchkis where he wanted to be dropped and drove fast to Earl's Court Terrace: a cavernous doorway beneath dozens of dimly lighted window squares.

Getting out, he gripped her hand and thanked her. He didn't even ask her to keep things to herself, and she was touched by his confidence. Something made her kiss him at the last moment, just as he opened the door. She found herself leaning forward quite automatically, pressing her lips lightly against his cheek. It was not convention. She really liked him.

She said, "For God's sake, don't get caught, will you?"

"No, not before time." He gripped her shoulder like one of her pathetic fathers. "Thanks a lot for the lift, Mrs. Foley. Mind how you go, now."

Bernard got out too and they walked into the building together, standing there in the doorway, talking. She heard them making arrangements to meet again.

Eventually Bernard got back into the car beside her and they drove off into Lowndes Square for drinks—for everything else she now so surely intended.

XVI

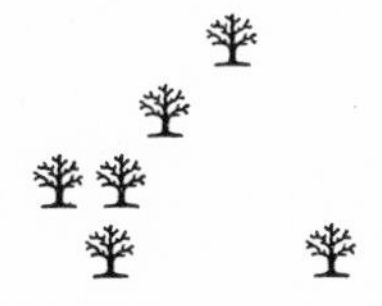

Criminals frequently co-operate with the police, Coles thought as he drove towards the cottage in Sumner on the Sunday night following the party. He'd been tempted by two police stations on the outskirts of London, the blue lanterns shining out in dark country, the words "POLICE STATION" in capitals. He had even imagined himself parking the Mini outside one of them and going in, saying to the duty sergeant, "My name is Randall Coles. Look here, I think there's something you ought to know."

So far the police appeared to have been incredibly remiss in their handling of Hotchkis' escape: not a word anywhere, not a single announcement or bulletin in the press, on the radio or television in three days. "Incredibly remiss": this is how he'd have put it to Bernard if he'd been able to contact him that afternoon from his office in Portland Place. At least he might have done; one never knew with Bernard: he might have taken exception to the phrase. But when he'd telephoned him, Presage had not been at home; nor had Helen. Only Cecily. "Daddy's away somewhere. Mummy thought he was probably still with you. You see, he hasn't come back since your party."

"Extraordinary!" Coles had said before he could stop himself. Now he wished he had not rung up in case he'd let Bernard down. He wished too that he'd had time to ask Cecily more questions, but with Lettice's coldness since the party and Malcolm's sulks, he'd been forced to shelve speculation about Bernard and the Foley girl in order to concentrate on his own affairs—or, rather, Hotchkis'.

He couldn't help feeling that it was "unfair" of the police to have done so little about the escape, or at least to have kept so quiet about it. Their silence had made him a kind of collaborator; now, he suspected, he was either an "accessory" or else he was "privileged," and he'd much have preferred to have been "uncommitted"—a private person doing his best to satisfy conflicting loyalties, officially blameless.

On the other hand, on this particular night, driving through the mysterious Sunday traffic of the coastal road, he had to admit that the sense of being in a curious moral gap had its compensations. Ever since Hotchkis' escape he had found himself imagining that they were both characters in a slightly dated spy story.

Seeing it like this changed everything for him: England ceased really to be England and became the fictional Europe of his boyhood—underscored by memories of Dornford Yates and Sapper: an era of chivalry and certainty. He imagined hooded limousines, foreign capitals, the still forests and dramatic mountains of the Continent. He even saw the snows and the green slopes on which the bells of animals rang softly in the dark. In this landscape he and Hotchkis moved significantly: the hunter and the hunted.

There was resentment too, of course—just enough; otherwise he'd never have considered going to the police. He didn't lack insight; he realized that resentment presupposed fear—not Presage's suspicion of some metaphysical trap but a rational prudence, explainable in human terms. Things had changed, grandeur had gone; his interest in crime had been forced on him by the national decline. Apart from this, on Friday, Hotchkis had broken into his life like a burglar, confident of "winning," appearing even to have been amused by his discomfort. He had visited him as if he, Coles, were now the prisoner and challenged him to involve himself once more with Betty.

Thinking of her, he knew he was going to have a drink. Usually he avoided alcohol on his evening visits to the cottage because Betty disapproved of it. She'd said: "I don't like drinking fellows—not since Paul. You never know what they're going to get up to and they don't neither."

Tonight he was unsure of his position with Betty, whether this might not be his last visit to her, whether on the other hand she might not say things like, "It's not going to make any difference, is it, Randall? You won't stop coming?"

He drew up at the next pub, rolled with a flourish into the cinder-covered car park beneath the sodium lighting and went into the saloon bar. He was wearing the white mackintosh but not the blue worsted—instead, his tweed, the suit Betty had once admired. "It's rough," she'd said; "nice when you put your cheek against it."

"The rough male kiss of blankets," Coles had quoted from Rupert Brooke.

He ordered a double scotch and sat down at a corner table beneath a supporting pillar covered with horse brasses. The room was full of local commuters, pull-overed minor public-school men, older businessmen with their wives, who were drinking gin and french or wine by the glass. They didn't appear to notice Coles sitting there alone, and although their indifference made him feel "meager" he bore them little resentment. He was accustomed to being a producer on the other side of the studio glass.

Who, amongst these people, nowadays, would listen to religion on sound? There might be one man who would turn out to be a Christmas and Easter Anglican and have "views." There might even be a Roman Catholic hidden somewhere among them, who, unless sufficiently "far on," would either be cautious or aggressive. But really, as far as his job went, he was out on a limb; he was an anachronism. If he could have told them about Hotchkis and Betty, the subject of forgotten breakfast conversations eight years ago, it might have been different; he might have held the floor. But as it was there was nowhere to start; his adventure, like the obsession from which it had sprung, was a secret.

Angry suddenly, he wondered who now was his radio audience anyway. He imagined a few thousand listeners in hospital beds, not too sick for religion, not quite well enough for politics or sex; a few vicarages perhaps, teacher's training colleges and voluntary patients in mental hospitals—all of them a suspect minority. The subject needed a twist somewhere, something that would make it relevant again, or, if not that, at least vexatious in the way that Bernard was vexatious.

He was wondering what on earth Bernard might be up to at that moment, imagining him in Lowndes Square with Hera Foley, when lust hit him. It came from somewhere at the back of his head, from a kind of hollow space in the hind part of his skull, trickling forward towards his eyes and, measurably later, down through his chest to his groin. His heart speeded up, his mouth dried, and the whole aspect of the saloon bar instantly changed. The horse brasses glittered promiscuously, the older men appeared suddenly to be sly while the younger men's voices took on a baying note. The girls and wives they were with seemed to be standing like lay figures, or sitting, ring-clad hands on laps, awaiting some primitive ceremony, part religious, part sexual.

He downed the rest of his drink and went out on to the road. There was a parish church on the other side, its tower catching some of the yellow floodlighting in which the pub was bathed. He could see old tombstones leaning in grey grass, the dull-golden cock on the east corner of the tower wavering in the night wind against minute winter stars.

He drove fast to Betty's cottage, parked his car beside the Assembly of God, and walked up the high street past the crooked curtained windows, glowing blue with the lights of their television sets. He could even follow the programmes as he passed: a murder rap on one channel, Sunday-night variety on the other. There was no other sound in the village at all, just the two programmes and the silent families listening and looking.

He went up the concrete path to Betty's, to "Honeycomb's." He still thought of her as "Honeycomb" Hotchkis. It was his secret name for her, instinct with the rural and a kind of innocence, wholesome.

The path was fringed with the saxifrage and aubrietia she had planted two summers ago in memory of her mother. She maintained her mother's grave like this, with cottage flowers, sweet William, clove carnations and stocks, transferring them from this garden to the cemetery at Easter. It was one of the things he liked in her, almost loved. By such means she seemed to say, "I know my place; I'm old like you, through mother. But we're cottage people. We remember."

He knocked on the black-painted door with his usual knock, the signal he had established: two raps, a pause and two more.

She opened it at once, the scent of the room coming out with her of a coal fire and washing-up liquid. Her eyes fell as he stepped in, a little sulky but ready to smile to herself at some joke she would never analyze. She was wearing a pink jumper, very finely knitted, a dark-blue or black skirt and her Cleopatra sandals. Her transistor set was playing on the floor beside the small sofa; the fire in the tiny grate was too hot: a curly black sheepskin rug lay in front of it with an empty cup and saucer tilted on the fleece.

She always greeted him as if he lived there, with some quite matter-of-fact remark to cover the span of his absence. It occurred to him that in Lettice's greetings there was usually reproach, that it was a mark of the middle-class marriage.

"The telly's packed in," she said, "bloomin' thing. I don't watch it anyway. I was listening to the radio. Thought I might hear your voice if you didn't come yourself."

"You weren't expecting me?"

"What do you think?"

"No, tell me, honestly."

She had slumped back on the sofa, her sandals off, side by side on the sheepskin, her shining stocking-clad knees curled up half under her, the round knees forward to the fire. "Well, I was, if you want to know. Pery wrote, said you'd be coming and that Chris was out."

"You thought it might be him, then?"

"He's not coming till Tuesday, silly devil. I knew if it was anyone it'd be you."

"Are you glad?"

Coles' knees were remarkably steady. Usually at this stage they began to tremble inside his trouser legs; but tonight, perhaps because of the whisky, perhaps because he had come to a decision, things seemed substantial. Betty looked solid, as inevitable as a statue, a waxwork, clothed, living, taking breath. She was wearing a pale lipstick, thick eye shadow. There were tiny curling black hairs in front of her small ears, fringing the margins of her cheeks.

"What do you think?" she said again. "I was wondering if you wouldn't have the nerve. Tonight."

"I had to come to tell you about Christopher."

"Lucky for me, then, wasn't it? If you depend on him? No Christopher, no Randall."

"I didn't mean that."

"Go on; who are you kidding? You'd have come anyway."

"Have you heard anything from the police?"

"They were here Saturday. They wanted me to promise I'd get on to them if he turned up."

"Did you?"

"Did I what?"

"Promise."

"I don't make promises."

"Well, what did you say, then?"

"I'm not telling."

"I've got to know, Betty."

"What business is it of yours? You only come here for kicks. Me, I'm only what killed the cat."

"You know that's not true."

"Isn't it?" She shifted on the sofa; her upper leg, lying on its fellow, moved up towards her stomach. He could hear the silk stockings rasping like a cat's tongue on a plate. The stockings were not silk stockings, of course; they would be nylon. It was Lettice who had worn silk stockings up at Cambridge before the war. He kneeled suddenly on the sheepskin rug and put his arms round her shoulders, looking into her somber eyes.

"I said I'd let them know." She yawned. "It's best in the long run; they said so themselves."

"Did you tell them he was coming here on Tuesday?"

"I didn't know then, did I? They came before the post. I hadn't had Pery's letter. Besides—"

"Besides what?"

She was smiling again, not to him, not at him, but at something secret inside herself. He could see each of her teeth, remarkably clean, as clean as television teeth, between them the tip of her tongue, the individual papillae bright as strawberry pips. She had a small mouth, almost a little girl's, as greedy.

"Besides what?" he asked again, shivering.

"A promise is a promise if you're soft enough to make it; but it's up to you when you keep it. I might want to talk to Chris first. He might want—"

He waited for her to say it; but she was silent. She had a widow's peak. It was more pronounced than usual, exposed because she had brushed her springing hair a little further back. He kissed the small mouth and felt it expand slowly, the bored touching of her tongue against his own. She drew back and pushed him away a little, as if to study him.

"Pery liked you too. She said a lot in her letter."

"Did she?"

He tried to kiss her again, but she moved her head to one side. It reminded him of a green day with Lettice: the first time he had taken her up the Backs. Willows were drooping over the water with wrack like birds' nests caught in the branches. Lettice fought him on the punt cushions, infuriating him so much that he had nearly given up. Several times he had kissed the dusty cushions instead of her lips.

"She liked your dancing," Betty said. "I reckon she saw you the way I haven't; but then she's a Pery, isn't she?"

"What do you mean?"

"Only some people have all the luck. I knew you first; but you don't take me to the night spots. I have to sit here and watch it on telly: Ginger Rogers and Fred Astaire." She laughed contemptuously. He saw again the fractional squint he had first noticed months ago.

He got up.

"No wonder she's laughing," she said.

"It wasn't like that. Your sister works at the Dolphin. I had no choice."

"*Works!* That's good. You ought to see her letter."

"I want to."

"It might make you mad."

"Where is it?"

"I'm not telling."

"Come on; show it to me."

She lay there, looking into the fire, scarcely breathing. He sensed the enormity of the boredom he had interrupted and realized that her stillness was a furious activity, something she would remember like an athlete much later when the trial was over. He was getting used to this fencing. He supposed it should have reminded him of his honeymoon; but Lettice had never gone in for it once she had accepted him. Hints she had dropped suggested that her mother had brought her up to acquiesce completely. She had said once, "Sex play simply isn't done when one's decided." He had made one or two halfhearted attempts in the second or third year, he remembered, and she had told him not to be absurd. He had felt absurd even before he started, but now he realized it was only because such nonsense was outside her canon. With Betty it was different, not because she started it, but because he knew that in the end she would allow him to win at the right moment, as if a clock were set somewhere inside her exactly tuned to his need.

"Please," he begged, "let me read it. Where have you put it?" He started to run his hand up to the welt of a silk stocking, and she jerked her legs away and stood up.

"What a sauce! I don't wear that sort. I'm not that old."

He realized with a shock that he must have been thinking of his mother over forty years ago; she had kept her little handkerchief in the leg of her bloomers, slyly taking it out to blow her nose in the far-off garden where the bees droned among the phlox and sweet william.

"Where then?" he asked, his face pale. In those days the plants in the border had been as tall as Brazilian forests, his mother as certain as summer.

"Where do you think?" she said. "Over the road. I keep all my letters there."

He picked up the white mackintosh.

"You won't need that," she said. "Wait while I see if the kids are all right."

He supposed one might become accustomed to this sort of thing, the masterfulness, the certainty, as if like his mother she had his life arranged for him, tea by the tennis court.

"What about your father?" he asked Betty.

"He's at the pub. Won't be back till eleven."

She looked at herself in the mirror above the mantelpiece and pushed a springy curl back behind her left ear. Then she went upstairs and he heard her sandalled footsteps pad across the thin floor boards, the sound of the neighbouring television set coming through the party wall. He imagined her head, fleecy as the sheepskin rug, leaning over the two sleeping children, Marc and Debrah, and remembered suddenly a line of Tennyson's:

> Shine out, little head brimming over with curls,
> To the flowers, and be their sun.

Then the lavatory flushed and she came down again. She chucked her chin at him and opened the front door.

"You've had something tonight," she said as she passed him. "Did you stop on the road?"

"I had a whisky in the Cross Keys."

"At Sumner?"

"Yes. Why?"

"That's where Mother's buried. Just opposite. If you went in the saloon you must have seen the stone coming out. It's just over the wall there."

"I parked on the right. There was quite a lot of traffic."

"I always go there Christmas," she said. "Not the Cross Keys, the cemetery. Mother died Christmas. That's why I've got no time for it."

They walked a hundred yards up the road together, very casually, as carelessly as if they had been loitering with intent. They went in at the gate of the other cottage.

Holding it open for him, she paused there. "I knew there was something. The sergeant fellow that came with the others to see me Saturday—"

"The police, you mean?"

"Yes. You'd never guess. He's Paul's young brother. Peter, they call him. He's been in the police ever since, nearly seven years. Wasn't half funny seeing him again in uniform."

Coles looked at the face of the unlighted cottage, the steep roof crinkled with old tiles, each row etched sharp in the light of a narrow moon. He hesitated.

"Come on," she said. "There's no one in there. Honest."

"The policeman–"

"Peter Caine's a sergeant."

"Did he seem resentful?"

She looked at him a little scornfully. "He made a joke of it."

She walked up the path away from him and looked back suddenly. He saw her white face, her frown. "Well, make your mind up! We haven't got long–not all night anyway."

How had she last spoken to Paul? The cottage was grey and white, the roof shone with recent rain, and a gutter dripped into a water butt. She was a dark figure now, poised against the light-coloured front door. In the absolute stillness the village seemed to move slightly, not when actually looked at, but a fraction of a second before, like the players in grandmother's footsteps, stock-still every time you turned to look at them, but creeping up on you nevertheless.

He thought, *If Presage were sitting there somewhere across the road or in a car, he would say, "The trap, Coles! The setting is immaterial, but the bait is always live."* He disliked Presage. At this moment he should have been at home in his flat with Helen and Cecily, but instead the bloody man was somewhere in London making a fool of himself with a girl young enough to be his daughter. He must dismiss him from his mind. He must decide.

He ran up to Betty and together they slipped in through the doorway. The cottage living room was in total darkness, no fire in the grate, only the smell of damp brickwork and strong tobacco.

"Dad," she said. "Poof! He doesn't half smoke Sundays, getting through the papers, dirty old devil. Wait while I open the door or you'll trip over something."

He stood dead still while she moved ahead of him. He had time to think: "a waste of time," not in the sense of extravagance but of enormity; a desert, St. Anthony. Wildernesses threw one back on the God concept, God and harems. Her father's tobacco reminded him of the prison, the smell of Hotchkis' cell when he and Bushnell had been in there together, smoking and talking before his arrival.

Across the space between them she switched on a red-shaded bedside lamp and the "dream" bedroom lighted up, the curtains already drawn, a small electric stove glowing in front of the flounced dressing table. He shut the door behind him and grasped her round the shoulders, his nervy hands slipping down to her thick waist. She lay there, leaning heavily against him, so that he had to brace his knees as he "lost" himself kissing her.

One had to lose oneself in a kiss even if, initially, it came a little hard: the difficulty in lying effectively, in making a present divorced from the past, from Lettice's kisses during the sweet, excruciating honeymoon and those later ones in the Half Yoke bedroom when the house had been new, when they had been poor together, the rooms barely furnished. A kiss had to be permanent: entry to the palace, lust and poetry hand in hand, beauty and the beast conjoined, equally believed in until the body took over. Given the chance, the scruples overcome, the body always did succeed as inevitably as an heir; one had only to make the undivided effort for a few moments.

She kissed him back with a trace of boredom. He could feel it in her heaviness, in the actual weight of her body, her substantial neck, her indolent lips, her bored tongue. He felt the habits of marriage in them both, no tentative honeymoon, but a gross intemperance, very adult.

She went with him to the bed and they arranged themselves skillfully: more kisses, a fancy he had to stroke her cheeks, massage them deeply with his unsteady fingers. There was no need to tell himself that it was new, that the old motions gave different results: her lethargy was new, her patience, her dumb response. She waited and waited as he let himself go frantically as if he had been deprived for a lifetime. He pulled up the finely knitted jumper and undid the buttons of the black skirt clumsily. She helped him apathetically, leaving everything else to him, laughing once or twice until he whispered, "What's the joke?"

She didn't answer; her eyes were half closed and he saw that she was looking away from him, gazing at something over his shoulder.

"What are you laughing at?"

Her eyes closed as though she had sighed, then opened again, focussing upon him with polite hostility, as if he'd had no manners. He was a little shocked but whispered once more: "Tell me what is so funny."

She frowned; her black eyebrows, thickened with a little pencilled paint, contracted; her lips tightened.

"Oh my Gawd! Nothing!"

He kissed the angry eyes, the big breasts, the patient lips before, suddenly, she nestled her head into the crook of his shoulder, turning her face away from him into the scented pillow as if he were inessential to her or she had left the room, absented herself. The gesture alarmed him; he came to a dead stop as when, years ago, in some game of hide-and-seek or sardines in an attic or a cupboard, he had gone too far with little Sylvia or Daphne.

He could hear his own boyish breathing and feel the fresh sweat on his forehead as he tried to see her face. He had an idea she might be weeping with closed eyes, very nervous of her mother or father. He tried to reach her mouth but could see only the corner of it, the lips curling up beneath the full white cheek. He dared not say a word but listened, waiting as she had waited, hearing her murmuring something to herself. She was no little girl; she was a woman, old perhaps, ill. He was as desperate as if she were dying, trying to catch with his ear the last thing she might say.

Awe overcame him: the half-smile, the whispered phrase he could not catch, the stubbornly closed eyelids—all as secret and private as death.

"What is it? For God's sake, tell me."

She turned her face up to him, raising her head from the pillow, pressing her lips against his mouth. Her hands came from somewhere and rested on his naked buttocks, not smooth palms but roughened and firm, a housewife's with years of work in them. His own eyes closed as he felt her calves cross over the back of his knees and slide slowly up towards his thighs. Rocking there with her in the absolute silence, he rocked himself in and out of his mind—alternations of exultation and nothingness, the sky and the ground equally sweet: the seesaw of his childhood, with a girl on the other end. He could think of nothing but women, of bodies, of hers in particular, of Lettice's, as if refined by death, of his marriage as distant as if he had been an old man remembering.

"Move over," she said when he had finished. "Coo! You aren't half heavy when you're in action."

On his elbows he was taking what Lettice called his "cat nap," the moment of pointless exhaustion when nothing could be done for him, a sick man's emergence to dawn. He thought of it sometimes as a scene in a First World War ambulance: tin hats and cigarettes, the sweat of the dying, the case who would never reach base alive, but he bundled out south of Poperinghe, some orderly saying, " 'Ere! Old Nobby's bought it. Tell Jack to stop."

He got off her obligingly, managing a smile and a buss on her cheek. It would be too damned ill-bred to be ungracious at such a time, slumping back beside her into the measured oblivion without acknowledgement. He hadn't done a good job; he knew that—too quick or something: the signs were all there. She was twitching at herself, pulling on her clothes slyly; and he, the man put out for dead, was going to recover by the roadside of poplars blasted level with the top of the sunken road. Not a blade of grass, only mud and ruts and men. His legs were cold and his buttocks: what novelists called "the singing in the groin" was subsiding.

She slid along her side of the narrow divan bed and padded across her thick rose-coloured carpet. He opened his eyes for a moment: the carpet was white, of course; the skirt she was fastening round her hips was made of some black stuff, rather creased; everything else was red—too red because of the scarlet lamp shade. He closed his eyes again: poor old Nobby, thinking about the Bethune brothel on his last forty-eight; someone would have to come and pick the bleeder up. There was a retreat on. Every man would be wanted for the counterattack. He'd better attract attention.

He wondered what her scent was: a bit too obvious for Lettice. "With a fair skin one has to be careful. Brunettes can get away with heavy scents—the pigmentation." He'd have to wash somewhere before he got back. His left wrist reeked of whatever it was. Also Dad's tobacco was filtering under the door, strong as the prison stuff. He caught some sound out there, a rustle in the living room, quite distinct, and sat up.

"What was that?"

She was fastening her suspenders. "Nothing."

"Where are my trousers?"

She had finished with the suspenders and was looking into the circular mirror, her red-bathed features floating beneath one off-red plastic camellia. "They're where you left them. On the floor."

"I heard something."

"That'd be Kipper, Dad's cat."

"It was too loud."

"Nervy, aren't you?"

She turned her face to the left and then to the right, checking the fresh lipstick she was applying, "repairing the damage." Lettice always said, "If one doesn't go in for cosmetics in the first place, there's no damage to repair." She would be sitting in the drawing room listening to his programme, deciding on her weekly verdict: "I thought you rather overplayed the revivalist; three minutes would have been ample." He looked at his wrist watch: no, he was wrong; it was only ten minutes past ten. With five minutes to go, Lettice would be making the little pot of china tea they always shared before the programme started.

"Want a cup of tea?" Betty asked. "You look as if you could do with it."

"I'd love it, but I haven't really got the time."

"Suit yourself." He'd got his trousers on and thought it would be all right to kiss her on the back of the neck in front of the mirror, watching their reflected faces as he did so.

"Haggard!" she said. "You're looking your age tonight."

He remembered his spectacles but couldn't find them.

"Try under the bed; they might have dropped off in the struggle," she suggested sourly.

"I thought I'd put them on the dressing table."

"Well, you didn't, or they'd be there."

He noticed the folk-weave counterpane and started to straighten it, searching the folds.

"Leave that," she said sharply. "I'll do it later; I always do."

Beforehand he would have taken her up on that, but there wasn't time now. On hands and knees he fumbled in the six-inch space of darkness beneath the bed and found something, a Sunday newspaper.

"Dad's," she said. "I was having a read this afternoon."

"I can't find them. Where the devil are they?"

He found something else and brought it out: a heel-flattened sandal of crêpe rubber and white plastic. She saw it.

"Do *you* mind! There they are, just by the leg. You must be half-blind."

"Without them, I am." He paused, listening again. "What was that?"

"Nothing. I told you; there's nobody in but us."

"Quite distinctly I heard somebody out there."

"Gawd!" She switched on the transistor, turning it down low on the Light Programme.

"What about your father?" he insisted. "How can you be sure he's not back early?"

She shrugged at her reflection, watching it, speaking over her shoulder to him: "You ought to take tranquillizers. Before and after. The way you're going on, you'll have us seeing things next."

"Just take a look outside," he begged. "I can't very well."

"I can see that, with your flies the way they are."

His hands shot down to them: that damned zipper on the tweed suit. He and Lettice had argued about it at the time; he remembered the whispered altercation in the tailor's dressing room three years earlier—an absolute fact, a real detail of his real life. What the devil had happened to him now? Nothing around him had anything to do with him, with his past or his present.

She laughed unpleasantly at her reflection. "I've got my reputation to think of. Imagine Peter calling and finding me like this. You with your trousers hanging open."

"Peter?"

"The police, silly! Paul's brother—I told you."

"Good God! You said they weren't coming back." He juggled with the new facts, which in reality had nothing to do with him. Where was his mackintosh? It should have been at home in the boot room. Where had he parked the car? They could be taking his number out there in the dark. What a bloody fool he had been! He could have been sitting in his own life with Lettice as usual. There was no war on, no national disaster. The programme would just be starting, John Forbes' sly interview with the Negro Baptist in Oak Ridge.

"Well, they could, couldn't they?" she said, tucking at her hair.

"I'm not their keeper, and that Peter's a fast mover or they wouldn't have given him promotion."

Promotion? He had never met "Peter." He was a part of her life, her wretched, quite different existence: a story he wouldn't even have wanted to read.

"Look here," he said. "I really think we ought to get out of here."

"Nobody's stopping you."

Oh, aren't they? he thought. *I'm stopping myself, a mistake somewhere along the line; must start working my way back to where I would have been.*

"You must make sure we're alone first," he said.

"Catch!" She threw him a white nylon hairbrush he had never seen before. "Your hair's a mess. If you're going out in the street, there'll be fellows coming back from the pubs."

He poked at it, the waves she had admired. Her transistor was tuned in to the Light Programme, thank god. He simply could not have overheard his own programme in this room, even though the only alternative was the Congregationalist ladies' choir singing "Jerusalem" in a Cheadle Hulme chapel:

> "And did those feet in ancient time
> Walk upon England's mountains green?"

Two or three dozen women, girls and matrons, with swelling bosoms, pushed out dead Blake's words, blocking Coles with memories of school concerts over thirty years ago. They both hated it: as Lettice had always said, that first "and" was special pleading, rhetorical. "Without it the answer would be 'no'—clearly."

He had to get Mrs. Hotchkis to see if the coast was clear. He had an idea that she was enjoying "torturing" him like this: a strong word perhaps, one that Presage would not have accepted, but, with so much at stake, valid nevertheless. He checked his buttons and zipper again as, outside Manchester, the women sang:

> "Give me my bow of burning gold,
> Give me mine arrows of desire."

He pushed the white plastic sandal out of sight under the bed and fussed once more with the counterpane. The whole place looked "historical" in some way, like an out-of-date film, the kind of setting they had both always tried to avoid. He realized that their taste, his and Lettice's, had always been set against just this, a room that lent itself to moral interpretation—a kind of victorianism. On the way home he would stop at a respectable pub, have a wash and a drink, chew cashews or something and not get too close to poor little Lettice.

There was a tap at the door and they both froze. He remembered it forever afterwards: Betty's raised arm arrested like Lot's wife, his own absurd gesture with the counterpane before he grabbed at the newspaper and sat down on the bed to make the wrinkles look natural, Betty's reaching for a cigarette and turning up the transistor louder before she called out: "Who is it?"

"It's me; Chris."

Hotchkis came in with a gun pointing between them and swung it slowly round at Coles. He spoke out of the side of his mouth, the lower part of his face fixed and flat beneath a porkpie hat pulled well down over his eyes.

"This is a stick-up!" he said.

Coles swayed on the bed. Betty drew on her cigarette and blew the smoke over towards her husband.

"When did you get in?"

But Hotchkis ignored her; he was still looking at Coles, the round eye of the revolver steady in his fists, his own eyes invisible beneath the brim of the hat.

"So you made it, did you?" he asked Coles.

The words, almost whispered, came out of the burlesqued mouth, the lips barely moving, the lower half of the face bathed in the scarlet light. In Coles' dark double-breasted suit, a white handkerchief in the breast pocket, Hotchkis looked very "Detroit," a figure out of the cinema myth of Coles' teens. But he was real; the turn-ups of Coles' trousers rested on black pointed shoes, the left leg was slightly bent at the knee, and he gripped the revolver not with the right hand but with both together so that he looked very professional.

Betty stiffened on the dressing stool. Coles distinctly sensed a change in her attitude and experienced some kind of a flash back, the sort of thing he would have attempted to describe to Presage:

"One of those quarrels people have had before," he would have said. "But although they're used to them they're never not in earnest." Worse than this, he believed that if Betty had not been frightened she would have been insulted, and this made him feel that he might easily be killed.

"You got a minute," Hotchkis told him, "before I plug you, so you'd better get thinking."

Coles stood up, the newspaper shaking between his hands.

"Look here, Christopher—"

"Fifty seconds and then you get it."

"If this is an act—"

"It's no act. It's no rehearsal. That's been done, remember? You've got just thirty seconds to say your prayers."

"You're mad, Hotchkis."

The revolver clicked: a cobra, some snake twitching into final position for the strike. Coles thought he could smell the smoke from it, the firework smell of cordite; but that was impossible. Only they would smell it after his death. He thought of holes in his shirt front and of his parked car, of Lettice having to come over and drive it back with Malcolm. He'd never counted on anything, but he was owed at least twenty more years: his retirement, his unborn grandchildren.

"Standing, you get it in the chest," Hotchkis said. "Kneeling, between the eyes. Take your pick."

"They won't bend," Coles said as if to his dead Christian mother. "For God's sake, Christopher, for Christ's sake, don't fire!"

"Get down there; you got twenty seconds."

Coles kneeled on the newspaper and the mouth of the revolver tilted.

"Hands together, lips moving. The proper position: Our Father . . ."

Betty screamed behind both hands: just louder than "Jerusalem," a false note ugly as a bad joke and as credible. There was no possible way of knowing until afterwards. The great stage, the scene shifters changing the settings. The drawing room gone and the china tea; instead the dream bedroom and the absurdity.

"A Christian with a gun," Hotchkis said. "We're not allowed them. Our Father . . . !"

"Our Father," Coles repeated, cranking it up from somewhere. "Which art in Heaven."

"Who," Hotchkis corrected him. "He's someone. He's not a bloody which."

"Who art in Heaven," Coles said. "Hallowed be Thy name."

The revolver sailed over his head, landing smack on the wrinkled counterpane. The porkpie hat followed it and Hotchkis, restored to his prison shape, pulled Coles to his feet.

"My God! He's done it. Old Randall, praying, kneeling on his knees."

"You bloody fool," she said, swirling about in front of her mirror, somewhere to Coles' left. "You're a raving madman coming in and doing things like that."

Coles hit him full on the mouth and he stepped back, one hand to his lips, his big green eyes smiling.

" 'Ere! Steady up! I'm going to need my kisser before the night's out. We still got uses for it, haven't we, darling?"

He kissed her lightly on the forehead, leaving a bloodstain there like thin lipstick. She smacked his face, a sidewinder that shook his curly head, and he took out his blue prison handkerchief to mop his split lip, speaking through the gag of its folds.

"It wasn't a joke, you know," he said. "People don't like them. You got to be serious to get loved, and I've never been anything but—serious, I mean. Solemn as death." He handed Betty his handkerchief. "Here, darling; you got a bloody forehead after all these years."

She chucked her chin at him. Quite distinctly, Coles observed that there was nothing anyone could do with her.

"What's that thing?" she said. "I've got tissues in the drawer."

She pulled it open and took out a handful, smoothing away at the pink blood on her just-lined forehead.

Coles was feeling apologetic. One of Hotchkis' teeth had cut his knuckle and the skin seemed to remember, on its own, the sensation of the smashed lips. Whenever one acted intemperately it was because one had first thought inaccurately. Panic was always blind. He saw that the windows were completely covered by the curtains and had been so all evening. No one out there in the garden could have seen anything, and any conversation they'd had had been *sotto voce.*

"You can understand," he said stiffly, "that under the circumstances—"

"Circumstances! Life's circumstances. I told you I didn't think you'd make it, Randall."

"I really don't follow you. We came over here to see Pery's letter."

"What you wanted, I meant. A bit of drama like the murder game at home. Outwitting the police, masked men and all that. If I'd thought of it, I'd have made it look even better by tying my handkerchief round my jaw." He looked over at the transistor. "Gawd! That singing! Turn it off, sweetheart."

"Bringing a gun!" she said in the quietness. "You want your head testing."

"Very foolish," Coles agreed. "You realize that if the police had arrested you with that weapon—"

"They'd have been disappointed without. You've got to fill the bill. Everyone's got to act up so that people know where they are. Escaped killers should be armed." He picked up the revolver and kissed the barrel stagily, the two of them watching him with hostility. "Only thing is, it's not loaded and never will be. I didn't bother with ammo. Once you've done a thing once over, you're rich like that, if you get me?"

"Don't be daft," Betty said. "Of course he doesn't. Mr. Coles isn't that kind."

"You get across something inside, what we was always discussing in the prison, the big dark that people read about and think to theirselves, 'What would happen if I?' And if you do get into it, you feel good. My God! You don't half feel good to begin with. Life settles down as if you was dead. You go floating out the other side of what you've done and you make the discovery. Here! I'll tell you: a dead man's master of life. He's the boss, no respecter of persons as they say, a tyrant, the man of the world. He's got it all wrapped up; he doesn't remember anything he's done before because the only continuity he's got in him is his death."

"It's turned your 'ead," Betty said. "I knew you'd go nutty in there. If you don't do anything else while you're out you want to see a doctor, doesn't he, Randall?"

"Listen, sweetheart, I'm not talking to you—not now; there isn't time. I want a day or two with you and the little boy and the little girl before the fuzz catches up with me. That's why I came over to your Dad's first, the back way, across the gravel pits. What you've got to do is get back home and give me a signal, a light on in the bedroom or something. If you're not happy, if there's any fuzz about, do nothing; don't come over till morning, when your Dad's back."

She looked at him lethargically, slack-bodied, and he put his hands on her shoulders and ferried her towards the door. "Well, get on then," he said. "But no more smackers, mind, or I might get angry—with you looking so good. She looks all right with those flushes in her cheeks, doesn't she, Randall? Like she was pleased? Like she wanted all she could get."

She was acquiescent, a woman who seldom made a gesture, whose excitement occasioned only stillness in her, a kind of apathy. They stood there together, Hotchkis altogether larger, enclosing her by the breadth of his shoulders, the size of his body. Coles saw them as if they had been guests at one of the parties, politely leaving, coats in the hall, a car ticking over in the drive. He saw himself interposed between them, smaller and older, white-fleshed.

"I don't know what you think you're up to," she said to Hotchkis. "I want my things." She dodged out of his embrace and went back to the dressing table for her lipstick and handbag, but left the transistor. She switched off the electric stove and foolishly went over to the bed, checking herself and then changing her mind. She straightened out the counterpane, picked up and fluffed out the flattened pillows.

Hotchkis watched her, and she sensed his attention, looking back at him slyly, the quick glances of a little girl in the presence of her father. When she had finished with the bed she caught his eye just as if they'd been alone, as if Coles had not been there with them on that particular night. Then, trailing her handbag, she went out through the door, her heels clicking fast down the concrete path beyond the window, the gate creaking as she opened it.

"My mackintosh," Coles said. "I left it over there."

"Evidence," Hotchkis said. "It's all evidence, isn't it?"

"Of what?"

"It's evidence of where you went and what you did. But don't worry, Randall. If you don't want to take any more chances tonight, you can always pick it up another time. It's not raining."

"I'd like to take it tonight."

"But you'll be coming again?"

"Of course," Coles lied.

He would have to, he supposed; but, my God, he would be reluctant. He would come in the flesh, in the Mini, but he'd leave everything else of himself behind. He would reappear as a shadow, a hollow man, programmed in advance.

"Betty's fond of you," Hotchkis said. "I could see that. You may have made mistakes, but you've done a good job just the same."

"I did my best; that was all. It was a little difficult perhaps to avoid personal involvement."

Taking refuge in the cliché, he saw Hotchkis suddenly as a wronged man, very pathetic in the borrowed suit—his own—his flesh tired, his shoes not polished, his hair human. A weight of pity shifted in him as when he'd been very young and looked at a tramp. He wanted to call out something or abase himself on the bedroom carpet. When he spoke he heard his voice crack embarrassingly.

"My God, Christopher, I wish you hadn't done this. I wish you'd waited until your release."

Hotchkis spared him by looking hard and cold, by a touch of the gangster. "I'll bet! Been all right, wouldn't it? Nice and neat. Time for everyone to get things in order."

"But the complications," Coles said. "They were all totally unnecessary."

"Don't be bloody silly. What's a man without complications? People have to do things sometimes. They get a pressure inside them and they wait until the time comes. Sometimes it never comes, or if it does they don't see it and they go on being nothing or thinking they are while they're waiting to get out and start; but they got to be careful, though."

"That was precisely what I meant."

"Oh, was it? Well, I'll tell you what I meant. It's this about death. If you was to throw yourself into what I'm saying, you'd get it. You'd see that it's only the dead that do things, right or wrong. It's only the dead that are complete, whether they get dead while they're still walking or only when they turn their feet up. You've got to be dead to be a villain or a hero or people won't be sure either way. You can die the way a bad man does and master the world, or you can die the way a good man does, the way God did, to bring life to everyone else. What'd be the good of a God who knew nothing about hell and never died? Here, I wouldn't 'ave no use for 'im if he hadn't of died, I tell you. I don't want only a living God in my life; I want a dead one too, and that's the argument."

Coles was silent, calling on his "poetry": "The Poetic Apprehension of Religion," a talk he had just read, commissioned for the Third Programme from a Cambridge don, a friend of Lettice's girlhood, an annual weekender. Lettice never allowed Coles to forget his poetry and did in fact often tell her friends: "I never allow Randall to forget that he's a poet. From the first it was part of my original contract with him—or, rather, ours."

To get at it, to tap the source, he had always to return to his childhood, the first seven years or so, the remembrance of his dead mother, Violet. She had been religious, a scented edwardian christian with a christian sadness beneath her joy. There had been those Good Fridays in the stony parish church, the third pew on the left, the unavoidable images of the dying Christ and the long-thorned crown. On that day, once a year, Coles had tasted Calvary vinegar as if it had been sour wine at the bottom of the bottles in the pantry. In imagination he had felt it spill from his lips and trickle down his naked chest.

Hotchkis was filling the room with himself, not the prison any longer, not any longer a hopeless man, but some bulging-shouldered rough fellow with dangerous eyes. The eyes of a tramp, Coles thought; the particular one who had called at his parents' home every year round about Easter. He had stood in the back kitchen with only the rim and peak of his cap like a crown on his tangled woodland hair. He had smelled of the country and there had been something frightening about his bearded lips as if in the night they had sucked at the cowslips studding the fields and prayed while everyone slept.

"There was darkness over all the land," he remembered, "and the veil of the temple was rent in twain."

Something gave in him for a moment, ripped like silk. He could smell the night outside the cottage, still and full of winter. The sky was a crucifix pinned with stars, a shadowy body impaled there, gleaming, the reason for his childish safety. For an instant he felt he might run beneath it anywhere he chose, perfectly free. It was nothing to do with christianity. It was simply necessary that one man, the tramp, out of the earth, should die for the people. "These things," Lettice's don had suggested, "have the power to move us all. There can be little doubt that the dynastic origins of Judaism, their later incorporation in early christianity, have withstood the tests of time and the developments in natural science."

The railings bounding that early garden, dividing it from the experimental landscape behind it, had given place to an even more limited safety, to Lettice and twenty years of china tea. *We have huddled,* Coles thought, *safely. There's our yew tree and the three conifers and the herbaceous border with the plants laid brick by brick ahead of us. One leads out to the hospital and her friends and the other to my own life, my job; it sneaks through the railings where I filed one of them away over many years so that I might break through into the landscape I call "experimental."*

In her Cleopatra sandals, what would Betty Hotchkis be doing at that moment, just beneath the cottage roof three hundred yards away? He saw her washing in the bathroom, then going back into the bedroom to look at the bed in which she would spend a night with Hotchkis. She would be tired; somehow she would be anticipating the morning and the rest of her life with him until for her, as for them all, the breathing ended and the grave opposite the Cross Keys, beside her mother's, was sealed.

"What I have written, I have written."

The words came back to Coles not like a clap of thunder but like the silence of mountains, that fact of rock or granite, ice-capped, which makes of noiselessness a voice speaking no known language. Rage rose in him, not the kind he was accustomed to controlling, but a violent and destructive protest, desperate as a prisoner's. He only just mastered it, the fury that made him want to wreck the bedroom and kill Hotchkis, his persecutor.

Rage, like laughter, he had read somewhere, was the outcome of imbalance, the juxtaposition of opposites in the mind. His anger had sprung from the enforced prayer and its associations. Hotchkis was a madman, the one he had needed; but the thing to do now was to cut loose from him and all he represented, a gentle washing of the hands, not in public, but in private.

With all his accustomed reasonableness he began to speak smoothly: "I know what you mean, Hotchkis. As far as it's possible for an unbeliever—frankly, an atheist—I know what you're implying. But you must realize we're speaking different languages. Even if in our childhood we shared certain beliefs, I've grown away from them; England has." He looked at his wrist watch. "It's quite fascinating and I'd like to go on with it, but not now, for god's sake. We've got to decide what your next move is to be. The immediate question, I think, is to—"

As so often before, in the rectangular cell, Hotchkis was waiting for him to finish. So earnest a man, both of them, so patient and earnest, Coles with his lined face and Hotchkis with his smile. But now he wasn't smiling, he was heavy in the face, as absent as his wife had been during the love-making. Repeatedly he pulled back a corner of the bedroom curtain, watching out through the window for whatever signal they had agreed upon.

Coles observed his big back; the borrowed suit would never look the same again and there would be no point in hinting for its return. He could keep it; my god, couldn't Hotchkis keep it! As the tramp had kept things, walking away in them and returning, a year later, hungry as a dog with no word said about what he'd been given last year. Coles would have given Hotchkis anything that night, any material thing, even to the car if necessary, all his savings, a pint or two of his own blood, so long as he moved away with the blood inside him and wrote no letters or ever came back.

"You'll be going now," Hotchkis said. "You'll be wanting to get home, Randall."

"There's no hurry," Coles said.

After all, when volcanoes exploded and ships sank or ambulances arrived, there was never in the first moments any hurry. People waited on the edge of tragedy, frozen and polite, their urgency static. "But I ought to be getting back. You've rather taken things into your own hands, you see, and at the moment there's not a lot I can do. Also, Lettice—"

"That's all right. You don't have to worry about me any more. In a day or two the jacks will come and pick me up, and by that time I'll be ready for them. I'll make it easy."

I don't care if you don't, Coles thought. *Whatever you do, whatever they do, is of no possible interest to me for my day or night thoughts.*

Yet he suddenly remembered the sergeant and found himself visualizing the arrest. Perhaps in all decency, out of loyalty to his own past, he ought to warn Hotchkis about Peter, the sergeant. The arrival of the brother of the man he had killed was a complication that Christopher, intuitive as he was, would not have anticipated.

XVII

Arriving back at Half Yoke House, Coles was feeling gay and very responsible. The immediate past crowed in him like a cockerel; he even imagined this bird in some Palestine back yard, its spiky wings close-held as its throat expanded to let out the cry, some image, he supposed, touched off by the conversation with Hotchkis and the threat of death. Yet it was not the contemplation of the past which contented him so much as the prospect of the empty future. He saw himself getting on with things again, reconciled to the second half of life, to a time in which he would settle down with Lettice until the end.

In this mood, clear and mildly exultant, he could not forget what Hotchkis had said about feeling good in the "big dark." The night lay behind him like another creation, a separate event in which he had been something, fallen into some kind of love, slammed his fist into a human face and kneeled in recollection of his own beginnings. His mother was mixed up in it and his father too, that silent man he could best remember standing one morning in the garden beneath a lime tree and giving him a bag of sweets. The tree, he remembered, had been thick with tiny yellow flowers, its foliage powdered with golden pollen, the whole air so scented that for as long as he and his father had stood beneath it, fragrance of everything had seemed the natural condition, a world so sweet that it was only in his loss of it that it had ever existed.

Now, as he turned into the Half Yoke drive, he hummed the tune of "The Foggy, Foggy Dew," beloved of himself and Lettice ever since their honeymoon. He hummed it in order to avoid the words, because he knew they never again would apply to Lettice solely, but to Betty Hotchkis as well—whom he had not saved from anything. But he hummed it with a light in his eye, a kind of wink, as if the sentiment the tune conveyed had been for the first time really known to him, naughty and very English. He hummed it still as he drove the car into the garage and stopped to fasten the bottom bolt into the floor, only breaking off when Tyndal came out to him.

The dog was suspicious at first, grumbling somewhere in the darkness, then bounding up to him, sneezing with delight and springing about his waist. His coat was soaked with dew, foggy with it, and his breath plumed out of his open mouth.

Coles liked talking to dogs; he and Lettice were full of guiltless sentiment about them and agreed that nothing too farfetched might be entertained about man's most faithful friends. "Dumb!" Lettice had once said unguardedly to Harriet Harvey. "They speak with everything they've got." "That," Harriet had replied, "is precisely why I won't have them in the house." "She's coarse," Lettice had told Randall later. "Harriet's got a very coarse streak."

But now in the close winter's silence outside his house, where, he noticed, the lights were still on in the drawing room, Coles talked intimately to Tyndal in the low, gravelly voice he always used for animal conversation. He said: "So she locked him out then and he's a wet fellow. There was no room at the inn for Tyndalman, so he has to hang about in the foggy foggy dew for his naughty old master. But he's a loyal, faithful old fellow who knows when to bark and when to keep his mouth shut."

Tyndal capered about out there with him, coughing at the ground, leaping up with the mirey paws which as hands would have been quite unacceptable. "Unacceptable" was one of Lettice's words, and Coles confided this too in Tyndal's left ear: "But to tell old Tyndal the truth," he whispered, "there's nothing unacceptable about *him!* He's a good friend; he sees all and he says nothing. Oh my, oh my! Oh no! Not Tyndal."

He grasped the dog's head as he said this and directed it round at the drawing room. "Sniff! Sniff!" he said. "Tyndal smells trouble. Oh dear yes, plenty heap trouble. He knows what's going on in there, but he's not telling nobody nothing!" Then he cocked up Tyndal's ears for him and said, "Is she sitting or standing? And why, oh why, is she up so late? Is she alone or is one of those bloody awful lady-dog women with her? Can Tyndal smell a big black coat with an astrakhan collar hanging on the bannister? Are there ladies in there talking about his master? Tyndal knows but he won't say."

With delightful bestial obedience the dog stayed like that, ears cocked, nose working as if he were really tuned in to the drawing room. Then he broke free and danced round Coles in a stealthy circle before returning once again to hear what more he had to say.

Coles was feeling ever more rebellious, ever more reluctant to enter the house, as alert as Tyndal, as deprived, as if somehow they had communicated moods. He was moved to confide in him still further. "And Master's been a naughty fellow; he doesn't deserve his Bonios tonight. Oh, he's been a bad old dog. No, not chasing chickens, or yowling to the moon—because tonight there isn't one. So not that, not putting back his lined old head outside some lady dog's back yard, but worse, much worse. He's been on the rampage, the randy, randy rampage, and he's come back all tousled and torn and smelling of lady-dog scent."

Tyndal snorted and tried to get away for another silent dance, perhaps to put his muzzle on the ground between his front paws and wait as still as death but for his tail. But Coles seized him by the big wet leather collar and admitted: "That's the truth of it, old friend. Master's been out across country on this dark and moonless night and found someone ready and willing, a naughty, untreated hot, hot lady dog, to roll with him in the ivy. And now he's come home and is he downhearted? No! Is he even guilty? Not a bit. He's just a wicked old top dog of fifty who's had his onions in the country and come back home to his cozy old kennel with his tail held high."

Tyndal licked him, caught his ear and his right eye with the sweep of his tongue, and Coles said, "Now that's not necessary. Sympathy's one thing, old fellow, but sentiment's another. Oh dear me, yes. If Tyndal's going to be a priestly dog and hear Master's confession, he must be worthy of his collar; he mustn't put his tongue through the hole in the box and lick his penitent's face. Oh dear me, no! He must keep strictly to the letter of the law or else he'll get himself unfrocked and then what would Master's friend, Presage, say?"

This last speech really amused Coles greatly. He let Tyndal go and for very little would have joined him in a midnight scamper round the garden. At the first opportunity he would tell Bernard about it. He would say, "Well, old man, you'll be pleased to hear I took your advice after all. I made my confession to a deerhound, and he seemed to understand."

But Tyndal did not want to scamper around the garden; he was intent on getting back into the house as was Coles on remaining out of it, delaying until he was quite sure of himself. Hotchkis, he remembered, had cased the place before knocking, and for a moment he was tempted to do the same himself; but this would have been too uncomfortable, too absurd, to steal round his own home like an escaped prisoner. So he forced himself into more merriment and good fellowship, seeing himself as a romping husband with a fine big dog, a man returning late to the wife who had waited up for him. He even considered his dishevelled appearance, Tyndal's footprints on the tweed suit, realizing with all a criminal's cunning that, as Hotchkis would have said, they were "evidence"—evidence of an easy mind, of doggy innocence.

"Such a welcome!" he would tell Lettice. "Your old watchdog guarded his mistress faithfully. Look, darling, at the marks of his affection." She would smile and he would add, "Heavens! What a mess he's made of me. I must go and tidy up."

Then, naturally, he would run upstairs to check up on things, to make sure there were no dark hairs on his shirt collar, no traces of that heavy scent. "My, my, what a guileful fellow he was."

He found himself resuming this idiom quite naturally, as if he were still addressing Tyndal, and played with the idea of keeping it up in Lettice's presence, of continuing to talk partly to her and partly to the dog. Then he decided that he must pull himself together, achieve a basic seriousness, a hint of tiredness after his working Sunday at Broadcasting House. He must even remember to ask her what she'd thought of the programme that night, give her a lead for criticism of the interview with the Negro revivalist. On the other hand—one never knew—it was just possible that in his absence there might have been additional cuts in the script. He could be caught out and it would be wisest to allow her to make the running.

He slid his key into the lock and found that it would not turn because she had fastened the safety catch on the other side. He paused, then, totting things up: Tyndal out, the lights still on in the drawing room, the front door locked from inside. He'd been right. There was "plenty heap trouble" awaiting him. He'd known this intuitively, he realized, and had wanted to make a challenging entry, but Lettice had outwitted him, forcing him to defend rather than attack. He'd have to knock and wait; but if he had to wait he'd use the moments of delay for a fresh appraisal of his attitude. He would discard both jollity and seriousness in favour of reproach. "What on earth's the idea?" he would grumble. "The dog's soaked through and you know I hate you to wait up for me on my Sunday stints. Why? Because it makes you tired the next day, tired and snappy. Dammit, darling—"

I'm a poor old fellow, he thought now, *trapped, not in Presage's sense, but like a Picasso clown, a twentieth-century dupe, here in his own drive, trying to work things mournfully out. Now why the devil did she have to lock the door?*

Lettice tripped across the hall to open it. He heard her, the "crisis" tripping of her heels he knew so well—Brett's mastoid, Malcolm's failed A Levels, a sound fast and anxious, very slightly aggressive. Tyndal got in first. He was a fool dog who knew nothing, nosing straight through into the drawing room, leaving his master undefended in the hall. So Coles sought to embrace Lettice, to give her a quick tactical hug, but she stepped back before he could reach her, not even closing the front door or smiling at him. She was pale and cold-looking, not merely emotionally, but physically too, economizing on fuel but not on anger. She left him there, joining forces with Tyndal, following him through into the drawing room, and Coles did not hesitate; he started immediately on his reproaches.

"What on earth's the idea of locking me out? And the dog—he's wet through. Dammit, darling, you know I hate you to wait up for me on these Sundays."

He dropped his brief case on to the hall chest and brushed with his red hands at his suit. Pointedly he closed the door and walked over towards her in the thinly scented drawing room, still rubbing at his jacket, picking off dog hairs in a finicky way, very put out.

"Covered with mud," he continued. "Absolutely covered with it. You know what he is when he's locked out."

She looked at him; he saw her eyes sweep down from his lapels to his turn-ups, crossing the barrier of his zipper almost palpably, if it was not his guilt, his unease, which made him interpret things in this way. His mother had been thin too, a tall thin little woman with the same quick gaze as Lettice's.

"Where's your mac?" she asked.

"My mac? I left it at B.H."

"Liar!" she said.

Coles stopped rubbing at himself and looked down at Tyndal, stretched out now as if they had never met out there, as if he had been hogging the heat throughout the evening.

"Now look here, darling!"

"Nasty dirty stinking liar! You left Portland Place three hours ago. I telephoned and they told me."

"I don't see what that has to do with my mac."

"Where have you been?"

"In the country."

"What country? Where? Who with?"

"I had a job to do."

"What job? Who with? I want the truth."

He saw her shiver. What thin shoulders she had, poor little thing; what a tiny jaw, how much pale-grey hair. Why, there was not much of her at all at forty-seven on her last birthday, and it was dressed in such sad little clothes, a wisp of grey blouse, the silver filigree brooch he'd given her when she got her degree, a yard or so of tweed skirt and one of the winter cardigans. All that little body and those mortal opinions so unpretentiously clad against the cold November. "Mortal opinions," an unbidden thought, made him see their coffins suddenly, long and narrow, not many men needed to carry them. Then he remembered that they would be very temporary, the fittings of plastic, because cremation was one of the things they had always been agreed upon. So that the more final coffin he had been visualizing must have been his mother's seven years ago, a northern burial.

He stepped over to Lettice, to plead with her if she would let him, to see his red hands on her shoulders, to shake them with affection and resolve while she was still there with him. But again she dodged him, furious, clay-faced and shivering. He looked over towards the walnut cabinet left her by her mother, uncertain whether or not it was worth it to weaken his case still further by having a drink.

"Don't come near me again until you've told me the truth. Everything!" she said, misinterpreting his indecision. "Everything that's been going on since you got mixed up with them both. You've been lying to me for months, haven't you? Lying and deceiving me, doing your damndest to wreck everything—all our ideas and all our sacrifices."

"Sacrifices? Darling—"

"Keep away! I mean it. If you approach me once more I shall ring up the police now. I want the truth. You've got to tell me everything."

She waited as, years ago, in a remote climate, his mother had waited for his confessions of theft and smut, of cheating, of undergraduate drunks and debts. As he was to tell Presage later: "She was magnificent. I had to admire her authority, her courage. It all came out just as it had done with poor little Vi."

"Vi?"

"Violet, my mother."

Lettice had locked up the house and put Tyndal out because she'd seen the six o'clock news on the children's old television set in Brett's "boudoir"—that last room of her girlhood. There had been an announcement of Christopher Hotchkis' escape and a police photograph of him looking shut-faced and vicious, clearly the man "Bicknor"—their guest at the winter party.

"How was I to know he wouldn't call again?" she demanded. "I was alone in the house, and when I rang you at Portland Place to ask you to come back early you'd already left. You'd taken your mac with you, so they knew you wouldn't be returning."

"Darling!" He could think of nothing else to say, playing for time, trying to tell her that it was over, the long night, the adventure.

"Where were you? There's no more time for lies; they're too dangerous. The telephone's been ringing all evening—Harriet Harvey and Mrs. Scott-Roberts, the magistrate, both nearly certain they'd recognized him. So it's got to be the truth."

"A drink! I'm sorry, but I've got to have a drink."

"You've had one already. You reek of whisky."

"That was hours ago." He poured it out stubbornly, a half-glass of her "crisis" gin, the unsweetened.

"And cheap scent," she said. "You've been out with his wife, haven't you? That disgusting working-class tart who has sex with commercial travellers."

"Commercial travellers?"

She picked up one of her most precious bowls, an early terracotta Wedgwood, Rossa Antica, enamelled with flowers, and dropped it into the hearth. "That was the staggering thing," Coles would tell Presage; "her control. She didn't throw it; she dropped it. And it represented something—everything! It had belonged to her grandmother, one of the Caleys, and was full of potpourri, as if she were dropping her life in the hearth, all her standards, all the secret part of herself I'd always respected, loved really, without knowing it."

"Liars, when they're waiting to lie, invariably repeat things," Lettice said. "Malcolm used to do it when he was at his prep school and now you've started. You've been repeating things for months; I've noticed it ever since you met your murderer. When I say 'commercial travellers,' I mean Mr. Smeed, one of your country tart's other customers. He was here, weeks ago, dropping hints, preparing for blackmail, no doubt."

Coles looked down at the potpourri and the lovely earthen fragments of the bowl on the quarry tiles of the hearth. He could distinguish the crinkled petals of her mermaid rose, beads of lavender, heads of sweet basil, flakes of verbena and the thyme they had gathered on the slopes behind Alassio in the summer of '57.

How splendid it was, such pain, such significance, as if in the pot-pourri something had been resurrected, all the concealed sweetness of their lives together, and more—that blinding memory of his father beneath the lime tree. *I count,* he thought. *She and I were buried together in there beneath those eternal flowers. Nothing was ever wasted.* He would tell this to Presage as soon as he saw him again. He would say, "It was a splendid moment—splendid, if you'll allow such a word. I knew suddenly how much I'd enjoyed everything."

But now he apologized to her for his confusion, saying, "I'm sorry, darling, but I'm out in the deep field, long leg or somewhere. I've never heard of Mr. Smeed."

"He's a man who sells carpets. The worst type of 'rep,' a real bounder with a gluggy voice, and he made it quite clear that he knew all about *you!*"

"What did he say?"

"Oh, what does it matter? Can't you see he's only a symptom, a warning of what will happen if you go on playing about with criminals?"

Out in the deep field at his prep-school cricket matches Coles had not been alert; he had picked daisies and achieved renown as a dreamer.

"I don't 'play about' with criminals," he said, still out there with the ball speeding towards him. "My interest in penology is purely—"

"With their wives, then! You play about with their wives, don't you? You haven't even denied it yet because you can't. You know perfectly well that everything Harriet suspected is true."

"Harriet?" *These shadows,* he thought; *who the devil was Harriet?*

Before he could correct himself or dodge her, Lettice spat at him accurately. Tyndal, who had half risen when she'd dropped the Wedgwood, now got up and watched them with both ears cocked as Coles wiped away the cuckoo-fleck from his lapel, utterly astonished. In twenty years Lettice had never done such a thing before, there had never been any tacit violence, only the odd little accident. But now she looked about eleven, a flashing white-faced little girl quarrelling with him at a party.

"Yes, Harriet; Harriet Harvey," she said. "She knows all about it, simply because I had to confide in someone. The whole of Coniston Road knows all about it. We'll be the laughingstock of the entire community, of all my friends, or, rather, I shall be. *You* haven't got any friends here. You may not realize it, but where they're concerned you're just my husband, the father of my children."

He was lost. As he would tell Bernard weeks later, after the funeral: "I was absolutely at sea. I hadn't the remotest idea that she thought like that, that she nursed such ideas, such astonishing grievances."

"She didn't tell you the half of them," Presage would say. "My dear Coles, you mustn't blame yourself. Very few Englishmen have any idea of the resentment of modern women, their anger!"

"What on earth do you mean?" Coles asked Lettice. "Of course I've got friends here."

"Who?"

"Well, Harvey, for one."

"Edward's no friend of yours. He's a pub type, a proper one, a decent unregenerate womanizer. If he ever thinks of you at all, it's probably only with pity. Harriet makes it quite obvious that for Edward you're just a wet."

"Cattermole," Coles said angrily.

"Geoffrey's *my* friend! Recently we've become quite close in a way you'd not understand. For him you're not even a bore, only someone rather sly."

Coles jerked back his gin. "Well, my god! What do you want? Do you want me to drink and womanize out in the open? Read Hemingway and play golf with blasted Cattermole? My god!"

"Don't try to be blasphemous; it doesn't suit you. I want what I've always wanted."

She smiled to herself, not bitterly, but with appalling confidence, reminding him of those afternoons on the Cam when he'd been beside himself with lust and poetry. For a moment he saw her as she had been before their marriage, an English virgin, the daughter of her parents, the Pecks.

"I want to go on as we have done," she said. "I don't find it lonely, because I've never been in competition with anyone. I accept things. I like you to lead your life and me to lead mine provided there's no cheating, that we do it with dignity."

"But you don't like my life. You've been disapproving of it for years."

"Not for years, only recently. And, anyway, your life is nothing to do with me so long as it's decent, so long as you don't let it get out of control, so long as we continue to prove that we're right to expect nothing beyond ourselves."

Coles wandered over to the cabinet again. He knew she wouldn't stop him this time, that she couldn't afford to do so even if she wanted to. "It was a moment you would neither understand nor accept," he would tell Presage. "It was a communion without any divine principle, something at which you'd be bound to sneer because it was purely human."

He filled a glass for Lettice too, smelling the fragrance of the last wood block on the fire, the redolence of the spilled potpourri on the warm hearth. He poured half a bottle of bitter lemon into her glass and the remainder into his own; then he walked back to where she stood in front of the mantelpiece with the blue Chinese funeral dog in the center. They touched glasses and drank in silence, not kissing one another, saying nothing, but only looking into each other's eyes with what Coles later termed "refreshment."

"Well?" Lettice asked.

"I had to take a message to her. Christopher wanted to see her and his children before the police caught up with him."

"I wish you wouldn't use his christian name like that. It falsifies your relationship."

"As a matter of fact," Coles said, "I do it because he's distasteful to me."

She didn't say, "I'm glad to hear it," but he saw that she nodded to herself as if he'd said the right thing.

She said, "And, anyway, he was due for his release very shortly, wasn't he?"

"Yes, darling."

"Then he must be mad, he must need treatment of some sort."

"That's the point. That's why I got so deeply involved. It was a religious question, some kind of conversion. It wasn't that he wanted to take things into his own hands so much as to see what 'God' would do if he cheated at the end of his sentence."

She looked at the funeral dog. He saw her gazing at it as sometimes she studied the arrangement of furniture in her room, as if deciding where things might safely be.

"How ricidulous," she said, her eyes still on the dog's ceramic haunches. "Don't tell me any more. I simply don't understand how you could have let yourself get mixed up with such nonsense."

"Darling, how could I possibly have helped him if I hadn't been prepared to accept his beliefs as true for *him?*"

She ran her finger over the dog's blue back and examined it for dust.

"Taking things into his own hands, indeed!" she said. "He'd done that once already. He was a murderer—convicted."

"You don't understand."

"I don't want to. Everything you're saying is quite unacceptable. It's too late."

They paused there, a little shyly, even embarrassed by the last involuntary words. Coles was wondering how one might be too late for something that had never happened. Lettice was wishing she hadn't spoken.

The moment retreated, as if into the Chinese past, the splendid moment of the wood smoke and the incense of the potpourri. "A gap opened up between us," Coles would tell Presage. "I so desperately wanted her to understand that I hadn't broken faith with her, but she couldn't see it. She's always been so direct, absolutely direct. Women are, I suppose; they have to be."

"And his wife," Lettice said. "I don't want to intrude on your privacy; you needn't tell me if you don't want to."

"He encouraged it," Coles burst out. "Hotchkis connived at it. I didn't realize it at the time, but from the first he deliberately involved me with Betty."

"And why not? It's just the sort of thing psychopaths enjoy. You've told me so yourself heaps of times. You told me years ago that was the reason for your attempts to help these men, to prove your conduct without reference to religion, to beat them at their own game."

With steady fingers he saw her put her glass down on the mantelpiece as she said, "I think I have to know how far you went."

"I had to take this message for him—that was all."

"I mean with *her!*"

"But you said just now that you didn't want to know."

"Well, I've changed my mind. I do want to know; I've got to." She was thinking of Harriet Harvey with fury, remembering her complacent certainty that they were sisters under the skin.

Coles remembered his Cambridge days, his half-blue for running, the winter changing rooms and the simple company of vanished athletes. "The whole hog!" he said. "I'm sorry, darling, but I have to admit it. I stuffed her and I enjoyed it. It was bloody marvellous, even though I did a rotten job, worrying about you, I suppose."

She said nothing. She was as receptive as Tyndal, and he was compelled to go on, to walk, as Presage had suggested, into the indigo jaws of the underworld. At all costs he wished to continue to amaze her, to pay her back for the broken bowl, the grievances, the years of her suppression. She'd had the sexual details now, all she was ever going to get, and he'd frighten her with something else.

"As a matter of fact it was what Hotchkis had been waiting for. I mean *actually* waiting. He was there outside the cottage god knows how long and came in just as I was putting my trousers on again. It was extraordinary, staggering! We were together in this fantasy bedroom of Betty's and I heard something outside—several times. I was feeling guilty—I don't mind admitting it. I suppose one does if one's never done it before. Anyway, while we were dressing or jolly soon afterwards, he came in—"

He continued talking, telling her odd bits and pieces as if he were silently addressing someone on the stage. He watched her go over to her white telephone and dial a number as he refilled his glass.

"He's still there, then? With her at the cottage now?" she asked.

"Obviously."

She was moving a little too fast for him. He had the sense that the programme had got out of hand, that he might have to flash the studio light before the telephone calls started to come in to the

Duty Room. She was running away with it, he realized, and he must make some show of stopping her.

He said, "But look here, darling," and she ignored him, speaking not to him but into the telephone. "Is that the police station? Give me the officer on duty, please."

Coles ran across to her. There was an ugly little struggle as he covered the mouthpiece with his hand.

"You're going too fast. It's dishonest, irreverent. Hotchkis has got to have tonight. I want him to have his night at home. We've got to give him it, both of us."

She wrestled with him, amazingly strong, her sharp elbows and thin arms, her blazing eyes.

"You fool!" she whispered. "Don't you realize this could be the end of us as people? They'll trace the call. Everything we've ever been will be given away."

They stood there, panting over the telephone, the cable stretched between them.

"If you stop me now," she said, "I shall leave you and let you ruin yourself on your own."

He stood back, suddenly very courteous, a stranger who felt he might be in the way, an onlooker who was relieved to see that he was not needed after all.

"I have a message for you," Lettice said into the telephone. "It's with reference to the announcement on the B.B.C. tonight." She paused. "No, I'm sorry, but I can't wait for you to write it down. It's only that I happen to know that the escaped prisoner you're looking for, Christopher Hotchkis, who was sentenced for murder, has just returned to his home in Sumner. I can't tell you how I know this, I'm afraid; but he's there now." She paused again, listening to some question from the other end. Then she covered the mouthpiece with her hand and spoke to Coles. "They want to know if he's armed."

Coles "had" it; he experienced certainty. At last there was a moment where a single word might be used as a lie or a truth, where he could say clearly the word "no" or alternatively add one or two other words, make an inference, and so change it forever, never confiding it in anyone: never in Presage, in Lettice, in the dog, but only in himself as far as his grave. Just before he replied he had an image of himself peering through the letter box into the hall of his childhood home, the remembered furniture all in place, no new tenants yet, his entire family dead.

He said, "He was fooling about with a gun. But—"

"Yes," she said into the telephone. "Mr. Hotchkis has a gun."

"A revolver," Coles said. "But in fairness I think you ought to tell them that—"

She would never hear it; she was ticking through their relationship like a clock and he knew the customary relief.

A moment later the ease of the betrayal appalled him. He expected to feel faint; he expected the mantelpiece to shift, the funeral dog to slide from the center to one side or the other. He found himself demanding that things should never be the same again for him; but nothing happened. He watched her replace the receiver on its cradle as he sat down on the sofa to go on with it all before they went upstairs to bed.

As they started in on the careful justification of the betrayal he was really thinking about Presage, wondering where he was, wishing to god he could get in touch with him.

XVIII

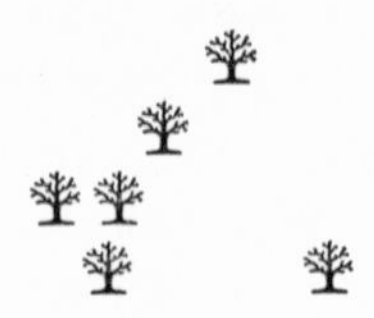

A hundred and twenty-five miles away, Bernard was lying awake in a French boardinghouse in the bed he was sharing for the second night in succession with Hera Foley. The bed was narrow, its head and foot constructed of metal sheeting grained to simulate pitch pine. Twanging like an old-fashioned cash register every time he moved, it made an effective accompaniment to his thoughts.

His principal mistakes, he realized, had been three in number: first, he should have saved or borrowed enough money to take Hera further than Calais; second, he should have had the guts to forget his religion; and, third, he should have realized that she was not greatly interested in him.

Her love-making on the first night, the Saturday, had been terrific; in the morning the lobes of his ears had been swollen to twice their normal size. "Exactly like fuchsia buds, you poor darling," she'd said at dawn. "I don't seem to be able to stop myself. I mean to be gentle, but something gets into me at the last moment and I simply can't resist a proper bite."

How busy she had been. In the small hours Bernard had reflected that one never knew about the young. In each generation they threw up the quirks which were so discomforting to their elders. He had been astonished not so much by her energy as by her matter-of-factness, the prosaic way she had clambered about on him as if she'd known him for years, from childhood, in fact. In one of the sudden sleeps she took he'd lain there beside her feeling old for the first time in his life, looking at her riven cheek not with either tenderness or satisfaction but only with happy surprise.

Originally the night had been calm—a clear, faintly luminous sky over the orchards of Kent—but, as they had approached the coast, dew had thickened on the carriage windows and they had put out from Folkestone in a sad sea mist full of appropriate winter melancholy: not a sound out on the water, not many passengers, and only the occasional braying of the ship's foghorn.

"Outward bound!" Hera had said, leaning gracefully against an ivory suitcase. "I know it's absurd, but I've never known whether to envy or despise these ghosts. They're so lucky to be dead, and yet it's so miserable for them that even on a sea journey they can't do a thing."

Gratified in some way, Bernard had nevertheless felt guilty about the expectancy of her luggage, that large suitcase, the matching vanity box and the little valise. They constituted some kind of a reproach, their shining efficiency, their acquiescence, each piece labelled in her own hand "PARIS." He had felt that very soon he'd have to tell her about Calais and, as a preliminary, had taken her down to the ship's bar to drink Americanos and stock up with tribute at duty-free prices: two hundred English king-size cigarettes and a bottle of scent.

He had been relying on what he would later describe to Coles as "the dialogue," not of their souls but of their fornication, an agreement that whatever happened externally would be accepted out of the prior unspoken contract.

"Old-fashioned of me, I suppose," he would explain. "But with so much at stake I'd been quite certain she'd accept my limitations."

"And didn't she?"

"That's the point. I'm not sure. I never shall be, dammit!"

He would say no more because later, long afterwards, he'd been as nonplussed as on that first night in the twanging bed with Hera in her ankle-length nightdress beside him. She'd appeared to take it well when, at the last moment, he'd explained that they were not getting on to the half-empty train, that Calais, even though it was not Paris, was still France and, incidentally, as much as he could afford. "Infinitely more original," he'd suggested. "The British make a great mistake in rushing through it. And," he'd added slyly, knowing how she prided herself on her accent, "the French they speak up here is second only to that of the Walloons."

She had said nothing; and because he'd loved her silences he'd not been uneasy as she'd sat opposite him sipping her pitch-black coffee. Her shadowy glance, her apathy, the reticence that bordered so closely on boredom had utterly seduced him. It was his preference for deathly beauty that had so responded to her, he had supposed—his demand that loveliness should be passive. "So little interests her," he would tell Coles. "And it's not in order to interest her that one acts. It's merely to confirm her in her own vision of things."

Throughout the rest of the evening he'd imagined that this fulfillment of her fantasy was his real function, that he was paying inescapable homage to her apathy.

"Once we'd got to Calais," he would tell Coles, "there seemed to be total understanding, no question of hurry, none of the hole-and-corner stuff that usually bedevils adultery. One gave oneself to the imposition of her dream with nineteenth-century conviction."

Time had thinned out and the mist thickened as they'd sat there in the Gare Maritime with everything round them quietening down for the night. They'd watched the ship darken beside the quay, the train moan out of the station and the restaurant staff take final drinks before slipping back to their French homes.

Outside there'd not been a taxi to be had, and for a time, Bernard, wrestling with their dream, had done his best to find one. He'd made inquiries from sleepy waiters, telephoned the dying exchange and sought out the absent stationmaster. In the end, with Hera gliding beside him, he'd carried the pretty luggage across yards of quay into the modern, concrete section of the town.

Too late by this time for a decent restaurant, they'd eaten veal and yellow *haricots verts* in a closing café, washing the food down with awful claret. Across the table, eating suddenly with extraordinary appetite, Hera had cleared her plate and gazed at him with glowing eyes. Neither then nor ever afterwards had he been sure whether this brightness were anger or distrust. At the time he'd hoped that it was the gaze of "the dialogue," that emphatic understanding in which she'd seen, as he had, the spell she had cast over Calais. The thought that it might just have been her eyes, the way they were made, had occurred to him; but he'd rejected it.

"It's horrible," she'd said of the second carafe of wine, "but let's have another."

Amid silent jukeboxes and battered football machines they'd sat on in cloudy understanding, two people united by the conspiracy of their expectation and the grey, gallic mist.

The taxi had taken them round the hotels, and at last they'd found this one somewhere on the outskirts of the town: a tall pension with blue linoleum in the corridors, a single lavatory on each floor, tiny washbasins and the metal beds. Here, beneath the steep roof on the topmost floor, the discrepancy had begun as Hera started to unpack.

"You'll want these," she'd said. "I knew that being a Roman you wouldn't have brought any." And she'd handed him not the packets of his youth but a grey plastic box, adding, "It's simply that I don't trust the pill. Mummy's gynae man is dead against it."

Undressing, she'd asked, "D'you like scent? I mean at night?"

"Of course."

"Why 'of course'?"

"Well, naturally."

"Some men don't."

Briskly she'd put on a most incongruous, a most "fetching" nightdress. Looking at it and feeling already a little out of date, Bernard had been slightly reassured—as if together they'd slipped back a generation, as if he were now some edwardian buck setting out for the "Frog" capital with his London mistress. But, dammit, he'd liked that nightdress! It had been so tactfully chosen, so right for the occasion. He'd have liked to have been able to describe it to Helen: "a kind of fine flannel, just very slightly yellow and buttoned high like those vests one wore as a child, but with a chaste little ruff at the neck."

In bed there'd been no delay about the fun and games. They'd started almost at once, catching him quite off his guard. Even before he'd put out the light or given her any preliminary caress she had started to muzzle his neck. He had managed to give her just three kisses before suddenly she was on top of him, her teeth fastened on his left ear.

"Things might have been different," he would confess to Coles, "if I'd realized. But she never gave me a chance. I got off to a thoroughly bad start and never made up for it."

"Honeycomb—Mrs. Hotchkis," Coles would admit in his turn, "was quite dissimilar. It was her lethargy that made one feel so inadequate. . . ."

Beyond the dormer window, high above the unnamed street, the mist had thickened in the small hours. Somewhere beneath them a fellow guest had snored his way into Sunday morning and Bernard, only half exultant, had drifted into sleep.

She'd awakened him almost at once, sinuous, gentle and very considerate. For a moment he'd imagined it was Helen, a confusion not merely of the place and person but of the year as well. For whenever, these days, Helen awakened him he was always thrown back to the infancy of his children, to the misery of the teething nights: the bickering, the sudden detestation of the wailing child, and the gossipy cup of tea. So now, as then, he woke cautiously, reluctant to admit to anything.

"Yes, what is it, darling?"

Her hands drew him to her, her breath was in his ear, and exultation returned; but he wondered where he'd put his wrist watch. He'd have liked to know what the time was, hoping that his misgivings were false, that he'd had his four or five hours of sleep so that this time he might take the initiative.

"You're so sweet to wake up to," she whispered, clinging to him.

He kissed her with all the conviction of uncertainty. "How long have I been asleep?"

"An hour. I thought you were never going to come back to me."

"Darling!"

But he refrained from kissing her again. He wasn't sure what its effects might be. Presumably even the young appreciated the aftermath. With any luck an encircling arm, that delicate face on his big shoulder, might gain him the time he needed. But already she had begun her climb.

Saddened by what he had called "the bruising disparity of the years," he was nevertheless extremely quick, shifting his great weight adroitly, the bed clanging to his move. But she pursued him across the narrow space and he flattened her suddenly, resting his head beside her on the pillow, kissing her neck and lips with somnolent affection, but holding her down, pinning her there beneath him, a giant not exhausted but only a little huge and careless.

He longed for the ultimate honesty, the courage to tell her that he was still *hors de combat;* but could not reach it and had to feign the sleep which was eluding him. Whispering inarticulately, he continued his kisses and allowed himself to slacken like Goliath falling, to slide almost imperceptibly off her and so delay until dawn.

It was four A.M. when she next woke him, rolling him gently on to his back, sliding on to him hardly perceptibly. The long nightdress was ruffed up round her neck and shoulders like a stole, and for a moment he was confused, imagining he must have got his head under the blankets.

"God!" she whispered between kisses. "I want you so much."

"What time is it?"

"Four; we've wasted hours."

He struggled courteously with the folds of the nightdress, trying to get it away from his mouth, and she whipped it off completely without even momentarily changing her position. He craned his head over her shoulder to look towards the window and see if there were any glimmer of Sunday morning out there. Her lips were nuzzling his injured ear, and as he dodged her he heard her laughter echo the twang of the bed.

"Were you afraid I'd bite?"

"Yes."

"You didn't give me time, you beast."

She relaxed then, slipping from him to lie absolutely still beside him; but he didn't trust her. He'd never realized before that he had developed habits. Helen, he thought angrily, had betrayed him.

"Please!" Hera said.

He hadn't shot his bolt yet; but he was going to be honest: the good old missionary position—all the conventions. "A gentleman," Helen had said, "always takes the weight on his elbows," and sometimes she'd asked him, too, if he'd been thinking of anyone else.

Quite certain of himself, as much justified as he ever would be, he'd begun to make love in the accustomed style until suddenly he realized that she'd kicked off all the bedclothes and that both her legs were in the air. He hadn't noticed it at first, but, searching for the eider down, he'd caught sight of a shadowy foot just above his head.

It annoyed him. He realized that for some time now he'd suspected her of overplaying the hand, of implying that he was not a success. This, after all, was not Paris, he thought. No tricks were needed, no professional simulation. Either he had to teach the little wretch manners or else instruct her in passion; and both, under the circumstances, were beyond him. The dialogue, if it ever existed, had broken down.

Later he'd mourned something in the graceless aftermath, an idea he'd had of eternal conversation, of real complicity. And it was as he realized that even the body resented lies that he'd seen the devil of his childhood, the one he'd been brought up on, not suave at all, unexpected rather than intrinsically evil, a clown rather than a serpent. As in those days when he'd hurried into things, those precocious haystack games, those tunnels in the bracken, those desperate thefts, the clown had seemed to spring out of the action itself, deftly cheating him of full satisfaction, smiling broadly, comically determined that next time, if he'd only try again, it would come off.

Tonight he could almost smell the powder and paint. Even before it was over he could see all the props: the buffoon bed, the dated nightdress so perfectly chosen, the romantic, intransigent mist. Agile, flour-faced, the clown—master of the empty ring—had watched the collapse of the elderly party.

He had awakened again at dawn, and somewhere out in the mist a bell was tolling for mass. He lay there in the cold bedroom, trying to resist a lifetime of habit, the need to define the day, to put up some kind of a marker to the week that had ended. Of late there had been reminders that he was more than halfway through his life; of late, he remembered, he'd found himself becoming more curious about the aged than the young.

The church was quite near, nearer than the nearest French bell buoy, warning of shallows or some sunken derelict in the Calais roads. The bell tolled steadily, without fluctuation, as if across a windless sea—a message as remote as morse, as personal.

He dressed irritably. He'd left it too late; he didn't even know in which direction the church lay, and at this hour there'd be no one to ask. He should have recognized his decision before the bell stopped; then he could have tracked it down in the mist, loped towards it and found a place decently, not at the back, but to one or other side of the chancel, whence he might watch. He needed time for this sort of thing too, he realized.

Behind him on the bed Hera awoke. He'd imagined that she was still asleep, that it might even be safe to kiss her before he left.

As he hesitated beside the door, she asked: "Where on earth are you going?"

"To mass."

She stared at him for a moment, most beautiful, her long eyelids blurred with mascara, her lacquered hair dark against the pillow. She closed her eyes and yawned; he saw the morning pallor of her tongue against her pale-mauve lips, a shred of tobacco between her white teeth.

"Why didn't you tell me?"

"You were asleep."

"I wasn't. I was watching you."

"Do you want to come with me?"

"To mass?"

"Yes."

"Darling!"

She laughed then, not into the pillow, not at him, but as insultingly as possible.

"You'll be awfully late, won't you? Or doesn't that matter?"

"I don't know." He'd been "early" twice during the night, and she would have agreed that this did matter.

"In any case, there's no time to decide," he said.

"What about me?"

"I'll pray for us both, I expect." He twitched at his awful Portland Place sports shirt, the one he wore for encounters with Coles. He hadn't shaved; in mid-November he looked like the most transient kind of summer tripper.

"You old hypocrite."

"I know."

"You don't really believe in it, do you?"

"No. But sometimes I weaken."

He wanted to ask her if she really believed in sex; but he was afraid she knew that she didn't.

"I was looking forward to our morning together," she said.

"We'll have it when I come back."

"No! Now!"

"Not now."

"But I want you; I mean it."

So do I, he thought. *I reciprocate everything you feel for me and probably, since I'm older, more; but you're not a fact for me; facts are bad enough, but non-facts are lethal.*

"Darling, when I come back we'll make up for it," he promised.

"It won't be the same—not you, I mean, but me: I'll be different."

"Little one, get some sleep. It's still frightfully early and I'll lay on a delicious breakfast for you—fresh croissants."

"I don't want breakfast. I want you."

"You promised me you were never reasonable."

"This is different," she said. "It's so absurdly practical, as practical as some of Charles' gambits, but even more offensive. We came for each other, not for a lot of mumbo jumbo."

"For me it isn't mumbo jumbo; it's a necessity." More of an enormity than sex, he wanted to say, and older if anything. How have you managed to escape it all? But he only said: "It's what I am, and we did agree to be honest."

She sat up, naked, pathetic—her young breasts, her tiny collar bones, her newly shaven armpits, all as fragile as their argument.

"You really are an astonishing man. Don't you realize that this is the only unforgivable thing you could do to me? The only really selfish and sordid thing? Just look at this ghastly room, this lousy bed, the foul dinner we had, the whole horrible north frenchness of Calais, when we'd agreed on France."

"I know."

"And the only sure way of making yourself what you really are—old and set."

Better now than later, he thought. He knew he was being drawn away as if he were out there on the sea in a subtle inescapable current. The hateful accuracy of her description made him see himself as a comic bather in a seaside post card.

He said, "Darling, couldn't you pretend to yourself that I'm only going out to get the newspapers or fresh milk or something?"

Her face changed, frozen for a moment and then cross-browed, her forehead hatched with waxen lines. He saw her shudder with fury and then collect herself as she asked: "How can you be so damned dishonest with me? With yourself?"

Anger would have helped him, but not guilt; he was too accustomed to it. If he'd been able to argue or explain out of some accepted emotion, he might have been able to make her understand; but nowadays his emotions never burned themselves out, his distrust of them always let him down.

"It's a habit," he said, "in the bones. You must have something like that yourself, some ritual or other? The difference between us is that although I'm stuck with belief in God I don't any longer see it as unlikely—as weakness. That's what middle age is: it's the moment when you no longer want to be free, when you start to hug your own bones."

"I haven't got any. I don't want any. I don't even want to be free, because there's nothing to be free from."

"How on earth can I argue with you?"

"You can't. You're not just a hypocrite; you're a coward. You're not even that really, because you're not a man. And to think I came away with you only because I was sick of all those little London pimps!" She laughed falsely. "Ha-ha! What a joke!"

She lay down again, pulling up first the bedclothes to her neck and then, with those reddened finger tips, the fold of the sheet until it covered her face completely. He saw that she lay perfectly still beneath it, a little girl playing possum or acting out a crude imitation of death.

He ran back to pull the sheet down again; but she held it from beneath, convulsively. "Go away! I don't want you. You're a bore."

Pausing by the door, he saw his face in the mirror above the washbasin: mottle-cheeked, jowly, ludicrously hurt. He closed the door quietly and went slowly down the stairs past the sleepy landlord and out through the bar into the grey street.

On the way back he cut loose. A little sunshine was penetrating the mist, illuminating a distant square—the town center perhaps. It seemed as if somewhere the morning had begun, not in his immediate vicinity, but at a little distance, at the end of the street in which he was. He pursued it, the suggestion of dyed awnings, of shops and cafés open, of flower sellers. But when he reached it there was little sunlight, less activity, and it was not the town center.

An hour or more had elapsed and he was not going to return empty-handed. This was the time for generosity, for youthfulness, for a new beginning. Distinctly he was coming into a more live part of the town. He could hear the rumble of a cart, the horn of a taxi, the sound of shutters being opened. In the distance the sun had broken through, there was colour, frenchness. He hurried along towards it, a square with railed gardens and autumnal flower beds not yet cleared. He went into a café and drank coffee, awaiting the brioches they had promised him. He found a patisserie and bought tiny éclairs filled with Saturday's cream. In a tabac he bought her a hundred french cigarettes and the latest magazines full of dubious news about the Royal Family—the kind of thing she most enjoyed, a chance for her excellent french and her fashionable republicanism.

He went into the hotel by the side door, climbed the stairs nervously, his gifts in their tissue paper, a kind of shield. But the bedroom was empty, last night's clothes still on the back of the chair and on the floor, the nightdress draped over the head of the bed, the dressing table a mass of bottles and face powder. On the mirror in her lenten lipstick she had written:

ARE WE SHRIVEN?
SCRAMBLED EGGS AT THE RITZ.

It was signed with an arrow pointing downwards.

She had been into her suitcases. They were both half-open, underclothes protruding from beneath the lids.

He found her in the bar with the landlord, who was still in his shirt sleeves, his thin mud-grey hair *en brosse,* his eyes fixed and reproachful. Bernard recognized the nature of the reproach: the man was sixty or more and unhealthy, his face blotchy with the *fines* of Saturday night; but even at this hour his heart was stirring to the soldierly glory of Hera.

She was drinking pernod and talking too fluently for Bernard to follow accurately. He recognized only her determination: at intervals her "hein?"—as velvety and inquiring as if she'd been born in Meudon. She wore a startling make-up: her face white, her lipstick off-white, her hair, eyebrows and eyelashes pitch-black. She sat on the high stool as if someone else had posed her there, pulled back the sleeve of her jacket to expose the fine bones of her wrist, selected for her the crude pink of her coat and skirt, the violet military frogs round the buttonholes—some fashion photographer who'd advised her to wear no stockings but to allow an edge of victorian lace to push beyond the hem of the skirt. One of her sandals was off, the other a mere stirrup over which she curled her ugly little toes.

She gave Bernard a casual glance and a wave and went on with her conversation, utterly absorbed in it, as, stealthily, the patron drank his mandarin in pursuit of her. His pursuit was as obvious as her artifice, an undeniable thing—an old man in a dream that was neither good nor bad but only inescapable. The man was spellbound. He hoped that soon he might size up the situation, see it as "du business," and decide what, if anything, he was being offered. But Hera didn't wish him to catch up with her, and he sensed this too. She was running free, neither a fox nor a hound: a young woman on the loose and probably angry.

"I thought you might like these," Bernard said.

"What are they? Not cakes?"

"Why don't you open them and see?"

She did so, patiently, with a kind of parental indulgence, as if she were offering to share the tribute, however inappropriate, with the landlord.

"Éclairs?" she asked. "In the *morning!*"

"You don't have to eat them now. I thought we might have them with coffee later on."

"I *never* eat them. Does Helen?"

"Helen?"

"Your wife, Bernard. Surely you remembered her too at your mass?"

She apologized for him to the landlord: a *moue,* very practiced. *"Hélène,"* she explained, *"sa femme. Il est mon oncle."*

"Darling!" Bernard began.

"Mon beau-père. Plutôt," she decided, explaining to the landlord that he had just been to mass. *"Il est croyant, voyez-vous? Les vieux sont tous croyants, n'est-ce-pas?"*

The landlord refilled his glass with a mineral. There was something a little unusual here, something reminiscent perhaps of the works of Monsieur Simenon. On the other hand, it was possible that the girl was pulling his leg, and had it been later in the day he'd have known how to respond. Certainly, whatever their relationship, these two had quarrelled.

Hera turned to Bernard courteously.

"Well, did you enjoy it?" she asked.

"The mass?"

"Yes. Was it satisfying?"

"Not particularly."

"Tell me about it."

"It was very clean and precise. I enjoyed the vernacular."

The celebrant had faced the people at a fenestrated altar backed by grey and pink. There had been many memorials on the walls and many black-clad widows in the congregation—an impression of the nearness of the two wars.

"Clean?" she asked. "No dirty lace, you mean?"

There was hope for them yet, he thought. She had recognizable prejudices, and therefore he could not resist confiding in her.

"I meant the priest. It sounds absurd, but he looked like one of those old-fashioned dentists, crisp and very professional."

She turned away from him and explained this to the landlord. He heard the starts and glides of her tongue as she told him that her *beau-père* was a writer, a little eccentric. He was not "of a certain age, you understand," he heard her say, but "an original." "He has just described the mass to me and said that *Monsieur le Curé* was like a dentist!"

The landlord picked up a corkscrew and Hera opened her mouth for him while he pretended to probe a molar. Then he gave Bernard a drink and together, for half an hour or more, they watched her turn over the pages of the magazines. . . .

Later she had slipped from her stool to go, as Bernard had supposed, upstairs. But she did not return, and when, eventually, he went up to the bedroom to tell her that he'd ordered a car for a trip to some dark inland village he found another message on the mirror. It said:

I HAVE GONE FOR A WALK.

This message was the beginning of that unforgettable Sunday over which he brooded as he lay beside her on the second night, listening to the rise and fall of her drugged breathing. Initially he had no idea that worse things awaited him.

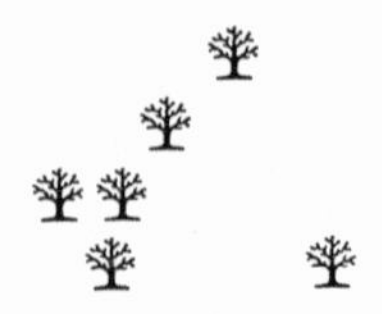

In Sussex the police cordoned off the village soon after Sunday midnight. They came in black Humbers and on grey Villiers-engined motorcycles. A number of them were equipped with two-way radio, and the two plain-clothes men under Sergeant Caine, charged with the actual arrest, carried revolvers. Caine stationed them in front of and behind the Hotchkis cottage, peered through the window into the empty sitting room where the fire still glowed, and tried the front door. It was not locked and he stepped inside, waiting there for a few moments to place the furniture with the aid of his flashlight. He located the light switch but decided against putting it on. Instead he stood beside it at the foot of the narrow staircase, well to one side in the doorway leading through to the kitchen.

He leaned forwards and called up to the tiny landing, where he could see the closed bedroom doors. He heard someone get out of bed and saw the latch of the left-hand door lift soundlessly. He stepped back into the kitchen, out of range.

"Make it sharp, Hotchkis!" he advised. "And don't bring your gun with you. The village is cordoned and the men outside this house are armed."

Betty had thrown an old country overcoat over her black nightdress, and he heard the rustle of it as she descended the stairs. He flashed a torch beam up at her, saw her naked feet and her white sulky face. At the bottom of the staircase he caught her hand before she could switch on the light.

"No lights, please!" he said. "Where is he?"

" 'E's not here."

"Come on! It's no good wasting time."

"I wasn't expecting you till morning."

"We got a tip-off."

"Dad?" She yawned.

"Your father's waiting in one of the cars."

"Dirty old beast! What business is it of his?"

"No business. He knows nothing about it."

"Well, what's the connection, then?"

"We picked him up outside the Cross Keys. He'd been breaking the licensing laws with old Walters."

Coles then, she thought. Toffee-nosed little drip.

"We don't know who it was," Caine went on. "It was anonymous, but it doesn't alter your position. You could be in trouble, you know, for not reporting it."

"I could, could I?"

"But you can make up for it now, by saving us time."

She brushed past him to the fireplace, standing there with her hands in the pockets of the overcoat.

"You've got nothing on me. Chris isn't here and you don't even know if I've seen him."

"Where is he?"

"How do I know? You can search the place so long as you don't disturb the kids. You can search me too, but it won't do you no good." She shivered. "Coo! It isn't half cold in here. Why didn't you make up the fire while you were at it—breakin' and enterin'?"

She stooped and poked at it in a bored way.

"I want him, Betty. There's a lot of men waiting outside, and they're liable to get nasty if they're kept there unnecessarily."

"How many?"

"Enough."

"Outside the cottage, too?" she asked.

"I told you."

With vague interest she looked over towards the window.

"Looking in, I'll bet. Keeping an eye on you."

He kept a tight hold on himself but said nothing.

"Eerie, isn't it?" she went on. "It makes you feel embarrassed—like being on the television or something." She pushed a curl behind her ear.

"Now listen," he said. "Do you want the kids waking up and the neighbours disturbing or are you going to be sensible?"

"I'm always sensible. I'm not frightened, see? Men don't frighten me, in uniform or out of it. If you want my help, you'll get it quicker if you don't rush me."

"Nobody's rushing you. I'm being very patient, but I want Hotchkis and I want him now. You understand that much, don't you?"

She smiled to herself. "Of course I do. You're Paul's brother, aren't you? And between us we got him killed."

Caine felt a kind of certainty in himself—not lust, not a substitute for it, but something he'd known ever since his school days. He hated criminals, but he never lost his temper either with them or with their "associates," by which he meant not only their friends but their families too. In his trouser pocket his hand found and held the head of his night stick, slung inside his trouser leg. It was firmer than his genitals, more useful really, more rewarding. His father had always approved his ambition.

"If you'd left it till morning, as you said," she went on, "it would have been easier for you. But men don't keep their word. And cops—"

She left it like that and they watched each other.

He said, "And have all the press mixed up in it? Radio and cameras?"

"Why not?"

She hadn't thought of that; she'd been near to it when he mentioned the police outside, but now the idea really reached her, affected her. She could be in a play, she realized: the prisoner's wife. She could be judged by people; either she could stand by

Christopher or she could act bored, like Pery. Pery always acted bored.

"It's better at night," Caine said. "These things are best done quietly. In the long run publicity does no one any good."

"Regular night birds, aren't you? Just like the Nazis."

"There are others who work at nights," he said before he could stop himself.

"Who?"

"You ought to know."

She slackened by the mantelpiece: old, giving up.

"Right," she said. "Go and get him. He's over the road at Dad's place and I'm tired."

She was; she was very tired. She didn't feel like dying, though she wouldn't have minded if they'd all come in to carry her out the way they had Mother that Christmas. There wasn't much to life if you didn't count upstairs, Marc and Debrah; and she wasn't sure if they were enough. She'd been with the kids more lately, surprising herself by watching them. "Not watching over them," she'd told Bill Smeed; "nobody can do that. But just looking. I like looking at them because they don't know anything." She didn't want them to know anything about this yet, either; that was why she'd given in.

"The gun?" Caine said. "Hotchkis has got it with him, has he?"

"There's nothing in it."

"How do you know?"

"He told us."

"Us?"

"Me," she said. She wouldn't betray Coles, poor little fellow, frightened of his own shadow. She wasn't sorry for him; she was just tired of him—and, anyway, she'd led him on all right, deliberately, but more out of boredom than interest. Besides, she'd wanted to go on mixing things for Chris.

"Did he open it for you?" Caine insisted. "Did you see inside the chambers?"

"What're you talking about? What chambers?"

"The chambers of the gun, the revolver."

"I wasn't that interested. It was a joke really, one of his capers."

Like the caper that killed Paul, Caine thought, his hand falling slack in his pocket. He said, "Well then, you don't know whether it was loaded or not?"

She smiled. *"I* do. It's you that doesn't know."

"If you believe that, you'd believe anything."

"It's what Chris said. If I was to tell you it wasn't loaded, you wouldn't believe me neither, so what's the difference?"

He'd thought for a moment that she was coming to it, that she was going to have said: "You don't believe me because you don't want to." But she hadn't bothered. Had she done so, he'd have played it off the top of his head. We ask, he knew, not to find out precisely, but to weigh up probability. Probability's all you get with people these days. He'd enjoyed discussing things like that in the sixth form at the grammar school; and but for Paul's death he'd have made university, instead of going straight for the pale-blue hatband of the police cadets.

"But he's got it with him?" he repeated.

He wanted to be quite certain of this. It justified everything: the transport allocation of three cars and four motorcycles, the two radios and twenty-five men, all out there in the dark, waiting to clear things up. It would ease him a little to know that another mess had been mopped up. It wouldn't be final, because nothing ever was, not even fairness. He believed in fairness because it was the one thing they had over the others: certainly criminals were never fair. In his position a criminal would have been nursing hatred—and not only a criminal, but society too, for that matter. But he was only doing his job; his fairness had his hatred strapped inside it like his truncheon.

"Well?" he asked.

"Well, what?"

"Just tell me whether he's still got it with him—that's all." He was getting a little nervous. It would not be enough that Hotchkis should only have been thought to be armed.

"Oh, sod his revolver," she said. "I didn't even look at it. I wouldn't know the difference between a revolver and a gun, and anyway I'm sick of you men and your weapons."

"He didn't give it to you to hide? He didn't hide it himself?"

"Why ask me when you never believe a word anyone says? Why not go and find out?"

"And if someone else gets killed?"

"Oh, all right!" she said, giving up for the second time. "The last time I saw it it was on the bed, and the bed's opposite the door, on the right as you go in, and Chris'll be waiting by the window for the light to go on: once, if he's in the clear—twice, if you're here. Anything else you want to know?"

It had been worth waiting for and he hadn't put a foot wrong. It could even have been taped and played over in court without trouble. It had worked beautifully, the way things usually did if you kept your head.

He said, "You'd better get upstairs. You could watch from up there, and in case there's any rough stuff you could tell the kids a story."

"Unless you frighten him, Chris won't give you no trouble. All you've got to do is tell him you've come and he'll come out to you. If there's any rough stuff, I won't be telling the kids stories; I'll be telling the press."

He looked at her and she narrowed into focus like a target on the range, properly identified.

"And be believed?" he asked.

But she said: "I know all about your ways. You never mark them when you're roughing them up, do you? Not when you've got them down at the station."

"What about that 'us' just now?" he asked stolidly. "What about the telephone call, the tip-off? Someone else must have known. Someone else must have been here with you."

"But this isn't the station, is it?" she said. "So you've got to be careful. Just imagine me screaming out—the neighbours, all the witnesses there'd be."

"Never mind that," he said. "Just tell me for a change who was with you when he arrived."

"I dunno what you mean."

"You've had a man in." He winked and rubbed at his eye immediately afterwards as if a speck of dust had troubled it. "But I could forget that, couldn't I?"

She started up the staircase, loose, barefooted, in no hurry. "What a brother!" she said. "If Paul had been anything like you, he'd have been safe from us. I wouldn't have touched him with rubber gloves on."

His straight blue eyes blinked under the shining peak of his cap as they watched her go upstairs again. As soon as she had shut the bedroom door he put his hand lazily up to the light switch. He switched it on and off once, counted three, and repeated the warning flash. He wanted Hotchkis to know that he was coming; it was the last little touch, the reward.

Outside the door in the empty village road he told the other two, "Yes, he's got it with him all right. She doesn't know how many rounds."

Back at Divisional Headquarters, an hour after the ambulance had left, Caine and the two constables "straightened" their notebooks. It was three A.M. and they were drinking tea prepared by one of the night staff. There was neon lighting at H.Q., but they had ceased to notice it, though unconsciously they were each in the presence of older people, because the light aged everything: the tea looked weaker, the sugar and their scalps and faces greyer. Only sounds were unaffected; their lack of confidence no older, their voices the same.

Caine read aloud to them from his preliminary notes: " 'The prisoner appeared to go down suddenly, striking the back of his head on the paved floor adjacent to the window.' " He paused, not to drink his cup of tea, but to be confirmed by their attention.

" 'In the course of making the arrest,' " he went on, " 'the prisoner tripped me and I therefore fell on top of him.' "

"No carpeting under the window," Constable Brown said. "You should make that clear, Sarge."

"Paved floor," Caine said. "Giving evidence, never tell more than is necessary." And he went straight on in the same twenty-nine-year-old voice. "Re the interview with Mrs. Hotchkis: I've said, 'Immediately prior to the arrest I interviewed the prisoner's wife—' "

"He was long enough, wasn't he, Charlie?" Brown asked Constable Smithers. But Smithers was discreet. "Stow it, Brownie. We've got to get this straight up before morning."

Caine started again. "Re the interview with Mrs. Hotchkis: 'Immediately prior to the arrest I interviewed the prisoner's wife. She was unable to tell me whether or not Hotchkis' gun was loaded. I was under the impression that it was. It certainly sounded as though he was loading it during the exchange through the door. All I know was that the prisoner was armed.' "

"Exchange?" Brown asked. "You mean remarks?"

"I mean what Hotchkis said through the door before we bounced him."

"A click," Smithers said; "a sort of a click."

"Sort of nothing," Caine said. "Hotchkis had opened the magazine, or he'd cocked it."

"The latch," Smithers said. "We agreed we'd say we thought it was the latch, remember?"

Caine read from his notes. " 'In resisting the arrest the prisoner had bolted the window and locked the door.' " He looked at them. "That being the case, there was no object in him trying the latch, was there? Get it in your notes."

"Yes, Sarge. We heard him put the revolver on cock?"

"Off the safety catch," Caine said.

"Not too much cock," Brown said. "We don't want them to get us wrong."

"Here, Sarge; do we have to list the remarks? What he said before we got in?"

"It was newspaper stuff," Brown said. "He was reading it out of *The People*. That stuff about the Muscle Man. I was reading it meself to Hilda after dinner."

"No need to be specific," Caine told them, remembering the arrest.

Hotchkis had called out, "Did you get your Sunday newspapers, Sergeant?"

"Open that door, Hotchkis."

"Got to give you the word," Hotchkis had said. "What about this from *The People?* I quote: 'My body certainly led me into trouble with women. I suppose it was being married to a film star and having good muscular development. I did not have the body beautiful exactly, but what they call magnetism, personal magnetism; and I must confess, like Errol Flynn, that this led me into many difficulties with what they used to call the fair sex.' "

"The village is cordoned, Hotchkis. If you've got a gun in there, either throw it out the window or hand it through the door, butt first."

Hotchkis had ignored the order, carrying straight on with the life story from the newspaper.

" 'Had I not been invited to Hollywood, things might have been different. There were many times when I wished I had remained on the building site, married to my English wife, Jenny; but the money was tempting and I had no idea what the offer would entail.' "

"Open that door, Hotchkis . . ."

Caine spoke into the three-A.M. silence of the H.Q. Duty Room: "This tea's cold."

"You let it go cold," Brown said. "He forgot all about it, didn't he, Smithy? Lining us up. Look, Sarge, do you want a report of what was said prior to the bounce?"

"Only about the book," Caine said. "There'd be no harm in referring to him reading from that book. It shows disturbance, really."

"He means the poetry. Where did he get it, Sarge?"

"The Scrubbs probably. He was in the library there for six months. No need to give any details, though. Just mention that the prisoner read out this French stuff or whatever it was."

Hotchkis had come close up to the other side of the door. He'd said, "I'm sorry for what I did to your brother. I can't explain it. It was something inside me that got out when I knew he'd had our Betty."

Caine had written in his report: *"Personally I bore the prisoner no resentment. I did not volunteer for this arrest. I was merely obeying orders."*

Smithers and Brown had moved over to the cottage fireplace, where the wood had still smouldered on the hearth, just after Hotchkis had started on the personal stuff.

"I must ask you to open that door immediately," Caine had said, "having first satisfied me that you are no longer armed."

But Hotchkis had continued: "I've got something better here, Peter—a book I got from the Nick library. It's a prisoner talking to his heart, and it's good. He hears his heart speaking to him and he says:

" 'Who is this I hear?'

"And his heart says:

" 'This is I, thine heart that holds on merely now by a slender string. Strength fails me, shape and sense are rent apart, the blood in me is turned to a bitter thing,
Seeing thee skulk here like a dog shivering–'

" 'Yes and for what?' the prisoner asks.

"And his heart says:

" 'For that thy sense found sweet?'

"And the prisoner says:

" 'What matters it to you?'

"And his heart says:

" 'I feel the sting of it.'

"And he says:

" 'Stop up. Leave me at peace.
I will repent when I grow wiser.'

"And his heart says:

" 'I say no more–'

"And he says:

" 'I care not though thou cease.' "

"You're only wasting time, Hotchkis. I've given you fair warning. If you don't open that door you'll have to take the consequences."
But Hotchkis went on.

"This prisoner's heart said to him:

" 'Is it hot lust that spurs thee with its sting?
Grasping thy throat? Knowst thou not anything?'

"And the prisoner said:

" 'Yes, black and white I know when milk is specked with fly, this I can make out.'

"And his heart says:

" 'No more?'

" 'No, in no wise,' he says.

"And his heart says:

" 'I say no more.'

"And the prisoner says:

" 'I care not though thou cease.' "

While Hotchkis was still reciting it, Caine had called Brown and Smithers back to him. When Hotchkis finished, Caine called them up and they came briskly. They had all three heard something move in there.

"Don't try the windows, Hotchkis," Caine had warned, "unless it's to throw out your gun."

"That poem's all right, isn't it?" Hotchkis insisted. "You've got to admit it's the way a man thinks, as if he was a whole person with two voices."

"Ask him what he's got in the gun," Brown suggested.

Smithers said, "Leave it to the sergeant."

They had heard a dead silence in there, as if Hotchkis were mewed up in it. They felt that the time was very significant—the silence like the cocking of a gun.

Brown had broken at this point, stepping right out of line. He'd called out to Hotchkis: "Look, mate, are you coming out or d'you want us to come in and get you?"

"What did he say?" Smithers asked.

"He's nuts," Brown said. "He said he'd prefer the garden."

Caine faced them, his back to the brown door.

"Hotchkis isn't nuts," he said. "He's classified as a hysteric, and you remember something about that from your lectures."

"A hysteric is unpredictable," Smithers said. "They think themselves into things."

"And you go in and get them," Brown said, Caine's eyes on the revolver in his hand. "Yes, Sarge?"

"No, Brown; no shooting unless I give the word."

He led the way back to the fireplace, a good distance from the door. "We'll have to rush him," he said. "Someone might get one in the leg, but it's not likely; and that door's sheer television, the sort one man could bust. Are you ready?"

They went in through the door like dogs through a paper hoop and straight across the carpet towards the window, where Hotchkis was standing. He raised his arms to shoulder level "like an old Jew in the market," as Brown later told his wife, Hilda. "He looked real comical with his head on one side. He said something like, 'Steady on, boys; there's only one of me. If you want the goods, don't maul them.' "

He went down like a pin in the bowling alley with Caine on top of him, and they all heard his head crack as sharply as a coconut.

"Well, that'll about do," Caine said now, looking at the Duty Room clock. "It's not so much what you mention in a report as what you leave out, and as things stand it's a question of not contradicting each other."

"Of course," Brown said. "If 'Otchkis comes round in the hospital he could make a statement. Did you brief Mac before he went on the bedside watch?"

"I briefed them both," Caine said. "But don't forget that in concussion it's the proximate memories that return last."

"Proximate?"

"Brownie!" said Smithers. " 'Proximate' means 'nearest.' It means that even if the bastard does recover it'll be months before he gets back to Sunday night. He'll be living his honeymoon over again and all that jazz before he gets up to the present."

"Your lectures," Caine said. "Didn't you take any notes, Brownie?"

"It's words like 'proximate,' " Brown said. "Why can't they say what they mean? It's a turn-out, though, isn't it? A fellow only remembering the past. You can't help wondering when he'll catch up with the last thing that happened to him, can you?"

In the hospital, with Constable McTaggert on watch behind the screens, Hotchkis retained the image of many men falling upon him. He knew he was dying and found it very easy and happy, at once a surrender and a relief.

XX

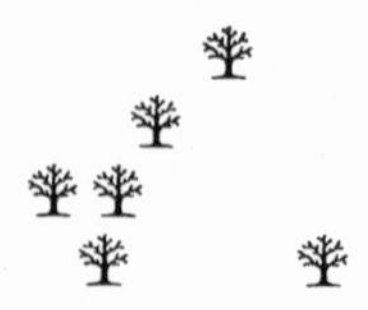

After the inquest an uncle of Christopher Hotchkis, one of his few surviving relatives, got in touch with the parish priest and arranged for a funeral mass. Betty Hotchkis wrote to Coles angrily, asking him to intervene, and he refused.

Now, discussing it with Presage in Shirreff's Wine Bar on the Thursday, Randall was fidgety about attending the ceremony himself; but Presage, who had just opened a bottle of nonvintage champagne, was truculent.

"We can neither of us dodge it. We let him down."

In Coles' longing to tell him how much he had let Hotchkis down his foot jerked beneath the table. He must be careful not to drink too much, to remember Lettice's warning: "Whatever happens, don't be tempted to drop the slightest hint. People always know."

"I can't honestly see what it's got to do with *you,* Bernard; you only got interested at the last moment."

"Tell me of a better. Tomorrow morning we must see him out, Coles."

"It's absolutely pointless and, in my view, in rather bad taste."

"It used not to be. Before the divorce."

"What are you talking about?"

"Secularism—death being in worse taste than adultery."

"And, anyway, I hate weddings—funerals, I mean."

"Burials," Presage said.

"It's the champagne. I didn't mean that death was in bad taste; I meant that our attendance at the funeral would be an invasion of privacy. And, in any case, Lettice is dead against it."

"Dead!" Presage repeated, taking a good gulp of the wine.

"So far I've been extremely lucky not to have been involved in all the publicity."

"The brouhaha!" Bernard said, thinking of Calais.

"She'd be furious if it ever got out—if there were any newspaper reports."

"Ah! The inquest. Sergeant Caine was pretty smooth, I thought. I suspected a certain amount of homework. Did you read his evidence?"

"No," Coles lied.

Presage refilled his glass for him. "There would be no need for Lettice to know. We could sneak off together in the morning; it's only an hour from Victoria. We've had a lot of practice lately."

"All that is over. We agreed not to refer to it again."

"Also," Bernard went on remorselessly, "it mightn't be a bad thing from the point of view of the Corporation."

"What the devil's it got to do with the Corporation?"

"I believe it's been suggested that you ought occasionally to participate. The Suite's got the idea that by the nineteen seventies you're going to be in again in quite a big way."

"You mean personally?"

"I mean the department—R.B. There are signs of a revival in the ratings, a suspicion that the present policy's getting a bit dated—all this peripheralism, this softly-softly-catchee-Baptist approach."

"And therefore I ought to go to the funeral? In order to conform to Corporation trends?"

"No," Bernard admitted; "I was improvising."

"Well, it's in damn bad taste. You know that within three years I'll either have taken over from George and be running Religious Broadcasting or I'll have been given the push."

"There's always retirement."

"I can't afford to retire. Lettice doesn't want me to."

"I'm sorry, Coles. It's only that I wanted you to come with me. I'd been rather looking forward to it."

Coles was mollified; but it was a pity that these things invariably happened too late.

"Why on earth should you want *me?*"

"I need your support." Bernard began to occupy the tabletop, his thick, tweed-clad arms pushing glasses and empty bottles ahead of him. "As in the other business—our adultery."

Coles took off his glasses and put them on again, waiting.

"We were able to compare notes all along the course," Presage continued, "right up to the final fence."

"A great mistake. We should have had the guts to keep it to ourselves."

"Next time—"

"For me there won't me a 'next time.' The whole thing was quite absurd and rather sordid."

As Bernard picked up the bottle Coles put a hand over the mouth of his glass, but Bernard poured the champagne through his fingers as if he were the server cleansing a celebrant's hands.

Coles fussed with his pale-yellow silk handkerchief, mopping himself dry; he pushed his chair an inch or two back to get Bernard's face into focus.

"In any case," he said, "I'd have thought the two situations were scarcely comparable."

"They are very similar, if one is honest: two gentlemen in season paying their final respects to a third."

"I don't think Christopher Hotchkis ever thought of himself as a gentleman."

"He was more; he was an aristocrat."

"Oh well," Coles said, nearly simpering.

"I don't know about you, but I'd brooded about my own infidelity for years, right up to the final moment, the trip to France."

Coles was silent.

"I did tell you about Calais, didn't I?" Bernard asked.

"You told me far too much."

"I couldn't have done, because there are parts of it I haven't even told myself yet. I mean there were."

Coles edged his chair a little further back from the table. He couldn't quite make the decision to go.

"What did you miss out?"

"It's extremely confidential, extremely painful. How's that bottle?"

"Empty. I can't spare too long because I promised Lettice–"

"Extremely!" Bernard repeated, pushing the whole table ahead of him. "Extremely confidential and extremely painful. Order another. I haven't yet worked out a good straightforward confession. There was a moment in the middle of the night when I thought Mrs. Foley might be dead."

"Good God!"

"Dead, Coles. Lying there beside me in the dark in Calais. Where's that waiter?"

"I'm sorry, Bernard, but I'm out of funds. Lettice is keeping me rather short at the moment."

"I thought Hera had taken the evening boat back to Folkestone; but I had to hang on because her luggage was still in the bedroom. When I eventually got back there on the Sunday night after searching the entire town, I found her already in bed, very uncommunicative, very sleepy. I undressed and got in beside her, and it was then that she told me she'd taken tablets– If you're short of cash, tell them to chalk it up."

"I'll do it on the way back. I have to go downstairs for a moment."

But Presage swooped across the table and pinned him down by the shoulders.

"You can do that later. I want you to concentrate. There was a moment there in the November darkness, with the gallic mist closing in on the single window, when it suddenly occurred to me that I didn't know how many tablets she'd taken. I felt her shoulder and found it unnaturally cold; her breathing sounded primitive, elderly. I began to examine her, not as a lover, not even as a first-aid man, but as if I'd been a total stranger. Open that bottle!"

"You should have asked her!" Coles said angrily. "Surely, when she'd told you that she'd taken sleeping tablets, you should have asked her."

"We weren't on those terms. I hadn't realized that the sexual contract still presupposes intimacy, familiarity. With Helen I'd have known what dose she'd taken, or, had she been depressed, I'd have been able to ask her. But when it's someone who's really a stranger, good manners can fatally delay you. And besides—"

Bernard relapsed into a silence which Coles was quite unable to interpret.

"Besides what?"

"She was such a liar," Bernard said fondly, wagging his head. "Such a little liar!"

"Well, of course she was. She wouldn't have gone with you otherwise."

"And so reckless, Coles. So damnably reckless. The young are, you know—so reckless and so generous." He sat up. "What the devil am I talking about? Where's that bottle?"

"It's in your hand. No, don't give me any more. I've got a train to catch."

"Later, please, later. Can you see what I'm driving at? The connection I'm trying to establish? The point is that we've both done it, we've joined in and can no longer dissociate ourselves from the consequences, however remote they may seem. Do you realize, for example, that at the precise moment when I was giving her black coffee and trying to find her pulse in that frightful french bed, Hotchkis was dying?"

Coles wanted to be on the train, moving out of it all. The champagne hadn't taken yet, and if he drank enough to make the difference he'd be there not for the night but to the end of Bernard's pleasure in him. He was a trifle tired of being used by Bernard; he was disappointed in him really.

He said, "I don't see how you can be sure."

"I worked it out. I knew there was a connection somewhere and I've found it."

His impatience betraying him, Coles got up. "Oh, don't be so damn silly. Of course there have to be coincidences of time. I might as well start working out what we—" He hesitated.

"What *were* you doing, in fact?"

"Going to bed." The answer came out pat.

"With Lettice," Bernard said, not interrogatively.

Coles sat down again, controlling his voice. "Of course with Lettice. You don't imagine it happened then, do you? It was days before that, weeks."

"His funeral," Bernard said, "will be a fact. At our age we shouldn't shrink from the final embrace. We've achieved the other and must move on now to the earlier fantasy. There must be no more playing about with it, no more dreaming, no one-night stand."

"You're drunk."

"A full-scale confrontation with death at its best, Coles. Infinitely more real than Calais or Sumner, unbedevilled by deception, properly arranged and overseen—sacramental. By the way, did I tell you that Emily's coming?"

"No."

"I'm seeing her this evening. She followed the case in the papers and was very skeptical about the inquest."

"I can't see that it's got anything to do with her. She never met Hotchkis."

"Emily believes in strangers. Also, she has a private devotion to the victims of sudden death. In Hotchkis' case she feels it necessary to do more than her usual 'Salve Regina.' She was very touched by the Villon verse quoted in court and believes he was betrayed."

"By whom?"

"By circumstance. All traitors are the victims of circumstance: they know not what they do."

"Casuistry," Coles said, shaking. "Damnable dishonesty. A man's either responsible or he isn't."

But Bernard was bland. "Afterwards, of course, we'll have lunch at the nearest pub: Helen, Cecily, Emily, myself and you. We'll eat corned beef and pickled walnuts washed down with the best bitter."

"I'm not coming," Coles said.

"With the exception of Emily, who will want something special."

"We're sending a wreath. Lettice has already ordered it."

"You can't face Honeycomb? Is that it?"

"Her sister's going with her—Miss Bowles-Johnson. There's no need whatsoever for me to be there—and it's quite against my principles."

"I'm sorry," Bernard said. "I'd hoped to persuade you. I daresay I went the wrong way about it." He picked up the new bottle of champagne. "Perhaps, after all, there's no point in opening this one. What's in the wreath, by the way?"

"Chrysanthemums. White ones. Lettice grew them under glass. She was hoping to keep them going into December."

"Very sweet of her. Give her my love."

They parted awkwardly, with unaccustomed politeness, Coles to catch his train from Charing Cross, Bernard to sit over his empty glass before taking the tube out to Emily's flat. . . .

She was very *affairé* when he got there, kissed him affectionately and took him straight up to her music room. "I'm glad you've come, Bernard," she said on the staircase; "though I do not usually receive my friends when I'm working, there are times when I make exceptions. Now don't sit down anywhere; all my seats are occupied."

He saw the books scattered on the floor, the sheets of music scored and unscored, the instruments reclining on the Scandinavian chairs.

"I'm not a romantic," Emily explained, "but I like my instruments to be present when I'm planning things for them. Though I've never given birth either intentionally or inadvertently, and though I don't confuse them with offspring, they have their place in my life; they are consulted."

"Of course." Bernard loved Emily most of all when she was showing off. "What are you up to?"

"I am rediscovering François Villon. In a moment I'm going to read him to you."

Emily was always "rediscovering" poets she had never read. Her French was even worse than his own.

"In French," she said. "Parts of two of his ballads. They are almost too appropriate."

"I'm rather off France at the moment. If you have a translation—?"

"I'll do that for you. No, on second thoughts, I'll read from John Payne."

"Never heard of him."

"He is not as felicitous as Swinburne; but he, as you know, only did a few."

"I didn't know he'd done any."

"For a literary man, Bernard, you're a little ignorant. Swinburne translated ten, and they are not included amongst those I shall use for my song. Now, are you listening?"

"If I had a drink—"

"You shall have that later. Thus far we are working."

"I'm not. I'm only standing."

"When listening to poetry it is very much better to stand."

"Couldn't I move the lute?"

"My lute has been there all evening; I have frequent recourse to it. And there's the tuning. Ever since the New York central heating it has been a bugger."

"The zither?" Bernard suggested.

"At this time of night my zither is hardly ever out of its case. It is very much neglected, and you, if I may say so, are being ungracious. You do not seem to realize that I'm giving my time on your behalf. Now listen to this for your friend, Christopher Hotchkis:

" 'Wantons who all their charms display,
That so more custom to them be led,
Brawlers and jesters and tumblers gay;
Clowns with their apes and carpets spread;
Players that whistle for lustyhead,
As they trudge it 'twixt village and town and hall;
Gentle and simple, living and dead—
I cry folk mercy, one and all.' "

"Very lovely," Bernard said. "What's it called?"

"It's the 'Ballad Crying All Folk Mercy,' and I shall combine it with his 'Ballad by Way of Ending.' "

Emily pushed up her hair and took a sheet of music from her table. "At this point I shall change into G-minor. I'll give you the air as far as it goes."

Childlike and sad, she sang for him:

" 'In such ill places his life did fall
He had but a rag when he was sped:
And (yet more luckless) when death did call,
Love's prickle galled him; its wounds still bled
In him. His heart was heavy as lead.
And salt tears stood in his dying eye:
At his despair we were wondered
Whenas he felt his end draw nigh.'

"The *envoi* is very touching," she said, "and I've found most poignant chords for it."

She picked up her lute, stroked the strings and, as the sounds ceased, sang on:

" 'Prince, that art gentle as a yearling gled,
Hear what he did with his latest sigh:
He drank a long draught of the vine-juice red
Whenas he felt his end draw nigh.'

"Now, don't you think that's appropriate?"

"Emily, it's glorious. And it's so very sweet of you to concern yourself."

"We're all concerned, Bernard, even though we may have no tears."

Emily, never known to have wept, always said that she had been born without the gift of tears. "It is little different," she said, "from lacking that of laughter."

"Is Randall coming to the funeral?" she asked now.

"That's what I was going to tell you. He can't face it after his affair with Mrs. Hotchkis."

"I hope he doesn't think of it as an 'affair.' He should be told that it was simply a word that *I* seldom use."

"Quite."

"And your own, if I may say so, was little more. When I think of it I am astonished that I continue to meet you. Does Helen know?"

"I think she may have guessed."

"You haven't told her?"

"No, only you."

"That is as it should be. The true role of the mistress, Bernard, is to carry the moral can for married women. You haven't told Randall either?"

"No," Bernard lied. "I've thought about it, but—"

"It would be letting down the Church. Never forget that the optimism of humanists is nourished by their continual disappointment in us. Also, I have a feeling that Randall was more closely concerned than he cares to admit."

"In what way?"

"In that poor man's death. Whereas you took an indirect part by influencing Randall's behaviour, he, I believe, may have had a direct hand in the betrayal."

"Oh, I don't think so."

"I am quite certain of it," Emily said, snapping the locks on her lute case. "I know these things. When you told me he was dodging the funeral I was confirmed in my suspicion."

She took him through into the sitting room and gave him a drink.

"For instance," she went on, "although you haven't told me as much, I know that your disgusting liaison with that Chelsea whore is over."

"How?"

"Because she was sick upon you for the second time. You cannot deny it, can you?"

"On the boat," Bernard said sadly. "*The Saint Patrick.* I had to take her up on deck, and the wind—"

"I do not want a description."

Bernard drank deeply of his whisky. "How on earth did you know?"

"It was necessary and right: the breaking of the original spell."

"But—"

"Besides," Emily added, "tarts like that can never hold their gin, and I read that there was a gale in the Channel. Now you must finish your drink and go home to Helen. I don't want her to suffer on *my* account too."

"Helen is very fond of you."

Emily ignored this. She said: "We'll met at Victoria by the departure bookstall in time to catch the eight forty-five. When you are getting the tickets don't forget that I always travel First . . ."

XXI

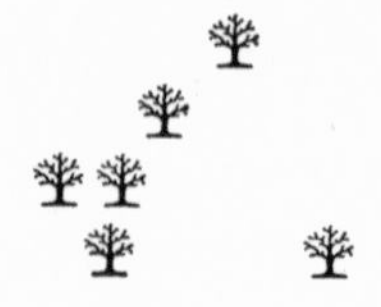

At the high altar of the parish church of St. Cyprian, thirty feet east of the coffin, the Reverend Cyril Faggott followed the Order of Mass for the Dead, praying God that He would not deliver Christopher Hotchkis "into the enemy's hands or put him out of mind forever."

Father Faggott, a squat man, old but black-whiskered still, objected to the whole business of death and his need to participate in it at second hand so often. He didn't like coffins in his church and dreaded even Remembrance Day, when the box, a mere replica stored from year to year in the presbytery cellars, was always empty.

This morning, vexed with cold and rheumatism, he was looking forward to completing the mass, wishing he'd been able to farm it out on the curate so that he might himself have remained comfortably in his study, logging the parish finances. He was, indeed, so irritable that he had to cheer himself on his way with various quips and secret diversions, such as, for Christopher Hotchkis, the words of absolution—only three pages ahead of him in the big missal on the altar. In the case of the dead prisoner they would be strangely appropriate:

"Therefore we pray that in passing judgement
Thou wilt not let thy sentence fall too
heavily upon one who is commended to Thee. . . ."

Although the joke was facetious, a remote kind of pun, Father Faggott did not on that account object to it. Growing older, he found that puns were one of the few means left him of redressing his private situation without impiety. While they were safe and superficially as "absurd" as his vocation, they reflected the essential disparity of all things and so redeemed for him a little of his habitual ill temper.

In his younger days, he realized now, he'd have found it harder to be lighthearted about this particular funeral, tending to brood over its implications, feeling it his duty to define them. But at sixty-seven—and with a recurrent chest pain that was almost certainly angina—his own faith had lightened.

He thought of it sometimes as a part of his youth, forgotten for many years but now ever more disturbingly remembered—as if old people of his boyhood had suddenly returned to him across the sands of his mid-life to be recognized again, not as friends or acquaintances, but as angels of some kind, dream beings.

The people of those early years were all like this: ghostly, neither warm nor cold, in some way more live than any he had met since. Death came amongst them too—a tall man continually taking on and off his black hat, someone who might have been one of his father's uncles or a visiting cleric, an angular figure who called Father Cyril's whole life into question: the faith and hope that had ceased to trouble him, the vows he'd kept so long that he'd quite forgotten them.

Praying officially for Christopher Hotchkis, he thought about him personally scarcely at all. In his death his features had become intermingled with those of the children he'd baptized, confessed or prepared for first communion down the years: gentle faces, full-cheeked and ardent—emissaries dispatched ahead of him into the world against his own sickness and longing for heaven.

Had it been possible, he'd have addressed the dead man in the coffin in such terms. He would have pleaded for him. Still keeping his own face to the altar, he'd have spoken of him to God as if he'd been one of his boy servers, a little wretch only just behind him, only temporarily in some kind of trouble.

Thinking of him like this in the chill and ugly church, with old snow still slipping like a soot-starred quilt from the corrugated roof, Father Faggott warmed to his jaded intention—the legacy of hundreds of such masses—and ceased to anticipate the cold journey to the cemetery.

Behind him, the mourners, to whom he'd not yet spoken, stood in two groups in the painted metal pews beyond the coffin. Emily Minck and Helen Presage were close together, with Cecily, nearest the aisle, beside them. Bernard, in the same pew, stood two or three feet from them, a nice distance, to emphasize his distrust of their renewed friendship.

Like postgraduates at a lecture, the two women often whispered together, and he overheard Emily telling his wife that she found it odd that the Order of Mass for the Dead should follow immediately upon "Occasional Prayers."

"For, after all," he heard her say, "what's this if not an occasion?"

When Emily was with Bernard and Helen during these recurrent warm phases in their unpredictable relationship, she always paid most attention to Helen. "It's not that we're ganging up on you," she told Bernard. "It's simply that we neither of us like you very much—you're such an untrustworthy old bugger."

But this sort of thing didn't disturb him half so much as the metal pews. Distinctly, if people sat down too heavily or rubbed their backsides against them when kneeling, they twanged like the french bed he'd shared with Mrs. Foley in Calais.

"Clearly," he told Coles the following evening, "you made the right decision. God didn't intend you to be amongst the mourners. Those pews were put there especially for me."

But Coles was only interested in Mrs. Hotchkis, wanting to know what she'd worn and how she had looked.

"Pale, Coles, and ill at ease, I'd say. She and her sister were both wearing black lace mantillas. They stood at the back beside one of the iron pillars, as embarrassed as if they'd been lower servants compelled to watch their betters at dinner."

"You're getting old, Bernard; you're beginning to parody yourself."

But Bernard had been right. All the way from Sumner in Pery's MG, Betty had insisted that it "wasn't decent" to wear the mantillas. "It's dressing up," she'd said. "And, anyway, how'll we know what to do with them during the ceremony? Now he's dead, why couldn't they have let Chris alone and be cremated the way Paul was?"

"You want to travel more," Pery had told her mildly. "They make quite a party out of a funeral on the Continent—a sort of black wedding. And you looked smashing in the Lisbon mantilla when you tried it on after breakfast. You know you did, or why would 'Reen have been so snarky?"

But Betty had persisted in looking for grievances. "And this other fellow coming along too," she'd said. "Bushnell or whatever they call him. What's his game?"

"He was one of his mates, darling. Chris asked for Bushy in the hospital. Even coppers can't refuse a last request."

"But he's coming with an officer," Betty had wailed.

"A screw, you mean."

"It isn't decent. They might be 'andcuffed together. What are people going to think?"

"Unless you start telling them, nothing. It's all being kept quiet. This is England, not America."

Ten pews in front of them, Cecily, who felt she was entitled to be bored by this half of the trip, was counting the things round the coffin. She picked out one handle on the head end, three along the nearest side, so eight in all. Then there were two tall trestles, five mass cards on the lid, a brass crucifix over where Mr. Hotchkis' face must be, and three dull-orange candles in oak holders north and south of him. By standing on tiptoe on the foam rubber of her trestle kneeler, she could just see that there was a name plate over his chest and six large yellow screws holding everything together.

Practicing her mental arithmetic, she gave herself one prayer's length to add all these up. She found that, apart from his coffin,

Mr. Hotchkis had two trestles, six candles in six candlesticks, five cards, six screws, eight handles, one plate and one crucifix to see him on his journey into the second world—thirty-five things altogether. For good measure she threw in Father Faggott and the six mourners, a mystical seven, made inaccurate by the late arrival of the friendly prisoner she'd heard the others discussing on the train.

Bushnell, who had shaved off his beard on hearing of Hotchkis' death, appeared to Cecily as a flat-faced man in a thin blue suit and an out-of-date overcoat. He stood with his warder in the very last pew on the opposite side of the aisle. Officer Dalrymple was wearing his uniform of ambulance blue, and they stood so close together that she thought at first they must be casually handcuffed, as on television.

But they weren't; Mr. Bushnell was resting both hands on the pew in front of him, leaning forward a little, his gaze apparently never moving from the trestles at the far end of the nave. Every time Cecily looked back she saw his flat face with its small black eyes fixed unmovingly on the head of the coffin. It unnerved her a little and, eventually, unable to keep her discovery to herself, she confided it in Emily Minck, who in her turn peered round at the two men.

"To stare is rude," she told Cecily. "At mass it is impious." But she tittered as she added, "Clearly that is the Good Thief. Or, more probably, the Bad! It depends upon his dispositions."

Cecily stole yet another glance, this time to look at the warder. With his hands to his sides, he stood at attention with the shiny black peak of his cap clasped to his side, efficient, determined not to seem embarrassed.

The mass followed its appointed course and she grew very bored. At the conclusion, when their party went off to the nearest pub to eat brisket of beef and winter salad, she noticed that the warder and the prisoner remained behind. The warder stood there, looking neither to the right nor to the left, blue-eyed, and, as Cecily told Emily later, "rather pathetic." Beside him the prisoner kneeled with his hands quite covering his face and his head dropped between his shoulders.

Alone in the chancel, Officer Dalrymple tapped Bushnell on the shoulder a few minutes after the others had gone. Now that it was empty, the church seemed colder than ever, and Dalrymple, who was off duty from midday, wanted to get back to Married Quarters. But he was used to waiting, and now that there was no one to watch him he stared round at things—at the Stations of the Cross, painted in blue and brown on the distempered hardboard; at the tabernacle on the altar and the coffin on its tall trestles.

"Come on, Bushnell," he said at last. "You've done enough knee bends."

"I'm waiting for the rest of it," Bushnell said through his hands. "Seeing him up to the cemetery."

"Oh no, you're not, Bushy. They're not covering him over till after dinner, and mine'll be in the oven by now."

Bushnell got up from his knees and gestured at the coffin or the altar.

"Well, will you come up there with me, then? It's in prison regulations that mourners is allowed to say good-by."

They moved up the narrow aisle to the communion rail, where the bitter smoke of the extinguished candles hung in the frosty air. Dalrymple stood chin up a few feet from the head of the coffin while Bushnell, leaving him there, kneeled down at the rail and prayed despondently.

He wasn't sure whether he was praying to God or to Hotchkis, but he felt it was enough to have done something. Rising, he crossed himself in imitation of Hotchkis' old gesture when something had knocked him, and then he walked round the coffin, whispering over his lower lip as if they'd been at exercise in the Inner Ring back at the 'Ville.

"I done what you asked; but they won't let me up for the last of it," he said. He waited a moment and then asked: "You all right, mate?"

The silence was as if Hotchkis had been kipped up in his peter, dead to the world after too much surgical spirit, or simply pressing his trousers on a Sunday evening. On an impulse as strong as if he'd been back on "A" Landing, Bushnell felt bound to give him the tap. He looked over his shoulder to see whether Dalrymple was watching him and saw that the screw was waiting patiently, absorbed in picking the fluff from the linings of his overcoat pockets.

Waiting until a lorry passed in the street beyond the chancel, Bushnell rapped twice on the side of the coffin, just level with the dead man's right ear. He hissed once and waited. Then he whispered: " 'Otchkis! Anything you want, mate? You all right?"

But there was no answer, nothing certain at all, though there could have been a creak from somewhere, a small dry sound, a shifting of something—of the dead legs or the sound of a hand falling from the chest. For Hotchkis had told him once that when they were finished, catholics chained up their hands with beads, to hold them like that even after they'd rotted, with the bones and the beads a kind of prayer. And because of this small noise he'd heard, it was possible that someone hadn't put Chris's chain on properly.

It shook him all right, more later than at the time, as if in the silence the noise was getting louder, like a signal—the tap on the ventilator shaft or the double knock of the thumb joint on the cell table.

"And what do you think you're doing?" came Dalrymple's voice, loud in the frost.

Bushnell jumped. "Christ! I'm not doing nothing."

"Then come away from that box, then. Stop knocking on it."

"I wasn't knocking."

"You was knocking."

"If you heard it, it was him. It was Chris. Here! Officer, I thought I heard him moving. I thought there might've been a mistake."

"Come off it, Bushy; you knocked. I heard you."

"Only to start with. Straight up, it wasn't all me. There's something moving in there. I gave him the tap and he gave it me back. I 'eard 'im. We both did."

Dalrymple didn't sigh. He wagged his head, looking high over Bushnell at the grey plain glass east window with tired eyes, scanning it as if he'd been back in the Bag Shop watching the duty clock.

"You do read about it," Bushnell insisted. "There was that case in the papers back in October—an old girl with catalepsy or something nearly buried alive."

Dalrymple shrugged. "Come on now; no more mucking about. Time's up."

Their breath was just visible as they confronted one another three yards apart, stock-still and undecided. In the total silence the coffin creaked and their heads jerked as they glared at each other. "Well," Bushnell said, "that was it. You 'eard it yourself that time, and Chris wants to come out. 'E's still alive."

"Are you coming, Bushnell, or do I have to come over and get you?"

"For Chrissake, knock him up yourself, sir. Just once. Give 'im 'is chance."

"Go on like this and you'll be taken straight to the doctor."

"Well, why not? So long as you give Chris his chance. Just once."

Dalrymple moved forward smartly. He glanced at the sacristy door, then over his shoulder to the west end and the ugly little font. Satisfied that they were alone, he put his cap down on a pew and, bending from the waist, rapped officially on the head of the coffin.

In the silence they waited, Dalrymple at attention, Bushnell slack-shouldered, his face down, smiling to himself. Up above, melting snow slipped inch by inch, rumbling as it gathered speed over the corrugated-iron roof. It thudded like dropped bibles as, yard by yard, it hit the asphalt.

"I told you," Bushnell said. "He's there all right. Nobody got him. He's wherever he is and he knows."

Dalrymple didn't reply. He half marched back to his cap and fastened it on to his military head there in the church as if he were about to leave a landing craft again, tin hat in place. One behind the other, they went down the aisle away from the candle smoke and the coffin. They went out in orderly fashion through the folding plastic doors to the taxi which was waiting for them in the cold street.

Betty and Pery did not wait for the burial. On the pavement outside the church they made their excuses to Bernard, Pery gracefully and Betty in sad silence, sniffing with cold or embarrassment. She was in fact embarrassed by Mr. Presage's accent and her mantilla, which felt sillier than ever now that she was wearing it round her neck. In the uncharitable cold, so grey and undramatic, walking stiff-legged to Pery's MG, she looked very black and white in her mourning, classical despite herself.

They went together to the Wicked Lady Café for a long-drawn-out lunch. Though she comforted herself with food, Betty wouldn't talk to her sister at all and, over the coffee, refused even the black cigarettes. Pery, supposing she must be feeling guilty at not waiting for what she and the undertakers called "the interment," started to make excuses for her. She said, "It's only natural, darling. They understand, and so does Father Faggott. They know about the kids and how we had to get back to them for 'Reen. So, for goodness' sake, stop worrying."

"I'm not worrying. I just don't want to look a bitch for not waiting."

"Don't be silly. They know what you've been through; they all do. That Miss Minck said over and over again that you'd done the right thing, that all this graveside stuff was only pagan and barbaric."

"Oh, her."

Pery blew out Russian cigarette smoke. "Mind you, I don't know who she thinks she is. She acted like someone at the Gas Board or a hospital almoner or something. She was lecturing me while you were sitting in the car. She kept on saying, 'Mrs. Hotchkis has prayed, Miss Johnson, and that is enough.' The only thing that did seem to put her out was that you wouldn't let us go for a drink with them."

"I didn't pray. You know bloody well I didn't. And no more did you, neither. You were just waiting like me for it all to be over."

"You did your duty, Betty. Miss Minck said you did. She said something like, 'God always expects too much of us all, Miss Johnson. He's very spoiled.' "

Betty at last took a cigarette. "I don't know what it's got to do with either of them—Miss Minck or that old Faggott up at the altar. Randy Coles said it would be like this, a thorough imposition on my privacy, mine and Chris's, and I don't want to talk about it any more, so let's get back home."

If there's one thing worse than being shut up with a man in a mood, Pery thought as they drove back to Sumner, *it's a woman.* And she decided that as soon as they reached the village she'd start in on her own excuses; she'd leave 'Reen to handle Betty and get off to London before the fog got bad. So that her haste should not be too apparent, she took her time on this first journey, driving slowly through the twisted well-remembered roads between the bare hawthorn hedges and the tarnished snowdrifts.

She parked the car in the usual place, and together, in their high heels and narrow black skirts, they tripped along the high street from the Assembly of God to the cottage. Already the street lamps glowed gas-green, ready to light up the start of the fifteen hours of winter's darkness. The curtains of the cottage's five windows were drawn and had been so all day, with the pattern outwards and the yellow door tight shut.

When they opened the door, the smells and warmth hit them, the heat of the coal fire in the hearth, the scent of the wax candles on the crowded table, and the noise of Marc, Debrah and the other children.

'Reen had brought her own two with her from next door, her Robin and little Muriel Sarah, the two most difficult children in the village. She'd had her hair done in the town and was wearing glass earrings clamped tight to the lobes of her big ears. Over her ivory satin, her face glowed—her heavy lips, her benevolent eyes and wide cheeks.

She'd been better than her word that morning and had filled not only the children's table but the cocktail cabinet as well. There was a bottle of advocaat, a half of cream sherry, a bottle of scotch, another of gin and a half of Activity Cocktail. On the white cloth of the table were jellies, cakes, chocolate fingers, favours and crackers. Holly was piled up round the candlesticks.

"Well, I told you I was going to give them a party," she said, seeing their faces. "With them getting no Christmas this year, they're having it now, the lot."

"You said high tea," Betty said. "You didn't say nothing about all this."

"Of course I didn't. It's a surprise."

"It's disgusting."

"And, what's more, it's what Chris'd have wanted when he came out. 'E promised it them—you know he did—out of his Buffaloes."

"Nobody's 'ad his Buffaloes yet."

"And my club," said 'Reen. "I drew half of it out and put it with the family allowances—so the drink's on me." She turned to the children. "Now come on then; get on with your jellies and pull your crackers while I make Mum and Auntie a cup of tea."

"I don't want any," Betty said.

"Tea when there's Scotch?" Pery asked her. "It's just what you need, after all that."

"Well, it's up to you," 'Reen said. "Personally I always like a drink better once they're in bed; but the glasses are on the side and the whisky doesn't need a corkscrew."

All the children were watching, not missing a thing, and Debrah shouted, "Go on, Mum; you 'ave some. It's what Dad would have wanted."

"Your Dad's dead," 'Reen's Robin said.

"You shut your mouth, Robbie."

"But he is, Mum; you said he was."

Debrah turned on the little boy. "Well, he wouldn't mind, anyway. Our Mum's cold; she's been in the cold and she needs cheering."

"What did they do with him?" Robin asked Betty. "Go on; tell us. Did you see him lowered?"

"Robin, if you don't stop your noise, you'll go back home."

"He was cremated," Debrah said, "wasn't he, Mum? They burned him up in a big oven."

"All in flames?" Robin asked her. "Was it gas, Debbie?"

"No, electric, silly. It's all electric, isn't it, Marc?"

"Prob'ly," Marc said. "When can we pull the crackers?"

He was half watching the television flickering over in the corner with the sound turned down, a man with an aqualung stalking a groper fish amid clouds of bubbles.

"We want the eggs," Muriel Sarah said. "When can we 'ave the eggs, Mum?"

"Greedy," 'Reen told her. "That's what you are."

"Oh, go on, Mum. Give us the eggs. We want the eggs," Robin shouted.

"Eggs?" Pery asked, drinking her whisky. "Are they having eggs to their teas as well?"

"Choc'late," Marc said, starting his jelly, "proper choc'late eggs."

"Well, I did bring them one each," 'Reen admitted, "from the traveller, Charlie Roach. It's a new line his firm's putting out for Lent."

"Lent?" Betty said. "What you mean, Lent? It's not Christmas yet."

"I didn't say it was, Betty. Charlie Roach is putting them out Lent, but this is a sample line he gives to his favourites."

"Easter eggs Christmas," Betty said. "It's not right."

"Please let us have them," Robin said. "Mum promised we'd have them today, didn't you, Mum?"

"Charlie Roach said it was a marketing project," 'Reen explained. "And he always let me in on them." And she told the children, "Of course you can 'ave your eggs, but not till afterwards. With kids you've got to distract them, Betty! Like that Coles fellow was always saying."

"Oh, him."

Betty looked over all their heads for a moment, as if 'Reen and Pery were no taller than the children. Her eyes caught sight of her face in the mirror, sprigged with a piece of mistletoe, and she said, "For God's sake, can't we get the kids out of here? You can't hear yourself think with all this noise."

"They're going over to my place," 'Reen told her. "Robbie can manage the telly, and they want I.T.V. in any case. Now look, children, so long as you don't play with the fire or kick up too much of a racket you can take your crackers with you and watch the telly till news time."

Debrah was eating a slice of cake as if it were very dry. Through the visible crumbs she said, "We don't want to go. We want to stay here, don't we, Marc?"

"No," Marc said.

'Reen picked big Debrah up and planted her crumbed cheeks with kisses. "Go on with you," she whispered. "It's the same serial you saw last night, Debbie, and you could play over there. There's more room, so take them over like a good girl for your Mummy's sake."

Debrah, with her woman's hands, smudged at her dry eyes as if to squeeze tears from them. She smoothed down the flounces of her party dress and went over to stand by the coats hanging on the back of the front door. When she opened it, all the children streamed out after her into the quiet street. Their noise went with them like the end of daylight or a vessel leaking its contents away. The village received their sounds as they lingered, playing with the snow beside the palings, whooping it up in the twilight with a kind of stubborn reluctance.

Alone, the three women settled down, Betty slumped in her black on the little sofa, 'Reen in the armchair beside the cocktail cabinet, and Pery graceful and slim beside the mantelpiece.

Pery always did look graceful and slim, Betty thought. She looked "London" wherever she was and whatever she was doing. Over her glass of advocaat, full of yellow eggs and brandy or whatever it was, Betty let her heavy eyes wander up and down the length of her sister, so slender and towny.

Nobody cleared the table, but 'Reen pushed it back against the wall with its load of plates and crumbs, cakes, holly and jelly cartons.

"Cheer up, Bet," Pery said. "You're not on your own, you know, and it's nice and quiet now."

Betty said nothing.

"I don't mind admitting it," Pery told 'Reen, "that I wasn't going to have stayed, really; I didn't think I could stand it, and that goes for marriage too."

"Gawd!" 'Reen said.

"There's too much attached," Pery went on; "you don't see that when you're young and you don't see it if you're married yourself; but if you're neither, you do see it sometimes and you're thankful."

"It's roundabouts and swings," 'Reen said, "leaving aside the larks." She looked over at Betty. "There is that, isn't there, Betty?"

"How do I know?"

"Go on; you tell 'er, tell Pery. She doesn't know what she's missing."

"There's nothing to it," Betty said. "It gets you nowhere. It's just a bloomin' waste of time."

"Pery wouldn't know," 'Reen told her. "That's one thing she can't know."

"Kids, you mean?" Pery asked.

"No, bed. It's better when you've had them. Your feelings is changed."

Pery applied her lipstick. "Plenty of the girls I work with have had kids and it hasn't changed *them.*"

"Well, it wouldn't, would it? Not without a husband."

"Do you mind!" Betty sighed.

"Oh, I'm sorry."

"Don't bother apologizing," Betty told her. "Don't imagine I thought I had a husband with Chris in prison all the time, and don't imagine it's that I wanted—"

"What?" 'Reen asked. "Sex?"

"No, don't imagine I was even sure I ever wanted him back."

Pery and 'Reen looked at each other and Betty saw them do it.

"I wasn't sure to begin with, and I'm less sure now," she said. "So you can both say what you like, because it's not me and Chris you'll be saying it about, because as far as I'm concerned we was never married."

"Don't be silly," Pery protested, suddenly angry. "What a way to talk. Of course you were married. Chris was a sailor. He had his job to do and that meant being away for long stretches and doesn't make any difference; but you can't say he wasn't your husband, because he was and you went to the altar with him."

"Lewisham Registry Office," Betty said.

"It's the same thing."

"He wanted me to; but I wouldn't go to church with him, not at first."

"But you did later, in March. That Saturday."

"Ooh, listen to her!" said Betty, looking at no one. "Whose wedding was it, anyway? You in that pink grosgrain."

Pery finished her drink and refilled her glass. "It's just that I don't like lies," she said more calmly. "You can't tell them when you've just buried somebody; it brings bad luck."

"Well, if I did go to the altar, it was only to keep old Faggott quiet."

"And to satisfy Chris."

"Satisfy Chris?" Betty put her head back, slid low on the sofa to laugh at the ceiling. "That's good. That's a real laugh, that is. Old Chris wasn't never satisfied—not till now."

With her head still in that same position of appealing to someone out of sight, she paused before adding, "Were you, ducks?"

They sat watching her, wondering if it was their drink or hers, not able to touch the hems of their skirts, to smooth them down, to take a sip from their glasses. They found themselves looking at Betty's sharp nose, her closed eyelids and half-smile.

"You ought to cry—didn't she, 'Reen?" Pery said in the end. "A good cry. That's what's the matter with her."

"I don't cry. You know I don't. I didn't over Mother or that Paul, and I'm not starting now."

Pery felt there ought to be someone else there, the club manager or someone. She cast round in her mind for advice and began, "That Miss Minck said . . ."

Betty jerked her head up. "Oh, sod her! Nasty poky little bitch, taking charge of everything. The past's the past, and what I'm thinking about's next year, after Christmas."

"Well, that's right. So you should."

"A job," Betty said.

"Or another man," 'Reen said. "Never mind work."

"Why not?" Pery said.

"You're young still, isn't she?" 'Reen said.

"Of course she is," Pery said. "Oh, for heaven's sake, let's have another drink and a biscuit or two. It gets real depressing when you can't help someone."

"And who's asking you?" Betty said. "Me sitting here listening to you both as if you were a bloomin' programme or something. Gawd! Men! The old wedding stick. I'm shut of it. I'm finished with them, and it's not just the way I feel now. It's the way I've always felt. Playing up for something I don't want." She turned on them suddenly. "Look at the two of you. One with and one without, and you feel the same as me really about them. The only difference is that you can't admit it because you don't know it; but I do and they do too: they're getting to . . . men are getting to know I'm worse for them than they are for me. Give me a gin, Pery."

"Not gin; they don't mix. Stick to the advocaat."

"Gin, I said!"

"You can have mine," Pery said, watching the quick way she drank it.

"You don't like it," Betty said, "because it's what you've thought. You've both been sitting there thinking, 'Look at her, not thirty-five yet, and she's killed off two of them.' "

"We never," 'Reen said. "And you didn't neither. You didn't do nothing to them except be a little bit free with yourself."

"Free!" Betty said. "You don't know what you're talking about. Who's free so long as they've got theirselves?"

"She ought to eat something," Pery said. "Do her a scrambled egg or a sandwich."

But Betty told the mantelpiece, "I killed them both. Something in me killed the poor devils. I know it did, and she does too, if she'd tell the truth. A sister always does."

She slipped off her shoes and stretched out her legs towards the fire, lolling her head back on the sofa again, saying, "Why don't you admit it, Pery? Why don't you tell her what you used to say—that I never liked men, that I don't approve of what they are, that *we* don't, that we only make do with them because we have to?"

'Reen got up and started to make the sandwich, reassured by the touch of the bread and the knife. "You want to stop this. You don't want to think of yourself as different from the rest of us. You want to think you've just 'ad bad luck, that's all, because if you go on like this you'll end up down at the clinic 'aving them asking you about your dreams and school days."

"Dreams! I don't know what dreams are, except to order. It's the only kind I have, the sort where you see what you want to see and nothing else, the sort you do on purpose, out of bed."

"Well, eat this then. It's only paste, but you want something in your stomach. Your dreams is what they call fantasy, and it's the same for everyone—even for us."

"Working-class!" Betty said. "I don't think."

"We've got the money now," 'Reen persisted. "And the time. We can go nutty as fast as anyone else, and if you don't watch out, my girl, that's what's going to happen to you. You'll end up mental."

Pery took a biscuit. "Oh, leave her, 'Reen. Don't let her upset you. She only wants time to think things out and she'll forget all this, won't you, darling?"

"Well, I might and I might not."

"You will. But you've got to give it all a rest first. As you said just now, you've got to think about practical things like wages and housekeeping. You've never even said if Chris left you anything or how you were fixed up here—for the cottage."

"Well, he left only what he'd put in his Buffaloes and the chance of a whip-round on the trawlers. That's all I know, apart from National Assistance."

She sat up suddenly. They watched Betty's feet and toes as, independently of her, they moved forward in the fleece of the rug to enter her abandoned shoes.

"What's up?" 'Reen asked. "What's the matter?"

"Only someone's coming."

"Outside? I didn't hear nothing."

"That's because you don't listen. You're not ready the way I am. You're the same as everyone else. You don't know when things are going to start up again."

They both listened, trying to dissociate their ears from the sounds coming through the wall as she moved indolently round the small room. They watched her apply make-up and put on the mantilla from the back of the door, adjusting the point of it carefully so that it covered her widow's peak as she said, "A visitor, for instance—some fellow coming to call."

"Randy?" 'Reen asked.

"Coles? Don't make me laugh. You won't never see him again. He's too sharp."

"Then who, then?"

Betty ignored her and spoke only to Pery. "It's going to be all right. Don't do your nut about me, will you? I'll drop you a line to the club."

Pery kissed her. "All right, ducks; I understand."

"Well, go on, Betty; just give his name."

"Bill Smeed," Betty said. "Old faithful! I'd know his car anywhere." She topped up her glass with 'Reen's gin. "Be a sport," she told her. "Keep the kids over there with you a bit, just half an hour or so, while 'e's talking."

"Talking!" 'Reen said. "Well, I don't know. I'll never get to the bottom of you, Betty. Just look at her! One minute she says she's finished and they are too and the next she's telling me to keep the kids out of the way. Just as if nothing had happened."

"Well, it hasn't. Nothing has. It's what's called consoling yourself, doing your duty, I don't think." She moved over to open the door, saying, "Watch his face when he sees the three of us, and then get out fast."

She opened the door just as Bill Smeed, outside, was raising his hand to the latch.

As in the old weekends they sat there alone with the television turned off, with only the gabble and music of the next-door set coming through the wall. Because she knew that tonight he wouldn't dare to, Betty turned out the light and did the teasing.

She let him talk in the light of the candles on the cluttered table and the intermittent blaze of flames on the hearth, waiting for him to tell her his tale and work round to herself.

Bill Smeed was at "a loose end." He kept saying so himself. "I'm at a loose end," he said, "so I thought I'd drop in." And he went on to tell her that his wife, Norma, had gone into hospital the week before to have her operation, telling her this as if she must have known that one was expected.

"What operation?"

"The womb. The whole lot, even to the office chair."

"Don't be dirty," she said.

"Well, you know! It's only a way of putting it, as if you were telling someone in a pub."

"Well, it's still dirty. I don't like it."

He swept on to the complications, phlebitis and bladder trouble. So, being at a loose end, he'd come to know if there was anything he could do.

"Like what?"

"In your loss," he said. "In your own loss, sweetheart."

She flapped her shoe against her heel. "It's a bit late in the day, isn't it? You didn't even send a wreath." And she turned her face away towards the blank television set as he came clean.

"Well, to be honest, with the house empty, I was lonely, Betty. I knew you'd be lonely too. I thought I could leave it a bit and not intrude, or I could chance it and just see if there was anything I could do."

She said nothing.

"I mean I wasn't going to have done this area this week, but something in me kept nagging and I had to take the chance. In the end I had to, sweetheart."

"What d'you mean 'chance'? Was you scared or something?"

"Well, I didn't think it was proper. I didn't know how you'd be feeling. I thought I could either leave it a fortnight or come at once—on the day."

"Makes a difference, doesn't it?"

He dried right up. She had him in a corner, poor devil, and now if they were to go on she had to get him out of it again.

"You weren't scared then, Billy?"

"Billy!" he said. "That's better. That's my Betty."

But she drew away from him. "Go on, then; were you or weren't you?"

"Scared? Of coming?"

"Sort of," she said. "I'm not talking about accidents, you know. I'm only asking if you were scared of coming to see *me?"*

"You, Betty. You mean your loss?"

"No," she said, drawing it out with scorn so that she could feel him shrink back once more into his own corner of the sofa.

"And I'm not your Betty," she said. "And I'm not Norma and I'm not in hospital with complications. If you want to keep on coming, you oughtn't never to forget that."

"Sweetheart! I didn't mean—look, I was only trying to explain why I came when you'd—"

He gave up and she felt him looking for his cigarettes.

"Well, go on," she said, flapping the shoe again. "When I'd what?"

"When you'd only just buried him—today, I mean."

She looked round at him. He saw her face fully for the first time that evening, and it alarmed him. He wasn't sure if it had ever been worth it. He wasn't sure that when he left he wouldn't put a red line through Sumner—slap through her name in the order book.

"Well?" she said. "What's the matter with you tonight? You don't finish nothing. You keep breaking off."

"I told you: I've had a bad week—Norma and everything and the papers and your Christopher. We get tired too, you know. We have our off days same as everybody else. Selling's not easy. People think that because we come in brightly, as if we believed, as if we had no troubles, faith in ourselves, they think—"

But she cut him short. "Oh, forget it. I'm sick of all this talking. Everybody's always talking like a bloomin' programme that never stops."

"I know, darling, I know. Now, why don't we have a cup of tea and a cigarette or a drink?"

"No," she said, "not yet, not now. What I wanted to ask you was, 'ave you seen Randy again?"

"Randy? Randall Coles?"

"Yes, old Coles. Have you seen him since?"

"As a matter of fact, I have. Something made me. I was in the area last week and I saw them both. She tried to give me the old shut-door treatment and I countered with the raised voice. He came out, polishing his spectacles, and ordered an Axminster for the bedroom."

"How do you know?"

"Know what?"

"That it was for the bedroom."

"I measured it, didn't I? All round the furniture with my tape measure with her sniffing down in the kitchen."

"Mrs. Coles, you mean? That Lettice?"

"She acted as if I was poison. I got real satisfaction selling him that Axminster."

"And what about him, then? How was he looking?"

"Sharp. Right on his toes. He got me down ten per cent on a close weave, three by four and a half."

"And he looked strong?" she asked.

He took the drink she handed him and sampled it, watching her. "Old," he said, "but a good risk. Why? What are you driving at, sweetheart?"

"Nothing," she said, sipping her drink and looking into the fire. She added, "He is old, all right; I've noticed that with them. You don't see it in the summer; but in the winter, round about now, when they've lost their tan, it sticks out a mile."

He patted the sofa seat beside him. "Come and sit down, sweetheart. Let's forget it all, just this once. Don't talk about winter now we're together again. Pretend everything's all right for us both."

She obeyed him, steadily drinking away her gin and lemon. "Not just the winter," she said. "It's when they get old without knowing it that it shows; but Randy's all right. He knows when to stop." She leaned against him, slipping her shoes from her feet, one arm stealing gently over his winter pull-over and along it and over and underneath the left lapel of his off-duty jacket.

"But you don't, do you?" she asked, kissing him on the neck.

"I never learned."

"You didn't—and neither did I." And before he put down his glass, empty, she added, "Without it, there's no fun; but don't say I never told you."

He emptied her glass for her and put that down too, remembering as he did so that the booklet, in the last paragraph, had catered for the situation:

> Never forget that time is not of the essence. The good representative allows for this. He calls again. The morning's most unlikely prospect can be the evening's optimum.

With only twenty minutes gone since he'd chanced his call out there in the street, they got down to it on the sofa, without another word said.

Off Bayswater, in her bedroom in the top flat, Cecily Presage was working on her Great Love Stories. She was all alone under the roof, with her small electric stove glowing by her feet, with her supper on the bureau beside her bible, which she had only just opened.

She was not exactly lonely; she could, if she'd wanted to, have gone with her parents and Emily Minck to supper in the italian restaurant in Blandford Street. Emily had, in fact, tried to persuade her, saying several times over, as she was inclined to do, "I'm trying to persuade you with pizza, Cecily. In New York young girls prefer pizza. Therefore I'm trying to persuade you with pizza." And her father had said, or, rather, whispered, "Tonight there really is a chance that she might pay for us; she's mentioned it three times."

But Cecily was tired of all their talk and lost in her dream of marriage. She felt, though she never told them so, that they were all too old for it and that really they had nothing to say for her—only things for themselves. She didn't feel in the least superior or, on the other hand, inferior, but more like a new girl at her third school, who knows that it's no good asking questions of the sixth form. Therefore she was quite happy to look for a new love story in the Old Testament.

Down below her she could hear the sounds of the new tenants moving about in Flat G. They had arrived three days earlier in a scarred white sports car with a moses basket and a four-month-old baby on the back seat and with no furniture. The wife had worn a three-quarter-length scarlet facecloth coat over a tight navy-blue skirt. She had worn, too, a close-fitting hood over her head and made up only her eyes, which Cecily knew were very beautiful indeed. Her husband was young and had a beard.

She could hear through the floor faint music and a little quarrel going on, which was preventing them from attending to their baby daughter, who was screaming more faintly in another room.

On this night Cecily couldn't make up her mind whether to do David and Jonathan or David and the wife of Uriah the Hittite, or Tobias and Sara. But the bible came open at the book of Tobias in the Apocrypha, so she started to read again the story of Tobias and his bride, Sara.

Before she married the splendid young Tobias, Sara had been married seven times before, and each of her husbands had died on the first night of the honeymoon. In Cecily's opinion, Raguel, Sara's father, wasn't so much pessimistic as experienced, while Tobias was inspired and Sara, quite simply mysterious. On the other hand, perhaps, in their obedience they were all three mysterious; as if they knew that in any marriage there might be devils and angels moving about just behind the moods and promises.

> "When the feasting was over," she read, "bridegroom was led to bridechamber. And now, remembering what the angel had said, he took out from his wallet a piece of the fish's liver, which he burnt on live coals. With that, the evil spirit fled; it was overtaken by the angel Raphael in the waste lands of Upper Egypt and there held prisoner. Next Tobias must plead with his bride; Leave thy bed, Sara; today and tomorrow let us pray God for mercy. These three

nights are set apart for our union with God; when the third is over, we will be joined in one, thou and I. We come of holy lineage; not for us to mate blindly, like the heathen that have no knowledge of God.

"Side by side they kept vigil, and prayed together that no plague should mar their mating. 'Lord God of our fathers,' Tobias said, '. . . When Adam was made of Earth's clay, it was by thy hand; when Eve was sent to cheer him, it was of thy gift. Thou, Lord, art my witness that I wed this sister of mine not from love of dalliance; only in the dear hope of leaving a race behind me, in whose destiny thy name may be ever blessed.'

"And Sara prayed, 'Have mercy on us, Lord, have mercy on us; safe from all harm grow we old together, he and I.'

"And now it was cockcrow and Raguel had all his men out early to help him dig the grave. Like enough, he thought, this one will have fared no better than the other seven. . . ."